WICKED BECOMES YOU
A May 2010 Top Pick of *Romantic Times* magazine

"So much fun . . . Charming and deliciously sensual from beginning to end."

—*Romantic Times* magazine

"Witty, often hilarious, sensuous, and breathlessly paced . . . [an] engaging mystery-enhanced escapade [with] charmingly matched protagonists."

—*Library Journal*

"The book to beat for best historical romance of the year . . . Sexy, inventive, and riveting, it's hard to put down and a joy to read."

—*All About Romance*

"A fascinating, passionate tale . . . you won't want to miss."

—*Romance Reviews Today*

"Rousing . . . delightful . . . *Wicked Becomes You* enthralls with particularly likable characters and a heartwarming romance with deeply affecting emotions."

—Single Titles.com

WRITTEN ON YOUR SKIN
An August 2009 *Romantic Times* Top Pick . . .
Nominated for the *Romantic Times* award for
Best Historical Romance Adventure

"Remarkable . . . Meredith Duran is one of the shooting stars of romance."

—*All About Romance*

"Mesmerizing . . . a glorious, nonstop, action-packed battle-of-wills romance."

—*Romantic Times* (4½ stars)

"Wildly romantic."   —*Dear Author* (Grade: A+)

"Everything a great historical romance should be."

—*Romance Junkies*

BOUND BY YOUR TOUCH
One of the Best Books of 2009 in
All About Romance's Reviewer's Choice column

"Entertaining . . . Historical romance fans will enjoy the adventure."

—Publishers Weekly

"A story that packs a powerful punch."

—Fresh Fiction

"Sophisticated, beautifully written, and utterly romantic."

—The Book Smugglers

"A great love story . . . I found new layers and meaning each time I read it."

—Dear Author

"Sizzling sexual tension."

—All About Romance

THE DUKE OF SHADOWS
A 2008 Finalist for the *Romantic Times*
Best Historical Debut award

"Evocative and enticing . . . a luscious delight."

—Liz Carlyle

"Fascinating, emotionally intense."

—Romantic Times (4½ stars)

"Riveting . . . emotion-packed . . . A guaranteed page-turner."

—The Romance Reader (4 stars)

"Without a doubt the best historical romance I have read this year."

—Romance Reviews Today

MEREDITH DURAN

THAT SCANDALOUS SUMMER

Pocket Books

New York   London   Toronto   Sydney   New Delhi

Pocket Books
A Division of Simon & Schuster, Inc.
1230 Avenue of the Americas
New York, NY 10020

This book is a work of fiction. Names, characters, places, and incidents either are products of the author's imagination or are used fictitiously. Any resemblance to actual events or locales or persons, living or dead, is entirely coincidental.

First Pocket Books paperback edition February 2013

POCKET and colophon are registered trademarks of
Simon & Schuster, Inc.

For information about special discounts for bulk purchases, please contact Simon & Schuster Special Sales at 1-866-506-1949 or business@simonandschuster.com.

The Simon & Schuster Speakers Bureau can bring authors to your live event. For more information or to book an event contact the Simon & Schuster Speakers Bureau at 1-866-248-3049 or visit our website at www.simonspeakers.com.

Manufactured in the United States of America

10 9 8 7 6 5 4 3 2 1

ISBN: 978-1-4516-0696-6
ISBN: 978-1-4516-0702-4 (ebook)

For Aunt Jan,
a born storyteller

ACKNOWLEDGMENTS

Maddie and Steph for genius suggestions on the beginning and ending, respectively; Birnholz for bringing me my glasses and sparing me the indignity of 86 point font; Janine, as always, for a myriad of kindnesses; Faren Bachelis for her skillful copyediting; Lauren McKenna for her enthusiasm and endless inspiration; Alex Lewis and the entire team at Pocket Books for turning a dog-eared manuscript into a beautiful book. My thanks and admiration, always.

PROLOGUE

London, March 1885

His brother's town house felt like a tomb. Beyond the brightly lit foyer, the lamps were turned down, the windows shuttered. One would never have guessed that the sun was shining over London.

Michael handed off his hat and gloves. "How does he fare today?"

Jones, Alastair's butler, had once been the epitome of discretion. But this question had become their daily ritual, and he no longer hesitated before answering. "Not well, your lordship."

Michael nodded and scrubbed a hand over his face. Two early morning surgeries had left him exhausted, and he still reeked of disinfectant. "Any visitors?"

"Indeed." Jones turned to fetch the silver salver from the sideboard. The mirror above it was still covered with black crepe. It should have been taken down already, for his brother's wife had died more than seven months ago. But those months had unearthed a series of revelations. Infidelity, lies, addictions—each new discovery had darkened Alastair's grief for his duchess into something more ominous.

That the mirror remained shrouded seemed fitting. It was an accurate reflection, Michael thought, of Alastair's state of mind.

He took the calling cards from Jones, flipping through them to note the names. His brother refused to receive company, but if the calls were not returned, the gossip would grow louder yet. Michael had taken to borrowing the ducal carriage and one of his brother's footmen, waiting on the curb for a chance to leave his brother's card without being seen. Had the situation not been so dire, he would have considered it an excellent farce.

He paused at a particular card. "Bertram called?"

"Yes, an hour ago. His grace did not receive him."

First Alastair had cut himself off from friends, suspicious of their possible involvement in his late wife's affairs. Now, it seemed, he was spurning his political cronies. That was a very bad sign.

Michael started for the stairs. "Is he eating, at least?"

"Yes," called Jones. "But I am instructed not to admit you, my lord!"

That was new. And it made no sense after the note Alastair had sent last night, which he must have known would provoke a response. "Do you mean to throw me out?" he asked without stopping.

"I fear myself too infirm to manage it," came the reply.

"Good man." Michael kept climbing, taking the stairs by threes. Alastair would be in the study, scouring the afternoon newspapers, desperate to reassure himself that news of his wife's proclivities had not been leaked to the press. Or perhaps desperate to *find* the news—and to learn, beyond a shadow of a doubt, who else had betrayed him.

But he would not learn the names today. Michael had already checked the papers himself.

A wave of anger burned through him. He could not believe they'd been reduced to such measures—reduced *again*, after a childhood in which their parents' marriage had exploded slowly and publicly, in three-inch headlines that had kept the nation titillated for years. It went against the grain to think ill of the dead, but in this instance, he would make an exception. *Damn you, Margaret.*

He entered the study without knocking. His brother sat at the massive desk near the far wall, the lamp at his elbow a meager aid against the larger gloom. His blond head remained bent over his reading material as he said, "Leave."

Michael yanked open a drapery as he passed. Sunlight flooded the Oriental carpet, illuminating motes of floating dust. "Let someone in here to clean up," he said. The air smelled of old smoke and stale eggs.

"God damn it." Alastair cast down the newspaper. A decanter of brandy stood uncorked by his elbow, a half-empty glass beside it. "I told Jones I was not at home!"

"That excuse would be more convincing if you ever left." It looked as though Alastair had not slept in a week. He took after their late father, as fair as Michael was dark, and normally he inclined to bulk. Not lately, though. His face looked alarmingly gaunt, and shadows ringed his bloodshot eyes.

Some wit had once dubbed his brother the Kingmaker. It was true that Alastair had a gift for wielding power—political and otherwise. But if his enemies had looked on him now, they would have laughed from relief as much as from malice. This man did not look capable of governing even himself.

Michael pulled open the next set of drapes. Not for a very long time—not since his childhood, spent as a pawn in their parents' games—had he felt so helpless. Had his brother's ailment been physical, he might have cured it. But Alastair's sickness was of the soul, which no medicine could touch.

As he turned back, he caught his brother wincing at the light. "How long since you've stepped outside? A month? More, I think."

"What difference?"

This being the ninth or tenth occasion on which they'd had this exchange, the impulse to snap was strong. "As your brother, I think it makes a great deal of difference. As your doctor, I'm certain of it. Liquor is a damned poor trade for sunshine. You're starting to resemble an undercooked fish."

Alastair gave him a thin smile. "I will take that under advisement. For now, I have business to attend—"

"No, you don't. I'm handling your business these days. Your only occupations are drinking and stewing."

With his harsh words, Michael hoped to provoke a retort. Alastair had ever been mindful of his authority as the eldest. Until recently, such jibes would not have flown.

But all he received in reply was a flat stare.

Damn it. "Listen," he said. "I am growing . . . extremely concerned for you." Christ, it required stronger language. "Last month, I was worried. Now I'm damned near frantic."

"Curious." Alastair looked back to the newspaper. "I would imagine you have other concerns to occupy you."

"There's nothing in the papers. I checked."

"Ah." Alastair lowered the copy of the *Times* and looked dully into the middle distance. In his silence, he resembled nothing so much as a puppet with its strings cut. Damned unnerving.

Michael spoke to break the moment. "What was this note you sent me?"

"Ah. Yes." Alastair pinched his nose, then rubbed the corners of his eyes. "I did send that, didn't I."

"In your cups, were you?"

The hand dropped. Alastair's glare was encouraging. "Quite sober."

"Then explain it to me. Some nonsense about the hospital budget." Michael opened the last set of curtains, and in the process, discovered the source of the smell: a breakfast tray, abandoned on the floor. Jones had been wrong; Alastair had not touched his plate of eggs. The maids were probably too frightened to retrieve it, and too fearful to tell Jones so.

"Whoever told you that we're lacking funds was misinformed," he said as he turned back. Devil take these gossips. He should never have let that journalist into the hospital. But he'd assumed that the article would discuss the plight of poverty, the need for legal reforms.

Instead the reporter had fixated on the spectacle of a duke's brother personally ministering to the dregs. Ever since, the hospital had been overwhelmed by all manner of unneeded interest—bored matrons raised on tales of Florence Nightingale; petty frauds hawking false cures for every ailment under the sun; and, above all, his brother's political opponents, who mocked Michael's efforts in editorials designed to harm Alastair. Had his attention not been occupied by his brother's troubles, he would have been livid with irritation.

"You misunderstood," Alastair said. "That was not a report of rumors. That was information. You are about to lose your main source of funding."

"But you're my main source of funding."

"Yes. I'm withdrawing it."

Michael froze halfway to the seat opposite the desk. "Forgive me, you . . . what?"

"I'm withdrawing my funding."

Astonishment briefly silenced him. He lowered himself into the chair and tried for a smile. "Come now. That's a poor joke. Without your funding, the hospital—"

"Must close." Alastair folded up the newspaper, his movements fastidious. "There's one inconvenience of treating the poor. They can't pay."

Michael groped for words. "You . . . can't be serious."

"I am."

They locked eyes, Alastair expressionless.

Christ. He knew what this was about. "The hospital was not her idea!" Yes, it had been named after Margaret, but that had been by *Alastair's* suggestion. Yes, Margaret had encouraged Michael in the idea, but it had been *his* project. *His* creation. The one thing he could do that his brother could not. "The hospital is *mine.*" The result of nearly a decade of his sweat and toil, with the lowest mortality rates of any comparable institution in the country. "Good God! Simply because she favored the project—"

"You're right," Alastair said. "It has nothing to do with her. But I have reflected on it at length. And I have decided it was an unwise investment."

Michael shook his head. He could not believe this. "I'm dreaming," he said.

Alastair drummed his fingers once. "No. You're quite awake."

"Then this is *bollocks.*" He slammed his hands flat on the desk and stood. "You're right—she deserves no legacy! I'll call in the stonemasons today. We'll chisel her name right off the damned façade. But you cannot—"

"Don't be juvenile." Alastair's words might have been chipped from ice. "You will do no such thing. The press would have a field day with its speculations."

His laughter felt wild. "And you think they won't when the place suddenly *shuts down*?"

"No. Not if you manage it with some subtlety."

"Oh, and now you mean to enlist *me* in this madness?" He drove a hand through his hair, pulling hard, but the pain brought no clarity, only added a sharper edge to his disbelief. "Alastair, you cannot *seriously* think I'll help you to destroy that place—the place I *built*—simply to sate your need for— God knows! *Revenge?* She's *dead,* Al! *She* won't suffer for it! The only people who will suffer are the men and women we treat there!"

Alastair shrugged. "Perhaps you can persuade some other charitable institution to take in the sickest of them."

A strangled noise escaped him. There was no other charity hospital in London with the resources—resources funded chiefly by Alastair, the fifth Duke of Marwick—to minister to every patient in need. And Alastair *knew* that.

Michael turned away from the desk, pacing a tight circle to contain this savage uproar of feeling. This was more than anger. It was a burning mix of shock, rage, and *betrayal.* "Who are you?" he demanded as he spun back. For Alastair always had been a fount of encouragement, both verbal and financial. Study medicine? *A grand idea.* Open a hospital? *Very well, let me fund it.* Alastair had been his protector, his champion . . . his *parent,* when he was young, for God knew their mother and father had been otherwise occupied. "This is not you speaking!"

Alastair shrugged. "I am as I have always been."

"To hell with that! You haven't been that man in— months!" He stood there a moment, his thoughts spinning wildly. "My God. Is this to be her legacy, then? Will you let Margaret drive us apart? Is *that* what you want? Alastair, you *cannot* mean to do this!"

"I anticipated your distress, and I do regret it." Alastair was studying his hands where they rested, loosely linked, atop his blotter. A *bare* blotter. He hadn't looked over his ledgers, or read his correspondence, in weeks. All of it, *all* of his business, had fallen to Michael.

He'd not minded it. As a boy, Alastair had shielded and protected him. He'd been glad to repay that debt. But now . . . now the thought of all he'd done recently felt like salt in the wound. "My God. That you would do this to *me*—"

"You're precisely the reason I do it. And I offer a solution, if you'll be calm enough to listen to it."

"Calm!" A strange laugh seized him. "Oh yes, let us be *calm!*" At Alastair's pointed look toward the chair, he gritted his teeth and sat again. His hand wanted to hit something. He balled it into a fist.

His brother eyed him from behind that desk—that overlarge abomination of a desk, from which their father, too, had lorded it over the world—like a king considering a tiresome petitioner. "I am prepared to make a very sizable settlement upon you, large enough to fund the hospital for decades."

What in God's name? "That would be more than *large*." The hospital treated the poorest citizens of London, and ran entirely on charitable donations.

"Indeed. But there are conditions."

An uncanny feeling ghosted down his spine. A minute ago, he'd felt as though he did not recognize the man across from him. But perhaps he recognized him too well. *There are conditions.* That had been one of their father's favorite phrases.

"Go on," he said warily.

Alastair cleared his throat. "You are generally regarded very warmly in polite circles. Accounted . . . *charming,* I believe."

His premonition strengthened. According to Alastair's hierarchy of virtues, discipline and enterprise ranked first; charm appeared somewhere below a firm handshake and basic hygiene. "I won't like what's coming."

Alastair's mouth twisted, less a smile than a grimace. "Perhaps *too* charming. You must know your reputation. Being glimpsed entering a widow's town house before noon—that was poorly done."

Done *three years ago,* in fact. "Christ, but you've a memory like an elephant! I've never been so sloppy again!" He'd never given another lover cause for complaint. He'd refined discretion to a bloody *art.*

"Your disinterest in politics does not help matters." Alastair settled his fingertips atop the rim of his brandy glass, turning it in increments. "You are not taken . . . seriously, shall we say. But that must change. You are thirty years old. It is time you overcame your objections to marriage."

Michael could no longer follow even the smallest bit of this conversation. "What objections? I have no objections. I've simply never met a woman to inspire the thought." Perhaps he never would. Their parents had offered a very good lesson on *that* count. But what difference? "Whether or not I marry has no bearing on any of this!"

"Not so." Alastair took up his drink and bolted the remainder. "It bears directly on the family. Unless you marry, the title will go to Cousin Harry's future offspring. And that is not acceptable."

"Wait." Alarm sharpened his voice. "What of *your* future offspring?"

Like a light going out, his brother's face shuttered. "I will not marry again."

Christ *God.* "Alastair, you did not die with her."

He might as well have not spoken. "And so the choice falls to you," his brother went on, his cadence curiously flat, as though he recited from memory. "I will require you to marry before the year is out. In return, you'll have the aforementioned settlement, enough to safeguard the hospital until your death, and to make your life quite comfortable besides. However, I reserve the right to approve your choice of brides. Your taste in women to date does not recommend your judgment— and I will not see you repeat my own mistake."

Michael felt as though he were underwater, hearing through a great distortion. "Let me be clear," he said. Let Alastair hear how much a *lunatic* he sounded. "I must marry a woman of your choice. Or you will see the hospital closed."

"Precisely," Alastair said.

He stood, the ground beneath him seeming to shift. "You need help, Al. More help than I know how to give you." God help him, he did not even know where to *look* for the kind of help that Alastair needed. An institution? Every instinct in him recoiled at it. And how would he even enforce such treatment? His brother was the bloody *Duke of Marwick*. No one could force him to do anything.

Alastair rose, too. "Should you refuse my conditions, the cost will be more than your hospital. You will need to look for new lodgings; you'll not be welcome any longer in the flat on Brook Street. Also, of course, some form of employment. When I cut off your allowance, you'll require an income."

Michael's laugh felt like a razor in his throat. He had not been treated this way—bullied and ordered—since their father's passing. And to endure such treatment from *Alastair,* of all people. "You can't take the allowance. It was designated to me in our father's will."

Alastair sighed. "Michael. You'd be quite surprised by what I can and cannot do. That said, I do not expect to deprive you very long. Given a taste of poverty, you will no doubt revisit your intransigence."

Intransigence? He took a ragged breath. "Let's not pretend, here." So difficult to keep his voice even, to speak in a manner that might persuade his brother to listen, when anger was bidding him to scream. "Your threats, my . . . *intransigence*—they have nothing to do with your concern for heirs. This is about *you*." He'd assumed this isolation to be a passing phase, a peculiar manifestation of his brother's rage and grief. But for Alastair to make such threats . . . why, it was his soul they were battling over. "You've let her win. You've given up. On your *own life*. My God!"

His brother shrugged. "I must plan for the future. Once the news comes out—"

That again? "*Let* the news come out! Let the entire world know that Margaret de Grey was an opium eater—let them think she slept with entire armies! What of it?"

His brother's slight smile chilled him to the bone. "Our father's story taught you nothing?"

"That was a different time. And he *earned* his fate." He'd abused their mother. Flaunted his mistresses and reneged on his debts. "His own actions ostracized him." Alastair's only fault had been to trust his wife. "What Margaret did had nothing to do with you. You're innocent in it!"

Alastair's smile widened, becoming grotesquely cheerful. "She made me a fool, no doubt. But I invited her to do so. I fed her the secrets she shared with her lovers, and we lost the elections, twice, because of it. God knows—perhaps we lost more than that. She did have a fondness for Russians, if you'll recall. So tell me, Michael: are you truly so naïve as to believe I'll emerge unscathed?"

Michael bit hard on his cheek. It would be rough going. There would be a scandal. "But you have allies—"

"No matter. What's done is done." Alastair flicked a dismissive finger at the newspaper. "I recommend you consider Lord Swansea's daughter. The mother is everything proper, and by all reports, the daughter is handsome and mannerly. Should reports reach me of your attendance at their ball this Friday, I will take that as a sign that you'll cooperate."

Silence opened. He could not agree to this. *Would* not. But something—*something* had to be done, quickly. Alastair could not go on like this. "I will attend," he said, though the words grated so sharply they should have properly drawn blood. "But I have one condition of my own: you must come with me."

"No. My terms are not open to debate."

God above. "You step outside with me, right now—into fresh air—and I'll attend."

"Alas." Alastair gave a one-shouldered shrug.

His temper snapped. He lunged forward and grabbed Alastair's elbow. "You are coming outside!"

Alastair tried to jerk free. "Get your hands off—"

With brutal force, he dragged Alastair a step toward the door. And then another. Alastair rocked backward, cursing, clawing at his grip. But three months of confinement did no good to a man's strength. Michael locked his arm around his brother's head and hauled him on.

For long seconds, he made headway. Closer and closer came the door.

A fist snapped into his chin. He stumbled backward, still gripping Alastair's lapel. The cloth tore in a long, ugly sound.

Alastair backhanded him.

The blow knocked him back a step. He staggered and caught his balance, his hand clamped over his eye.

"Get out," Alastair said very softly.

Shock briefly paralyzed him. Then he forced his hand to fall. No blood on his fingers. That was something, at least. "Bravo," he said through numb lips. "Your father's son."

The words, their truth, caused his stomach to roil. For a moment he feared he would be sick on the floor. *Your father's son.*

He swallowed. *No.* Alastair was nothing like their father. This was a temporary insanity, a sickness. It could be healed. Somehow. It *would* be healed.

Alastair walked past him back to the desk. Glass clinked. Brandy gurgled.

Michael pushed out a breath. "Listen to me. I won't let—"

"Don't you grow bored of your own voice?" Alastair's drawl was cutting. "Make your idle threats elsewhere, to someone who mistakes you for a man with the power to enforce them."

Michael sucked in a breath. "There, you're wrong. That newspaper article gives me all the power I need."

Alastair pivoted toward him. Michael advanced a single step, and God forgive him if Alastair's retreat did not gratify something very dark in his soul.

No man struck him. Never again. He had vowed it as a boy, when first leaving his father's domain for the safety of school. Now that he was prepared for the possibility of violence, his brother would never again have the upper hand.

If the echo of that thought scored through him like a blade—if, for a moment, bewilderment and hurt swam through him like a toxin—he did not allow them to show. "The hospital is a great credit to you. A loud advertisement for your politics. Tell me, with the elections approaching, how do you think it will look if the world learns that you're responsible for the hospital's destruction? For I'll write to the papers myself to announce your role in it. My hospital, your party's hopes—my legacy, and yours—they will fail as one. Once again, you will cause your party to lose."

Alastair's smile did not linger. "Impressive," he said. "But forgive me if I'm not persuaded. You see, I think here of your precious patients. In the end, you'll concede—for their sake, if not your own."

"Test me." For now he meant it: he would not humor this madness a moment longer. Seven months now—he should never have let it go so far. "Indeed, perhaps it will be a relief to you if I spill this tale. No more waiting for the news about Margaret to break. Your name will be ruined long beforehand, along with your party's trust."

Alastair slammed down the glass. "You will go now. Remove your property from the flat on Brook Street, or I will have it disposed of."

By God, that did it. "Here's a better idea. I'll leave London entirely. You go ahead, destroy the hospital. Give the public a jolly good show. I won't be here to see it."

Something dark passed over his brother's face, twisting his mouth into a savage smile. "Oh, you'll be here. Where would you go? *All* my properties will be closed to you."

"To hell with you." Michael turned on his heel for the door.

"Although . . . it would be amusing to see you try to hide. I give you three weeks. Perhaps four. You can't imagine what it means to make your way in the world without my influence. You've absolutely no idea how to go on."

The remark was like a hot lance through his chest. Or through his pride. He paused, his hand gripping the door latch, and took a hard breath. This room. He had always hated this study. It was where their father had been at his most comfortable. Lord of the manor. Tyrant extraordinaire.

"I am not your puppet," he said. "And I will not dance to this tune. For *your* sake, Alastair, as well as my own."

He walked out, slamming the door shut behind him. The sharp bang triggered an ache in his chest, a bruise that spread deep beneath his skin.

For his brother's sake, he meant it: he would leave town. And he would stay gone until Alastair left this godforsaken house to come find him.

CHAPTER ONE

Bosbrea, Cornwall, June 1885

A drunkard lay snoring in his rosebushes. She looked inexplicably familiar, though Michael did not think he would have forgotten such a face. She was one of the more beautiful women he'd ever seen, all creamy skin and long, spiraling, chestnut hair—and she was dressed as though for a ball.

He stood staring down at her for a long moment. How peculiar. She was unbearably lovely, and . . .

It's a trap.

He took one step backward before catching himself. Christ, what a wild thought! A *trap?* His brother was not quite so Machiavellian as *that.*

Her diamond tiara, one hoped, was made of paste.

He cleared his throat. "Ho," he said. "Wake up, there."

No response.

He rubbed his eyes, feeling insufficiently awake to manage such novelties. The scent of bergamot still lingered on his palm from his morning tea. It was not yet seven o'clock—no time of day to be drunk. And she *was* drunk, was she not? He did not think it was the flowers exuding the stench of whisky.

He cast a look around the garden, but no help was forthcoming. It being a Wednesday, the gardener and job-boy were both at their homes in the village for the morning. Meanwhile, all around him, the sun was splashing brightly across glossy green leaves, and birds sang in the flowering branches of the camellias. Not the season for drunkenness, really. Summer in Cornwall was better suited to lemonade.

The woman's body jerked on a snore—not a small or kittenish sound, that, but a phlegm-filled snort, the more startling because her rib cage didn't look large enough to produce a whisper. She was laced within an inch of her life.

Michael frowned. This fashion could go to the devil. Half of his female patients would have returned to instant health if only they were willing to cast off their corsets.

Sleeping Beauty snorted again. Her arm flopped out. The bloody scratch bisecting her inner elbow would need dressing.

Well, at least she passed out in advantageous spots. Better the bushes of a doctor than a baker. *Or a candlestick maker,* his tired mind helpfully nattered.

Dear God. Rustication was rotting his wits.

He stepped forward to grasp the woman's wrists. She was wearing only one glove, long, elbow-length, delicate lace. The other was missing.

Foreboding crept over him, prickling along his scalp. But what an absurd instinct. She had drunk herself silly, and then she had stumbled down the hill from Havilland Hall in search of God knew what. A water closet, probably.

He lifted her into his arms, discovering with a grunt that she was not as light as she looked. "Mmm," she said. Her head lolled into the cradle of his shoulder, and he felt the wetness of drool.

A laugh slipped from him. Such an effect he had on women! He kicked open the garden gate, then shouldered his way through the front door.

"Mercy me!" This shocked exclamation came from the depths of the hallway. Mrs. Brown hustled into view, visibly appalled by the bundle in his arms. "If it isn't Mrs. Chudderley!"

The bundle in his arms was married? What kind of man would let his wife wander off in such a state? And such a woman, too—

He closed his brain to the path his mind had started down. He was doing a very good job (he congratulated himself) of avoiding *particular* notice of the woman herself. Missing glove, expensive gown, possibly real jewels, very tight lacing: these details would occupy his brain rather than the feel of her in his arms, the curve of her arse surprisingly substantial.

No women. Not until his brother recovered his wits. Michael would give him no inroads for trickery. Alastair would have to sire his heirs himself.

He cleared his throat. "Mrs. Chudderley, you say? Well, then—send for her husband." He started down the hall, the rustle of starched skirts announcing his housekeeper's pursuit.

"Oh, she's got no husband," said Mrs. Brown. She sounded as stern as those occasions when she discovered dust on the mantel. "Don't you read the newspapers, sir? She's a widow—and an infamous one at that!"

To his discredit, he recognized a stir of interest at

this announcement. *Infamous. Widow.* So many ways, so many words, by which to label a woman fair game. Widows had always been his favorite type . . .

Don't be a bastard, Michael.

Granted, if Mrs. Chudderley was infamous, she herself probably had no small hand in it. A woman who passed the night in a stranger's garden, drooling on her diamonds, clearly felt comfortable flirting with an ill fate.

As he mounted the stairs, the boards underfoot squeaked like small creatures being tortured. The thought crossed his mind: *need to fix those.*

Ludicrous. He would not be here long enough to make such improvements. And as Mrs. Brown constantly reminded him, the household budget could not accommodate such luxuries. He'd leased this house— five rooms and a garden, no land attached—for six months, all his small savings could afford. But surely that was all it would take. Michael's continued absence would goad Alastair like a thorn in his side. He would bestir himself from that creaky mansion and come looking soon enough.

Until then, Bosbrea made an ideal place to hide. The only other medical man in the vicinity was over seventy and glad for the help. Furthermore, Michael had no connections in this area of Cornwall. It would take time for Alastair to find him here—enough time to properly prick his temper, and, so Michael hoped, goad him out of that house.

I give you four weeks, Alastair had predicted. Pompous bastard. Michael hoped he was enjoying his feast of crow.

He deposited Mrs. Chudderley on the bed in the front room. The depth of her sleep concerned him somewhat. He laid two fingers to her pulse. Her skin felt clammy from the alcohol poisoning her system, but her heartbeat was steady and strong.

Her upper lip looked to have been drawn by an artist's hand, so precise were its peaks on either side of her philtrum. Her lower lip was . . . lush. What color were her eyes?

Brown like her hair, he supposed. A rich, dark shade, like Parisian chocolate. Bittersweet.

But highly edible.

Christ almighty. He stepped back, both amused and appalled. In London, he'd always known a woman willing to entertain him. But here, in the chaste countryside, he was learning ever so many things about himself. For instance: abstinence made him a very bad poet.

"Too pretty for her own good," Mrs. Brown muttered. Michael glanced over in time to catch the edge of his housekeeper's uneasy look, just as she flicked it away. He supposed he'd been staring. That would be typical behavior around the widow.

His housekeeper's next remark confirmed it. "Photographs of her, sold for money." Mrs. Brown's tight jaw telegraphed her opinion of this industry. "You see them in all the city shops. She's a, what do you say? A *professional beauty,* they call it."

"Ah," he said. This was *that* Mrs. Chudderley. He knew of her. She ran with Viscount Sanburne's circle, a very fast crowd. He'd been to school with Sanburne, but in the years since, their circles had rarely overlapped: even with a generous allowance, he'd lacked the funds to keep up with that sort. Also, the interest. Wild parties did not appeal to him.

For this one, though, he might have made an exception. Unconscious, she looked like a figure from a fairy tale, her long chestnut hair suitable for wrapping around a man's wrist, her pink lips slightly parted in invitation of a kiss. Something far more touchable than classical beauty, here.

He made himself look away again. "Her color seems healthy." Poor form to ogle a woman who was not even awake.

Out the open window, over the trees, loomed the turrets of the estate from which she had tumbled. Sleeping Beauty's abode. It looked less a mansion than a miniature castle, with banners streaming from the towers and a widow's walk encircling the roof. Gaudy, confused architecture—not an old home, or an established one.

He smiled at himself mockingly. What a *very* grand judgment for a country doctor to issue.

"Shall I fetch your kit?" asked Mrs. Brown.

"Please do. I expect she's scratched all over."

All over.

Good God. That his mouth went dry appalled him.

"Scratched all over her arms," he said grimly, by way of clarification. Any other scratches, he would let Mr. Morris tend. Morris was the doctor preferred by the denizens of Havilland Hall. Michael was glad to let him have them. He must keep as far from his brother's world as possible, for now.

Her head hurt.

Liza kept her eyes closed, though consciousness stole in with unmerciful speed, scraping like a knife over the wooden lump of her wits.

Recollection was slower to come. Breath held, body tense, she waited for the memory of whatever had happened to give her such a terrible headache. It would be very mortifying, she felt sure; this felt like a two-bottle headache, and one did not drink two bottles unless the need was great. Already she felt humiliation crawling under her skin, anticipatory, ready to sink in claws.

"Good morning," said a voice. A pleasant voice, not loud enough to antagonize her aching head; a smoky, low, male voice . . . which she did not recognize.

She opened her eyes and her breath caught in her throat. The man standing over her looked like a wolf in the lean season: hollow cheeks, dark hair, burning eyes. His carnivorous mouth offered her a slow, unsettling smile.

Fear flashed through her. The man was in his shirt-sleeves. She had no idea who he was.

"Sleeping Beauty awakes," he murmured, and then his smile disappeared, as though his own words displeased him. Without the smile, his angular face became severe. He had tremendously bold cheekbones, and a nose like the prow of a ship.

Swallowing nervously, she became aware of a tremendous thirst. Her mouth felt like a desert. Who was he? "Have you any water?" she whispered.

When he nodded and turned away, she pushed herself up by one elbow. Only then did she see the tall, well-padded woman hovering in the doorway—a housekeeper, judging by the key ring tied to her apron. The woman looked vaguely familiar—a face from the village, perhaps. The narrow look she cast Liza before leaving also felt familiar. It was filled with disapproval.

Well, then. Liza's reputation had preceded her here—wherever *here* might be. *Here* also obviously was a place located firmly on the moral high ground—that look from the housekeeper proved it—so she needn't fear her wolfish interlocutor, either. Men bent on rapine did not employ aged women with consciences.

Good God, her head hurt! Why couldn't she remember—

The man turned back. She tried out a smile. He did not reenter the room, but took up his servant's former place in the doorway. Some look on his face—a flash of wariness—gave her the odd impression that he did not wish to come too close.

Her intuition faded as she studied him. He did not look prone to intimidation by a woman. Lean through the hips, broad at the shoulders, he filled the doorway comprehensively. A touch underfed, perhaps—those hollowed cheeks suggested a recent illness. But it was nothing a month of Sunday roasts could not fix. She looked for such long, well-muscled lines in her public servants, and knew them very hard to find.

Alas, footmen must also have classical features and natural vanity. This one's hair was a gorgeous shade of brown, dark and glossy, sure to be soft to the touch—but unkempt, as though he often ruffled it. His suit was not only incomplete—where was his jacket?—but pointedly plain. His waistcoat and trousers, both a muted gray, were slightly too large for him.

When her survey returned to his eyes, she discovered that he was watching her, his regard steady and unreadable. For some reason, her heart tripped pleasantly. Well, the wolfish smile, of course. And men who did not babble and fuss over her—men of athletic self-possession—were rather her favorite type, though she knew they should not be. But who could resist a challenge?

How did she not know this man? He had a striking presence. Or perhaps that was only a trick of his nose.

"Where am I, sir?" It seemed more courteous than demanding his name.

"Outside Bosbrea, ma'am."

His respectful address eased the last of her fears. "Then you must be a neighbor," she said. The village of Bosbrea was only an hour's walk from home.

"I suppose so."

Taciturn, wasn't he? And she'd thought she knew all her neighbors. She cast a curious glance over the room. The bedspread was stitched together in homely fashion from mismatched patches of cloth. No carpet softened the polished wood floorboards. A modest, un-ornamented suite of walnut furniture stood guard on the perimeters of the room: chest of drawers, trunk, and armoire. The walls bore an old-fashioned print, little bouquets of flowers that suddenly swam together.

She frowned and knuckled her eyes. Clearly she was not on either of the neighboring estates. How had she gotten here? Last night—last night—

Nello had left!

Of course. God in heaven, how had she forgotten? She'd told him the disastrous news, and he'd then shared his own. He'd been *waiting* to tell her—waiting all day and most of the night, while he consumed her food and abused her hospitality. The memory flooded her now like nausea.

Wait—the nausea was *real*.

She swung herself off the bed so quickly that her balance went. A hard grip closed on her arm and pushed her back to a safer, sitting position. The man must have lunged across the room in a single pace. Very impressive, no doubt, but balance wasn't of much value to her when her stomach was still protesting. Sharply she said, "I'm going to—"

The man dropped to his knees to rummage beneath the bed. He popped back up with a chamber pot—clean, thank God, smelling of vinegar. She grasped it to her belly, feeling its coolness even through her gown and corset and linens. And then she closed her eyes and fought to retain her dignity.

He left. It was final, this time. She'd thrown him out on his ear, for the very moment Nello had discovered her financial troubles, he'd decided to propose marriage to that—that child, that timorous miss who could not even pronounce her own name without stammering—

"*Yes, Elizabeth, an* innocent. *What other kind of woman should I marry?*"

How casually he'd said it, while examining his nails. By that point—shredded by his coldness, by his utter indifference to her tears—she had known better than to speak the reply that came to mind.

She took a deep, ragged breath now. *You were meant to marry* me.

"Are you in pain?"

The quiet voice was edged with concern. As she opened her eyes, she realized why. A tear was slipping down her cheek.

Good God, what drama! How mortifying. Wiping it away—feeling, to her regret, the warmth of a blush forming on her skin—she shook her head. "No," she said, and then cleared her throat. *Be cheerful, Liza. Nobody likes a bore.*

She lifted her chin and smiled. In reply, the man frowned. It was not the first time she'd had cause to reflect that the onus of being charming generally was borne by women alone.

I grow bored with this, Nello had said. As though her distress were performed for his amusement! As though he had not been *begging* to marry her six months ago!

The man was waiting for her reply. She took a deep breath. "Forgive me, sir." Her smile did not want to balance properly; it kept slipping off her lips. "It's terribly awkward, seeing as we're neighbors, but I'm afraid I don't know your name."

His eyes were striking, a smoky bluish gray, the pupils ringed by starbursts of gold. Their steadiness seemed increasingly judgmental. "I'm the new doctor," he said.

"The new . . ." She hadn't known there was a doctor in the area apart from Mr. Morris.

He saw her confusion. "Michael Grey, at your service."

"Oh." She wiped again at her eyes, still appalled by that brief moment of tears. Nello did not deserve them. What a fraud! He had not meant one word of his promises. And all the dreams she'd spun for their future . . . they were fraudulent, too. She should not mourn for them. It was clear now they had always been as hollow as spun glass. "Well, Mr. Grey." She cleared her throat. "How do you do, then?"

"At the moment, I'm concerned," he said evenly. "Does something hurt you in particular?"

"What?" She could not imagine how she hadn't noticed his eyes instantly. Such unlikely beauty. His nose, she supposed, had overshadowed them. "No, I'm quite well indeed." Nello's nose was straight and narrow, but his eyes were a very plain brown. The color of *pig* muck.

The doctor's dark brows arched, a message of skepticism. "Did you injure yourself in some way I cannot see? There's no call for modesty."

Evidently her reputation did *not* precede her, or he wouldn't imagine she had any modesty. "No," she said, "I'm quite fine." But of course he did not look convinced, having seen her weep. "It's only that the light is so bright in here." As he cast a doubtful glance toward the window, she rushed onward. "And I do hope you won't think too *terribly* of me, but I confess, I don't recall *precisely* how I came to be"—*in your bed* sounded a bit indelicate—"here."

His gaze returned to her. He really did put her in mind of a wolf, or some other predatory creature. It wasn't owed so much to the sharpness of his bone structure or the darkness of his coloring—for he was quite tanned—as it was to his absolute and obvious ease with her discomfort. "I can't say how you arrived here, ma'am. But I found you in my rosebushes."

His . . . *rosebushes?* She sucked in a long breath, wrestling for composure. Good heavens, had she slept outside in the dew? This was . . . humbling, even by her own recent standards.

He was still watching her, the steadiness of his observation somehow clinical. She forced herself to meet his gaze. She could not control her color, but she certainly wouldn't duck her head like a meek little girl. "The rosebushes," she said brightly. "But how novel!"

He laughed, a low, slow, husky sound. "Indeed," he said. "Novel was precisely the word that came to my mind."

That *laugh.* And the smile that lingered on his mouth now! Slow to spread, it assumed a mocking edge that—

to her amazement—made her breath catch. She reared back a little, and his head tipped as though to see her better, and that smile . . . continued to spread.

Goodness. For some reason she suddenly felt certain that he knew *precisely* what effect his smile worked on her. Moreover, he was *enjoying* it.

She swallowed. How unexpected. "The new doctor, you say?"

"Here to tend to your scratches," he confirmed with a bow so slight as to be insulting. His low, smooth voice made the task sound distinctly . . . unchaste.

Her bewilderment increased. Such a raw, animal presence did not generally belong to *doctors*. Now she was awake to it, she could feel its effect, thrumming through the air between them like curling tendrils of electricity, reaching for her.

This one . . . this one would say very nasty things in bed, and laugh at her when she protested, and make her like it anyway.

She pushed out a breath. Obviously her night in the bushes had scrambled her wits. "I hope the roses did not suffer overmuch for hosting me." Pray *God* this doctor did not incline to gossip.

"I believe they will survive," he said. When he reached out to take her hand, the contact of his bare skin on hers made her fingers twitch as though she'd been shocked.

His light eyes met hers. Perhaps this attraction was only in her imagination, for his expression remained bland. "If you would follow me downstairs, I'll see to your scratches."

She let him pull her to her feet. He was taller than Nello, his shoulders broader. And those long, long legs . . .

She eyed them as she followed him out, putting her hand once to the wall to catch her balance. His trousers might have been tighter, but as he walked, she could glimpse sufficient hints to form an ardent appreciation for his musculature. Nello looked very well with his clothes on, but this man would fare the better for losing them.

She bit her lip, amazed by herself. But . . . why hesitate? To the devil with Nello! What she required was a distraction from heartbreak, and this mysterious neighbor might keep her *well* entertained.

CHAPTER TWO

Thankfully, Mr. Grey was a bachelor: that was clear from his drawing room, which was small and well dusted but spartanly furnished and barren of curios. A lady never would have allowed the appearance of that flower-patterned carpet, either. It was too thick and garishly bright to be anything but new, and factory made at that.

Yet the dearth of valuables perhaps moved his staff to a more relaxed attitude than Liza's household adopted, for the curtains were thrown wide, allowing the light to damage what it might. As a result, the room felt cozy, sunlit and cheerful, despite the awful carpet.

Mindful of her tendency to freckle, she took a seat in the only corner where the sun did not reach, in a pretty green velveteen chair so generously upholstered that she felt as though she were sinking. Were it not for her corset, she would have slumped into a boneless heap.

Mr. Grey, standing over her with kit in hand, frowned. "You should not lace so tightly, Mrs. Chudderley. It will injure your health."

Goodness! She swallowed a laugh at his frankness.

How endearingly naïve! Her doctor clearly did not know much of London fashions. For that matter, he didn't seem to know of *her*. In town, men would have lined up at the door to glimpse her in this dress. She could only imagine their reactions to the notion that she would do better to expand her waistline by five inches.

Mr. Grey settled the kit on the floor and then knelt before her—and began to roll up his shirt cuffs. Her mouth nearly fell open. What a barbaric thing to do! He was a savage. A savage whose bared forearms . . . made her mouth go dry.

His wrists were broad, lightly haired. His forearms looked to be carved from pure muscle. The veins on them stood out distinctly as he unwound a length of gauze.

Adorably barbaric. She wanted to trace those veins with her fingertips. Surely his arms could not be as hard as they looked.

Her fingers curled into her palm. She could not assault innocent country doctors. She would give him the vapors. "It looks to be a . . . lovely day," she said.

"Indeed." Without warning, he grasped her arms—a little sound catching in her throat as he held them out for inspection.

He glanced up. "Are you all right?" he asked.

His voice was pure courtesy. But he gripped her bare skin very firmly, his palm hot and dry and a little rough.

"Yes," she said faintly. What in God's name ailed her? This reaction was nearly *animal*.

She forced her attention elsewhere. To the dreadful carpet. But that only brought into view his lower half. His squatting position made the lawn of his summer trousers strain over his thighs.

His thighs looked even more well muscled than his arms.

She shook her head slightly. Rustic, untutored Mr. Grey gave new meaning to the notion of a diamond in the rough.

"I see nothing that requires stitches," he said.

She manufactured a laugh. "Lovely. I confess I've no fondness for needles. Why, my needlepoint would give you terrors."

"Oh? I'd no idea I seemed so cowardly. Must work on that."

Was that a *giggle* that slipped from her? She bit her lip, appalled. She was Elizabeth Chudderley: she did not *giggle*. "No, I assure you," she said. "It's dreadful. I aim at a simple flower, and I achieve a . . . well, a *blob* would be a generous description for it."

His smile was brief, and he made no reply as he bent his dark head once again to his task.

Her mild disappointment mixed with puzzlement. Perhaps he thought himself too far beneath her to flirt. The poor dear! She must correct him.

Once again, he turned her limb without permission. In bed with a woman, would he manipulate her body in this same way? Commanding, but not cruel; he would not accept any shyness, nor any reluctance, either. He would have his way with her, calmly and deliberately. *Methodically.*

With a small shock she registered her own thoughts. It was not her way to dream of such intimacy with a stranger. Why, apart from her husband, Nello was the only man—

A pang shot through her. *No. Do not think of him. He doesn't deserve a single thought. Ass, cad, pig!*

How could one's own judgment err so terribly? She had felt so certain that at last she'd found love. So *certain*!

She should never have told him of her troubles. Never should have gotten involved with him in the first place. All her friends had warned her of his motives. *Fortune hunter. Rake.* But even fortune hunters and rakes could fall in love. So she had told herself. So she had believed.

You terrible, unforgivable fool.

His face, when she had told him of her financial troubles . . . She had never seen a sneer form so quickly.

If Nello told tales abroad, what would she do then? For there was no one less popular in society than a widow desperate for funds.

"You did not simply fall into the bushes, Mrs. Chudderley. It would appear that once there, you rolled."

As the doctor glanced up, a trick of the light turned his eyes to a deeper blue. The effect caught like a hook in her stomach.

She stared at him. He was not handsome, precisely— but his face rewarded study. Bold cheekbones. Striking eyes and a very firm jaw. He had a cleft in his chin that begged to be touched.

Something chemical seemed to be bubbling inside her, a reaction unbalancing in its vigor. She would embrace it, gladly. It was better than weeping. "How clumsy of me," she said. "Are you *certain* your roses didn't suffer for it?" She could offer to replace them with something lovely from her hothouse. Could deliver them herself, in fact.

"Oh, the roses are thriving," he said easily. "Certainly they fared better than your hands."

"Indeed." She tried for a teasing tone. "A lady should always wear gloves on her midnight ventures. How brazen you must think me!"

He gave her another brief lift of his brow, a look she could not read. Or perhaps she would only have preferred that it be unreadable, for it reminded her as strongly as words that he had not merely found her unconscious in his bushes, but drunk besides—a far greater brazenness than the lack of gloves.

Mortification burned through her again.

One could not blame him for condemning your behavior.

The thought seemed to announce itself in her mother's voice. She frowned and glanced toward the window, letting the brightness of the sunshine scald her eyes until she could swallow the knot that had come into her throat. *Enough. Don't think on that now.*

Mama would never have liked Nello. But she had liked Alan Chudderley, so her judgment, too, had not proved so sound.

What a hash I've made of everything. Mama would never have foreseen it. "My golden girl," she'd called Liza. Gentle, kind, misguided Mama. Nobody would ever again look at Liza with such faith.

The thought was too painful, and her sharp breath too loud; it caught the doctor's attention.

"Yes," he said, "this one is the deepest." His low voice had a rich, soothing, almost honeyed quality to it—the voice, she supposed, of a man born to sing.

Indeed, he was very well spoken for a doctor. She could not catch a hint of his origins. "Where is your home, Mr. Grey?" She would focus not on her own wretched state, but on making him comfortable. She would show him that it was all right to address her less professionally, more . . . flirtatiously. A distraction was what she needed.

He dabbed a length of gauze in the liquid his house-keeper had brought—sharp-smelling, almost like vin-egar. "North of here." Before she could insist on a good deal more specificity, he added, "This may sting."

As he laid the tisane to the long scratch bisecting her forearm, she sucked in an obliging breath. It didn't hurt, of course. Only a ninny would imagine that it hurt. But she supposed she had no cause for surprise if he imag-ined her an idiot.

Your recent behavior invites all manner of cruel judg-ments.

Liza bit the inside of her cheek to stem the next prick of tears. Even in death, it seemed, Mama could not hold her tongue. Would this nattering voice never leave her in peace? It seemed only to grow stronger with each passing day.

Dared she ask him for a peg of whisky? It would lessen her headache. Whisky was held to be medicinal, was it not?

"The headache will diminish," said Mr. Grey—star-tling her, until she realized that she was rubbing her temple. "Be sure to take fluids until it does," he added. "Broth and tea, preferably."

The dear, sweet bumpkin! He issued his instructions as though he imagined this was the first time she had drunk to excess. Only the kindness in his eyes stopped her from laughing at him. Indeed, as she looked into them, the ache in her heart seemed to ease a little.

"You are very decent," she said. "A true gentleman, sir." Perhaps they all inhabited the middling classes. That would explain their rarity in her world.

The compliment made him frown. "I'm a doctor, Mrs. Chudderley. This is what I do."

"Perhaps you see it so." But some men, on finding a woman unconscious in the night . . .

She laid her hand over his where it cupped her elbow. His fingers twitched, the only sign of his surprise. His knuckles felt slightly rough. Of course they did. He *worked* for his living.

The idea caused a flush to move through her. Exotic creature. Capable, skilled hands. This man did not merely know how to handle reins and hunting rifles. Pity that true gentlemen and handsome bank accounts so rarely coincided. "Thank you," she said.

Their eyes met. That electric current seemed to snap into place again.

"My pleasure," he murmured.

She drew in a great breath of him. He smelled so . . . *masculine.* A great, muscled laborer of a man, with no notion of proper fashions, no inkling that she might be one of the more famous beauties in the country. Ludicrous, perfectly absurd, but she felt a sudden, overpowering wave of fondness. He was just *lovely.* Pity she couldn't keep him—simply take him back with her to Havilland Hall, and have him tend to her arms and scowl very adorably at her *every* morning she woke up with a sore head.

The door opened. He pulled free of her and pushed to his feet. Had they been doing anything remotely inappropriate, or had there been a shade less grace in his movement, she might well have characterized him as *springing away.*

"Splendid," he said to the housekeeper, "thank you, Mrs. Brown," and waved toward the tea table.

Clearly he was unnerved. Why else should he imagine that his servant needed direction on where to set the tray? Liza watched him with growing amusement as *he* watched his housekeeper lay out the saucers. Evidently he also felt this magnetic pull—and it rattled him.

"Well," he said in something near to a mutter, meeting neither her nor his servant's eyes. "I will leave you to take your tea in peace, Mrs. Chudderley—"

The housekeeper cut him a startled look.

Liza came to her feet. "Oh, no," she said warmly as he turned away toward the door. "Please stay. I do so wish to learn more about my savior."

For a moment it appeared he would ignore her and continue his striding escape. But then the housekeeper said, in tones of pure disbelief, "Sir?"

He stopped. His shoulders squared. When he turned, he was smiling, as though Liza's interest suited him perfectly. "Of course," he said pleasantly. He came back to sit across from her, that false smile still riding his lips.

Mr. Grey took his tea with no cream and two spoons of sugar. His eyes met hers over the rim of his cup, then flicked away as though hers burned.

Warmth prickled through her cheeks. The wild thought came to her to say to him: *Yes, I feel it, too. Marvelous, isn't it?*

What a mortifying gaffe that would be! She gave herself an inward shake. She had rubbed shoulders with dukes and princes, and had no cause to be disconcerted into social blunders by a country doctor—no matter how handsome his forearms.

Clearing her throat, she said, "I'm not surprised that a man so charming as you should hail from a place north of here." When he glanced at her, frowning the slightest bit, she offered her kindest, most encouraging smile. "There are so many lovely places in that category—why, nearly the whole country, I believe. We are, after all, in Cornwall."

His laughter sounded rusty and surprised. "So we are," he said.

That was not a very helpful contribution to the conversation. Luckily for him, she felt patient. "Must I guess, then, which part of our lovely north was blessed by your birth?"

"The coldest part," he said.

The housekeeper was looking back and forth between them as though watching a tennis match. Liza could not much blame her. Mr. Grey's elliptical replies verged on a spectacle. The dear heart was shy! "So you come to Cornwall for the warmth," she said.

"For the peace and quiet, in fact." His eyes slipped down her body, returning to her face so quickly that she might have imagined it. But she hadn't. Her skin burned where his gaze had wandered.

He was very aware of her as a woman. And he did not like it.

Her answering disappointment seemed to scrape along the raw wound opened by Nello's betrayal. She had all the patience in the world for shyness, but no tolerance whatsoever for moralizing curmudgeons. She had vowed it over her late husband's grave: she would never again apologize for herself to any man.

Tucking back her shoulders and arching her spine the smallest amount, she leaned forward. Granted, this formal gown was not suited to nuncheon teas, but it certainly displayed her bosom most admirably. "I hope I have not disrupted your peace too terribly, then."

Now his eyes met and held hers with a steadiness that caused a little shock of warmth to explode in her stomach. He knew exactly what she was doing. "I expect I shall recover shortly," he murmured.

That frank, appraising look could not belong to a prude. Her pulse began to thrum again. "I must thank you for your ministrations with an invitation to dinner—tonight, if you're free." It was her social duty, after all, to welcome newcomers to the district.

"Alas," he said, "I've a prior engagement at the vicarage."

This news gave her brief pause. She was not certain she was prepared to flirt with a man who willingly consorted with men of God. Such an undertaking would no doubt be riddled with lectures.

But . . . one must take risks to win rewards. A pleasant distraction, a harmless flirtation, would be very welcome. "Tomorrow, then?"

For the brief space of a moment he merely looked at her. And then he gave her a strange, knowing smile that utilized only half his mouth. "Mrs. Chudderley. I think that would be unwise."

She blinked. The answer was so unexpected—and, if interpreted in a particular way, so frankly *impudent,* as though he assumed that if he did come, he would have his way with her over the dessert course—that it briefly took her breath away.

His smile widened into a grin. "And now I've shocked you," he said, and set his cup back into his saucer with a definitive click. "I am bad company, I confess it. This is precisely why I must decline your invitation: I should not like to ruin your good opinion of the north."

He rose then and sketched a bow that belied his own words, for it spoke of polish and breeding, and an education in the niceties of society. But before she could point this out—and she might have done; he was intolerably blunt, which meant she might be blunt in reply—he had turned on his heel, throwing over his shoulder the discouraging: "Mrs. Brown will show you out, ma'am."

And then he was gone, leaving her puzzled about whether she should be terribly offended, or determined to answer what surely *must* have been intended as a challenge. For nobody said no to her—especially not men who were considered bad company.

CHAPTER THREE

At the house, in the entry hall, the rap of the butler's heels echoed off the marble dome high above. Undoubtedly it was a remonstrance to Liza that neither he nor the footman seemed surprised by her bedraggled state, her lack of cloak and hat and gloves, her seven hours' absence, or her failure to have appeared at breakfast.

"Good morning, ma'am," said Ronson. The butler's voice was terribly bland as he clicked his heels together in a bow. His face, hatched by lines that grew deeper when he frowned, currently looked as though it had been carved with an axe. Dear Ronson did not approve of her. "I see that Miss Mather does not accompany you."

Her secretary? "No, of course not." Mather tended to disappear when the liquor came out—last night being no exception.

Liza took up her mail from the salver proffered by a footman. A dozen envelopes, many of them invitations forwarded from London. She had closed up the town house three weeks ago, after that disastrous meeting with her solicitors. Creditors knocking right and left . . . they all seemed to be in cahoots, for the crisis had manifested with such shocking suddenness. Her first instinct had been to flee to where she felt safest. *Hide and regroup.*

Now she had a new reason to stay away. In London, the beau monde would make a sport of watching her reactions as Nello courted his heiress beneath her nose. She could not go back to town. It would be a summer in the country for her.

She cleared her throat, breathing deeply to stave off a welling loneliness. *It doesn't matter. Let her have him.* She knew how much his promises were worth. Oh, he'd been full of sweet words at the beginning. He had promised her everything—the moon, the stars, marriage, and everlasting love. And in the wake of her mother's death, she'd been desperate to believe him.

But she'd also been too recently widowed, and too well educated in how quickly marriage could go wrong, to commit herself so quickly. *Give me time,* she'd begged him. *A little time is all I need.*

Thank God for that! For his motive had not been love, after all. No, what he'd been looking for was money.

She should probably do the same.

Her throat closed. What choice did she have? It wasn't simply her own welfare that hung in the balance. Everyone who worked her land—though the value of their crops kept falling; everyone whom she employed—and the children whose educations she funded, and the parish, and the village school—

How could a handful of bad choices have sunk her so quickly? Her accountants had seemed amazed. *Can it be that your solicitors never reviewed your late husband's investments?* But the solicitors said it had been the accountants' duty to do so. For her own part, she might have kicked herself for assuming that such matters didn't require her oversight. But really, what did *she* know of stocks and bonds?

The silence felt heavy. She glanced up. Ronson's lifted brow screamed with significance. "Ah, yes," she said. "You were speaking of Mather?"

"Indeed, ma'am. When Mrs. Hull could not account for your whereabouts at the breakfast table, Miss Mather went in search of you."

Liza sighed. A hundred times she had chided Mather, but the girl had a gift for fretfulness: at the slimmest possibility of trouble, she was off like a dog on the scent of a bone. "I do wish you had stopped her, then. *You* knew I was fine."

"Of course," Ronson said blandly. "Shall I dispatch someone to locate her?"

"Yes, tell her I'm well. Though I—"

"Elizabeth!" A figure appeared at the top of the staircase, hands clasped dramatically to heart. Jane Hull was a fellow widow and new friend whom Liza had encountered when taking the water at Baden Baden. Oh, glorious winter! She'd been so innocent then of the troubles to come.

Clearing her throat, she made her voice bright. "Good morning," she called. And the sight did cheer her. From this angle, Jane looked like a hovering angel, for as always she wore white, and her blond hair fell to her waist, unbound. A very winsome discovery. She would be great fun to introduce to everybody at the next party. *Provided I'm invited, once the news breaks.* She pushed that thought aside. "I hope you didn't miss me too terribly last night."

"Thank heaven you're back safely!" Jane replied in a high, trembling voice.

A snort came from Ronson's direction. Liza turned her smile on him, glad to see real life in his expression—but then he averted his face, the bulldog.

How absurd to feel wounded. He was only a servant, after all. She hiked up her chin and gave him her back.

Jane came rushing down the stairs to embrace her. "Did you find him?" she whispered into Liza's ear. Her cheek was cool and smooth where it pressed against Liza's, soft with youth, and she smelled unbearably wholesome: rose water, soap, and the lavender that the maids folded into the household laundry.

Conscious that she herself did not smell so sweetly, Liza pulled back—or attempted to; Jane would not permit it. "Come," the girl said, clasping Liza's waist and drawing her up the stairs. "Tell me all of it. Your maid says Mr. Nelson has left. Did you throw him out? Or"—Jane's voice dropped, and a pretty pink stained her cheeks—"were you *with* him all night?"

Liza did worry about Jane's ingenuous mannerisms. They would not be counted at all fashionable. "Neither," she said. After their contretemps in the drawing room, Nello had left. Simply . . . walked out without so much as a backward look. So much for *his* heartbreak. Whatever beat in his chest, it was probably made of stone.

As for herself, she barely remembered her mad rush through the wood. Had she spent some time by the lake? Yes, that seemed right—staring at the moon and thinking of her mother as she wept, wretchedly and dreadfully, so that her throat, even now, seemed to ache in memory. And then . . . somehow she had found her way to Mr. Grey's garden.

A shiver passed through her. Sometimes she frightened herself.

"What is it?" Jane asked as they crested the stairs. "The look on your face—"

Liza spoke quickly, for she did not wish to know about the look on her face. "In fact, I met a man."

Instantly she regretted that confession, for the thought of the doctor triggered a physical throb, an echo of the attraction she had felt—which, in the cool, spacious elegance of her home, seemed all the stranger and embarrassing. A *country doctor.* Terribly dressed. Who had spurned her invitation to dinner!

"Oh!" Jane clapped. "Oh, do tell! *Who?* Is he in love with you already?"

Liza made herself shrug. "Quite the opposite, I think."

Jane made a face. "Then he must be made of clay."

"Or arrogant," Liza said. "Full of self-importance." To turn down her invitation so bluntly! "As for Nello, I imagine he caught the last train toward London. And good riddance to him."

"Gracious!" Jane's blue eyes opened wide with curiosity. "Such vehemence!"

"Yes." The whole world seemed vexing, suddenly. "I'm done with him."

"I see." Jane sounded skeptical, which pricked. "Well, you must be exhausted. We'll have a bath drawn for you, and a cup of tea for us both, and . . ." She lifted her brows. "The whole story, perhaps? Of this arrogant jackanapes?"

They turned into Liza's rooms, where Jane released her to bustle toward an already-waiting tea tray. The sight gave Liza a moment's pause: had Jane been waiting here for her? These were her private apartments!

Jane glanced up. "I saw you through the window

from the gallery, walking up from the lake. I thought you might like to take your tea in peace—I hope you don't mind?"

"Oh! No, of course not. How perfectly thoughtful of you, darling." Liza took a seat at the tea table, which pressed against the window to offer a view of the surrounding parkland. On clear days, one could see to the coast.

She fixed her eyes on the distant sparkle and sighed. Perhaps it was time she took a sea journey. Where would she go? America? Plenty of millionaires for the taking there. If she meant to do this—and she didn't see she had much choice in it—an American husband would be as good as any other. More difficult to pry into her financial state from abroad, too. The key would be to make him fall in love before he learned the truth.

What a fool she'd been to tell Nello everything. If he did not keep his mouth shut, she was doomed.

"But tell me," Jane said as she poured the tea. "Who is this mysterious, arrogant man whom you met?"

She cleared her throat. "Oh, just a doctor. A newcomer to the district."

Jane nodded and crossed to the dressing table, uncapping a crystal decanter from which she splashed a bit of whisky into the steaming cup. "This will fix your head," she said sweetly. "Is he married, then?"

"No." Liza took the cup gratefully. "Much obliged, darling."

"How old is he?"

"His thirties, I believe."

"Oh, then he's old," Jane said dismissively—ignorant, Liza assumed, of the age of her hostess.

Yet it still irked. Jane had been married at nineteen, and widowed last year, at twenty-two. But not every husband exercised such splendid good timing. Why, some of them monopolized a woman for years, though they showed no interest in her bed, her company, her desire to be a friend and companion . . .

No, her husband had taken a different course. His only interest had been in chiding her. *You mustn't do this, you mustn't do that, shameless, vulgar* . . . The next one would need to be far more manageable.

She took a large, bracing sip of her tea—sugarless, not as she liked, but as her waistline demanded. Jane had taken to following suit, though she was inches taller, and already slim as a whippet. "Yes, I suppose a man in his thirties *is* old," she confirmed, by way of experiment. *Am I old now?* For if a gentleman was accounted old, a woman of nearly the same age—a woman of thirty-two—must be positively *ancient*.

The thought made her anxious. She needed to find a husband *quickly*—before news of her troubles broke; before her age started to show.

"But handsome, still?" Jane persisted.

Her interest seemed peculiar. A vision flashed before Liza's eyes: Jane, blond and blue-eyed as a china doll, drifting down to the good doctor's cottage and promptly winning him with her blemishless complexion and virginal white gowns—all of them, so Liza had noticed, cut an inch lower than current fashions advised. "Why does it matter?" Country doctors were as marriageable as . . . furniture.

"It matters if you mean to bring him to his knees," Jane said. "If he is ugly, you'll have to attack his intellect, for he'll never believe you deign to notice him otherwise. But if his looks are passable, why, then you can trick him into loving you and then break his heart!"

Laughing, Liza set down her teacup. "My goodness! A very cold approach!" Yet it felt soothing to her vanity to be accounted still capable of breaking hearts. "Wouldn't it be kinder to ignore him altogether?"

"But he was rude to you," Jane said. "So tell me: is he handsome or not?"

Liza considered the girl for a moment. It felt uncannily like looking a decade into her own past, at a face smooth, unlined, alight with pleasure and ambition, unshadowed by doubts. The years ahead—the decade that had been lost to Liza—would comprise Jane Hull's greatest triumph. She would learn, no doubt, about the uses of kindness; having tasted her own defeats, she would develop compassion for those less blessed than she. But while disappointment was a fine tutor, it need not be her lifelong companion. She had beauty, breeding, and in Liza, a brilliant entrée to society: what else did she need to find love?

Perhaps, Liza thought, this was how she might have felt for a young sister: hopeful and impatient and protective all at once. She reached for Jane's hand, catching and squeezing the soft little fingers. "Darling. You trust me, don't you?"

Jane's eyes widened. "Of course, dear Liza!"

"Then let me make certain you are happy." She'd squandered her final chance at love. But she would make certain Jane did not. "As for this doctor—no, he's not handsome. Good heavens," she added with a laugh. "He's a *doctor*. Let the poor man be!"

Jane looked slightly disappointed. "Then you don't mean to break his heart?"

"Oh, I didn't say that." Smiling, Liza released Jane's hand and reached again for her tea, which really did fix her head marvelously. "It entirely depends on how bored I am."

CHAPTER FOUR

Had anyone told Michael three months ago that soon his most constant companion would be a vicar, he would have choked on laughter, or predicted the end times. Religion, along with all other forms of creaky propriety, was best left to firstborn sons, who could afford such noble indulgences. Yet here he was, gladly sharing a tankard at the village pub with a man who wore the collar.

Lawrence Pershall was that rare churchman who had been drawn to his position by faith rather than by financial considerations. But God did not figure much in their conversations, and today, as usual, it was politics and sport that engaged them. They shared an interest in racing, perhaps strengthened by the fact that neither of them could afford to indulge in it. They both believed—quietly, for they were not suicidal—that rugby trumped cricket for athleticism. And on matters of empire, they also concurred: the Irish question had become a great burden, best discharged by granting independence to that nation. However, the army was a damned fine institution, regardless.

"Soldiering was my other calling," Pershall confessed as they exited the pub into the bright daylight. "At fourteen, I was convinced I'd be a general one day."

"I remember that phase," said Michael. Nothing like the prospect of wielding a rifle to cheer up a boy raised on vengeful fantasies. Only, as Alastair had pointed out, duels had been outlawed decades before—and the fight would not have been equal, their father having been a crack shot in his time.

"What stopped you, then?"

Michael shrugged. "Decided to save lives, rather than take them." That, and he'd ultimately found his attempt to enlist in the infantry foiled by Alastair's interference. What his brother had arranged instead—a commission in the Horse Guards, a regiment that rarely stirred beyond the shadows of Buckingham Palace—had not suited him.

Damned difficult to make something of oneself when one's brother consistently purchased one's successes. For years, during university and shortly thereafter, Michael had chafed beneath Alastair's doting regard. But with age had come a new view. In their boyhood, Alastair had played the role of father and mother both, protecting Michael from the worst of their parents' excesses. Such a very old habit was hard to break.

And until recently, Michael had been content to let his brother do as he might.

"Well, I call it good luck for us both," said Pershall. "Had we enlisted, we no doubt would have died of dysentery in the first week." As Michael laughed, he added, "And how could I complain? I ended up in God's own village—if you'll forgive me the blasphemy."

Michael followed Pershall's look as it traveled over

the scene. Bosbrea was pitched along a gentle slope of limestone. The bright faces of shops and flower-fronted cottages clustered along either side of the main road, which led upward to the old cairn marking the apex of Bosbrea Hill. In the opposite direction, the cobblestone lane spilled downward to span the River Cuby, a gurgling rush of water that glittered in the noonday sun.

"Picturesque, indeed," Michael murmured. The beauty made him feel downright itchy—smothered, almost. His calling lay elsewhere, with people who depended on him because they had nowhere else to turn. Alastair might fund the hospital, but it was Michael who saved lives there, and formulated policies that had produced the lowest mortality rate of any medical institution in the country.

Damn it, he wanted to be in London. The air here was too clean, the residents too healthy, and his time too idle. He knew his brother well enough to guess that the mystery of his whereabouts would goad Alastair into a healthy temper, but the waiting was hard, indeed.

And a line had been crossed now that Michael could not tolerate.

As though the other man had read his thoughts, Pershall said, "Any word from your brother, then?"

Michael shook his head. Pershall knew the bare outline of the story: a violent quarrel, an untenable demand, no choice but to retreat as far as possible from his brother's range of influence. What he did not know was how very far that range extended. "It would make no difference if I had done. If he wishes to reconcile, he'll have to come himself."

Pershall's eyes widened. "As bad as that, is it?"

A very good question. Michael did not think Alastair would follow through on his threat. Through all their parents' travails, the affairs and the depositions, the whole nasty divorce that had kept the public so titillated—through it all, Alastair had been there for him: a rock in an otherwise stormy sea. Over the past year, Michael had done his best to return that favor. Even this act of concealment was ultimately for his brother's sake. Surely Alastair would see that, soon enough. He would not betray the trust between them.

Yet if he did . . .

Interference was easy to bear, so long as it was the work of love. But closing the hospital would be nothing more than brute malice.

Frightening thought: Michael might never be able to forgive him for it.

"Let us say, he would win no prizes for congeniality," he said to Pershall.

The vicar snorted. "And you would?"

Michael, grinning, was about to retort when a cry rang out: "Ho there! Mr. Grey!"

The upper-class drawl caught him off guard. He stopped in his tracks and spun on his heel, thinking for a moment—well, that he'd been found. Such ironic moments did tend to proliferate in his life.

Instead, approaching them was none other than his uninvited visitor from last week. Uneasiness bolted through him. Mrs. Chudderley was a tremendous flirt, as much a temptation as a pie left in the windowsill during a famine. Looking over her scratched, dirty arms a week ago, he'd battled an overwhelming temptation to lick her clean.

Not sanitary, of course. He'd settled on antiseptic instead.

"A heavenly sight," sighed Pershall. "Aphrodite arisen from the waves."

Michael cut the man a wry glance. "The wrong heaven for your church," he said. "And should a man of God notice such things?"

Pershall laughed. "Not dead yet, Mr. Grey."

Mrs. Chudderley came floating toward them. She was dressed ludicrously for a walk in dusty village lanes, in a delicate, billowing gown the color of a ripe peach. Behind her hurried a tall, red-haired maid, out of breath and visibly cross, who carried a hamper on one arm and used the other to hold a parasol over her mistress's head. The ludicrous confection, too thin to properly shield out the sun, was trimmed with fluttering ribbons that precisely matched Mrs. Chudderley's gown.

Michael nodded to the overburdened maid before making his bow to the widow. It was a small jab, but one that the widow caught: he saw it in the way her eyes narrowed briefly before her smile determinedly widened.

As simply as that, his heart skipped a beat. *Damn it.* Would that veils were in fashion! He had imagined, a week ago, that the widow's eyes would be as brown as her hair, and so it had come as a shock when she had opened them to reveal irises of a pale, uncanny green, the shade of Chinese jade when held to the light.

It came as an equal shock now to look into them again and realize his imagination had not embroidered upon their loveliness.

He took hold of his breath, which wanted to escalate, and his intentions, which wanted to sharpen. She would never know how terribly she'd humbled him in his drawing room last week. Her every movement had sent a suggestion of perfumed warmth toward him that had made his body tighten like a crank. By the time Mrs. Brown had handed him that damned tea, his hands had been shaking.

It happened sometimes, this instant attraction. But never with a *patient*. God above! Country life did not agree with him.

"Mrs. Chudderley," he said. "Good day to you."

Graciously, she returned his greeting—then surprised him by turning briskly toward the vicar. "All the animals are accounted for?"

A gentle breeze moved past them, fluttering the ruffled neckline of her gown, offering teasing glimpses of smooth, pale décolletage. Michael dug his index finger into the pad of his thumb with savage force, making a small but adequate distraction.

"Oh, indeed," Pershall was saying. "And I've already had a dozen inquiries about the pies. The kitchens at Havilland Hall have been busy preparing delicacies for our little bazaar at the school tomorrow."

With a start, Michael realized this comment was directed at him. "Oh?"

"Yes, their strawberry pies are wildly famous. Rightfully so!"

"Mr. Grey would know this," said Mrs. Chudderley lightly, "if only he were to accept my invitation to dinner. Perhaps *you* can persuade him, sir."

At Pershall's questioning look, a flush crawled down Michael's nape. "Mrs. Chudderley does offer the finest table in Cornwall," said Pershall. "Why, just last week, I dined on the most tender, succulent quail I've ever tasted."

Ah, very good. Now a man of God was persuading him to accept an invitation that would end only one way: with Michael devouring his hostess. He had given it some thought these past few nights; he knew exactly how he would do it. He would start with her fingers, sucking them into his mouth one by one . . .

"Mr. Grey was invited to that same dinner," Mrs. Chudderley said, her smile teasing. "Alas, I fear he thinks that to sit at my table will endanger his immortal soul. Being an expert on such matters, perhaps *you* will counsel him, Mr. Pershall."

"Ah, but I think nothing of the sort." Damn it, his tone was all wrong—low and flirtatious, to match her own. It was a reflex, of course. Second sons with over-large noses had to become quite skilled in seduction if they wished to snare a woman's interest. And in the normal course . . . by God, he would have spent a *great* deal of effort snaring this one.

But this was not the normal course. Michael frowned and cleared his throat. He did not understand *her* interest in *him*. She was not the sort to take a personal interest in lowly country doctors.

Aware of Pershall's interested attention, he bowed again, striving now to seem properly staid. "Ma'am, as I told you before, my only fear was to lower the tone of the company." *Recall I am a mere doctor.*

"Oh, I rather doubt that," she said with a lift of her brow. And then, when the silence drew on a moment too long and began to seem as pointed as her remark, she laughed and turned toward her maid to take the parasol. "Mather, I know you had some business in town. Hand me that basket and I'll go on by myself."

"Quite," said the maid, and dumped the basket into her mistress's arms. Turning on her heel, she strode off.

The abruptness of her exit did not strike him alone.

"Peculiar girl," said the widow as she turned back—sounding, to his mild surprise, amused rather than irked. "Mr. Pershall, you shall hear from me tomorrow morning; I mean to send the flowers and whatnot by ten o'clock."

"Thank you. But may I say, Mrs. Chudderley, I wish that someday soon we might meet on a Sunday. Our congregation misses you sorely."

"Oh," she said lightly, "one of these days, sir, the sinner shall return to her flock. And then you may reform me to your heart's content! Mr. Grey, will you walk with me?"

Very bad idea. He glanced to Pershall, who was beaming like a young boy whose cheeks had just been pinched by the most buxom dairy maid in the milking shed. No help there. "In fact, I may have patients waiting—"

"But that's precisely my concern," she said. "The Browards' boy has been ailing. I'm certain they would appreciate a professional opinion."

He eyed her narrowly for a moment, suspicious of how well she'd crafted her lure. But her smile was bright and guileless, and he'd look like an ass if he declined. Moreover, ethical obligations forbade him to do so. The avoidance of flirts and preservation of one's virtue did not take priority over sick children.

He took a deep breath. Restraint: he would have to practice restraint. A true novelty, along with all this bleeding fresh air. "Of course," he said. "I'll be glad to have a look at him."

"Lovely!" She thrust the basket into his arms and walked off without so much as a by-your-leave. The foamy gown transformed her gait into something more like a . . . strut. The wind kicked up again, and his fevered mind thought it glimpsed the outline of a well-shaped hip, sloping inward to a shapely thigh.

Long before Alastair came calling, chastity was going to kill him.

Young Daniel was running a slight fever, but Michael felt it safe to declare him on the mend, particularly after the boy evidenced a healthy appetite by attacking Mrs. Chudderley's basket of custards. Mrs. Broward, heavily pregnant, insisted on tea, and a half hour and two pots later, Michael sat on a small chair, desperately trying to rearrange his limbs in a way that did not suggest the extreme discomfort occasioned by furniture designed for a much shorter man.

Or perhaps his discomfort came from the slow dissolution of his best defense against the widow. Lady Bountifuls did not impress him; too often their good intentions were diminished by their transparent distaste for the objects of their compassion. Yet Mrs. Chudderley seemed easy in the Browards' company, and her attitude fostered an atmosphere of informal good cheer. Mrs. Broward, one hand on her great belly, wondered if Mrs. Chudderley hadn't any suggestions for names. Young Miss Broward solicited her opinions on London fashions. Various little ones tugged at her skirts. At one point an ominous ripping sound was heard, but while Mrs. Broward gasped and yanked the offending tyke away, Mrs. Chudderley only laughed.

This was clearly not the first time she had visited the Browards. Nor would it be the last, judging by the warm invitations that followed them as they finally took their leave, all of which centered on the prospect of her return as soon as the babe was born.

"Well," he said as they stepped back into the village lane. So she enjoyed the company of farmers. So he rather liked her for it. No matter. Circumstances dictated that he take his leave all the more quickly as a result. "I must get to my other patients. I'll bid you farewell."

Mrs. Chudderley, caught in the process of untangling the ribbons of her parasol, slanted him a look. "Running off so soon?"

He hesitated. "That's a great lot of ribbons on that parasol. Do they serve any purpose?"

She laughed. "Beauty," she said. "That is their purpose."

Then the ribbons weren't required. Her eyes were the only adornment she needed. They were extraordinary, such a pale shade of green, and they tilted ever so slightly at the outward corners. They put him in mind, somehow, of the cat statues in the Egyptian wing of the British Museum. Ancient eyes, much older than the face they graced.

Out of nowhere, he recalled her tears upon waking a week ago. What, or who, had made her weep?

It is none of your business.

"Anyway," she said, "your home and mine lie in the same direction. Shan't we walk together?"

Shaking out the parasol a final time, she started down the road without a backward glance—assuming, as women of her beauty usually did, that he would follow.

Their respective destinations did lie down the same road. He could think of no excuse to go back into town. And so, with a sigh, he followed her—as men, he supposed, usually did.

"You seem to know the Browards well," he said as he fell into step beside her. It struck him as unusual. Most country gentry strove to distinguish themselves from their tenants.

"Indeed," she said. "I fund their eldest sons' educations. Very bright lads, one at Harrington, the other at University College in London. And I've known Mary and Thomas—Mr. and Mrs. Broward—since we were children."

"Ah. You grew up in this district, then."

"In the winters, yes. Didn't you know?" She sighed. "And here I imagined that nobody in Bosbrea had *any* topic of discussion more interesting than me."

Her rueful smile lent her remark a self-deprecating air, one he liked very much. His better instincts warred against habit. Habit won. "That *is* difficult to imagine," he said.

His reward was a flutter of mink-brown lashes. "How kind of you. In fact, I'm kin to the Browards through my mother. My father bought Havilland Hall to keep her from growing too homesick."

A mésalliance, then. Startling to hear her divulge it so casually. "I see."

She lifted a brow. "Yes, I'm sure you do. Not the most glorious match for Papa, of course. His family was most displeased. But . . ." Her mouth pulled in a sideways smile. "Mama and Papa loved each other dreadfully. Eventually they won over even the stoniest of his relatives."

The cynic in him rather doubted that. But it made a good tale for circulation. "So you're related to some of your tenants. That's bound to be messy."

The slightest edge entered her voice. "I suppose it might be, if the landlord is unjust."

In return, he felt mildly annoyed by her accidental

implication: that his own family behaved less than justly with their own people. Of course, she thought him a mere doctor. Nevertheless . . . "With crop prices sinking, economies become necessary. One might say that causes an inevitable tension between those who own the land and those who work it."

She gave a little laugh. "You sound like a university lecturer."

Good God. What he'd sounded like was *Alastair*. "Perish the thought, Mrs. Chudderley."

"Or . . . like a man who has some personal experience of land management?" Her pause plainly invited him to elaborate. When he did not, she added pointedly, "In the north, no doubt."

Ah. He allowed his smile to widen. Clearly his reserve had pricked her. "What an excellent memory you have. In the north, indeed."

Her eyes narrowed. "I do believe you're teasing me now."

"You might be right." It gratified something foolish in him to be the cause of her rising color—and to be studied so closely by such magnificent eyes. He lifted a brow, and watched her blush deepen.

Really, she was surprisingly easy to ruffle for a professional beauty. A man could make a hobby of it.

"Now you're staring," she said tartly.

"Surely you're accustomed to that," he said. "I imagine it's almost obligatory."

No false pretense of modesty from this widow: she did not even blink. "I'm accustomed to a great many things," she said. "Polite conversation, for instance— which generally commences with a frank discussion of one's natal place. But perhaps such niceties are only common in the *south* of the country. I will leave it to you to enlighten me."

Oh, but she was clever. He vaguely recalled tales of her wildness, but none of her wit. Typical unfairness, that. "It's true, we northerners are famously reticent savages. But I promise you, we abandoned most of our more boorish customs once the Picts fell from power. You're quite safe with me."

"Oh, I do not think you a savage," she said sweetly. "In fact, you seem a much more evolved specimen— a man whose favorite subjects do not include himself. Why, I'm not certain I've ever encountered your kind before!"

He laughed. In fact, only the barest thread of common sense leashed his tongue, for a man's instinct, when holding such a woman's attention, was to babble endlessly, lest she find a reason to look away.

Christ, but she was beautiful. He wondered how wild she became, exactly. He had a brief vision of her dancing atop a table, garbed only in a string of black pearls. Alas, it seemed a bit too Parisian, even for her.

"You find me amusing?" She sounded pleased by the notion.

"I find you persistent—particularly in the face of such boorishly northern company."

Her nose wrinkled. "You are not nearly the *northerner* you claim to be. Your address shows breeding; the way you walk suggests a lifetime of sport. Cricket, I think?"

"Rugby," he answered before he could think better of it.

"Ah." She sounded satisfied, as well she might. Rugby was a sport most often confined to public school playing fields. But he had not given himself away.

"A common game in the north," he said. "Mr. Pershall also played it as a boy."

"Oh, I don't doubt it. Nevertheless . . . yes, I find your presentation suspiciously *polished* for a boor. Your apparel, on the other hand . . ." She shook her head. "You *do* know we have a very fine haberdasher in Brosbrea? You've just now met his wife."

Now his laughter was full-throated, impossible to contain. "A blunt-spoken woman! Mrs. Chudderley, if my kind is rare, yours is rarer."

Her smile widened to a grin. "Then what a pair we are! But you, I think, are determined to remain a mystery, while *I* am an open book."

Ah, but these lies left him feeling uneasy. It was not guilt that troubled him, precisely. He undertook this masquerade as plain Mr. Grey partially for his brother's sake: were he to use his true name, word would eventually reach London that the Duke of Marwick's brother had abandoned the hospital to live quietly in rural Cornwall, and speculation would run rampant as to the cause. He would not make Alastair the brunt of gossip until and unless his brother left him no choice. By the same token . . . to incite such gossip would be to squander one of the only weapons he had in this ridiculous little game they were playing.

But sound motives did not make for an easy frame of mind. He ought to be in London right now. This situation was absurd in the extreme.

"On the contrary," he said, "I am as you see me. The only mysteries in my life are medical. I did briefly entertain a different mystery last week, but in the days since, my rosebushes have disappointed me."

He expected a coy reply, or perhaps even a retort born

of embarrassment. Instead she looked at him in surprise, and then burst into laughter—and his breath stopped. *He* nearly stopped, the better to behold her. What kind of laugh was *this*? Not a polite and controlled sound, smothered behind a palm, as society ladies favored, but a surprisingly loud bellow: a laugh without a trace of self-consciousness. She laughed like a barmaid, with her entire body.

Perhaps she *was* Parisian at heart.

For a moment, he permitted himself to feel the full effect of this possibility: the hot leap of desire, the dazzled giddiness. To be walking in the sun with a beautiful woman, who gazed on him as though he were the most fascinating riddle she had ever encountered, and then laughed as though no one could amuse her better . . .

The next moment, he checked himself. His bloody romantic temperament had gotten him into enough scrapes to last a lifetime. *Perfection,* he always decided within the course of five minutes' conversation, only to conclude, two or four or six weeks later, that perfection was only a very good disguise for disaster. It never lasted.

Besides, she knew nothing of him. She teased and flirted by nature, and would have done so no doubt with the roughest-spun laborer. He understood that, and he approved of it. She was not a snob, Mrs. Chudderley. She took fun where she found it.

"Have you other patients to see?" she asked. "If not, I will show you around the area."

Damn the circumstances. In any other time or place, he would have been rampantly eager to amuse her. "In fact—"

"It will work to your advantage to be seen with me,"

she said lightly. "If you wish to establish your credentials, that is. You will find that people in these parts are inclined to mistrust a stranger, even if his medical skills recommend him."

"A very generous offer, for which I am properly grateful. But—"

"And I find myself willing, because the day is so fine, to show you one of my *favorite* places," she continued, and something gay and carefree in her manner tugged out a similar feeling within him, leaping and laughter-prone, much younger than he felt these days. He realized that he was grinning.

Well . . . why not accompany her? He was bored; he had neither enough patients nor books here to keep him occupied. Attraction did not require him to *act*. And prolonged acquaintance with her surely would cure this budding interest he felt.

Besides, to offend her would be unwise. If Bosbrea's most famous citizen set out to blacken his name, prospective patients would be deterred from consulting him. Then he'd truly be out of hand.

Oh, yes. Very sound logic, not at all self-serving. He bit his cheek. "Very well. If it's near."

"It's all near." They walked side by side, past the last few houses, into the open country. "In fact, my land begins at this hedgerow."

He looked out. Havilland Hall was not visible from this vantage, but the scene had its own charms. Summer lay like a warm breath over the fields, and butterflies danced up out of the long, quivering grasses. "A lovely piece of earth."

"More than a piece," she said. "Nearly five thousand acres—all mine now."

Did a trace of sadness color her words? "You have no siblings, then?"

"No brothers, you mean." She cast him an arch look. "No, I was an only child. Another way in which my mother disappointed Papa's family. But Papa never minded it. He spoiled me terribly, almost as terribly as he spoiled her."

Ah. Perhaps she wasn't romanticizing her parents' marriage.

At the thought, he felt the stirring of a very old emotion, disbelief and wistfulness entwined. As a boy on holiday at friends' homes, over dinner tables and in drawing rooms before supper, he had watched with amazement as the lord and lady of the house exchanged glances, or brushed against each other. What a rare and wondrous thing it must be, to have had happy parents. "It was a great romance, I take it."

"Of course! But I'm hardly an objective critic. I suppose most children idealize their parents." She gave him a merry look. "Yours were also perfect, no doubt."

He could barely fathom the fortune it required to produce such naiveté. "In fact, my brother raised me." For all intents and purposes, Alastair had played both mother and father to him.

Her expression instantly sobered. "I'm so sorry, sir. How awful for you!"

She imagined he'd been raised an orphan, he gathered. He could not permit that misunderstanding to stand. "My parents were . . . engaged elsewhere." Embroiled in their own private war, they'd had little time to spare on their children, save insofar as sons made excellent pawns. "Not often present in our lives. My brother saw to my . . ." *Safety. Sanity.* Not politic remarks. "Well-being," he said.

"Oh." She frowned a little. "Well . . . who knows, sir? Perhaps you're the better for it. I often suspect that a happy marriage is a *terrible* example to inflict on a child."

Surely she meant that as a joke. "A rather wonderful one, I'd think."

"Oh, for the husband and wife, no doubt. But imagine the expectations it creates! That anyone can have such love—or that a man who falls madly in love with a woman will never fall out of it. A child nursed on such fairy tales is bound to develop the *wildest* expectations."

The frank remark startled him only briefly. Over the past two months, he'd discovered that this kind of intimacy happened a good deal when people looked at him and saw only a country doctor. Where his reputation did not precede him, honest friendships seemed to proliferate.

"Such cynicism," he said. "Surely you're too young to be so wise."

She laughed. "Now your flattery grows transparent. I am, after all, a widow."

He opened his mouth, then paused. Did she mean that comment as an invitation to ask after her marriage?

If so . . . good God. His curiosity suddenly felt as large as any hunger he'd known. *Why are you hiding here in the country?* For she owned London's heart: her face was in the shop windows; society would throw itself at her feet if only she deigned to grace it with her presence.

What a pity that their paths had not crossed earlier. He might have approached her openly, with a frank invitation. His liaisons did not usually last longer than a few weeks, but with her, he could imagine making an exception. Most of London's fashionable beauties cultivated a coy air of mysterious reserve—or its reverse, an overblown sensuality that turned every other word into a veiled invitation. Her charm, on the other hand, seemed connected to her frankness. He found her honesty strangely . . . refreshing.

Paired with a lack of self-consciousness, honesty would be a great asset to lovemaking. *Tell me what you like,* he'd say. *Show me.*

"Have I shocked you?" she asked.

Her question amused him. If only she knew where his own thoughts had been leading. "Not at all," he said. *Beware, old boy. You are not free for seductions at present.* And she looked too impossibly vivid in her gown, like the spirit of summer itself, with the green fields rolling out behind her, for him to imagine that a friendship between them would be uncomplicated by baser temptations.

So he forced himself to make a neutral remark. "The realities of love aside, I suppose it must be useful to have an ideal in mind."

"Do you? Then we must debate on it. Do you enjoy debating?"

"On occasion," he said.

Her head tipped; she studied the clouds overhead. This new view revealed imperfections: a mole high on her cheekbone; the oddly blunted tip of her nose. Her photographs, he suspected, were never taken in profile. This was a view that would never be given to the public.

The thought strangely fascinated him. These were secrets waiting to be discovered. He found himself studying her more closely yet, avid to find more. The shape of her ear was not shell-like, her earlobe a touch too large for that pretty description—stretched, perhaps, by years of heavy earrings. But ideal for a kiss. The faint freckle on her throat sent another thrill through him. He wanted to touch it, to whisper against it, *I've found you.* For that matter, the slope of her neck begged to be brushed with a hand. *His* hand, before he cupped her nape and guided her gently backward onto a bed . . .

"Then let us debate this proposal," she said, blithely unaware of his rapidly developing . . . condition. "Love is one of the more *dangerous* ideals a young girl might have. Why, the first man who declares himself will inevitably appear to her like her destiny, leading her to ignore all manner of *other* considerations."

"Perhaps." He spoke slowly, for it was a battle now between his wits and his body, which wanted to embarrass him like a schoolboy. Good God. He'd never approved of men who used brothels, but if celibacy spelled the end of his dignity, he might reconsider his contempt. "Or perhaps . . . her expectations will guide her to the best of matches, and steer her safely past those roués who look for something less than love in a marriage."

That had sounded very virtuous. He smiled, pleased with himself.

Tilting her head, she said dryly, "How sweet. But do you truly think love so easily recognized as *that*? Why, a rogue may speak of love as easily as the morning editorials—more easily, in fact, for I find most rogues have a great distaste for reading."

His enthusiasm lessened abruptly. She was not a moralist, he hoped. "I take it your husband disappointed you, madam."

Ah, that was too blunt. The look she gave him changed as their eyes met; he felt as though he *saw* her decision to retreat from him in the way her smile firmed, like a wall hardening.

"But what a bore I am," she said. "I promised to show you a lovely spot, and instead I babble at you."

The strength of his disappointment amazed him. On its heels came wry resignation. She was not looking for a confidant, after all, but a silent ear, an audience that did not talk back. Ladies of her rank did not befriend their doctors.

"I imagine you very rarely bore anyone," he said. Gallantries were what she expected, and this one was easy to offer.

Her smile slipped a little. Ah, but wistfulness did lovely things to her face. Though she would not admire them in the mirror, the faint lines that fanned from the corners of her eyes lent her beauty a human quality that roused in him the most peculiar and unexpected feeling.

If not her husband, then who had disappointed her? Such clumsiness was unforgivable; he would bloody the man's face. No, he would do more than that: he would cup her face and smooth his thumb along her lip and whisper, *He was not worthy of you.* Then he would show her what she deserved: steadfast attention, a man who understood how a woman's body worked, who could name each of its parts and manipulate them to her pleasure . . .

Christ, man. Take hold of yourself. He had long ago accepted that his character placed him among the more rash and impetuous men on the planet, but these fancies were a very quick development, even by his own natural tempo.

As though she divined his thoughts, she said, "We're nearly strangers, Mr. Grey. I wonder why it is that I feel so comfortable with you? It seems to me that silences are particularly hard to share, don't you think? But not with you."

She liked flirting. That much was clear. Provoke and retreat; provoke and retreat. It was the natural tempo of the coquette. "That's a compliment, I believe."

"Yes, it is. Let us be silent for a few minutes, then."

And so in silence they walked onward, beneath a sky that deepened from a pale blue into a vivid cerulean as the sun slid a little lower. He felt the most absurd impulse to take her hand—his fingertips twitched with the anticipation of what her fingers would feel like, clasped in his—the warmth of her skin, the softness of her knuckles—and he made his hand into a fist, and then put it into his coat pocket, lest it slip the rein and seize hers without permission.

A smile came and went on her lips. She ducked her head to hide it from him, which made him all the more curious to know what had inspired it. Infatuation, of course, could spring up at any time: he had fallen in love with women he'd glimpsed out the windows of trains, or across ballrooms, or on the quay as his ship docked. And he'd fallen out of love just as quickly, as these women had walked onward—or, worse yet, as he grew to know them. Beauty was a toxin to the wits, infatuation its ally—but by God, the drug was heady when it hit. It blurred other eyes, other smiles, other faces, until only hers, in this moment, seemed distinct to him.

Ah, but his brain was *not* rotted. Surely it was statistically improbable that anywhere on this earth another woman existed whose smile curved with such breathtaking gentleness. He would gladly accept the inevitable disappointment for a chance to feel that mouth on his own.

He took a breath full of sun-warmed earth and fragrant hay and honeysuckle and exhaled on a disbelieving laugh. No women until Alastair wed again? He was *doomed*.

She glanced over but did not ask the cause of his humor. "Here," she said, and turned through an opening in the hedges onto an unpaved path. The trail led catercorner across the field into a wood where sunlight filtered through the branches and cast dappled spangles over a carpet of moss and fragrant, fallen leaves. Down a gentle slope they wended, to what turned out to be the bank of a well-hidden lake.

Lifting aside the fronds of a willow, Mrs. Chudderley beckoned him to follow her to the very edge of the water. From this vantage, the entire wood-shrouded lake revealed itself, glassy beneath the cloudless sky.

"May Lake," she said. "So called because it is never more beautiful than in May, when the trees are blossoming. But even in June, it suffices."

A breeze struck up, riffling the stands of willow, moving their fronds like fingers through the water. "Ah," he said softly. Yes, he understood why she thought this place special.

"Ah," Mrs. Chudderley echoed just as softly, and her glance toward him was radiant with understanding . . . and something more. He had studied women too long to misread that look.

He could not resist it. Why should he? A brief moment of indulgence . . . for both their sakes.

He reached out to cup her elbow. Best to move slowly, to communicate that she could refuse him. The choice was hers.

Her luminous eyes remained fixed on his. Her lips parted as he trailed his hand from the point of her elbow to her wrist. *God.* Her bare skin, that small, vulnerable patch exposed between cuff and glove, was indescribably soft. His thumb rubbed her pulse once, twice. A small noise came from her, the loosening of her breath, a sound as meaningful as the shushing of silk as a dress fell to the floor. This was how it began: how a woman came undone.

He drew her against him. The willow fronds whispered and snapped over the water. A little flirtation, that was all. Two fellow cynics, taking their summer amusement where they found it.

He lowered his mouth to hers, breathed against her lips. No hurry. They stood together, mouth against mouth, as his hand trailed up her arm, slipped around her small, fine-boned shoulder to palm her back. Inch by inch, his fingertips discovered the delicate ridge of her spine. The rhythm of her breath against his mouth grew more distinct. Her body was awakening to his, and the message made his own body tighten. He traced her spine downward, then upward again, reaching the warmth of her bare nape, the heavy weight of her chignon, the cool softness of her hair against his knuckles.

Her eyes were like light through the shallow waters of a lagoon. Green as the home of mermaids, wide, fastened to his.

He cupped her face, his thumb stroking her satin-smooth cheek. The space between their bodies—a finger's width, no more—told him how they would fit together. *Perfectly.*

Closing his eyes, he molded his lips to hers. A single lick along the seam of her lips won his entry. Her mouth parted. She tasted cool and clean, like water from a fresh alpine brook.

His hand found the small of her back again, that

graceful curve above her arse. A small stretch of perfection, worthy of worship in any language. He tasted her more deeply, his tongue meeting hers, and she swayed into him and began to kiss him back. Oh, she was hot and clever with her mouth. No moralist would kiss like this. His hand tightened; he felt the rigid boning of her corset, and beneath it, a dizzying softness. If she wore any petticoats, they were thinner than a breath of air.

More than a brief kiss, then. More voluptuous. More open-mouthed. Everything about her was edible. He wanted to taste her sweat. *Life, right here.* Life was short. Its sweetness, he would not deny. Was this not a legitimate philosophy? Seize pleasure where he found it. Leave the more complex considerations to others.

He caught her lower lip in his teeth and suckled it, hungry for the salt of her skin. Some low noise she made inspired him to chart the line of her jaw. Then the slope of her throat. God, she was *perfect*.

The thought broke his restraint. The kiss grew savage; her hands closed on his waist and tightened, her fingertips digging, and he answered the silent demand, ravishing her lips, her mouth, tasting her cheeks. His skin against hers would cure this hunger. He stepped into her, and she stepped into him; too much clothing, God, the way she smelled, he would eat her in bites, he would start here at her throat—

"Oh!" She set her forehead to his, dislodging his mouth. He froze, waiting, every sense focused, his breathing ragged, waiting to see if she had changed her mind.

She did not withdraw. But she did not lift her mouth to his, either. He took a long breath through his nose, schooling himself. *Calm. Calm.* His hands fell away from her, flexing on empty air.

The ragged puff of her breath against his cheek was a compliment. It made him feel savage with ambition. Given a chance, he would make her breathe harder yet. He would make her *gasp*.

"Good . . . ness," she said, the word broken into syllables by the small hitch of her breath. "Your talents extend beyond the medical."

His laughter felt slow and drunken. "I would be glad to demonstrate them at further length."

Her sigh tasted like cinnamon. "Oh, would you?"

Would he? With the sun gentle on his skin and the warmth of her body pressed tantalizingly to his, everything seemed very clear to him. He was no saint. Had never hewed to virtue or churchly regimens. Women liked him; he liked them. This woman, more beautiful than Venus, wanted him. Why deny her?

Widows were free to dally where they might. Dalliance held no threat of matrimony. An affair would harm nobody, and leave his vow and intentions intact.

Alastair would never know.

"Only repeat your invitation to dinner," he said.

She pulled away to look into his eyes. Her smile looked shyly pleased, perfectly designed to make a man bolder. "Tomorrow, after the bazaar, you must come to dine with me."

He caught her hand and brought it to his lips. "Madam, I gladly accept."

CHAPTER FIVE

The bazaar was always Liza's favorite occasion of the year—historically, the event at which she needn't worry if her dress ripped or some hussy was flirting with Nello, largely because Nello had never bothered to come. But now, as she stood at the back of the hall, she was conscious of a sharpening dissatisfaction that made her skin itch.

Frowning, she looked once again over the room, past the wilting chiffon swags of pink and yellow. The annual event, which raised funds for parish relief, had drawn visitors from as far away as Matlock, nearly a half day's drive to the north. They had eaten all the pies, bought up all the bric-a-brac—sunflower pincushions and cambric handkerchiefs, knitted socks and hand-painted cigar cases, embroidered chair backs and watercolor scenes. Little Dolly Broward had pocketed and been forced to return four doilies, much to her mother's mortification. The raffle was drawing a good crowd to the front of the room.

The bazaar was a success. But *he* was nowhere to be found.

Were she not so vexed by his absence, she would have laughed at herself. To think that the kiss of a country doctor had kept her up half the night! But she rather liked the notion of a man who recognized his good fortune in winning her attentions. His admiration was precisely what her sore vanity required. And did she not deserve a small romance, a brief bit of harmless fun, before she committed herself to the tiresome husband hunt?

For she had no choice in that. She had received another letter from her solicitors, this time written by joint effort with her accountants at Ogilvie and Harcourt. She'd enlisted her steward and secretary to help her decipher it, but the mystery of her bad luck was not so fuzzy, after all: her late husband's unwise investments, paired with a depressed agricultural market and, oh, a *touch* of indiscipline in her own spending habits, had put her close to the brink.

She would not starve. She would not even be forced to sell off property—*yet*. But should some misfortune befall her, or her friends, or any of the people of Bosbrea who depended on her—and should that misfortune happen to require a large amount of cash . . .

Well, she would be sunk.

Curious, how words on a page could make one feel as though the ground beneath one's feet no longer held steady. For a very brief time, she'd imagined herself in love with her late husband. Then she had learned to content herself with the luxuries he'd provided. But now, all those years with Alan Chudderley seemed doubly wasted. And as for her time with Nello, which had yielded nothing but heartbreak and notoriety . . .

Next to *that* instance of bad judgment, her attraction to the doctor felt nearly virtuous. At the least, the novelty of an honest, upstanding man's interest should be educational for her. *Medicinal,* really. An inoculation before she once again waded into the muck.

"I bear gifts!" Jane swept up, two glasses in hand. "Look what I found!"

Liza laughed as she took a flute. "Champagne? But from where?"

"I instructed one of your footmen to pack it—so we might celebrate the saving of the parish." A wicked smile tipped Jane's mouth as she touched her glass to Liza's. "Or to scandalize the parish, if you prefer. That lemonade was *very* weak."

With the first sip, Liza's nerves began to settle. It would be all right. There was no *immediate* hurry, her solicitors had assured her. She had a little time.

At the next moment, happiness washed over her: she spied Mr. Grey entering through the side door.

He looked a bit harried, his glossy hair ruffled, and he was tugging at his gloves as though he'd only just donned them. But he was here! He had come. His suit tonight fit him splendidly, molding quite closely to his broad shoulders and lean waist, and the white tie at his throat contrasted splendidly with his tanned skin. He had the bone structure of a Viking, she decided—cheekbones like the prows of a ship, and lips so precisely defined that a woman would be able to trace their edges in the dark. Not a pretty face, but a brutally attractive one.

She finished off the glass, her heartbeat racing. "Where is the bottle?" she asked. She felt reckless with anticipation. "Mr. Grey can join us in a toast."

Jane had followed her eye. "Ah! Is *that* the doctor who's to come to supper? Goodness—I recognize him!"

"Really?" The idea made Liza feel unaccountably cross. "From where?"

Jane's brow knit. "I can't quite recall. He looks *terribly* familiar, but . . ."

Ah, well. Jane did so wish to know everything. Liza handed off her glass to the girl and started across the room.

Mr. Grey saw her coming. Those long, talented lips shifted into a smile. She would miss, when she was older, the way her approach could make a man's shoulders square, his chin lift, as though he strove to present his tallest and best self to her. Such a delicious sense of power it gave her!

But she did not wish to exercise her power over him too forcefully. It would not be fair, for he was only a doctor. And she rather liked his temerity; she could not separate it from the air of self-possession that drew her so strongly.

"Good evening, Mr. Grey!" She drew up before him, restraining the urge to smooth down her hair. Larcenous little Dolly was very fond of dancing, and their romp around the room earlier had no doubt left her looking a fright. "We feared you might not attend. How good it is to see you!"

"Mrs. Chudderley." He sketched a bow, his light eyes never leaving her. At last, she identified the main reason for their beauty: his lashes were so dark that he almost looked to be wearing kohl. "Forgive my late arrival," he said, but his eyes spoke a hotter message. "I set out at the normal hour, but I came upon an accident in the road, and stopped to give assistance."

"Goodness." A man who could be *of assistance*. A man of use! "I hope everyone was all right?" Her voice sounded breathless as a giddy girl's.

"Yes, indeed—a twisted ankle, a few scratches; nothing more serious than that." He glanced beyond her, and bowed again.

Jane had come up, one of the footmen in tow. Liza made the introductions, then watched as Jane snapped for more champagne to be poured.

"A very high-toned bazaar," Mr. Grey said neutrally. He shook his head at the glass Jane offered. "No, thank you, I will refrain."

That dimmed Liza's spirits slightly. This was a celebration, was it not? And it would continue at the house afterward. "Mrs. Hull, may I introduce you to Mr. Michael Grey? Lately of the north," she added with a game smile.

Mr. Grey caught that smile and returned it, knowingly, before glancing onward to Jane. "How do you do," he said, but Liza barely caught Jane's reply.

Her parents had excelled at these unspoken intimacies, these silently shared jokes. An odd pang ran through her, loneliness mixed with longing. She tried to hold on to her smile.

You do not love him, her mother's voice said. *Without love, it will be empty.*

"Mr. Grey, I feel sure we know each other," Jane was saying. "Your face is *shockingly* familiar. Yet I can think of no Greys who come to mind. Whence in the north do you hail?"

"Near the Scottish border," he said.

"Why, and I hail from York! So we must have acquaintances in common. Pray tell, where is your family settled?"

"Forgive me, Mrs. Hull, but I don't think our circles cross." He cut Liza a brief, unreadable look.

"Surely I would not manage to forget so lovely an acquaintance."

Jane preened, gratified by this compliment. "Well, I feel certain there is some connection. We may riddle it over dinner. I hear you're to join us?"

For an odd moment the conversation came to a halt. And then Mr. Grey said to Liza, "May I have a private word with you?"

Puzzled, Liza let him lead her off to a corner. Behind them rose ringing cheers as the raffle winners were announced. Mr. Grey's hand on her elbow, at first oddly formal, grew gentler; her breath caught as she felt the surreptitious stroke of his fingers before he pulled away. "I must once again beg an apology of you," he said softly. "I cannot come to dinner this evening."

A sharp bolt of disappointment briefly closed her throat. "But . . . why not?" Oh, good lord, she sounded the veriest schoolgirl. "That is, I've planned a very fine menu, and I was . . . I was very much looking forward to it."

"As was I," he said somberly. "In fact, I was . . ." He cleared his throat and glanced away. "Well," he said. "You understand."

No, she did not understand in the least. His manner seemed so changed. She followed his gaze and found it directed toward Jane, who in her white dress looked radiant with youthful good health. The expanse of her bared bosom had raised several sticklers' brows over the course of the last hours . . . and provoked more than one man's red-faced interest.

Jane gave them a sunny smile, then lifted her brows in a question. *What keeps you over there?*

"She is very lovely," Liza heard herself say.

"What? Oh, yes." Mr. Grey sounded distracted. "A guest of yours, I take it?"

"Indeed." Suddenly Liza felt ancient, and acutely aware of her own modest attire—a plain gray silk dress, with a neckline that might have done proud a matron of sixty. But, heavens' sakes, it was a *charity bazaar*. She always made a point of dressing modestly for such occasions, the better to ensure the townspeople's comfort with her. "I expect some pressing engagement has presented itself?"

If those last words had a waspish edge, she would not regret it. A pressing engagement at ten o'clock in the evening, in bucolic little Bosbrea?

"I fear so." He frowned a little as he met her eye, then shifted his weight like a guilty schoolboy. "Of course, I do wish . . ."

Her lips twisted to keep back the words that sprang to them. *You wish you had chosen a different lady to kiss. A younger one, perhaps.*

Her mother's voice rang through her head. *Beauty fades, Liza. What will you have then?*

She stepped back from him. Good God. Had that time already come? If so . . .

No. She had looked in the mirror today. She knew very well that he had no cause for complaint. As she exhaled, her uncertainty turned into a temper. Who was he? A country doctor. *Nobody*. "Very well," she said. "I wish you a good evening, Mr. Grey. I believe a few doilies yet remain, if you would like to support our little parish."

Turning on her heel, she stalked past Jane to the footman. The bottle of champagne was still half full. Until she got home, it would do.

*   *   *

"It's very poor form on Mr. Grey's part."

"I don't wish to speak about it." Liza sat on the ter-race, Jane lounging to her right, Mather awkwardly perched to her left. Overhead, the moon cut a bright path through the bruised clouds in the night sky. The breeze seemed to whisper secrets through the leaves of the trees.

"Very well," said Jane after a moment. "But I think it quite ungrateful. To be invited to dinner was a great honor to him!"

Mather's voice was as prim as a schoolteacher's. "Per-haps someone has taken ill. We mustn't judge without the proper information."

Jane snorted. "I believe I shall judge as I please! And I'm certain Liza agrees with me."

Liza had no such intention. Mather and Jane had taken a very entertaining dislike to each other, and she would not dream of discouraging it: heaven knew the rustic life offered few other diversions.

She reached for her glass, taking a long swallow of brandy. The burn felt like summer in her throat, a burning summer in a savage climate. "I should have traveled this season," she said. "The moment the last ball was held . . ." No—long before that. A year ago. The very moment Mama had died. "I should have boarded a ship to the farthest place in the world." A time-tested way to save money, too. Everywhere was cheaper than England.

"But that would have been impossible." Mather reached for the lamp on the little table. As she turned it up, her spectacles reflected the light, two dancing flames in place of her eyes. "Don't you recall? There were so many arrangements to be made—"

"Would that be China?" asked Jane idly as she lifted her hand to examine by lamplight the state of her pearlescent nails. "China seems very far away."

"I don't know." Liza mulled it for a moment. China did not quite catch her fancy; it seemed too straitlaced. "I've read that they are devoted to order in China," she said. "They have a mathematical system that guides even the placement of their beds."

Jane giggled. "How peculiar. Must one consult a mathematician before one turns over to snore?"

Liza mustered a smile, because Jane was attempting to amuse her. That was the proper task for a guest, and such efforts must be rewarded, even if they failed. Besides, it was not *precisely* Jane's fault that her mood was so black.

The breeze strengthened, fluttering their shawls. "Ma'am," said Mather, batting her own away from her chin, "I do wish you would come inside with me. This air cannot be healthy—"

"What an old woman your secretary is," Jane said.

"Not so much older than you," Mather muttered.

"Tell me, Liza, have you ever known her to frolic on a moonlit night? Or is it always too cold for her?"

Liza, sliding a glance toward Mather, repressed a sigh. At work, the girl excelled, but it was true that she lacked a talent for whimsy. Liza did not *blame* her for it, precisely—for she suspected, from Mather's rare hints, that the girl's history did not lend itself to a merry temperament. Nevertheless, she was paid very handsomely *now*. Surely she could spend a bit of her salary on grooming? But perhaps the prospect overwhelmed her, for there was *so much* in need of redress. The lamplight highlighted stray wisps of red hair that frizzed around Mather's square, pale face. Her glasses were atrocious. And her costume—an ill-fitting jacket, given structure by a belt that bore an overlarge buckle in the shape of a parrot—might have featured in a pantomime about suffragettes. Her jaw, meanwhile, telegraphed stubbornness: she had no intention of answering Jane's challenge.

"Well?" Liza asked. "*Do* you frolic, Mather?"

Her secretary frowned at her. Liza took an idle sip of brandy and waited.

"I suppose I did frolic as a child." The tartness in Mather's voice seemed promising. "But after sixteen hours of labor to promote a charity bazaar—no, I cannot say I have done!"

Ah. Liza shook her head. Such a disappointing retreat into moral superiority.

"Well!" Jane sat up, tossing her Indian shawl over her shoulder with practiced drama. "If the implication is that *I* was not of use today, I will most *strongly* object. I caught that child who was stealing doilies, didn't I? I believe that counts for *something!*"

Good heavens, it seemed sanctimoniousness was contagious. "Dear ladies," Liza said. Perhaps it was too much to expect them to keep her entertained. Jane had been here only a few weeks now, but it felt like ages. How on earth were they to rub along together for the rest of the summer? So soon after Mr. Grey's loss of interest, the prospect of remaining cloistered here troubled her. *Beauty fades.* She could not afford to waste any time.

She bolted the remainder of her brandy and reached for the bell to ring for more.

That's enough, Elizabeth.

Her mother had never been so annoying while alive. She toyed with the handle of the bell. "Perhaps I should invite friends to visit."

"A very fine idea," said Mather.

"Yes, isn't it?" She would put together a list, among them several eligible bachelors. Of course, she would need to lure them, for Cornwall lay in the opposite direction of most summer itineraries, which invariably concluded in the north for the August hunts.

Bah! She did not want to think of *the north* right now. She rang the bell.

"Who will you invite?" asked Jane. "Will I know them?"

"No, darling." But it would advance her prospects considerably to befriend them—*befriend* being the operative verb. Liza made a mental note to include several men not known to prefer blondes. Jane would have her chance, but being so young, she could afford to pursue it more leisurely. "We'll have a house party—a proper one, with a theme. A week at the least, to make it worth their while."

"A . . . week?" asked Mather. "That length of time would require a great deal of preparation—"

"Perhaps a fortnight," Liza said. A footman appeared. "More brandy," she said.

"Goodness!" Even Jane sounded doubtful. "Do you think anyone would want to stay so long?"

"Of course they would." Liza let a measured amount of asperity show in her voice as she looked between the two women. "*I* am the hostess, am I not? Besides, I shall *guarantee* their interest is held."

Mather took a deep breath, then nodded, shoulders squaring. "With six or seven weeks' notice—"

"No. A month at the most." August always left her terribly freckled. Best to do it before then.

"What theme shall you choose?" asked Jane.

The inspiration was so simple, yet so brilliant, that for a moment Liza was sure it had been sent from above. "I was reading a book on mysticism recently—something the Viscountess Sanburne recommended in her last letter. I believe we'll have a spiritual theme. All manner of experts. Demonstrations, experiments, lectures—and at the end of the party, we shall gather together and decide which practice is most credible!"

Jane wrinkled her nose. "A bunch of preachers! Have you gone mad?"

Liza burst into laughter. "Dear Jane, how put out you look! No, darling, I don't mean men of God, I mean *mystics*—clairvoyants and mediums and such."

"Such arrangements may take more than a month," muttered Mather.

"Oh, but how clever of you!" Jane bounced in her seat. "And Mr. Nelson will be mad with jealousy, simply green to be excluded!"

It took Liza a moment to follow Jane's meaning. Nello was the last thing on her mind at present. How curious. She tested herself, the way one might tongue a sore tooth. The ache was still there, but much diminished.

She supposed boorish northerners were good for something, after all.

"Mr. Nelson's feelings do not concern me," she said. Much as her worries had not concerned *him,* save to provoke him to drop her like a brick. "Mather, we must start on this at once." Telegrams must be sent; rooms must be aired; the staff must go up to London to make use of the telephones.

"Yes, ma'am." Mather bent down and produced, from the voluminous folds of her execrable skirt, a small notebook and pencil. "I suppose you'll want to hire a table rapper as well . . . and perhaps a Gypsy to read the cards—"

"A spirit writer," Jane suggested. "Oh, I saw a very chilling demonstration of that gift while wintering at Bath two years ago! I promise you, Liza, the man could not have known the things he wrote!"

"In short," Mather said repressively, "the usual variety of shills and rogues."

"Spiritualists," Liza corrected. "The rogues, my dears, will be *strictly* confined to the guest list."

CHAPTER SIX

The letter arrived in the midst of crisis. Liza was standing in the ballroom, overseeing the hanging of the velvet drapes she'd ordered from London. Twice now she'd rejected the shipment; lengthy notes and telegrams had flown to and fro; and now the footmen uncrated the boxes to reveal—*burgundy*. Burgundy velvet.

Jane gasped. "The horror!"

"It looks red to me," Mather observed.

"Red! You call that *red*!"

"I call that idiocy," Liza said coolly. "Must we hold a public lecture on the precise definition of the various colors?"

"I think we should hold a wake for Madame Huse!" Jane stamped a foot. "Scarlet, you said—scarlet or crimson, like the fresh spill of blood! Not *bordello* red! It looks . . ."

"Lurid," Liza finished. The red had too distinct an undertone of purple. But there was no time now to demand another exchange, so the lighting would have to be adjusted. "French lamps and candelabra, then. I will not be using Madam in the future." She had only used Madam because her usual draper was sending the most *aggressive* demands for payment.

"Oh . . ." Jane frowned, looking around the room. "French lamps *might* work, but in a space this size . . ."

Liza took her meaning. This room was large enough to hold two hundred people without a single foot being stepped on. If she required the footmen to trim the lamps as often as it would take to prevent a single one from guttering, they would never have a spare moment to breathe, much less to fetch new rounds of champagne. Also, wasn't it time she began to economize?

"Gas jets, then," she said with a sigh. "But I'm afraid it won't be nearly as atmospheric."

That decided, she opened the letter Ronson had brought her.

Had she foreseen its contents, she would have read it in private.

The blood drained from her head in one dizzying moment. She groped blindly for Mather's arm, unable to wrest her eyes from the page.

"What is it?" Jane seized her other elbow. Liza could not say how grateful she was for the doubled support, which seemed suddenly to be the only thing holding her upright.

"Mr. Nelson has announced his engagement." She cleared her throat. He must have proposed the moment he'd returned to town. Or . . . perhaps he'd already proposed before his visit here, in which case . . . he'd been planning to jilt her all along. Her financial troubles had nothing to do with it. He simply hadn't wanted *her*.

"Oh!" Jane drew her into a hug, but suddenly the

scent of rose water and lavender seemed smothering, unbearable.

Heedless of the rudeness of it, Liza pushed her friend away. "I can't—forgive me, I must be alone for a bit." Crushing the letter against her chest, she dashed through the ballroom, past a pair of footmen unwinding yet another bolt of the horrid burgundy cloth, out through the gallery and the open double doors into the gray afternoon.

The slight humidity of the fresh, mild air acted like a slap to bring her to her senses. She slowed from her mad dash, her steps uncertain on the crunching gravel of the long drive. A deep breath brought the taste and scent of the sea, the sharp salt and the sour brine of aquatic creatures. For all the cloud cover, the day was bright, a cool glowing sort of brightness that might have been the cause for the tears abruptly pricking her eyes.

She dragged in a breath through her clogged throat, unfolded the note, and read the lines again:

I must share the news of Mr. Nelson's engagement to Miss Lister. Will you not take it terribly amiss if I admit I am relieved? He never recognized your worth, Lizzie, nor deserved a moment of your attention. To wish Miss Lister joy would be like wishing for the moon to wear on a chain, for I know it can never be. The poor girl! I am so thankful that you never were trapped by marriage to him.

Miss Lister. Liza held that name in her mind the same way she might test her thumb against a thorn. *It does not matter.* She did not want Nello! Nobody should want such a deceitful, cowardly bully! Forever quarrelsome, always unsatisfied . . .

She turned and took one step toward the house, the wild idea in her mind to write the girl, to warn her: *He will never love you. If he could not love me after all the forbearance with which I greeted his bad behavior, all the many times I forgave him for his rude treatment of me, all the tolerance I showed upon learning of his betrayals, then he will never, ever love you.*

But what a cruel message! Worse yet—what if it were not true? What if Nello *had* fallen in love with this girl? What if he *could* be an honorable, honest, loving man— to someone else?

What if you simply can't be loved?

She crumpled the note again and walked blindly down the drive, the crushed oysters and gravel under-foot jabbing through the thin soles of her house slippers. The pain suited her. She stomped harder to feel it all the more sharply. Some people called her the most beautiful woman in England. She called herself the stupidest. What were words without actions to match them? Why had she ever gambled her heart on the strength of his *words*?

She lifted her head to stare down the drive toward the lake, shrouded from view by trees. A breeze ruffled through the tops of the branches, lifting them toward the sky, and she felt, with a sudden strange shock, the large-ness of the world: the ocean like a vast yawning mouth, some ten miles to the east; and the endless impossible distance of the sky overhead, bridging land and sea as it wrapped around the earth; and the empty space beyond it, an alien void sparsely scattered with stars.

How small she was, standing here. No more than a speck. All the turmoil in her breast was tantamount to the tap of the next pebble scattered by her step.

What was love, anyway? Soundless and ephemeral as a breath. This scene around her, which had witnessed her parents' contentment for their brief span of life—it would outlast everyone she knew, and their children, and their children's grandchildren. Why cling to love? It was a handhold amid the torrent, but everyone eventually fell into the river. Swept away, they were forgotten.

Why drive oneself to anguish, longing for such a handhold? Why bother? Better to look for comfort than gamble on a dream for which suffering was the more likely reward. Handholds were useless. And she would not find one anyway.

She took a deep breath. Very well. Practicality would be her aim from now on. She would never be stupid again. She vowed it: she was done with love.

She crumpled the letter. It was not even worth the burning.

Standing in the dusty road outside the postal office, Michael read the words again.

> *Lord Marwick's secretary had no official comment, but confirmed that an interim director had been appointed to implement an unspecific program of reform at the Duchess of Marwick Hospital. Of the former director, his grace's brother, no news is heard . . .*

Michael took a deep breath. The newspaper was half a day old, sent from London by the morning train. God knew what tidings tomorrow's delivery would carry. He could not imagine why Peter Halsted, his right-hand man at the hospital, had not written in warning. Halsted alone knew where he was. Until now, he'd made a very steady correspondent, full of reassurances. But yesterday he'd not written at all.

An oversized timetable was plastered over the front window of the post office. He found himself staring at the train schedules. The station was an hour's drive north. He could be in London by midnight. Go directly to Halsted's flat. Alastair need never know.

Unless Alastair had somehow enlisted Halsted in this business.

You would be surprised by what I can and cannot do. Alastair had already proved that, for despite the terms of their father's will, Michael's bank accounts sat empty. He could only imagine what Alastair had said to the bankers. In fact, he could imagine it all too well. *What will he do—take me to court? With what funds? You know whose money your bank depends on for its success.*

If Alastair could intimidate such men into doing his bidding, why would Halsted, a mere clerk with three children and a fourth on the way, prove immune? Perhaps threats hadn't even been needed. An extra hundred pounds would be a small fortune to Halsted, and barely noticeable to Alastair. Button money, really.

He tried to calm his thoughts. The hospital remained open. This *interim* director probably didn't exist. He was a ruse, a gambit designed by Alastair to force Michael from hiding.

Well, it wouldn't work. He'd be damned before he gave his brother the victory so easily.

"—absolutely insist on it. You cannot be seen in such rags!"

The familiar voice further frayed his composure. He

turned to discover Mrs. Chudderley stepping directly into his path.

She had not seen him until now; that was obvious from the way her expression abruptly smoothed into a mask of bland pleasantness. Her companion—the red-haired maid—did not bother with such efforts, giving him a scowl of undisguised dislike.

Ladies talked to their maids, of course. His behavior at the bazaar had blackened his name at Havilland Hall. "Mrs. Chudderley," he said. "Good morning."

"Mr. Grey." She herself carried her parasol today, a confection of rose silk trimmed in yellow, again to match her gown. The twirl she gave it set the lemon-bright tassels shivering. "What a . . ." Her smile quirked into something sharper as she trailed off, pointedly refraining from pronouncing it a pleasure.

"What an occasion," he suggested—an attempt at humor that fell flat as silence opened between them.

He sighed. He'd made a hash of the dinner invitation, but her damned houseguest's insistence that they knew each other had taken him off guard. He did not recognize Mrs. Hull, but it was possible they had met somewhere—and if so, he'd had no interest in giving her the opportunity to interrogate him, or to wrack her memories as she studied him at leisure.

He glanced past her. "Mrs. Hull does not accompany you?"

Mrs. Chudderley's eyes narrowed. "No, she does not. And I suppose our meeting might be termed an *occasion,* as you say. But if you prefer, we might instead consider it an incident, and move on without remark."

Well, that *was* blunt. And refreshing, strangely, after long minutes spent pondering his brother's manipulations. "Perhaps if I apologize again for missing your dinner," he said, "we may elevate the incident to an event."

"These are all different words with specific meanings," said the redhead sourly. "To be precise, I would call this an encounter."

"Have you met Miss Mather?" asked Mrs. Chudderley. The idle roll of her shoulders put him in mind of a great cat stretching in preparation for the kill. "My secretary, and an all-around bon vivant."

That joke seemed aimed at Miss Mather herself, who arched her brows. "I am a firm believer in the specific import of various words," she said primly. "It's a very fine quality in a secretary, so I've heard. Ah, is that the morning paper? Ma'am, you were wondering—"

"Yes, so I was." Mrs. Chudderley lifted her brow and extended one gloved hand. Belatedly he realized he was meant to hand the thing over to her.

He did, unhappily aware that he had not bothered to refold the thing. He'd gripped that specific page so tightly that his thumb had left telltale smudges in the ink.

Alas for him, Mrs. Chudderley was catlike all around: her sharp eyes fixed on this evidence of his interest. "Medical gossip," she said. "Goodness, I'd no idea that such a thing existed!"

He took back the paper before she could read further. "Yes," he said as he refolded it, "we doctors amuse ourselves where we may. I assume you were looking for the society columns?"

"Perhaps I was looking for a military editorial," she said. "Perhaps our imperial stratagems keep me awake at night."

He laughed. Truly, she elevated sarcasm to an art.

"For certain," he said. "I believe the front section will suit you, then."

"In fact, the last section is what she wants," said Miss Mather, only to close her mouth quite abruptly at her employer's black look.

"Then you must be seeking an announcement." He flipped the paper to the relevant page. "Births, deaths—ah, and the next page: a public ball in honor of the Queen—"

"I do not attend public balls," said Mrs. Chudderley coldly.

Snapping the paper down, he studied the flat line of her mouth. "News of a betrothal, then?"

Silence. Mrs. Chudderley shot another fulminating look toward her secretary.

Oh, but *now* he was enjoying himself. "Heavens. Never say one of your *countless* admirers has turned his attentions elsewhere. Now, that—and I believe even Miss Mather will agree—would be an *event,* indeed."

"You're very rude," Miss Mather said flatly.

He looked at her in amazement—and so, too, did Mrs. Chudderley. The girl colored as only a redhead could, violently, all of her freckles darkening. "Well," she muttered, and rubbed her square chin. "Perhaps I should be off—"

"Yes, off you go," Mrs. Chudderley said. "And do not come back until you've plotted something acceptable to wear with the milliner."

It occurred to Michael that the girl *was* dressed peculiarly. A grandmother of eighty might have made that bombazine look dowdy.

"Something immodest," said Miss Mather. "Yes, you've told me."

"Come now, I did not say *immodest*—"

Off stalked the secretary, leaving them both frowning, first at her diminishing figure, and then at each other.

Almost immediately, Mrs. Chudderley's glance bounced away. Her color was high, the light through her silk parasol adding to the rosy glow of her cheeks. Not even the most stylish French hostess could have faulted her dress, a confection of bright lemon silk that slipped over her curves as closely as a loving hand.

He shifted his weight. Rarely did he feel so discomposed around any woman, particularly one he'd much rather be kissing. For, yes—it took only a moment's exposure now, after a week of trying not to think on her, to recall why he'd wanted to share dinner with her in the first place. He did love a woman with wit.

"I will get my own paper," she said, and turned on her heel.

"No, wait." The secretary was right; he was a boor. He slipped out the section about the hospital and passed the remainder to her. "I bought the last one, I'm afraid."

She halted, then turned back, the slowness of her movements lending them a grudging flavor. As she took the proffered newspaper, she did not quite look at him.

That made his mood sink a little lower. He'd done many clumsy things in his time, but he'd never before made a lady reluctant to meet his eyes—save from delighted shock, and this certainly did not count as such.

"About the bazaar," he said. "I'm truly so very sorry to have broken the engagement."

"So you've said. Do you know the Duke of Marwick, then?"

He choked on his next words. "Ah—why do you ask?"

"The hospital in your medical gossip." She made a show of flipping through the paper, the pages rattling. "He's the benefactor of that hospital. It's his brother's pet project, you know."

Pet project? "What an interesting way to phrase it," he said. "From what I understand, they've made great leaps in the prevention of infections." That he did not proceed to cite the statistics should have earned him an award for restraint.

"Is that so?"

Her incredulous tone ruffled his temper. "Yes. Why should it surprise you?"

She gave him a one-shouldered shrug. "I admit, one does not imagine his grace's brother as a medical visionary. But perhaps he hires a very good staff."

What on God's green earth? She made him sound like a dilettante! "Do you know the duke's brother?"

She blinked. "I don't recall if we've met. But I know *of* him." Her faint smile, like her words, fairly dripped condescension. "London is a small place, Mr. Grey, for those in my circles."

"Oh, I can imagine," he said. He'd certainly heard of *her*. "And Lord Michael's reputation does not recommend him as a doctor? Is that what you mean?"

The edge in his voice appeared to amuse her. Her smile broadened. "Well. I suppose, if one is a lady in need of . . . *particular* attentions, he'd be just the man to call."

God's blood! Was anyone ever going to let him forget that single error of judgment? *Just go out the front door,* Lady Heverley had said. *It's barely light yet. Who's around to see?*

"I was unaware of that." He sounded like a stiff stickler of eighty, but it was not every day a man heard himself maligned as a lecher.

"How pleasant that I could educate you." She looked back to her newspaper. "I will say this for him: the hospital is quite pleasant. Full of light. Perhaps that helps with the—infections and whatnot."

Now he felt faintly lightheaded. "You've visited?"

"I went to the opening five years ago. His grace hosted a soiree in the rotunda."

"I . . . that must have been quite marvelous." It had been a nightmare. To have the entire place assembled and ready to open, only to have to wait for weeks for the start of the social season, all so Margaret could have her party first—

"It was passable," said Mrs. Chudderley as she flipped to the next page. She was making a great show of studying the paper now. "I did not stay above a quarter hour. The decorations were poor, the champagne was flat, and the crowd, I fear, was not select enough to hold my interest. But, yes, I suppose *you* would have found it marvelous."

He swallowed his startled laugh, for she could not know how closely her opinion matched his own—and, after all, she was attempting to insult him. He supposed, after the bazaar, he owed her the satisfaction of thinking she'd succeeded.

"Indeed," he said. "You're no doubt right." Would that he had known her back *then*. They could have spent the time merrily complaining to each other. Afterward, he could also have shown her how well he treated ladies in need of . . . *particular* attentions.

His reply had not satisfied her. She glanced up to frown at him. He supposed he should have seemed a bit more put out. "That is, I'm sure I'd have been quite overset by it," he said. This masquerade was rather wearing on his dignity.

She looked back to the newspaper. "Yes, well. You would not have felt comfortable in such a crowd, I expect."

"I thought you said it wasn't select."

Her glance flashed up again. "By select, I do not mean breeding, sir; I mean wit and good taste." She smiled.

Whatever complex recipe had produced that smile, it did a marvelous job of reminding him that he was playing a man too far beneath her to properly merit her notice. And for the first time, he found himself irked by it.

He wanted his apology to be taken seriously. He wanted, he realized, another chance at dinner with her. Country life was tedious. And really, what matter if Jane Hull recognized him? He would not encourage it—but if she did manage to identify him, he would relish the look on Mrs. Chudderley's face afterward. *I believe you've heard of me,* he would add.

"Are you ruminating?" she asked sweetly. "I can repeat my remark."

"No need," he said. "I believe you've just insulted my breeding. Do I have that right?"

"Yes, precisely." She snapped to the next page. Whatever she saw there made her go quite still.

"Did you find your announcement?" he asked.

Her eyes rose to his, then wandered over his shoulder before returning to the page. "Yes," she said. Where she gripped the paper, her knuckles were whitening.

Perhaps his speculation about a former lover had not been so far off the mark. "Are you quite all right?"

"Oh, *quite.*" She folded the newspaper and stuck it beneath her arm. "Indeed, the announcement was not for an engagement, but a death: the death of a pleasant stroll, the assassin being a northerner."

By God, but she was magnificent when she was cross. Put a sword in her hand and he'd be bleeding right about now. "And now it seems our encounter has turned into a rout. I cede you the victory, madam."

Briefly, her mouth seemed to tremble—but then it curved into a fierce, bright smile. "I do not believe one cedes what one has already lost," she said. "But take heart; you can complain of my rudeness in the tavern tonight. Be sure to tell them I did not say good day to you, sir."

She lifted her chin and walked past him. He turned to watch her go. It was not his imagination; her shoulders had assumed a decidedly dejected slope. What had she seen to dispirit her?

Curses. He was going to have to find another copy of that newspaper.

CHAPTER SEVEN

The pounding came in the middle of the night. Liza opened her eyes, then groaned at the bolt of pain that lanced through her head. Too much wine at dinner.

The knocking came again at the outer door.

The carpet felt chill against the bare soles of her feet. Her hand fumbled on the door latch. Behind her, from the boudoir, came the sound of rustling as her maid, Hanson, awoke. She yanked open the door herself.

Mather stood on the other side, her face pale in the light of the hand-candle she carried. "Ma'am, forgive me for waking you."

The clock in the hall was chiming half past three, and Mather was fully dressed. Dread spilled over Liza like an ice bath. "What is it? What's happened?"

"A boy has come—John Broward. He said you would wish to know that his aunt is still in labor."

Her breath caught. "What?" Mary had felt the first pangs almost two days ago!

Mather's face was somber. "It seems that she asked for you."

Liza's heart clutched at the implication. Her friendship with the Browards did not extend to such intimacy; properly, she had no place in their home at such a time. But if Mary Broward feared the worst, then of course she would wish to speak to the family benefactor. Mary was ever plotting the best for her brood . . .

Liza wheeled around. Her maid was gaping like a mooncalf. "Hanson, dress me quickly." Over her shoulder, she said, "Have a horse saddled. That will be faster."

"I've already given the order," Mather said.

Not again. This all felt too familiar. The journey through the dark of night. Her heart pounding with fear. She remembered boarding the train at St. Pancras, blindly fumbling for her ticket, the conductor's look of sympathy. She had arrived too late then. Her mother had already passed. And now . . .

She stepped inside the Browards' small bedroom. The air smelled thick with sweat and blood. Mary lay amid a pile of twisted sheets. The sheet draped over her waist and legs veiled the doctor who examined her.

This piece of typical prudery fixated Liza's attention. A startling wave of anger shot through her. She did not understand it, but it felt better, so much better, than fear. "Why was I not informed before this?" she asked. Too sharply, too loudly. Heads turned.

She realized then that the little room was crowded. Mary's husband knelt by her head, eyes closed, hands clasped, murmuring a prayer. And Mr. Morris . . . why, the old doctor stood at the window, breathing deeply of what air entered through the open pane.

"Mrs. Chudderley," he said, clearly flustered. The

man beneath the sheet, the man tending to Mary, straightened and revealed himself to be Mr. Grey.

She had not seen him in a week. His insult now seemed irrelevant. Only his skill mattered. "How is she?" she asked. "Can you help her?"

He had dark circles beneath his eyes, and glanced at her only briefly before Mary's moan turned his attention away. "You should go," he said.

"You should take that ridiculous sheet off her," Liza said. "See what you're doing!"

"Mrs. Chudderley," Mr. Morris began sternly, but Grey cut him off.

"Yes," he said coldly. "So I should. Once you step outside, madam, I believe I will."

"Mrs. Broward was very specific in her instructions," Mr. Morris snapped. "She wanted her modesty preserved."

She did not understand the black look that Grey gave to Morris, but it settled something in her. He would remove the sheet. "I will wait outside," she said, and stepped into the little hallway where most of the Broward family waited.

Her knees were trembling. Gratefully she took the chair that one of the sons made available to her. Paul Broward, home from school. He made a slight bow to her, to which she replied with a nod. Absently she thought, *They are teaching him manners at Harrington.* Her accountants had tried to talk her out of such expenditures. Boors.

No noise came from the bedroom. The silence in the hallway felt like a heavy weight pressing her down. Daniel Broward, nine years old, eternally grubby, clutched her wrist with a small, sweaty hand. "Is Mama all right? Did you see her?"

Liza peered at him through the dimness. The floor-boards creaked as someone went down the stairs. She had never been in this part of the house. She was kin, but not a true friend. Only the parlor for her, and the finest dishes, and the best of the Browards' tea. Family, but not *real* family.

"Yes," she said, "she'll be all right," but her voice was choked and the boy heard her uncertainty. His hand slipped away, making a fist, which he put into his mouth. Miss Broward, with a small noise of grief, picked him up and pulled him into her lap.

Here was love. Watching it, Liza felt grief wash over her. What purchase could it find amid the grim facts of life?

She grimaced. Too early, this despair. Unnecessary, indulgent. Her anger suddenly twisted, becoming self-directed. "Mrs. Broward will be well," she said. *There* was the steadiness she required, there in her voice now. "She has two doctors attending her. She will be well, Daniel."

"Thank you for coming," Miss Broward said. She sounded dull and hoarse, as though she had been yelling.

"Had I known, I would have come sooner."

"Of course. We did not wish to trouble you. Then she asked after you, but . . ."

Liza closed her eyes. The ache in her head felt like some intolerable evidence of her own lowness. Tonight she had sat in the drawing room, planning a party, drinking toasts with Jane to all manner of stupidity. Meanwhile, Mary had been lying on that bed, suffering . . .

A raised voice came through the wall, the words muffled but their mood clear. In the bedroom, men were arguing.

Liza cleared her throat. "I thought it would be fine."
At market on Monday, Mary had been feeling the first
pains. But she had seemed so calm. Six children borne
already. She'd never had any trouble with it.

"Yes," said Miss Broward, and then said no more.

The door flew open. Mr. Broward stumbled out. "I
can't watch this," he said, dashing tears from his face. "I
can't. Forgive me."

Behind him, Mr. Morris appeared. "Mrs. Chudderley," he said grimly. "If I may beg a word with you."

Mr. Grey was laying out instruments atop the chest that
adjoined the foot of the bed. With unaccustomed aggression, Morris pushed her toward him. "Tell her of
your plan. If Mr. Broward lacks the wit to defend his
wife, *she* will!"

Liza cast a bewildered look toward the bed. "What
is this about?" Mary lay quite still, the only sign of life
now her fluttering lashes, and the faint sheen of sweat
pearling her skin. "My God, is she . . ."

"No," said Mr. Grey. "Morris administered a small
amount of chloroform to give her ease. It won't last long."

Liza's eyes fell to the scalpel in his hand. He dipped
it into a small pot of liquid that bubbled. There could
be only one reason for such a blade. "You mean to . . ."

He glanced up at that. His light eyes seemed to assess
her. "The child is lodged too high in her pelvis," he said.
"Surgery is the only remaining option."

"A craniotomy is the obvious choice!" Morris spat.

Liza looked between them. "What is that?"

"A procedure that would save Mrs. Broward's life,"
Mr. Morris said after a moment.

That pause seemed telling. "And the child?" she asked.

His jaw ticked from side to side. "The child . . . would not survive. But she would. Something Mr. Grey cannot guarantee, given *his* way!"

"A craniotomy poses significant risks of its own." Grey bent, retrieving from his black doctor's bag a length of silver wire. He unwound the wire, dipping it, too, into the solution. In contrast to Morris's agitation, his measured movements seemed jarringly calm. "Conversely, a Caesarean section might save both mother and child. And that is Mrs. Broward's preference."

Morris scoffed. "*Her* preference—yes, very well, let us listen to a woman hysterical with pain! And while you're at it, tell Mrs. Chudderley the risk of infection, and how often a woman survives *that*! Not to mention hemorrhage! Why—"

"Uterine sutures," said Grey.

"Impossible. How will you remove them?"

Grey's smile was cool and sharp as glass. "It is not my job to educate you." Now, from the bag at his feet, he produced a needle and a length of white gauze. "Saumlnger wrote an entire monograph on the subject five years ago."

"No." Morris was shaking his head. "You would have me condone this madness on the newfangled tactics of some *German*? Absolutely not!"

Mr. Grey made no reply as he focused on his tasks. Liza glanced again toward the bed, anxiety tightening her throat. She did not understand why *she* had been brought into this quarrel. But surely Mary hadn't much time. Her face looked waxen, nearly bloodless.

"Do *something*," she blurted. "One or the other!"

"Reason with Mr. Broward," Morris said to her. "I pray you, persuade him to stop this! His thoughts are muddled. He will rely on your judgment!"

She swallowed. "But *I* have no idea which—that is, Mr. Grey, what is your argument?"

Mr. Grey looked up. "Mr. Broward gave the choice to his wife. And I would not support that choice if I did not think it the best way. I know the odds, and I will take them."

He spoke curtly, not in the manner of a man bent on persuasion. That, more than anything, decided her. "Then, if the Browards feel it best, we must respect their wishes."

Morris chopped at the air—a movement so violent that she took a startled step away. "A tailor and his wife! A *tailor*—do you hear yourself? Trust him to judge the cut of a coat, but this is a woman's life, madam!"

His contempt was sharper and more shocking than a slap. She stared at him. His face reddened but he did not look away. "I will have no part in it." Spittle flew from his mouth. "Do you hear me? I will *not* assist!"

In the brief silence that followed, panic coiled around her lungs, tightening until she could not breathe. So this was true fear. She had come to watch Mary Broward die. "You must," she whispered, but Morris averted his face, his lips pinching.

"You aren't needed," said Mr. Grey.

The breath burst from her. She turned toward him, savagely grateful to see the cold confidence in his face, as behind her Morris exploded, "Rubbish! You can't do it alone!"

"Your hands aren't steady enough." Grey's attention fixed on Liza. "I will need your assistance."

"What?" Shock splintered into horrified understanding. No, he couldn't mean— "You want *me* to help?"

"Outrageous," Morris said. "She will faint at the first drop of blood!"

Grey gave her a long look of assessment as he unwound a length of gauze. "Will you?"

Her stomach rolled in reply. No, *no*. He wanted to make her a party to a surgery that might *kill* Mary? "I can't! I've *never*—"

"The child." The voice came weakly from the bed. "Please . . ."

Morris, on a low oath, turned away. Liza stepped toward the bed, thinking to speak to Mary, but a hard hand at her elbow—Grey's hand—pulled her back.

"Let her be," he said. Then, lower, into her ear: "You are frightened. I understand that. But you must decide now, quickly. I would rather not involve her immediate family in the surgery."

She hesitated, turning in his grip to look directly at him. Strange, fleeting thought: she had thought his eyes so beautiful. But now they were bloodshot, deadly sober. She recognized nothing in him of the laughing flirt who had kissed her by the lake.

"If I make a mistake . . ." When had she ever done anything so important and delicate as this? She did not even do *needlepoint*. She did not even dress herself! "I am the *last* person you should be asking."

Something moved across his face, too fleeting to decipher. But his stern expression softened. "I would not ask if I did not think you capable. All you need do is take my instruction."

She could not do this. *No*. She glanced away—and found herself locked in Mary's agonized look of entreaty.

Her throat closed. How could she refuse?

"Yes." *My God.* "I'll help." She lifted her hands to test them. To her amazement, Mr. Grey was right. They did not shake.

Once Morris had stomped out and Mr. Grey had bolted the door, time seemed to slow. For an eternity Liza scrubbed her hands, disbelief like a panic in her blood, the sting of the antiseptic drawing tears to her tired eyes. Mr. Grey turned up the lamps. Everything became too bright, painfully illuminated. Her heart was pounding like a war cry before battle: what was she doing? He must be mad to ask this of her. She was a butterfly. A *professional beauty*, for God's sake.

When he held out a rag well blotted with chloroform, she faltered. "There is no one else who can help?"

He held her eyes. "I can send for someone. Pershall should be coming."

But that might take too long. "I can't do this," she said. "You don't understand." He had no idea who she was. Had he known her reputation, or understood the poverty of her judgment, he never would have asked this of her.

I will kill her.

"You can," he said. "I will explain every step."

She swallowed, certain she would be sick. But she took the cloth and crossed quickly to Mary's head, trying to match Mary's weak smile—God in heaven, an attempt to reassure *her*—before placing it carefully over the woman's nose.

Mary's eyes fluttered shut again. And then the whole world contracted to the bed, to Grey's quiet movements as he propped Mary's knees atop rolled blankets.

"Now the antiseptic," he said. "This is your task. I'll prepare the tubing."

Amazing that her hand did not shake. How had he known it would not shake? She focused intently on her job, limiting her awareness only to the moment: the pale curve of Mary's belly as she swabbed it down. The frightening faintness of the child's weakening kicks.

The sickly sweet smell of chloroform, as she administered a new dose under Mr. Grey's direction.

The coppery scent of blood as he made the first incision.

Through it all, she felt anchored by his voice—steady, clear, and free of doubt as he directed her. His voice made it possible to keep her hand steady as she assisted him with the india rubber tubing—"To direct drainage," he told her. His voice kept her calm as she watched him reveal the awful, ugly secrets the skin kept veiled from view. Somehow none of it, none of the blood and mess, affected him; at every turn he remained evenly spoken, transparently unsurprised; and so Liza, breathing deeply, remained collected, too, even as the blood spilled more freely, and his scalpel flashed again. It could not be bad. For he did not sound worried.

Yet when he wrestled the babe free—when he put it squirming and bloodied into her arms, and she realized it was a flawless little girl, with eyelashes and nails all intact—part of her awoke with a sudden jolt. Abruptly she was back in her body, and shaking indeed, in this stinking, close little room, as she gripped a living child who had come so impossibly close to not living at all.

My God, she thought. She looked between the babe and Mary, who yet slumbered, peaceful in her drugged dreams, and the man standing over her who now wielded his needle, silver wire flashing. He was piecing Mary together layer by layer, blood up to his elbows, no sign on his face of anything but focused intent.

The same man who had kissed her, and laughed.

She could not look away from him. He did not give up. Having saved one life, he was battling now to save another.

She felt her breath go. She had never witnessed anything so serious. Never witnessed any man performing a task of such import. A queer feeling seized her, a prickling all down her skin, curiously like wonder. She clutched the child harder to her breast. *I know the odds, and I will take them.*

The explosive wail made her jump. The baby screamed, red face contorting. Then footsteps pounded, the door rattled, and Mr. Grey looked to her, a hard look that was broken by his blink, as though suddenly he could see again.

"Well done," he said.

"Yes," she whispered.

"Hand over the baby, but keep them out—I'll need your help once more."

She flew to the door.

The surgery concluded, Liza returned to Havilland Hall only to bathe and sleep. At the Browards', endless tasks awaited her, for by God, she still had the money to make their troubles easier. A wet nurse must be hired, for Mary's pain required laudanum, which made her milk dangerous. Mr. Broward's tailoring shop could not be closed, for he was receiving a shipment of cloth from London. But Liza put together a schedule for the neighbors, young men called in from the fields who would man his shop once he had dealt with the shipment.

Almost the moment those matters were settled, nearly a full day after the baby's birth, Mary developed a fever. For the first time, Mr. Grey showed concern. And that frightened Liza more, even, than the great heat radiating from Mary's body.

The second and third days passed in a haze: ice baths to bring down Mary's fever; the constant administration of medicines; the vigil to make sure Mary's airway remained clear. Near noon on the fourth day, Mary grew delirious and had to be restrained. Shortly thereafter, Mr. Morris paid a call, requesting to look in on Mary himself. His manner was terse, his anger clearly undiminished. But Mr. Grey ceded his patient courteously, and after a brief conversation with Morris, Liza went to find him, eager to know his thoughts.

He sat in the small, stone-walled garden that adjoined the cottage. She took a seat beside him on the low bench; it was quite wide enough for another two men besides. The mellow sunlight and mild warmth, the bees drifting around them from flower to flower, made a welcome respite from the darkness of the house. Someone, Miss Broward in all likelihood, had brought Mr. Grey a simple lunch of cold beef, Stilton, and bread. He handed her a piece of cheese without comment.

She took a bite, but chewed without enthusiasm. "Do you think the fever will break today?"

"If we are fortunate." Mr. Grey picked at his bread, frowning.

"It's a bad sign, isn't it? That she hallucinates?"

The corner of his mouth hitched, not precisely a smile. "Has Mr. Morris been advising you?"

"He says you must cup her."

"Cupping will not help," he said evenly. "Mr. Morris languishes in the 1830s, I believe."

"But is he right that it's a bad sign?"

He sighed. "It is . . . not a good sign. No."

"All right." She took a hard breath. "I'll send a note to Havilland Hall, inform them I must stay on tonight."

He cast her a look she could not decipher. He also had returned home, once or twice, to rest and gather supplies. But by the shadows beneath his eyes, he had not allowed himself very much sleep. "No need for that. The others can help me where it's needed."

Strange that she should feel hurt by the notion that he did not require her. "But Paul is returning to school today, and Miss Broward must look after the little ones and the baby. And Mr. Broward is exhausted, and becomes so terribly upset whenever he sees his wife in such a state. It would be better all around if I stayed, don't you think?"

He turned on the bench to look at her. In the strong light, the shadows beneath his cheekbones were pronounced. "Your help is welcome," he said slowly. "But surely you have your own obligations to attend to."

She shrugged. Mather and Jane had the preparations for the house party well in hand—a good thing, for Liza could not think on it right now. As for the rest, Havilland Hall ran like clockwork: she was only an idle spectator to its operation. "Nothing of import."

He did not reply to that. Nor did he look away, though he angled his face a little, so the light suddenly struck his eyes, illuminating them. They matched the sky behind him, achingly blue.

She shifted a little on the bench, discomfited by

sudden awareness. For days now he'd been a remote authority: the doctor, issuing instructions, who must be obeyed. But now, suddenly, she saw him again as a man, his strong jaw shadowed by stubble, his glossy hair mussed beyond repair. And she saw, too, how his dishevelment became him. He was not classically handsome, but he had the body of a soldier, long and lean—and a sharp and knowledgeable mind, and broad hands that saved an infant and then gently cradled an ailing woman's head as he spoke to her, whispered to her, encouraged her to believe she would live to know her child.

Liza's eyes fell to those hands, tanned and long-fingered and capable, and something hot moved through her, something entirely overpowering and mortifyingly out of place. When she had kissed him by the lake, she had not known *anything* of him. Her admiration, her attraction, had been premised on her surprise: a country rustic with wit, a man who smelled delicious, whose lips were surprisingly skilled.

But then he had saved a child's life, and Mary's as well. And now he deprived himself of rest to ensure Mary's continued survival.

And now Liza wanted him for those reasons, too. He was not simply a diversion any longer. He was a man well worth wanting.

And he was still staring at her.

She reached up, tucking stray wisps of hair behind her ears, abruptly conscious of how much she had perspired while helping to hold Mary down. "What is it?" she asked, attempting lightness. "Why do you stare? Have I grown another head?"

He gave her a faint smile. "The one you have is already quite enough to draw stares. No, I'm only wondering . . . what is it that really keeps you here?"

Her throat closed. Did he somehow sense her shift in mood? That every inch of her skin was suddenly humming, longing to move closer to him? The thought was too awful. With Mary so ill . . . "You said the fever might be serious. But if you prefer . . ."

"No," he said instantly. "Don't mistake me. I could not hope for a better assistant. You are calm and clearheaded; you listen carefully, and you're methodical in carrying out instructions."

She could feel her face warming. What peculiar praise, to touch her so deeply. "Not the most difficult tasks."

"You'd be surprised. It was Mrs. Broward's good fortune, and mine, that you were here to assist that first night. But I confess I'm surprised that you've stayed so long. I know that Mary's health gravely concerns you. But I wonder . . . do you fear what might happen in your absence? Or are you kept here by the . . . novelty of it?"

She stiffened. But on a moment's reflection, she could find no judgment in his voice, despite his implication that she might be offering her help out of boredom— or suspicion of his abilities. His curiosity sounded too gentle to give offense.

"Of course I trust you to care for her," she said.

"Thank you." His voice was grave. "I promise you, I will hold that trust dear."

How seriously he spoke! As though *her* trust truly did mean something out of the ordinary to him.

The notion made her feel strangely shy. She looked into her lap, attempting to smooth skirts that were wrinkled beyond repair. "Perhaps part of it *is* the novelty," she admitted. Attending to Mary felt . . . *useful* in a way she had never experienced. She had offered money before to those in need. But now she had involved her hands and heart in it. She had held a child that her efforts had helped to save.

Who among her friends would have thought her capable of such feats? Nello would have laughed himself off his seat at the notion.

"I suppose," she said hesitantly, "I rather like feeling as though I'm . . . needed." She had not felt lonely a single moment over these past few days. Had not once heard the chiding voice of her mother. "Heavens. What a very selfish motive!"

"Not at all, Mrs. Chudderley." He crumbled a piece of bread between thumb and forefinger and tossed it to an adventurous finch that was hopping toward them. "You're speaking to a man who chose medicine for his living. Not the usual path, but one that guaranteed my services would be valued. That was important to me, to do something that . . . others couldn't."

She hesitated. "Perhaps you might call me Elizabeth. For the sake of convenience," she said quickly. "Mrs. Chudderley is so cumbersome." Suddenly she did not like him calling her by the name of her late husband. Alan Chudderley had nothing to do with her now. Nothing to do with *him*.

"Elizabeth." He spoke the name slowly. "An elegant name. It suits you."

But he did not invite a similar intimacy. She tried not to feel hurt by it. Perhaps he felt it would be too impertinent for a man of his station. "Was your father in some other business, then?" When he cast her a startled look, she repeated his words back to him: "Medicine was not the usual path, you said."

"Ah. Yes, he was a . . ." He laughed softly as the finch hopped closer yet. "Ridiculous bird." He threw another bit of bread. "My father was something of a . . . businessman. But of course that legacy went to the eldest son."

An odd note had entered his voice. She hazarded a guess. "Your father did not approve of you becoming a doctor."

"Oh, he approved of very little when it came to me. Save at the end." He looked down at the stub of bread, turned it over in his hands. His beautiful mouth firmed as though to hold back his next words, which he spoke, at length, very slowly. "When he took ill, he no longer had much use for cleverness with numbers, or righteous attitudes, or . . . loyalties. I was finally of some use to him then. I alone had the skill to ease him."

She bit her lip. It did not take a mind reader to guess at the pain that his neutral tone must conceal. She reached out to touch his arm. "You're a wonderful doctor."

He lifted a brow, glancing from her hand on his sleeve into her eyes. And as simply as that, her innocent touch seemed not so innocent. As though an electric switch had been flipped, the feel of his warmth beneath her fingertips made her whole body go hot.

How curious that her instant urge was to *remove* her hand—to withdraw and sit back. Now that she knew him better, this base attraction seemed dangerous, for it could go nowhere. Her future, and the future of boys like Paul and Harry Broward, could not be secured by a doctor's income. A brief dalliance, she'd thought, would harm no one—but if her heart became entangled in it, a great deal of harm might result.

Her heart had been broken too many times now. She would not willingly break it herself.

Still, she forced herself to keep her hand where it was—praying that he did not notice the warmth rising in her cheeks. For she did not wish any awkwardness between them. If wisdom forbade her to take this man as a lover, then above all, she wanted him as a friend.

Yes. That was right. Even her mother would have approved that.

"A wonderful doctor," she repeated steadily. "We are very fortunate that you chose our district, Mr. Grey."

He stared at her, his throat moving as though he prepared to speak—and then he looked away. "Thank you," he said. "That means a great deal."

Now she did withdraw her hand, feeling off balance somehow—oddly rebuffed, though his reply was in every way correct.

Then he said, "So you will stay, then. I'll be glad of the help."

And as easily as that, her mood brightened again.

CHAPTER EIGHT

Night was falling as Michael stepped out of the Browards' cottage. Mrs. Chudderley's carriage waited outside the gate. Michael tipped his hat to the coachman and looked down the road into the gathering darkness. The wind winding toward him carried the scent of fresh earth and green trees, and crickets were singing from hidden perches in the grass. An owl hooted, eager for the coming night.

He exhaled and felt as light as the air. Whether in London, rural Cornwall, or the remotest corner of the world—whether as a foreigner, a duke's brother, or a nameless traveler—he could help. People would turn to him, and sometimes, when luck was on his side, his skill would make the difference.

Today he had made a difference. The fever had broken and Mary Broward would live. As always, on such occasions, he thought no scene had ever looked as lovely to him as this one, here before him.

As though on cue, thunder rumbled.

He turned toward the sound. The scattered clouds,

stretched like long swaths of gauze across the dimming western sky, could not account for it. He cast a questioning look toward the coachman, but the man was well trained, studiously bent on ignoring him.

The front door opened. For a brief moment, Mrs. Chudderley paused on the threshold, her silhouette small and sublimely curved against the warm flood of light behind her. He felt a mild shock, as though he were coming awake.

By God, but Pershall had been right. Greek sculptors might have used her figure as the inspiration for a goddess.

She pulled the door shut, and her skirts hissed over the stepping stones as she came toward him. "I'm glad I caught you," she said. "I wanted to thank you. For . . . everything, I suppose."

"The thanks are mutual." He always had a sense of the ones who would prove steady in a crisis. But his intuition about her had come abruptly, in the very moment of his need. That he'd been right seemed surprising only now, when the crisis was over and his brain could once again focus on pleasanter matters—such as she.

Elizabeth Chudderley hid her mettle very well. But now he had seen beneath the outward trimmings, the ruffles and lace and feline eyes. She had been a magnificent aide, even in the worst of it: collected, unfailingly cheerful, untiring. *Tell me what I must do.* So calmly she had said it, night after night.

In the darkness, he had the sudden, curious feeling that he had never truly seen her before.

He cleared his throat. "And you," he said. "How do you fare, Miss Nightingale?"

She laughed softly. "Goodness. Very complimentary, Mr. Grey—particularly from a man whose name is being championed in a family's prayers tonight."

"Excellent news," he said. "I need all the help I can get to balance that tally."

The tilt of her head suggested surprise. "That's the first joke you've made since all of this began."

"So certain it's a joke, are you?" He gave her no chance to reply. "I tend to be very single-minded when I'm at my work." It was one of the reasons he had never looked among his hospital's Lady Bountifuls for companionship. At work, he was not charming. Though perhaps, had the Lady Bountifuls of London been as competent and lovely as this one . . . "And I don't compliment you," he went on. "You were a great help these last few days. I hope you know it."

"Thank you." She hesitated. "I wonder if you—"

Another explosion sounded in the distance. She looked toward it, as did he. "That's the second one I've heard," he said. "I begin to fear there's been some mining accident, in which case—"

Her laugh interrupted him. "Oh, no, it's not that. It's fireworks. Goodness—how had I forgotten? It's Midsummer's Eve!"

"Fireworks for Midsummer's?"

Her head turned toward him, a darker shadow in the darkness. "Goluan, we call it. Have you never seen our celebrations? But no, of course not—you being a northern savage." The laughter yet lingered in her voice, making her insult a friendly tease. "Shall I show you? You can write home to the north about our own savage customs."

They were both exhausted. Sleep and food, in that order, were what they required. And usually he preferred after his triumphs to bask alone in his satisfaction.

Yet from the close proximity at which she stood, her warmth translated to him like an invitation. She smelled like the soap with which she'd scrubbed her hands each time she'd approached Mrs. Broward's bed. It was a commonplace scent, one he knew better than most any other. Yet on her skin, it became something . . . more. Something that made him want to take a deeper breath, and step closer.

"I may not be the best of company," he said. He felt strangely unbalanced, uncertain of his own ability to recover the flirtation that had existed between them before that damned charity bazaar. He knew how to seduce women. But she had become, however briefly, a colleague. Respect made such an uncomfortable partner to lust.

"I know you're tired," she said. "We can take the coach to Bosbrea. Have you the strength for it?"

Oh, his *vanity* was not tired: he would drop dead before implying to her that he hadn't the energy for an evening stroll—or, for that matter, a mountaineering expedition. "Of course," he said. "Tally ho, then."

The coach trundled down the road toward the village. He sat across from Elizabeth, who gazed out the window, her profile illuminated by the glow of the coachman's lamp that radiated through the glass. The rumble of the carriage wheels over the tight-packed road produced a peculiarly pleasant vibration, one that made Michael relax further into the plush, tufted bench.

In his drowsy contentment, he might have ridden like this forever, watching her, his mind idle. He could not remember any other woman with whom silence had seemed such a pleasure. She had commented on that, too, once.

"Look here," she said as the coach slowed. "A procession."

The light through the window strengthened suddenly, revealing the small details of her beauty: a tendril of hair that had escaped her chignon to curl at her temple; the small mole high on her right cheekbone, like a beauty spot from an earlier century.

He cleared his throat and followed her attention to the roadside, where a long line of young men hoisted blazing torches that topped their own heads by a foot.

"Good God," he said. "How medieval."

With a smile, Elizabeth pressed her palm to the glass. In reply, cries rang out, and the men began to wave the torches in great looping arcs. The flame stained a blazing trail across Michael's vision; when he shut his eyes, he saw very briefly the symbol for infinity.

Elizabeth thumped on the trap. "We'll walk from here," she said. "Otherwise we'll only get in their way."

By the time they stepped out into the mild night, the men had already raced ahead up the road. They set a more leisurely pace, through warm night air that was alive with the dim music of cymbals and pipes and the cheers of a distant crowd.

Past the first houses of the village proper, a bend in the road brought into clear view the apex of Bosbrea Hill. Atop it, three bonfires burned, the two smaller ones flanking a blaze as tall as three men put together. They stopped to admire the sight. Now the lights spilling from windows illuminated her again, revealing her faint smile.

"You're going to explain this, I hope," Michael said. "Or am I to guess?"

"Oh, yes, please guess!"

"A minor revolution?"

"Against whom?"

"The local tyrant."

"But that would be me," she said. "And you'll note they greeted me quite cheerfully."

"Yes, well, they *are* men, after all."

She laughed. "Mr. Grey! You'll puff up my head with such talk."

"That would be a pity," he said, "for it's already the perfect size."

"Your next guess?" she asked as they began to climb again.

"Wanton destruction," he said. "For that matter, I don't recall the existence of a village fire brigade. Call me a pessimist, but shall we stop for buckets of water?"

"Good heavens! I hope it never comes to that! I'd have to indebt my heirs to the seventh generation, just to rebuild the town!"

It struck him how casually she assumed responsibility for this place. Perhaps Alastair would have liked her, after all.

The thought darkened his mood a little. He did not want to think on his brother tonight. "Does it weigh on you?" he asked. "Knowing that the entire district looks to you as their benefactor?"

"What an odd question! I would never wish it otherwise."

There, too, he heard an echo of Alastair. Perhaps he himself was lacking some vital part, for noblesse oblige had always baffled him. "I would find it very limiting, I think, to be so beholden."

She gave him a frowning look. "What nonsense.

You're a doctor! Lives depend on your decisions. I can't imagine being more beholden than that!"

"But it's precisely the opposite." Nothing bound him. No single tract of land could define his scope or shape his usefulness. "I may be powerless to prevent a fever, but I can certainly predict its arrival. And from there, my decisions are what dictate my course—not my tenants' concerns, or rude boys' carelessness with torches."

She reached out—and tweaked his ear. As he gaped at her in astonishment, she burst into a laugh. "They won't be careless," she said. "Oh, the look on your face—I do apologize, but I had not imagined you such a pessimist!"

Belatedly he smiled back, for he deserved the ribbing. "And now you've learned my secret," he said. "I'm an old woman in very good disguise."

The moment the words were out, he heard the grain of truth in them. He'd always imagined himself the carefree counterpart to his brother's rigid sobriety. But next to this woman, he felt almost staid.

The thought disagreed with him. "Perhaps I should ask for a torch of my own."

"Oh, I would wait on that," she said. "You haven't seen yet what they do with them."

"How ominous." He would have pressed her further, but a door slammed open nearby, and out rushed a breathless woman with two tankards. "Goluan!" she cried. "God save you from evil, Mrs. Chudderley! God save you, sir!" With a bobbing curtsy, she pressed the mugs into their hands.

"Goluan!" Elizabeth replied. "God preserve you!" Lifting the glass, she drank deeply before handing back the cup. Michael followed suit. Damned fine ale, thick enough to chew.

The woman retrieved his tankard, then turned on her heel and dashed back into the house.

"I think I like this holiday," he said. "Shall we be bombarded with ale at every doorstep?"

"Mrs. Matthews's husband is a brewer," said Elizabeth. "But I expect this will not be your last tankard, if that's your fear."

Near the bonfires at the top of the hill, her prediction proved true: stragglers at the edge of the crowd swept them toward a mass of barrels, where new cups were pressed into their hands. Around them, young girls in long braids were spinning each other in giddy circles, and farther off, a band of musicians with fiddles and flutes played accompaniment to young men who danced in a giant circle around the fires, their torches adding to the greater cloud of sparks scattering into the night sky.

Then one man broke free of the circle and hurled himself *into* the smaller bonfire—casting his torch into the flames before emerging on the other side to somersault across the dirt.

"Ah," Michael said. "You're right. I don't want a torch."

Her laughter was the sweetest reward that cowardice had ever received. "Yes, it's a peculiarly Cornish skill; I do not recommend that northerners attempt it."

"Perhaps this northerner should not have left his doctor's kit in the vehicle."

"Oh, there's no medicine so strong as Cornish pride." Amusement danced in her voice as she turned toward him. "Nobody will get burned tonight. But I would advise you to rise early tomorrow, if you can bear it. You'll have more than a few patients, then."

He had never seen someone so animated by enjoyment. She had a talent for happiness that struck him, suddenly, as childlike. He had a brief inkling of how she must have looked as a young girl, inclining toward the hearth on the eve before Boxing Day, roasting her chestnuts and dreaming of tomorrow's presents.

The wistful flavor of this vision left him uneasy. He had no interest in children, and he certainly did not see her as one. God, no. The light playing over her drew a shadow beneath the plump curve of her lower lip, and he did not feel fatherly in the least.

"I cannot imagine you in London," he said without thinking.

Her mirth visibly dimmed. "What do you mean?"

What could he reply that would not betray him? A country doctor would not know that the *ton*'s upper circles discouraged such vivacity—that the beau monde required ennui, not enjoyment, from its fashionable beauties. Certainly rumors of their frolics with farmers would not elevate their reputations.

"You seem to belong here," he said instead. And that, too, was true. What a curious creature she was. He'd always imagined himself freer as a second son, liberated by his lack of obligations to the family legacy. Yet somehow she managed to find pleasure in the very duties that made his brother's life seem so constrained.

"But I'm not this way in London," she said. "Perhaps you wouldn't recognize me there."

He wondered if the new soberness in her regard was only an effect of the flame-light around them. "What are you like in London?"

A reveler called out her name, and she returned the greeting with a nod and an absent smile. "Not . . .

happy," she said. "Not recently, at least. You guessed rightly, you know—that day outside the post office. I *was* looking for a marriage announcement. Or a betrothal, rather." Her mouth turned down at the corners, a rueful little grimace. "And I found it."

"Ah." Suddenly he wasn't sure he wanted to know any of this. The thought of her pining after another man made him feel . . . restless. He frowned toward the bonfire—then winced as yet another young idiot took the plunge.

Yet curiosity was an emetic. It brought words out of his mouth that he more wisely would have swallowed. "Whose announcement was it?"

She pulled a face. "A man not worthy of the ink spent on him—much less the year I wasted, imagining he might turn out to be honorable."

If her breezy delivery was intended to reassure him, it worked the opposite effect. "He did wrong by you."

"Nothing so Gothic." She shrugged. "My own fault, really."

He thought again of his brother. "Don't blame yourself. Love makes a poor judge of character. Best avoided, all around."

She laughed softly. "Indeed. Champagne is so much quicker, and *its* aftermath only lasts for a day or so."

He took her arm. There was no forethought in it: he simply wanted to touch her. "Shall we walk?"

They began to stroll through the crowd, past the fires. "Is that your policy, then?" she asked. "To avoid love? I suppose that explains how an upstanding doctor remains so long a bachelor."

Au contraire, my dear. Marriage makes the quickest cure for love.

He pressed his lips together, oddly irritated. He'd spoken that line to any number of women, sweetening the warning with a wink and a smile. But it did not seem like something a country doctor would say. In fact, it seemed far too close to what a cur like her former lover might have preached.

"Perhaps it's a matter of laziness," he said. "Cynicism, unlike love, rarely disappoints."

"I will confess, love drove me to some terrible moments," she said slowly. "Public moments, I should say. Moments that . . . rather shaped my reputation." She bit her lip. "Which is not, if you must know, particularly genteel."

Why, that was *bashfulness* on her face. The professional beauty was shifting her weight for fear of what he might think.

A strange feeling stirred in him—protective and tender and angered, all at once. He could not imagine the bastard who would willingly disappoint this woman, but he certainly could imagine several fitting punishments for such idiocy. "People say a great deal of nonsense. A wise man rarely listens."

"Oh, don't mistake me, Mr. Grey—I don't give a fig for what people say. That is *my* policy."

She gave him a cheerful smile. He might have believed it once. But what he had originally taken for brazen sophistication now seemed to him more like bravura. It felt familiar to him, for he'd once employed it himself, the better to endure the sly taunts of fellow schoolboys who had kept apprised, via the newspapers, of his parents' particular foibles.

The slope steepened beneath their feet. A misshapen pile loomed up against the night sky, an ancient cairn whose huddled stones were a monument to someone long since forgotten.

"A beautiful night," she said as they reached the cairn. She slipped free of his hold to set her tankard on the ground, then turned back to face him. Her features, in the darkness, blurred into an indistinct paleness, impossible to decipher. "A beautiful night, on which Mrs. Broward will live." She spread her arms and tipped back her head. "I feel like screaming it to the stars: A very nice try, but we foiled you! These specks of dust had their victory, after all!"

He laughed. "Go on, then. Scream! I'll never tell."

He heard her take a great breath. But after a pause, she exhaled gustily, and her arms dropped. "No. Mustn't tempt fate. I should hate for Mary to have my punishment."

He reached for her cheek. So smooth. "I can't imagine you would deserve one."

Her hand covered his, a warm, soft pressure. "Oh, but you have no idea if what they say is true. For all you know . . ." He ran his thumb over her cheekbone, and heard her breath catch. "For all you know, I'm a very wicked woman," she said.

His fingers slid easily into her hair. He could pull her toward him now . . . or tilt up her head to expose the line of her throat to his mouth. "I had been hoping so," he murmured. "Since the time Mr. Pershall chided you for failing to attend church, my expectations have grown quite wild."

Their breaths mingled. "I begin to think you're not a northerner at all," she whispered. "You're far too charming."

The words echoed his brother's. The coincidence felt

eerie. A strange foreboding tapped at him, like a finger on his spine.

The urge to kiss her still gripped him. But would that not make him as a great a cad as the man who had jilted her? For the intimacy born of recent days had led her to divulge intimacies he did not deserve. Had led her to trust him when she did not even know his true name. *Mr. Grey,* she called him.

He slowly loosened his fingers from her hair. God, what a tangle. Had they met in London, openly, he would have had her in bed by now. To *both* their satisfaction. "My name is Michael," he said. That was one piece of truth he could give her. The rest . . . he must think on. Wisdom told him that one did not share secrets until one was willing to hear them broadcasted. "If I'm to call you Elizabeth, you must return the informality."

She cleared her throat. "I would be honored," she said. "But only . . . only if I may also call you a friend." She caught his hand and his attention divided, half of it fixing on her words, the other riveted to her touch. "I know I've not always been kind to you." Her fingers were warm, as light as the brush of a butterfly. "Can you forgive me for that?"

The uncertainty in her voice fascinated him. Perhaps the true cause for his continued masquerade had nothing to do with discretion. He simply wanted to discover how far this odd affinity between them could extend. A society beauty and a country doctor . . . He had a way with women, but he was a realist: he knew that his family connections aided his seductions. Yet she, knowing nothing of them, still stood here in the darkness, touching him . . .

"Come," he said. "There's nothing to forgive." When

insulted, she took her own pound of flesh: he liked that about her. "You have spirit; there's no sin in that."

Her fingers tightened. Much like her stature, their strength was deceptive. He'd meant what he'd said; in spirit, in strength, she was outsized. And he was a doctor, after all. He'd never found frailty appealing.

He laid his free hand over hers, wanting with an almost animal intensity to move her hand to his hip, to feel her grip tighten as he pulled her against him. Hell, that was not where he wanted her hand. He wanted it gripping his cock as he leaned over her in bed, his tongue deep in her mouth. God, the things he would do to her.

Friend was a pale, pale word.

He caught her hand and lifted it to his lips, a gesture chaste enough to be performed in public. But between them, it could not remain chaste. He had ideas . . . and as he breathed into the web of her fingers, he gauged her pulse with his thumb, and felt how it began to thrum faster.

Doctorly skills: good for multiple endeavors.

He opened his mouth and bit her, very lightly, on the web between thumb and finger.

He heard the breath shudder out of her. "Perhaps . . ." But she did not finish the thought; her voice trailed away, turning the word into an invitation.

"Perhaps," he murmured against her skin, and tasted her again—slowly, tracing the ridges of her knuckle with his tongue, then settling his teeth very gently around her fingertip before closing his lips on her.

Salt and skin. The flavor of her. "Oh," she whispered. "I don't think—"

Thinking was the problem. They'd both done too much of it. He lifted her hand and placed it on his nape, then took her by the waist and pulled her into him. From down the hill came another explosion; overhead, bright lights glimmered briefly among the stars.

He saw her face by that brief flash—her wide eyes, her trembling mouth. He lowered his mouth to hers . . .

And she averted her face.

"Friends," she said breathlessly, "do not . . . kiss."

He tongued her earlobe. "Then perhaps we shouldn't be friends."

The line of her jaw tightened, telegraphing stubbornness. "What else can we be, sir?"

The question seemed disingenuous. He should not have to explain the alternatives to a widow, much less this one.

A very disagreeable idea struck him. "Do you still love this fellow, then?"

Her hesitation seemed to last minutes. "No," she said finally. But she did not sound convinced of it.

He let go of her. She took a single step back.

God help him, but he wanted to hunt down the bastard and throttle him. "What's his name?" he asked.

She blinked. "What difference? You wouldn't know him."

"No matter," he said. "It's the sort of thing *friends* tell each other."

"Oh, excellent. We *are* to be friends, then?" Her arm slipped through his again; she pulled him back down the hill toward the fires. "I should warn you, though, I'm a terribly *interfering* kind of friend."

What in hell had just happened here? He could feel her nerves in the way her fingers danced nervously on his arm. For that reason alone, he let her tug him along as she continued to babble.

"I'll always be hanging about," she said, "forever badgering, wishing to know every detail of your business. You'll have to grow accustomed to that."

"My business, I promise you, is beyond tedious." Unless it involved her. Her pulse or her skin. Her mouth. *Friendly.* "I will spare you those details."

"Yet I will insist on knowing them." As they stepped back into the range of the firelight, he saw that she was giving him the brightest of her smiles—the one, he was coming to understand, that she used to smooth over those moments in which she felt uncertain. She felt as much out of her depth here as he did. This current between them . . . neither of them knew how to manage it.

And that, more than her words, made him take a breath and control himself. For her comfort, he discovered, was important to him—and the sight of her so rattled stirred an instinct that felt strangely protective of her. *Shh,* he wanted to say. *You needn't smile.*

He set his hand over hers, forbidding himself to stroke the soft skin over her knuckles, and made himself say only: "Very well. If that is what friends do."

Friends, Michael learned, finished their ale and then walked decorously, arm in arm, back to their vehicle. Friends made comfortable conversation on the drive home, and shook hands before parting. Friends traded notes over the next few days, solicitously inquiring after each other's health, exchanging tidbits of news: Mrs. Broward's health continued to improve. Havilland Hall's strawberries were proving particularly sweet this summer. The weather continued very fine. Should they meet for tea on Friday at five o'clock?

Friends paid calls. They waited in the foyer as the butler went to confirm that the mistress was at home. They then concealed their surprise when shown upstairs, away from the drawing rooms, to a boudoir done up in pink silk, where three ladies sat in their morning gowns, folding paper roses, embroidering, and laughing so loudly that their voices carried all the way into the hall.

"Mr. Grey!" cried Elizabeth as he paused in the doorway of the small, sunlit room. "How good of you to call. Now catch!"

He reacted just in time, plucking a paper rose from the air.

"That is for your damaged rosebushes," she said. "Take as many as you like. There is glue, somewhere, if you wish to attach them."

He stuck the rose into his lapel as giggles rose from the other two women—the secretary and Mrs. Hull. Their presence should not disappoint him. *Friends* did not require tête-à-têtes. Although . . . surely even country doctors' calls were not usually received so informally.

Elizabeth swept out a hand to direct him to an overstuffed armchair, then nodded inquiringly toward the tea tray beside her. He shook his head as he sat.

"I hope you don't mind my receiving you here," she said. "As you can see"—she gestured toward the mass of paper roses clustering at her feet—"I'm rather boxed in."

"It requires pruning shears," said Miss Mather. She wielded a needle and appeared to be waging a battle against her embroidery hoop. Her needlepoint was . . . aggressive.

"I say." This from Mrs. Hull, who tapped pen against paper as she looked him over. There was a sly cast to her smile—or perhaps that was only a trick of her face, which was narrow and distinctly foxlike. He braced for another comment on how they might know each other. Instead she said, "Perhaps Mr. Grey might help us with our rules."

"Ah, yes—a gentleman's perspective," said Elizabeth.

"Might not be of much use," muttered Miss Mather. "I thought we specifically excluded all gentlemen from the guest list."

"Guest list?" He sounded stilted, and no bloody wonder. His chair was covered in pink damask. The carpet was lavender. Somebody wore too much perfume. Two china cabinets flanked him, each filled with small figurines of animals and peasants. If he moved too quickly, he was going to break something. Or sneeze. "Are you planning a party?"

Elizabeth laid down the sheet of paper she'd been folding. "Goodness, had I not told you? Yes, a house party in the old-fashioned style, a full week of fun."

To which he apparently was not invited.

He bit his cheek. Of course he was not invited. One did not ask the nobility to hobnob with an ordinary doctor. "How pleasant for you."

"Pleasant is not our aim," Mrs. Hull said eagerly. "Liza has planned the most cunning entertainments. Oh, and the guests! You would recognize their names, I vow it. Lord Weston, Lord Hollister, the Viscount Sanburne—some of the most famous families in the country!"

Brilliant. He'd known Sanburne at Eton, and Weston was an old friend. Hollister he hadn't met, but the man had done business favors for his brother, who in turn had supported Hollister's quiet—and ultimately successful—

campaign to be ennobled. "A week, you say?" That was a long time to slink about in the shadows, hiding his face.

"Perhaps longer," Elizabeth said. "Perhaps we'll all sail off to Paris together! One never knows with my friends. They make very good company—or," she added with a mirthful look at Mrs. Hull, "shall I say the very *worst!*"

All three women exploded into laughter. Either they'd been tippling at luncheon or there was some very good joke to which Michael was not privy.

He put on a game smile. "So, a party. With rules, no less."

"Oh, yes, the rules!" Mrs. Hull leaned forward, eyes bright. "Shall I read you what we have so far? And you may suggest amendments or additions, as the spirit moves you."

"Oh, the poor man," said Miss Mather. "Will you really subject him to this?"

The poor man? He was not quite sure he liked that title.

"He won't mind," Elizabeth said casually. "He's a very good sport."

Now he wanted to frown. No bevy of women had ever treated a duke's brother with such merry informality—rather as though he were not a man at all, but an oversized toy.

"Rule the first, then," said Mrs. Hull. "Charm is required."

"Our good doctor would pass that rule," said Elizabeth with a smile for him.

"Yes, that's a fine one to start—the bar must stay very low at first," Mather said as she once again skewered the cloth.

That was not the only thing she'd just skewered. How

good to know he passed the very lowest bar. Michael cleared his throat. "To what do these rules pertain?"

But nobody seemed to hear him. "Rule the second," Mrs. Hull continued. "Words must be matched *at all times* to actions."

Elizabeth nodded. "That's the most important one. I rather think that should be the tenth rule, in fact—the final hurdle to be leapt."

"I disagree. I think it a dangerously general principle, myself." Miss Mather bit off her thread as though beheading a very small enemy. "What if the gentleman threatens to shake you like a rag doll? Or tells you that he will always love his dog better than any lady? Should you really demand that his words match his actions? The poor dog!"

Mrs. Hull made a violent choking sound and slammed down her teacup.

"Good lord, Mather," said Elizabeth. "I think you've killed her."

Mrs. Hull frantically waved her hand. "Only you—" She held up a finger, coughing, her face quite red. "Only *you* would worry over such a thing! His dog, *really!*"

"But she does have a point," Elizabeth said. "Add a colon, then, with this notation to follow: we speak of romantic propositions, specifically. If he pledges his heart, he must also pledge his name and his bank accounts. Do you follow?"

Good God. "These are rules for *suitors*?" he asked.

All three women turned to stare at him.

"Did you imagine they were rules for livestock?" Miss Mather inquired.

"*Suitors,*" said Mrs. Hull. "What a delightfully quaint word!"

"He's northern," said Elizabeth—as though that explained anything.

"What would you rather call them?" he asked, aware, and not caring, that his tone had grown less genial. Probably he was living out a good many men's dreams, being invited into a boudoir to eavesdrop on feminine stratagems. But had they looped a bow around his neck and patted him on the head, he could not have felt more like a lap dog.

"I would call them likely prospects," suggested Mrs. Hull.

"Men of good character," said Miss Mather.

"Lovers," said Elizabeth.

The single word provoked shocked coos from the other women. Her smile widening, Elizabeth looked from them to him—hoping, he supposed, to reap his scandalized reaction as well.

He met her eyes and held them. "I do admire a woman of frankness."

Her smile faltered.

"Though if your lover is guided by a rulebook, I would suggest you aim higher." His glance dropped to her mouth.

Her face flooded with color. She looked down into her lap, plucking at a half-folded flower.

Yes, he thought. *Don't forget how well you liked my lips once.*

"Perhaps"—she paused to clear her throat—"perhaps we'd best discuss other things while Mr. Grey is here. We should not like to bore him."

"Oh, I'm far from bored." He rose, causing Miss Mather and Mrs. Hull to blink up at him, startled. Elizabeth missed his movement, her attention still on her hands.

He walked past her, deliberately brushing against her skirts as he reached for the teapot.

"Oh, let one of us," Mrs. Hull said, but it was Elizabeth who sat nearest—and when she looked up at him, she made no move to help.

"Would you like to hear my rules?" he asked softly—too softly for the others to hear.

Her lips parted. She stared at him, and he stared back. What other choice did he have? Her eyes were the most extraordinary sight he'd ever beheld. In every light, they seemed a slightly different color. Just now they were a vivid green, the precise shade of her gown.

This friendship business was not going to work.

"Or perhaps I should first hear your rules," he said. Lifting his voice, he continued, "Go on, Mrs. Hull. What else do you have?"

Elizabeth glanced beyond him, toward her friends, who had gone silent.

"I find 'lover' a very distasteful word," Mather said after a moment. "But I agree, perhaps 'men of good character' is too clumsy. Or exclusive," she added in a mutter.

"Why not 'eligible bachelor'?" Mrs. Hull chirruped. "Liza invited several of them, you know!"

He fumbled the teacup. Elizabeth reached out to catch it. For a brief, burning moment her fingers brushed his.

Not since he'd been thirteen had such an innocent touch knocked the breath out of him. Everything in him tightened in response.

Lovely. Just what he needed: the beginnings of an erection in this music box of a room, with three women looking on. Through his teeth, he said, "I've got it."

Elizabeth sat back again. He felt her attention lingering on him as he poured the tea. He was tempted to deliberately splash some on his skin. A burn would distract him, all right.

"Now, there's a rare sight," Miss Mather commented.

Good God. Surely she didn't mean—

"One rarely sees a man pouring tea," she went on, and he exhaled and set the pot carefully back in its place.

"Too true," Elizabeth said. "Perhaps one of the rules should address a man's usefulness." Her voice brightened, becoming brisker; she was recovering her composure. "Isn't it lovely when a man can be of use?"

Michael smiled to himself as he returned to his seat. "There's a fine ideal," he said. "Cheers to that." He took a sip of the tea. "Very fine oolong."

"What nonsense," said Mrs. Hull. "Mr. Grey might pour his own tea, but the gentlemen to whom these rules apply are *not* of a class accustomed to doing for itself."

Mrs. Hull grew more annoying by the minute. "Really?" Michael asked her. "Do you find the men of the upper class such a sorry lot that they lack the aim to land tea in a cup?"

"It isn't that they lack the *aim,* sir. It's a very different life, you know, among our sort. Men simply do not pour tea for themselves. Indeed, I think men rarely *drink* tea, save when in female company."

He almost choked on his mouthful. "Indeed," he said. "Liquor for breakfast, lunch, and dinner, is it? And water, is that also reserved for mixed company?"

Mrs. Hull gave him an indulgent smile. "You would be amazed," she said. "You've no idea how a man can indulge himself, given the time and means to do so."

Dear God. He began to wonder if one reason so many marriages failed to thrive was a generalized female ignorance that men, too, belonged to the human race. "Then I do have a rule to suggest, Mrs. Hull. Any man of worth must pour your tea when you request it."

Mrs. Hull laughed—a high, tinkling sound which she belatedly muffled with her palm. "Mr. Grey! I think you misunderstand the purpose of these rules."

"I quite like the suggestion," said Miss Mather. "A fine test of chivalry."

"Now, now," said Elizabeth. "At least demand that he add the cream and sugar, too."

Mrs. Hull tsked. "Well and good for a man who *works* for his living, as Mr. Grey does. But what Elizabeth and I require are men of *breeding*. Of refined tastes and standards! Not someone versed in how to be a *menial*."

A brief, uncomfortable pause opened, in which Mrs. Hull's remark echoed, becoming an unmistakable insult to him.

Then Elizabeth recovered her smile—bright, very bright as she directed it first toward him, then to the other women. "Have I told you how marvelously Mr. Grey managed with Mrs. Broward? What a fortunate day for Bosbrea when he decided to settle here!"

Murmurs of agreement from Miss Mather and Mrs. Hull—but nothing capable of reinvigorating the conversation.

He took pity on them, and rose. "I must take my leave."

Elizabeth stood, too. "I'll walk you out."

Her transparent relief did not improve his temper. Once in the hallway, he said, "It's no matter. I can make my way from here."

"But I feel—" She sighed, linking her hands together

at her waist. "I feel as though we've insulted you. That was not at all Jane's intention, I promise. A silly remark, spoken without thinking—"

"No, not at all." Now that he was out of that cloistered little closet, it struck him how absurd this was: not only his masquerade, but also this farcical moment in which she apologized to a duke's son for accidentally reminding him of his low station.

"I've never been ashamed to work for my living," he said. Indeed, for the first time in his life, he actually *was* working for his living. And as a result, for the first time, he felt . . . entirely certain of his own capabilities.

Here was something to *thank* his brother for. The thought lightened his heart. He offered her a real smile. "Truly," he said. "I took no offense."

Her hand rose, then hesitated, her fingers curling as they fell back to her side. Telling moment, that: a silent acknowledgment that there could be no simple touches between them. "You must let me make it up to you anyway," she said. "Will you come to dinner on Tuesday night? To meet my friends?"

"All the eligible bachelors, you mean?" Weston among them. Weston was highly eligible by any measure. Damn his eyes.

She hesitated, a small frown on her brow. "I—well, yes. I suppose some of them would count as such."

"Will you tell them of the rules you've made for them?" *Stop*, he commanded himself. *You are not in competition for her.* "Hand out the list at the door, perhaps?"

Her frown deepened. "The rules are for ladies," she said. "Reckless ladies who might be too quick to give away their hearts."

"As you were," he said. "With this cad whom you've yet to name."

A queer look crossed her face. She stepped away from him. "You don't know him," she said. "What difference would it make to know his name?"

What difference? His patience snapped. He would show her what difference it made.

He stepped forward too quickly for her to respond. Seizing her by the waist, he lifted her into the wall and laid his mouth on hers.

CHAPTER NINE

The press of his lips briefly paralyzed Liza. Her tame doctor, who had sat in the boudoir letting himself be poked like a housecat, had suddenly turned into a tiger. She tried to speak—to turn her face away; to call him back to his wits—but he would not have it. His palms framed her face, gripping her so she could not move, and his tongue penetrated her mouth.

As simply as that, she melted. Her muscles unraveled. Her bones dissolved. His large, broad body surrounded her, his grip demanding but not painful, his lips insistent and full of intent. He would have her mouth. And she had no say in it. That was the message of his mouth and his hands.

She let herself be had. With two women in the room behind her and her staff wandering the halls, she relaxed into his hold and returned his kiss. He tasted of the tea, of the sweetness of sugar; he tasted like a very bad idea that she would soon regret, but not now. Never now, while he kissed her yet.

His hand skimmed down her body, shaping her

breast. She opened her eyes and discovered him watching her, so blue his eyes were, and his palm over her stiffening nipple suddenly seemed to carry a message, too. The audacity of his touch, paired with the frank boldness of his look, made her laugh from sheer delight.

She felt him grin against her mouth. His hand slipped farther yet, seizing her by the waist and pulling her more solidly against him. Her joints felt like melting waxworks, incapable of supporting her. She flung her arms around him and let him have all of her weight—and hit the wall harder yet as he stepped straight into her. Now she was doubly pinned, the tight, taut planes of his body as unyielding as the plaster behind her.

Again he kissed her, harder yet, as though trying to convince her of something. What? What was the aim of his persuasion? She kissed him back eagerly, for did he not see? She was already convinced. She found his hair, soft and a touch too long, where it brushed against his collar. The skin beneath was hot and smooth. Her palm wrapped around his nape, and as she gripped him, she shuddered. This need felt elemental. Like hunger or thirst.

From the entry hall far below came the sound of voices. They froze. Her eyes snapped open. His were so very, very blue.

Someone would see them. They stood in plain view.

His face turned into her neck. She heard, felt, the great breath he drew. Very low, against her skin, the roughness of his jaw abrading her, he spoke.

"Friendship is not what I want."

Her hands broke free of her caution. They found his back, gathering in handfuls the soft wool of his jacket. *Think.* There were reasons, very good reasons, to discourage him. Money: he had none. Power: he had too much over her. He simply didn't realize it.

She would never tell him. He was a good man, but he was a *man*. She had learned not to offer a man weapons on the slender hope that he would never use them.

"You . . ." *You aim too high* was the reply that would snap him back to his senses. *Remember your station*. Effective set-downs. She could not speak them.

She lowered her forehead to his shoulder. As they stood pressed together, she grew aware of the small tremors that moved through him. A savage triumph swelled through her. It felt far from feminine. Too wild. Too expansive and hungry. She wanted . . .

She wanted to be responsible for everything that touched him. Her station *was* above his. And she . . . liked that. Whether he shuddered beneath her touch or laughed at her wit—God help her, when he took a sip of tea and pronounced it excellent—she wanted to know that she was the author of *all* of it. What delicious power, to grip this man, so much taller and heavier than she, and feel him tremble! But not to humble him—she would never do that. He was too beautiful, too capable, too strong. Like that night when he had put the baby into her arms, she wanted to be woven into everything he did, all of it so worthy. She wanted to aid him in all those endeavors.

But she couldn't.

She *couldn't*. She was not the carefree woman she'd been ten months ago. She had fewer choices now. And none of them included him.

"Listen," she said hoarsely. "This isn't safe."

His sigh burned her earlobe. "Yes. I know."

In stages they separated: first his hands loosened, then slipped away. She let go of his nape, her palm slid-

ing down the suggestion of his spine, coming around his
lean waist before falling to her side. He took a step back,
and her head lifted from his shoulder.

Their eyes met. Her heart jumped once, violently.
Then something in her seemed to settle, like a key turning in a lock.

One encounter. She could manage that. She could
have that for herself.

"My guests arrive the day after tomorrow," she said.
"If I could slip away beforehand . . ."

Some subtle transformation changed his face: his attention, which had been focused so wholly on her, grew
more intent yet.

"The christening tomorrow," he said. "Will they"—
he nodded toward the boudoir—"accompany you?"

"No, but . . ." She bit her lip. His glance fell to her
mouth. Heat blazed through her. She sucked lightly,
then ran her tongue over her lip.

His indrawn breath was a hiss. "Do that again and
we'll find a room here."

Her doctor was a savage. She adored that. She smiled
at him. She wanted to applaud.

"The christening," he repeated.

"I had not planned to attend." But suddenly . . .

"You're the *godmother*," he said.

She stared at him, temptation battling with cowardice. Since her mother's funeral, she had not set foot in
that church. But it was past time. And with such a reward to motivate her . . . "I'll go," she said quickly, before she could think better of it. "And—afterward, there
is a cottage by the lake, for the gamekeeper . . ."

He picked up her hand. She watched, breathless, as
he took her index finger between his teeth.

His tongue flicked out, a hot, wet, lazy stroke that made her stomach fall.

"Till then," he said, his eyes burning. He planted a kiss in her palm, then carried her hand very gently back to her side before taking a single, oddly formal step back.

He did not bow before leaving her. She stood motionless as he walked away, his shoulders straight, his gait limber and easy as he went down the stairs. Her country doctor moved with the arrogance of a prince.

And she was either braver than she knew, or the greatest idiot on earth. But tomorrow, at long last, she was going to live up to her reputation as a merry widow.

After two weeks of sunshine, the skies clouded over for the newest Broward's christening. Michael arrived late, taking a seat in the last row of pews. The windows had been left open to permit entry to the freshening breeze, and restive feet shushed and scuffed against the flagstones around him. He rubbed a hand over his eyes. He hadn't slept much. Impossible to sleep, knowing what would come after this event—not simply lovemaking, though God knew that was the main event, but also . . . a moment of truth.

Knowing nothing of his real identity, Elizabeth wanted him. It amazed him when he thought on it: one of England's most famous beauties, drawn to him without even the barest apprehension of his true station. But despite that strange pleasure, he could not, in good conscience, lie down with her until she knew everything.

So he would tell her. And once her shock faded, he imagined—he hoped—she would think it a very good lark. This was, after all, a woman who threatened to scream at stars; a widow of some infamy, who felt comfortable dallying with country doctors. He'd give her a marvelous *on-dit* to share with her friends when they arrived. And Michael would greet them by her side, as her lover.

Yes, the plan seemed sound in all regards. Pleasure for them both, and a reply to Alastair, who had planted that story in the newspaper as a transparent taunt. Michael had waited too long in the countryside for his brother to act. By revealing himself, he would ensure that word reached London, the message clear: *You want a chaste, demure bride? Behold the woman with whom I'm keeping company: a notorious widow . . .*

That was a proper goad, all right. That would bring his brother out of his priest's hole. For Alastair would never approve of a woman like her.

Even as he reasoned it, the idea perversely angered him. He did not like to think of her being so judged. No matter what happened, he would never permit Alastair to speak poorly of her.

Michael leaned left and right, trying for a glimpse of her. But he could not see anything of the activity at the baptismal font save the broad shoulders of Mr. Broward and some cousin who would stand as godfather.

The baby began to wail. A murmur of satisfaction ran through the parishioners. They came to their feet, all in their finest summer linens, to sing a hymn. Michael followed suit, though he did not recognize the song—an oversight that in other circumstances might have scandalized the people around him. Instead they had only smiles to offer. Since Mary Broward's recovery, he had learned what a true Cornish welcome felt like: everywhere he went, strangers stopped to speak to him, to offer their respects.

The melody was beautiful. He closed his eyes, at first to admire how well the music matched his anticipation. But then the smell of the stone, and damp paper and candle smoke, teased out a memory of his childhood, in the time before his parents' quarrels had grown public and their congregation had ceased to welcome them. He had loved the Sunday service then, for it had been the only occasion on which his behavior had won his parents' vocal approval. He could still hear his mother's exasperated remark to his brother, made with weekly regularity: *Why can you not behave more like Michael? See how still he sits!*

When he opened his eyes again, the sun had come out from behind the clouds, and the single stained glass panel above the altar was shedding pools of gold and blue over the bowed heads in the first pews. The beauty made his heart catch. He traced a particular ray of light down to where it made delicate contact with the crown of a summer bonnet trimmed in pewter ribbon. The bonnet turned, revealing a profile so pure that his heart clutched harder. He'd never had any defenses against beauty encountered by surprise.

As though his thoughts called to her, Elizabeth glanced over her shoulder. Perhaps it was a trick of the light that made her expression look troubled. When their eyes met across the dim interior of the church, he felt a smile break over him, and after a brief beat, she returned it before turning again toward the font.

The crown of her bonnet riveted him. It looked so . . . *typical.* Exactly the kind of hat that should be worn by a demure matron, a staid and passionless widow. What fantastical camouflage! And in a few hours' time— perhaps less—he would be unpinning that bonnet. Loosening her hair.

By God, he could already feel it through his fingers. The morning of their first meeting, he'd viewed it in its glory. It had seemed a cruelty then to be unable to touch her. He had not anticipated how much harder that act of restraint would become.

Not long, now. Luncheon at the Browards', and then . . .

The ceremony concluded. Those around him stayed seated to let others exit. First came the Broward children, and then Mr. Broward, his arm around Mary, who was still weak but walking well. She clutched her child to her chest, and when her glance grazed over Michael, she looked back immediately, beaming at him. He nodded to her.

Now came the gentry, Elizabeth at their head, retreating down the narrow central aisle in a single line.

Foreboding touched him. She did not so much as glance in his direction.

Liza stepped out of the church, blinking in the noonday sun. People streamed past her, dressed in their Sunday finest, laughing and chattering. The christening concluded, the celebrations would continue now at the Browards'. But Liza did not fall into step toward the road. She had an appointment with Michael . . . though her mood had rather turned. She feared he would not find her good company.

Discreetly wiping her eyes, she took a breath and made herself face the place that had occupied her thoughts during the baptism.

The graveyard lay a short walk down the gravel path. It had stormed the day they'd buried her mother there.

Amid the gloom and the gale, with rain beating into her face like needles of ice, Liza had felt the *wrongness* of it so sharply that she had wanted to scream.

But from this vantage, the graveyard looked shockingly peaceful, even cheerful—the grass thick and green, the headstones awash in roses.

She could no more approach it than she could the moon.

Passersby threw her smiles, curious glances, nods. She was accustomed to such interest, though the variety here felt more benign than in London. Nevertheless, and not for the first time, she wished the fashion were for veils. Everywhere she went, people stared and whispered. She was tired of always smiling for them.

She lifted her face to the sky, making the pretty array of clouds an excuse for her sudden detention.

A hand closed on her elbow. She ripped free and spun around, appalled even as she did so by the gracelessness of her response.

Michael stepped back from her, palms up and out, the ancient gesture to show no harm was intended. "Forgive me," he said. "I didn't mean to startle you."

She had the most appalling impulse to seize his hand—fall into his arms—put her face into his shoulder to block out the sight beyond him. As though that would solve anything.

Instead, stupidly, she said, "You came."

He frowned—rightly so. They had seen each other inside. "Of course. Did you imagine I would miss it?" He laughed softly. "God, what would *that* have taken? Some natural disaster, I promise you."

Yes, of course. No man would have turned down the harlot's invitation she'd extended yesterday.

No. That was not right; her ill temper was unfair. She had wanted this meeting as much as he had. Only, after the ceremony . . . now it seemed somehow wrong.

Without love, it is wrong.

Her mother's voice echoed so much more loudly here, so close to where they had put her into the ground.

"Are you all right?" he asked.

She pulled up a smile, lest he think her a lunatic for this strange mood. "I'm quite well," she said. "And you?" And to herself, she said, *Then it will be wrong. So be it.* For love could not enter this equation. For her own sake, there would be no love between them. But she was owed . . . something before she committed herself again to the staid path of the marriage-seeking woman.

"Oh, I find myself remarkably cheerful," he said, his tone playfully suggestive. "And may I say, what a *very* fine choice they made for the child's godmother."

The afternoon light revealed the creases that bracketed his mouth and radiated from the corners of his eyes. They spoke of a man who smiled often and easily, without the grudging hesitation she so often felt, the tired sense of obligation.

Loneliness leached through her, a cold and blue feeling like twilight. She would look for such lines on the faces of her eligible bachelors tomorrow. She would want a husband who laughed. "Yes," she said, "I was quite honored."

He hesitated, studying her. When he smiled again, she sensed the effort behind it, his puzzlement at her manner. "I was sitting at the back and couldn't make out their remarks. What did they name the child?"

She could do better than this. She took a ragged breath. "Rosemary," she said thickly. "Rosemary Adele."

He took a step toward her, briefly touching her arm. It was a casual, courteous gesture, nothing that would stir onlookers' suspicious. "Are you certain you're well?" he asked softly.

The light was temperamental at present, and a sudden wind tossed the branches of the trees around them. The shadows of these branches danced and slid over the bold, square planes of his face, lending him the illusion of perfect stillness: all else moved, but he did not. He seemed . . . *solid* in a way that contrasted with the fuss and prettiness of men of her class. She would not find anyone like him.

She could not bear to think on that. Something had lodged in her throat; she tried to swallow it. "Rosemary was my mother's name." Mary Broward had no doubt assumed that it would be a welcome surprise for the godmother. Any normal woman, any decent woman, would certainly find it so.

Any decent woman might have visited her mother's grave by now, too. But Liza had never gone. Like a coward, she dispatched footmen with roses and wreaths.

"My mother is buried here," she blurted.

"Oh." His expression seemed to soften, the skin around his eyes relaxing visibly. "I'm sorry. How long ago did she pass?"

"A year, now." Her throat felt tight. "Long enough, I suppose, to . . . recover."

To recover? Sometimes she feared that she had recovered; that *this* was normalcy. She was alone. Nello was marrying Miss Lister. She, too, would have to marry. And this man before her, whom she meant to take to bed . . . he was a stranger, in truth. He knew nothing of her real life, of the friends she kept, the things she had done . . . He was an honest, bourgeois gentleman, guaranteed to find such truths shocking. Her drunken brawls with Nello; collapsing from too much drink in the middle of a ball . . .

She felt ancient beside him.

"One tells oneself that such losses are commonplace," he said gently. "Inevitable. As though that does not make them all the more terrible."

Her indrawn breath stabbed like a knife in her throat. She absolutely would not weep. She would not think on it at all. This was not a conversation to be held in public.

"You—" Her voice was clogged. She cleared her throat and curled her fingernails into her palms. "Forgive me. It was ill bred to speak of these things on such a day. I am very happy—"

"No one will blame you if you don't go to the Browards'," he murmured. Such compassion in his face now; it hurt to look on him. "And as for our meeting . . . well. There will always be another day."

No, there wouldn't. He had no idea that her opportunities to go where she pleased, do as she pleased, were about to narrow. An aging woman on a husband hunt could not behave as a reckless, wealthy widow could.

But until tomorrow, she was free.

She called up the most dazzling smile she possessed. Its effect registered, as it always did with men, in the slightly dazed blink he gave, as though to bring her back into focus after suffering a hard knock to his head. "The gamekeeper's cottage," she said. "I've had it fitted out for us." She'd left a bottle of brandy there. She could almost taste it; could feel the nerves throughout her body thrilling in anticipation of the giddy indifference it would impart. She would feel better once she'd drunk a little.

"Perhaps," she said as she took his arm, "we can skip the Browards' luncheon together."

In silence they walked for several long minutes, Michael stealing occasional glances at her profile. She was lost in thought, stepping absently around the stones and dung that dotted the road. Not the most promising prelude to passion. But no matter what transpired—or did not transpire—at their destination, he would not have let her go off alone with such a look on her face.

It being market day, carts of produce and flocks of sheep choked the road into Bosbrea. Several times they paused on the embankment to allow passage to an over-burdened vehicle. Once, as the traffic moved onward, the driver of one pony cart slowed and doffed his hat, revealing a shock of white hair.

"Mrs. Chudderley." Mr. Morris looked down on them, unsmiling. His sunken face put Michael in mind of caricatures of Scrooge. Before the sag of his flesh had disguised it, the set of his jaw had no doubt announced his stubbornness. His idiocy, alas, did not announce it-self so plainly. "I hope you are well today," the man went on. "I would be glad to drive you to your destination."

Michael laughed beneath his breath. It seemed he had a competitor for Elizabeth's attentions, for that pony cart did not seat more than two.

"Thank you," she said, "I am very well, sir. But Mr. Grey will escort me."

A wave of vivid color washed through Morris's waxy complexion. It occurred to Michael that time might quickly resolve the dilemma posed by this man's ignorance. That cast to Morris's skin rarely foretold longevity. "Hmph," he said, and slapped his reins. The pony trotted off, carrying his buggy rapidly down the road.

"I don't believe he likes me," Michael said.

A strange little smile flitted over her mouth. "You mustn't take Mr. Morris's words to heart." Her eyes wandered over his shoulder, lingering on some object that did not appear to interest her much. "He is accustomed to being our local hero. With the Browards singing your praises, his vanity must sting."

He bit his tongue. But—no. She needed to know this. "It isn't his vanity that concerns me," he said. "He is incompetent to practice medicine." She cast him an appalled glance, which he ignored, pressing onward. "I understand your family sponsored him in his studies. That would have been your grandfather, I assume, for the last half century of medical advancements are unknown to the man. He must kill as many as he saves—if he's lucky."

"That's not true." She sounded strangely shaken. "Perhaps you were right to argue against his method for childbirth, but otherwise he is an *excellent* doctor. I have that on authority from Her Majesty's own physicians."

This ludicrous news made a laugh catch in his throat. "Is that so? I can't imagine where Morris found the money to purchase such a verdict."

She hissed out a breath. "What effrontery! Mr. Morris has been my family's doctor since before my birth!"

So it was like that, was it? The family's pet would be protected, and be damned to those he slaughtered. "The man is a butcher. To suggest otherwise is to place your allegiance above the welfare of every person in this district."

Her palm cracked across his face.

Such was his amazement that he took a step back. She glared at him, her mouth twisting—and then spun on her heel and stalked away. Ahead lay the hedgerow that opened onto the path to the lake. She slipped through it and out of sight.

His hand rose to his cheek. By God, she had a wallop in her palm! Or perhaps he underestimated women's strength. To his recollection, none had ever struck him before—though he had certainly done far more to deserve it.

"God damn it." No one hit him. Not even a woman. He turned on his heel—then came to a hard stop, staring blindly down the road.

Christ! He had no idea what ailed her. But the sting in his cheek left no doubt that she was badly distraught.

Friendship was not *all* he wanted. But he had agreed to be her friend. And friends did not abandon each other in times of need, no matter the provocation.

On a deep breath, he pivoted and started after her.

CHAPTER TEN

The old gamekeeper's cottage was clean and well swept, and freshly stocked with water and victuals. Cradling the brandy bottle, Liza took a seat on the single chair at the window, a relic of Mr. Pagett's tenancy. He had liked to sit here and gaze out at the lake. To watch out for her, he'd joked. He had not been of much use to her parents, who rarely hunted. Instead, Mr. Pagett had served as a sort of forest spirit, a kindly creature ever ready to entertain a curious young girl who often visited his cottage, thirsty for lemonade, after a long morning spent wandering the woods.

He had been gone for years now. The room held nothing of him.

Like so many ghosts, people passed through life. And the memory of them faded so quickly. But she remembered Mr. Pagett, even if no one else did.

A footstep came at the door. She looked up to behold Michael, crouched awkwardly in a doorway built to accommodate a shorter generation of men.

"You should not have followed me," she said, but

even as she spoke, she realized how relieved she was not to be alone. And that realization brought its own grief. How lonely she was, to be grateful for the company of someone with whom she'd just behaved abominably.

He hesitated. "May I enter?"

She nodded, watching as he ducked under the door frame. He moved with an easy strength—too masculine to be graceful, but pleasing all the same. Competence, she thought. That was what marked his every gesture.

She could not bear to think that he had spoken truly about Mr. Morris.

He looked around the space. She did, too. This place had always been called a cottage, but in truth it was a single room, the enlargement of which Mr. Pagett had always resisted. *I like simple things,* he had grumbled. *A bed, a stove, and a desk, that's all a man rightfully needs.*

When Michael's attention returned to hers, she saw the faint redness on his cheek where she had struck him. In her lap, her hand curled into a damp ball, a fist so tight that her knuckles ached. Until now, she had only hit Nello—a single time, when he had tried to shove and pull her out of a party at which she'd wished to stay. They'd been quarreling. She'd been drunk. She had no such excuses now.

The brandy bottle felt very heavy, suddenly.

She set it carefully at her feet. Perhaps the ugliness with Nello had irreparably altered her. Filled her with poison. Would she spread it now into the rest of her life?

Straightening, she took a deep breath. "I'm sorry for slapping you. It was quite wrong of me."

He studied her a moment. "You were distressed, I think."

"Yes."

"Tell me why, and we'll consider it forgotten."

It startled her that he would demand so little before accepting her apology. She supposed she'd known once that all men were not like Nello, sensitive and prone to grudges. But she'd forgotten, somehow.

Still, she did not deserve such easy forgiveness. She did not want to be the sort of woman from whom such behavior was expected or even imaginable. "It was quite wrong," she repeated. "But Mr. Morris—" She swallowed. "Mr. Morris tended my mother when she was ill. And I can't bear to think . . ."

Curious, how hard it was to share a simple truth; to trust that it did not somehow diminish her to admit her private fears. But he deserved honesty. She had struck him, yet he had followed her to make sure she was all right. "I can't bear to think that another doctor might have saved her," she said in a rush.

His face grew somber. "Oh," he said. "That is . . ." With a heavy sigh, he scrubbed his hand over his face, into his dark hair. It stuck up wildly, this way and that; a raffish effect, that became him greatly. "That is quite another matter, then. It is I who must apologize. Most humbly. I was . . . wrong to bring up the issue like that."

"You needn't apologize." As he glanced toward the door as if rethinking his presence, she added quickly, "It's all right, really. Please, do sit down."

He looked around, and as the faintest twitch of humor crossed his face, she realized there really was nowhere for him to sit but the bed.

"It's clean," she said. How stilted she sounded! How formal! "The sheets—sometimes I hire a gamekeeper temporarily, in case the guests wish to hunt. And I told the staff—well, that they should be changed this morning."

Her face warmed as she said it. After what had just

transpired, she felt very awkward alluding to their original intentions for this meeting.

She had ruined everything. She had a talent for it, she feared.

He sat down on the narrow pallet. Propping his elbows on knees, lacing his hands loosely between them, he looked at her. "How did your mother die?"

She physically recoiled. "No." She did not want to do this. That was not why she had told him of it. "That's a cruel question!" For what if the answer revealed that someone else—that someone like *him*—could have saved Mama? She would not be able to bear it.

"You needn't answer me," he said gently. "But perhaps I could put an end to your fear."

Fear? She took a shaking breath, for suddenly she recognized he was right, and not just about Mama. Fears seemed to hem her in on all sides these days. Maybe they were all of a piece—her cowardice now, and the other one that kept her from visiting her mother's grave, and the fear that kept her with Nello so long—months, really—after she'd first glimpsed the ugliness in him.

So say it, then. Quickly. "An affection of the heart. That is what they called it." She tried to smile and failed. "A queer turn of phrase, isn't it, for something so awful?"

He lifted his braided fingers to his mouth, gazing steadily at her over them. "How did it present? What were the symptoms?"

Her nails cut into her palm. She kept her voice steady. "Dropsy, foremost. A great swelling of her legs. It was painful for her to walk, and for months she was weak, short of breath. I tried . . . I did everything to help her. I took her to London, to Her Majesty's own physicians.

But she wanted to be here. And they said . . . they said Mr. Morris was doing everything he could."

Did the line of his shoulders loosen a little? She tried to keep the naked longing from her face. But her eyes, perhaps, begged for her: *Tell me they were right.*

"Yes," he said. "They were right, Elizabeth. I've seen the same. It's a common affliction in the elderly, and there's nothing that can be done. Only make the patient comfortable, which I know you did."

The breath went from her. For a moment she could not find her voice. Then she whispered, "You don't . . . lie, to placate me?"

"No," he said. A strange, rueful smile tipped his mouth. "I don't lie about those matters."

She exhaled. "Then . . . thank you." There were no words for it but these: "*Thank* you."

"I've done nothing," he said. "That is only the truth."

Such a truth! She turned her face away, toward the lake, to hide her tears. Were they of relief? She could not say. *Make the patient comfortable.* Mama had been so strong in the face of pain, but she had not liked Liza fussing over her. *She* had always been the one who fussed; to have their roles reversed had not suited her. And they had bickered because of it. *I am tired of your long faces,* Mama had told her. *You cannot remain shut up here forever. Go to London for the week. Bring me books; bring me something cheerful.*

She had forbidden Liza to mourn for her. *My life has been mostly sweetness, dear girl.*

She had said so many things. *If I could undo your father's decision . . . if I could go back in time, I would not have let you marry him. Dear Liza, please forgive me for that.*

But there had been nothing to forgive. Liza had gone to London for the books. But she should never have left. The very *night* she'd departed . . .

She had not made it five feet into her town house before the telegram came.

Bah! Such pathos! She dashed her hand across her eyes. What was done was *done*.

She forced a smile onto her lips as she turned. "Now you will be thinking—"

He had crossed the room to kneel in front of her. The look on his face stopped her throat. Naked on his countenance was such open, *affectionate* compassion—

"By God," he whispered. "Whatever makes you cry now . . . let me fix it for you."

A strange sound escaped her. She put her hand to her mouth but it was too late; the tears were upon her now and they would not be stopped. A hoarse sob burst from her, and she buried her face in her hands, horrified. Where had this grief come from? Why now?

She knew why. Tomorrow she would look for a loveless connection, which meant . . . Mama's love might be the last real love she would ever know.

Arms came around her, tightening to draw her close. Her nose came up against the rough wool of his suit. She shook her head and tried to pull away, for she *would not* be pitied, but his embrace only banded more tightly around her.

"Shh," he said. "Tears are medicinal, I promise you."

A ragged laugh escaped her, broken in half by another sob. "You contradict yourself. I thought you wanted to stop them." Once again, she tried to pull free. "I'm fine, I promise you."

Once again, he clasped her more firmly. As though

he wanted her there against him. As though he did not mind it. "You will be," he said.

The quiet confidence in his voice overthrew her last reservation. She let herself sag into him. His chest was broad and hard, and his hands on her back made firm, soothing strokes. She relaxed further, and his fingers found the line of her spine and dug in, a pressure that somehow dislodged the greater pressure on her lungs, and allowed her to breathe again, a long clear breath free of weeping.

"You are too decent," she heard herself whisper. "I haven't earned it."

"Not so decent," he murmured. "I would not mislead you."

"Kind, then."

"No. Only for some reason, I can't bear to see you weep."

She lay against him a long moment, letting his words repeat in her mind. *I can't bear to see you weep.* What a lovely world he must live in, to consider that anything other than the greatest proof of decency. She had wept a thousand times, and even people who cared for her—her closest friends—had grown impatient with her for it.

She could not blame them. How many tears she had squandered on cads! In the arms of an upstanding, honorable man, the memory made her feel angry with herself, too.

But as he pressed his hand down her back again, the feeling could not linger. How gently he touched her— how caressingly, as though the privilege were precious to him. Cheek to his chest, she listened to the steady beat of his heart and remembered the way Mama had flown into Papa's arms after a separation, and put her ear to his chest, and cried out to Liza, "There's the music I was waiting for!" And her father, in reply, had laughed and said, "It had quite paused until I saw you there, dear."

Liza had remembered that moment when ordering their tombstone to be engraved. *Set me as a seal upon thine heart . . . for love is strong as death.*

She straightened very slowly, catching his arm when he would have restrained her. Their eyes met. He looked steadily into hers, seeming not to notice the way tears made her face blotchy, seeming unafraid of whatever she might show him. In her grip, his sleeve was warm from his body, his wrist thick and sturdy.

Surely she deserved this. Just once.

She put her mouth to his.

He went quite still. The muscles in his forearm flexed; his entire body seemed to harden. His lips were soft, though, and his skin smelled clean and profoundly good, so profoundly right.

"You are distraught," he murmured against her mouth.

"Yes," she whispered, and threaded her hand through his silken hair, her fingertips tracing the clean, curved line of his skull. "But not alone. I don't wish to be alone."

As her thumb found the pliant lobe of his ear, his loosed breath bordered on a gasp. She kissed him again, harder, using her tongue to part his lips. Her own aggression somehow emboldened her further. It had never been her way to choose a man. Before, she had always been chosen. Before, it had never been right. But this would be.

She deepened the kiss, and the noise he made—a strangled sound deep in his throat, something between a gasp and a growl—caused warmth to flush through her.

She tasted his lips, his tongue, and for a brief, blissful moment he took the kiss from her, his mouth pressing harder against hers, bending her back in her chair as his palms around her waist supported her. Kneeling before her, he still topped her by a head; he was tall, broad, sheltering.

And then, on a loosed breath that sounded almost like a moan, he pulled back. "This is not right," he said hoarsely. He wore a dazed look. "You aren't thinking clearly. And I haven't—"

"So clearly," she said softly. "I'm thinking very clearly now, indeed." She framed his face in her hands, looking again into his eyes. Every touch she initiated made her confidence strengthen. Decency, kindness, compassion: here in his face were the things her mother had told her to seek and value. Fashionable friends, a fine suit, a town house in Mayfair, a pedigree—all of those stupid things that had dazzled her before, what were they beside this?

Here was a *man*. Bold and raw-boned. Muscled arms that could lift a woman so easily, and hands that could save her life. Firm lips that would never speak false promises. A stern jaw and hair like silk. So many contrasts. His body might have kept her fascinated for days.

She did not have days. But she had this one. This single day, and an opportunity to take what, for once, she knew she was *right* to want. For there was no doubt in her: Michael Grey was everything a man should be.

She leaned in to kiss him again, making the kiss a soft invitation, a temptation to him. "Do you wish me to be alone?" she said into his mouth. "Shall you go?"

"God, no," he whispered. "But I must tell you—"

"You are not kind," she reminded him. "Not decent."

His laughter was ghost-soft. "You have no idea."

"Show me," she whispered.

He took her by the elbows and drew her to her feet. Their bodies came together, a sweet contact that radiated in small shocks through her limbs, making her knees weaken. His grip shifted to her back, slid down to palm her buttocks through her skirt.

"There is something I must tell you," he said.

"Tell me later."

"No. Before we proceed—"

She seized him by the hair and brought his mouth down to hers. Now he did make a noise, a rough and desperate sound, and his mouth was no longer gentle. Yet once again he broke away to speak into her ear.

"I am not who you think I am," he said.

She smiled. Would he apologize for his lack of experience? "It doesn't matter." Nothing mattered but this moment. Tomorrow her guests would arrive, and before she went to greet them, she would sit before her dressing table and evaluate her flaws. The lines and spots that grew more numerous by the year, the blemishes her maid must conceal—she would disguise them, and reassemble herself piecemeal, with powders and rouges; she would put her beauty on the market for a wealthy bidder. But for now, in this moment . . . she was not a beauty, but a woman.

She slid her hand around to palm his buttocks, and her breath caught as they tensed, pure muscle. He made a low noise and his mouth found hers again, his arms wrapping around her as he stepped into her. Were it not for his grip, she might have swayed backward like a flower. She felt like a flower, something delicate and beautiful.

His mouth slipped down her chin, her throat, sucking and laving. "Farther," she whispered.

His growl raised goose bumps along her skin. His teeth closed lightly over the spot where throat joined to shoulder. He pulled down her bodice and laved the upper slope of her breast, sucking hard, and it caused her to smile, a strange smile of delight that only the ceiling witnessed. Her country doctor knew what he was about.

But when she pulled free in order to kiss him, she found the angle difficult. She was so much smaller. On her tiptoes she could not reach his mouth. "I want—"

He lowered his head to her shoulder and spoke into her throat, his voice purring. "What do you want, Elizabeth?"

He was too tall. But she knew how to fix it. She took his wrist and pulled him toward the narrow bed, tugging him down, reclining before him in an invitation he leapt upon, planting one knee by her hip, his hand by her face. His face was intent, hard with need.

She had never seen that look on his face before. For the space of a heartbeat, uncertainty dimmed her hunger. In some ways, all men were the same . . .

But when his head dipped, the gentleness of his lips on her neck made her sigh and forget her worry. Her eyes drifted shut. So delicately his mouth traveled down her throat, his hot, moist breath trailing to her clavicle, lingering there. His hand closed over her upper arm, drawing a firm, steady stroke down to her wrist, which he lifted. Turning his head, he planted a kiss on the sensitive skin at the base of her palm. For a moment he remained like that, the ragged gusts of his breath tickling her.

"You are certain," he said unsteadily. "*Certain* you will not regret this."

Tenderness uncoiled in her. What other man, lying over her, would think to ask such a question? What other man, so importuned by a widow, would hesitate?

"Never," she said.

"Thank God." His hands grew eager now, lifting her to unlace her blouse. She had dressed strategically, donning a suit dress for ease. It was an easy step from pulling the blouse over her head to unlace her corset, and then to free her of her linens.

Cool air washed over her naked torso. She watched his face as he beheld what he had uncovered, watched his lips part, his eyes fixed to her. Slowly he laid his bare palm over her breast.

She sucked in a breath. His skin was hot and slightly rough. *Calluses.* She arched into his grasp, then took his head and pulled it to her breast.

His lips closed over her nipple. *Yes.* This was what she had wanted. A fierce, animalistic urge made her slide her fingers through his hair, threading tightly, pulling harder to hold him in place.

His teeth scraped over her and she gasped. He wore too many clothes now. She felt down his torso, shoving away his jacket, tearing at his waistcoat. She pushed his suspenders off his shoulders and yanked up his shirt. And then—ah. He reared back on his knees to finish the job, and then . . .

God above.

She sat up, jaw agape, to touch him. His clothes had disguised wonders. He was raw-boned but lean, knitted together in taut ropes of muscle and sinew. His shoulders were heavy, dense and smooth beneath her palms.

His upper arms bunched with muscle. There was no give to him: his body might have been chiseled from stone. With one nail, she lightly circled his nipple—and then watched the effect as his flat abdomen contracted, the bands of muscle tightening.

A man's body could be beautiful. She would never say otherwise. Here was the proof.

He wrapped one of those muscled arms around her and pulled her up against him. The lovely shock of flesh on flesh rendered them both immobile for a moment. Then his mouth nuzzled through her hair, finding her ear. "If you knew how I had imagined this moment, every night since we first kissed—"

"Yes," she whispered. Slowly they reclined together. But he did not follow her all the way down. Propping himself on one elbow over her, he cupped her face in his broad palm. His expression was strangely grave.

"You are . . ."

But he trailed off, frowning, and when he opened his mouth again, she placed one finger over his lips. This was not the time for pretty speeches. "Come here," she said, in a voice she had not used in months, sultry with need. Oh, but she felt *aquiver* with anticipation. Sex could be pleasant. It had been pleasant with Nello, at first. But the prospect of it had never made her feel *famished* before. This man's skin—it had some recipe in it, some spell that awoke an elemental greed that his touch alone could not sate. Her hand traveled down his bare back, across his lean waist to close over his buttocks, and she pulled him hard against her. "Quickly," she said.

His low laugh caused her stomach to tighten. "Oh, not even soon," he said.

He slid down her body, kissing her as he went. His hand found the waist of her skirts, working cleverly over buttons, feverishly as his mouth coasted over her belly. With his forearm beneath her back he lifted her, and then she was completely bare. His head sank farther yet, and his mouth opened, hot and wet, on the back of her knee.

Ticklish! She had not known it. What man had an interest in *knees*? Giggling, she tried to roll away, but he pinned her there, untying and sliding off her knickers with one hand, then kissing his way up her bare thighs. Shivering, delicious kisses, like the brushes of butterflies' wings, only now and then the hot, moist flick of his tongue made her gasp—

His mouth closed on the juncture between her thighs. She nearly bucked off the bed, then shuddered as his low, indecipherable murmur—the tone clearly appreciative—warmed the most sensitive spot in her body.

"Shh," he said, "be good." And then he tasted her.

She put her knuckles to her mouth and bit hard. His lips closed around her most sensitive part—somehow he found it instantly, a near miracle, unprecedented—and his tongue flicked, and flicked, and then *pressed*—

She twisted beneath him, sobbing, then gasped as he delivered a long, slow lick—she could not bear it; even when he steadied her hips and held her still she felt as though she must writhe, that perhaps she would twist out of her skin altogether—

"Come here," she gasped. "Please, I want—"

She wanted to be pressed against him again. She wanted his body hard against hers, inside hers, reminding her in the most frank and physical way that he was here with her. She caught him beneath the arms and urged him up, attempting and then ceding to him the effort to unfasten his breeches. He sprang free into her hands and he was hard, hot, magnificent; he was *hers*.

"Please," she said, spreading her legs as she directed the head of his cock through the moisture there. "Please—"

"Yes," he growled, and then his hips flexed, and he was pushing inside her. Ah, God, such sweetness. She moaned and lifted herself to meet him, the unbearable exquisite stretching of his possession. He was larger than her experience had prepared her to expect. His hands slid up her body, his fingers finding and threading through hers. He lifted her hand and placed it by her head and looked into her eyes as he thrust into her.

She gasped. The sound excited her, and made him lean down and ravish her mouth; she let him swallow her next moan. A thought wanted to rise, words to frame this moment—but there were too many feelings swirling through her. His body moved against and into hers slowly, steadily, and with each stroke something in her seemed to come a small bit more unraveled, an incremental loosening that first felt like pleasure, and then like need, elemental as a firestorm.

His mouth found her ear, his breath hot and ragged. "Look at me," he whispered.

She opened her eyes. A hot shiver slid through her. He was looking down at her, *seeing her,* as his body took hers. His eyes seemed bottomless; she felt a curious sensation, something in her breaking and falling free, plummeting into his gaze. Wonder stole over her, exhilarating as desire. *I see you.* She saw him so clearly . . .

His hips twisted and she shuddered and moved

against him, lifting her hips to meet his. The last bit was coming loose . . .

"Ah!" The cry exploded from her as she climaxed. She threw her head back, but he caught her by the hair, directed her mouth to his. She took his long kiss and returned it with her lips and teeth and tongue, wanting to devour him. This, *this* was pleasure . . . it rippled through her, causing her to shiver again and again.

"Wait," he said, "wait—" Her turn now to grip his face, to force his mouth to remain with hers, to swallow his gasp as he thrust into her fiercely. But then, with a groan, he ripped himself off her, his seed spilling as he fell by her side.

Her eyes closed. As they lay together, the aftermath of her satisfaction kept her sated and relaxed.

"Aphrodite, they call you." He spoke into her ear. "But Rome being in fashion, I think I'll call you Venus instead."

She laid her hand to his bare chest, feeling the rapid beating of his heart. When her eyes opened, he gave her a slow smile. She heard now the singing of birds outside, the rustle of rattling leaves.

Contentment was a hum in her bones. She felt aglow, fierce and brave, as though she had accomplished something here. She leaned in to kiss him, very softly, on the mouth.

"A very fine beginning," he said against her lips.

Ah. She drew back. This had not been a beginning at all, but an event. Yes, more than an incident; so much more than a mere occasion. But an event all the same: profoundly memorable, but singular.

"What is it?" he asked.

He was so attuned to her. She wondered if any man

had ever watched her face so closely. A curious thought, when her face was everywhere. Those stupid photographs.

He was waiting. She smiled at him and slid her hand up his body. His chest hair was sparse, the shape of his muscles translated so clearly by his skin. What a wonder he was to touch.

But her opportunity to do so was drawing to a close.

She took a long breath. She would not regret this. He was lovely, absolutely lovely. And had matters stood . . . differently . . .

No. Don't think on it. Fingers curling, she lifted her hand away. "I should dress."

He sat up, watching as she gathered her linens. From the corner of her eye she gauged the depth of his frown, the likelihood that he was about to say something that would force her into an unpleasant speech. His mouth opened.

She bent over to retrieve her corset. Then hid a smile as she heard him exhale. Yes, it was quite a view she was offering him.

His hands closed on her bare hips, pulling her back onto the bed. Onto *him,* in fact. The intimacy, the sweetness of it, made her eyes close—and then open again in surprise.

"Goodness," she said. Surely he could not be ready again *already*. Were men so individual in that regard?

His smile was rueful. "No, not yet," he said. "I fear I'm too old for such feats." He touched her hair, gently, and then traced the curve of her ear, his eyes following the motion.

The tenderness in his face arrested her—and then lit a flame of panic in her, a strong instinct of self-preservation. She turned away from him again to hunt for her underclothes. "How old are you, then?"

"All of thirty," he said.

She froze for a moment. He was younger than her. The news . . . did not please her, which was silly. It made no difference how old he was.

She pulled on her linens, then slipped the corset over her head. "Help me tighten the laces?"

"Such a rush." She felt his hands at her back. "I'll try not to take it personally."

"Don't," she said. "It's only that there's so much to be done, and—"

"Your guests will be upon you soon. I know." The corset began to tighten. "I look forward to meeting them. But before I do, I must—"

"About that." She stared fixedly at the door, steeling herself to correct him. This, too, was a part of playing the merry widow, as much as the pleasure that had come before it. "I know I extended an invitation to you. But after this . . . I think it would be wiser if you did not attend the dinner."

The laces made a whipping sound as he finished tying them off. His hands fell away, and she turned to face him.

He looked at her, a square look that somehow seemed to delve into her and . . . expose her. She fought the urge to squirm, to glance away.

And then he sat back, putting one palm behind him to brace his weight, a posture that brought the muscles in his arm into stark prominence. "I see," he said slowly.

She swallowed. *She* saw as well, and he made a splendid sight: long legs, a flat belly, that gorgeous expanse of chest.

"You think I would make you . . . uncomfortable?" he asked.

He was making her uncomfortable right now, for she barely recognized herself. Her body was lighting up again, warming and loosening, as though she had not been sated five minutes before. His lips . . .

She forced herself to focus on the space an inch above his head. He could not come tomorrow. She feared she was not *quite* sophisticated enough to manage herself. If he sat nearby, her very body would vibrate to the sound of his voice. And eligible bachelors did not incline to women clearly in lust with their doctors.

"The company will be fast," she said. She had no intention of honestly speaking of her marital ambitions. Not at this moment. She did not flatter herself that it would be *cruel* to do so—he had never spoken of love, or even hinted at it to her. But it would be plainly tactless, all the same. "I should not like you to feel uncomfortable."

His brows rose. "I find it odd that our recent employment here should have given you cause to think me a moralist. If my behavior was not *fast* enough for you, by all means, let us try it again."

She felt a flicker of panic, which with an effort she twisted into resentment. He was not going to make this easy. But she owed him nothing. "Very well. To speak honestly, I find you . . . alluring, and I should not like others to notice it. Should rumors reach London, it would be awkward for me."

"But I thought you had no care for what people said." He rose off the bed, and despite herself, she looked him up and down and felt breathless again.

He gave her a half smile. "Yes. If you do that in public, I suppose there will be talk."

She went hot. Hot in the face, and hot . . . elsewhere. "But I won't," she said. "For I've withdrawn my invitation. My friends will not meet you."

"I do not accept the withdrawal. In fact"—he took a prowling step toward her, one she matched with a quick retreat—"you may be surprised how well I fit in with your friends. I told you I was not who—"

"*Madam!*"

The call, distant but distinct, made them both spin toward the door.

"Quickly!" Liza cast a frantic glance around for her blouse, then grabbed it and tugged it on. For his part, Michael had spun to grab up her jacket and bonnet.

"*Madam!* Are you out here?"

Closer, much closer now. "That's Mather," she said breathlessly.

Michael went to the window, then ducked. "Bloody hell, she's twenty yards away. What in God's name—"

"I don't know. She likes to come looking for me." She could do nothing for her hair; the pins were scattered everywhere. She crammed it into her bonnet, tying the ribbon with record speed. "Stay here. Don't leave yet. Give it ten minutes." She bent to cram her feet into her shoes, and then raced for the door.

She stepped out. Mather saw her instantly. She held up a hand, showing the flat of her palm, and her secretary stopped dead. Liza nodded, then lifted a finger to her lips. If anyone else was in the area—which they should not be—she did not wish her secretary to broadcast these curious circumstances.

Shaking out her skirts, she walked forward. Mather's curious glance roved over her, and everywhere it paused, it called to Liza's attention the signs of her guilt:

Her jacket was not buttoned properly.

A great chunk of her hair had fallen out of the bonnet.

She wore no gloves.

Her shoes were not laced.

Joining Mather's side, she took the girl's arm in a tight grip and tugged her away from the cottage.

"Silly me," she said. "I took a nap, and—well, as you see, I'm quite undone."

"Yes," said Mather slowly, with no attempt to conceal her skepticism.

Liza would be more to the point, then. "What on *earth* are you doing out there? Roaming the woods and shrieking my name!"

"The Browards sent a slice of cake to the Hall for you. But I knew you intended to go to their party. I was worried."

"Mather, I have *told* you—"

"I know!" The girl pulled free. Shoving her glasses up her nose, she blinked like an earnest owl. "But you haven't been to church since Mrs. Addison died, and I know it must have been very upsetting, and I worried that perhaps—perhaps—"

"This is Bosbrea, Mather! Did you think I was kidnapped by a farmer? I am perfectly safe!"

"Villains are *not* confined to cities! It is very naïve to think so, ma'am!"

Liza looked at her in astonishment. The girl looked to be nearly shaking with some suppressed emotion. Surely it couldn't be fear. "Are you quite all right, darling?"

Mather blinked, then shook her head and rubbed her brow with her knuckles. "Yes. That is—I'm very sorry," she said more quietly. "I shouldn't have raised my voice. But please allow me to worry for you. For I owe you a great deal, ma'am, and I *do* worry. You are far too trusting."

Her irritation died. How could she resent Mather's concern? It was so kind, and such an undeserved gift— for despite the girl's nonsense, she had done nothing to earn such fondness. "You owe me nothing, you silly thing. And—too trusting? *I?* I'd fear you were drunk, but you don't partake!"

Mather shook her head stubbornly. "Bad things might happen anywhere, ma'am."

"You are terribly cynical, dear. I do wonder the cause for it."

The girl shrugged and made no reply. Asking about her past was always the best way to silence her. Liza knew from experience that pressing further would yield no clues.

With a great sigh, she retrieved the girl's arm and kept walking. "As you see, I am—as ever—quite safe. Only very sleepy."

"Because you . . . fell asleep."

"As I said."

"In the gamekeeper's cottage."

"Well, you're quite right, it *was* unnerving to return to the church. And so I fled like a coward to a place where I thought nobody would find me. One doesn't wish witnesses to one's cowardice, you know."

Mather ran a hand over the top of her frizzing red hair, then down to her nape, which she cupped. This was her thoughtful pose, portending some revelation. "But I found you," she pointed out.

"Yes," said Liza. "And once again, I will remind you: you are a secretary, not a bloodhound."

Mather frowned. "And tomorrow I become a harlot."

"You can't talk like that," Liza said with a snort. But perhaps it was a sign of insanity that she followed the girl's meaning perfectly. "I'm so glad, though, that your wardrobe was readied in time."

Mather laughed. "Yes, it's a piece of good luck, isn't it?"

"Indeed." And so, too, was Mather's laugh, for it covered the noise that came from behind them, the sound of a door closing.

Which is a fitting sound, Liza thought, *very poetic and fitting.* For the door had closed on their event, never to be reopened.

And if that felt like a tragedy to her . . . well, then she would simply not think on it.

CHAPTER ELEVEN

Laughter spilled out from the drawing room into the dimly lit hall. Liza, returning from a brief conference with the spirit writer on the room allotted to him, paused and then withdrew behind a marble statue to eavesdrop.

She could hear Weston's ringing laugh, splintered by Hollister's cool voice and Katherine Hawthorne's sultry tones. Now from Tilney came a deadpan remark, surprisingly risqué for only—she checked the grandfather clock—seven in the evening.

Well. That boded brilliantly. She tried out her most carefree smile. She must seem light of heart, without a worry in the world.

The mirror across from her did not offer reassurance. The gown was lovely, perfection, the mulberry skirts a delicious confection of satin drapery, the underskirt and jacket of violet velvet. But the colors washed her out. Or perhaps she simply looked weary. To her frustration, she'd tossed and turned half the night, thinking of a man she could not have—and who, to her misfortune, had had her too well and too thoroughly to be so easily forgotten.

"Madam."

Mather came stalking up the hall, skirts swishing. She'd submitted to the ministrations of Liza's maid, even submitting to the "unnatural indignity"—as she termed it—of having her hair straightened and then curled. "You look absolutely marvelous," Liza said warmly. Redheads should never wear *any* color but mint.

As with all compliments, Mather became selectively deaf. "There's a problem with the room assignments. The medium has discovered that you placed the spirit writer next door to her. She says—"

"Did you tell her that he and the clairvoyant are mortal enemies?" So the spirit writer had solemnly informed her.

"Yes, I said so." Mather readjusted her grip on the heavy ledger in her arms, freeing a hand to nudge her wire spectacles back up her nose. The ridiculously thick lenses made her blue eyes look small and squinty and unjustly porcine. Countless times Liza had advised her to do away with them, but Mather seemed determined to believe that she would be blind without their aid. "It makes no difference to her," the girl continued. "She says she cannot lodge beside a fraud."

"What? You're joking!"

Mather shook her head.

Liza sighed. She was intent on housing *all* the spiritualists together, in the farthest wing from the rest of the guests. After all, it was very difficult to place one's faith in the mystical powers of someone known to snore.

What she hadn't foreseen was what a suspicious lot they would be! To a man, each of them assured her that the others whom she had invited were, in fact, con men and shills.

"I don't understand it," she said. "Even if Mr. Smith *is* a fraud, what of it? How can it harm Madame Augustiana's ability to contact the dead?"

Mather's brows crested the rim of her spectacles. "Ma'am, I am sorry to say that I have no insight into the workings of Madame Augustiana's abilities."

"You're not sorry at all, you cheeky thing."

A slow, owlish blink from Mather. "I confess, I may not be."

Liza snorted. "Well, let Madame Augustiana struggle with the spirits for a bit. I haven't scheduled her to perform until Friday at the earliest. And what of—"

"That is another message I am bid especially to relay to you." Mathers checked a notation in the ledger. "Madame Augustiana begs you not to use the word *performance,* as it may offend the spirits."

Was that the faintest tremble of *amusement* in her secretary's voice? "Mather, you're not *enjoying* this, I hope?"

The girl's square jaw firmed. "No, ma'am. That would not be my place."

"Oh, stuff *that*. It would be your place if you'd unbend enough to join the company." A peculiar creature, Mather. She seemed to have no concern about her spinsterhood, though she was quite pretty, despite her lantern jaw, when she made half an effort. And certainly there were men in the world who would appreciate her . . . *unique* brand of charm.

"It would not be appropriate," said Mather. "I have explained this. I agreed to the wardrobe, but—"

"Poppycock! You're a relation!" It had been such

a lovely surprise when they had discovered this a few
weeks ago.

"Sixth cousins do not count, ma'am."

"It must count for *something,* darling. After all, it's
countable: sixth, six—that's a number, I believe."

Was that a *roll of the eyes* Liza detected behind those
awful lenses? "Ma'am, you are to be commended for
your keen mathematical skills." Mather retreated a pace.
"Shall I inform Madame Augustiana that she may leave,
if the lodging does not suit her?"

"Oh, very fierce," Liza said. "Yes, and say it just like
that, with that militant tilt to your jaw."

Mather smiled. "I think I shall do," she said, and
spun on her heel, giving a little kick that made her skirts
froth as she strode away. Deny it though she might, she
was enjoying that dress.

Liza took a deep breath and once again met her own
eyes in the mirror. She must try for the same joie de
vivre. She pinched her cheeks and then pressed her lips
together to force some blood into them. There. This
smile looked more convincing.

She squared her shoulders and swept into the drawing room.

"There she is!" Tilney sprang off the sofa on which
he'd been lounging. She had hesitated before inviting
him—he was very close with Nello—but vanity had decided it for her. Not only was Tilney a bachelor, and
therefore good practice for Jane, but he was also sure to
dispatch to Nello very detailed reports of Liza's romance
and courtship. For that was what this house party held
in store for her.

"Good evening," she called brightly, "what a welcome
sight!" And one by one she went around the room, ex-

changing handshakes and, for the more French among them, kisses.

Jane had been captured by Baron Forbes, which was well and good, provided she was willing to flirt. Silver-haired and sixty and in denial of it, Forbes liked to befriend pretty young things and introduce them as though they were his pets—a habit his wife indulged, so long as he did not grow *overly* fond of them.

Liza exchanged only the briefest of greetings with them before moving on to Katherine and Nigel Hawthorne, troublesome siblings, who stood in conference with Baroness Forbes. The Hawthornes were tall and slender as greyhounds and colored to match, their eyes and hair a drab brown that blended into their skin, for they were great yachters and forever in the sun. As a result, they had a knack for merging with the woodwork—a skill they used to eavesdrop and garner gossip, which they enjoyed spreading as harmfully as possible.

Liza would not trust them with her middle name, but they made delicious company. "Darlings," she cried.

"Looking smashing," Katherine drawled as they pressed cheeks. "I see you've a new toy. She looks very young. Shall I encourage Nigel to play with her?"

Liza laughed. "I can think of no more dangerous man on which to cut one's milk teeth. Do be kind," she added to Nigel.

"Never," he said, flashing his teeth in a lazy grin.

"Very dramatic repartee," commented the Baroness Forbes. She was a larger woman, whose upper arm wobbled quite vigorously as she fanned herself. But a kind woman—warm and expansive in her interests—who would do well by Jane even if her husband's interest made her itchy. "I must say, it was good of you to give us a reason to flee London. You know my husband would insist on remaining until every house on Park Lane was shuttered."

The baron heard this remark. "I enjoy town in the summer," he called with a shrug.

This comment caused Katherine and Nigel to stare. "How bohemian," Katherine said, in the same tones that a doctor might use to diagnose a contagious disease.

No. Don't think of doctors. Liza smiled all the more brightly. "I'll be back in a moment," she said, and turned for the corner where, as fortune would have it, *both* her likely prospects lay.

In fact, it struck her as very good luck that Hollister and Weston should be standing together. She hadn't known they were friendly, but there was no quicker route to securing one man's interest than convincing him he was in competition with another.

"My lords," she said as she sailed up. "I hope your journey to the back of beyond went smoothly?"

Bows and handshakes ensued. "If only all journeys ended in such fair views as this one," said Hollister, with an admiring look that traveled from her head to her toes and back again.

Weston put his hand over his heart. "Hollister is a flirt, but I am a man of total sincerity. And I tell you, I would travel to Timbuktu if you waited there."

Her light laugh felt false. It *sounded* false. For a beat of panic, she hesitated. Had she forgotten how to do this?

Don't be foolish. "You're both too kind," she said. Both wealthy. Both attractive, though she did not favor blonds, which put Weston at a disadvantage. Hollister's black hair had a pretty wave to it. Their eyes, she thought, were not particularly beautiful, being a lack-luster brown and a muddy green, respectively.

Eyes did not matter. Their bank accounts did. And both were extraordinary in that regard.

"We were speaking of the Ascot," said Hollister. "Did you wager correctly? Weston claims he's never lost, but then, I trust no man who claims to be sincere."

"A lady never tells, sir." She'd wagered far too much and lost every penny of it. Such idiocy, in retrospect.

As she glanced around the room, it occurred to her that one couple was missing. "Where are the San-burnes?" She was eager to see James; he and Lydia had returned from their honeymoon only a week ago, after an endless sojourn in Canada, the purpose of which still puzzled her. Twelve months in *Canada*, of all places. Where next? And for how long? Siberia for a decade?

"They went for a stroll in the garden," said Weston. "Apparently Sanburne has developed an appreciation for foliage." He traded a wry look with Hollister, who smirked.

Liza did not like that expression on him. Advantage, then, to Weston, whose arm she briefly touched. "New-lyweds," she sighed. Had her touch raised a hint of color in his cheeks? Very promising. "Always stealing off to admire the ferns."

"Surely, after a year, one would think—" Hollister paused. "Ah, here they come now."

Her heart lifted. James was a childhood friend, and she had missed him terribly, and so much had happened in his absence, and she could not wait—

Half turned, she came to a stop.

Michael Grey was walking into the room.

For a brief, stupid second her heart soared. And then reality crashed in and she gaped.

Michael Grey was *here*. Dressed in *evening wear*.

Where had he found formal tails? The suit looked . . . very expensive. And elegant. The snowy white necktie set off his square jaw, his tanned face, to perfection. He was devastatingly attractive; he might have fit in anywhere. But not *here*. He was barging into her *party*!

Shock held her paralyzed, even as Sanburne called out a greeting to her, and his wife—who looked shockingly pretty, much prettier than Liza remembered, her dark hair done up in a stylish twist—lifted a hand.

She could not believe Michael's gall. To expressly ignore her wishes, to thrust himself upon her friends—for Sanburne leaned over and spoke something in his ear, as though they were not perfect strangers, and in response, Michael laughed and nodded, and—dear God but her heart turned over in her chest, for his laughter was low and rich and musical, and it spoke to parts of her ungovernable by good sense. His eyes met hers, and her skin seemed to come alive with heat.

No. No, no, no. Weston and Hollister stood right beside her! *Focus.* Focus on his brazenness—his presumption—simply because she had slept with him, he thought he could overrule her wishes, bully his way into her party?

Oh, but they had not *slept*. She could not imagine being calm enough, beside him, to *sleep*—

She lifted her chin. "If you'll excuse me," she said sweetly to Weston and Hollister.

"Oh, for certain," said Weston. "Didn't know de Grey would be here."

Her next step hitched. That—she hadn't heard that right. How would *he* know Michael Grey?

Sanburne and his wife had been intercepted by the Hawthornes. She strode directly for Michael. His gaze lifted. Their eyes locked and for the span of a heartbeat everything in her swelled like a symphony.

She bit her tongue hard as a punishment. What unforgivable *cheek*! Had he gone mad? What did he think he was about?

He did not look away from her as Nigel spoke to him, some remark that caused him to smile faintly. He would not be smiling in a minute!

She drew up before the group. Something in her movement must have betrayed her agitation, for the Hawthornes, ever alert to scandal, broke off their conversations to study her.

Sanburne stepped in front of them. "My God," he said as he looked her over. "Looking very purple tonight, Lizzie."

Sanity fell over her like an icy rain. She could not make a scene here. A scene would make the Hawthornes wonder. And the Hawthornes, set to wondering, did not stop until they solved the mystery. "Is that"—she cleared her throat—"is that *really* all you can say, James? Well, I suppose I should be grateful. After twelve months in Canada, it's a wonder you speak English at all."

"But that's the main language of Canada," said Lydia, Viscountess Sanburne, in tones of puzzlement, even as her husband discarded convention and pulled Liza into a hug.

Over Sanburne's shoulders she once again met Michael's eyes. *Get out,* she mouthed.

His smile broadened. "Lovely to see you, Mrs. Chudderley."

James must have felt her go rigid, for he lifted his

brow in a silent question as she pulled away. "I hadn't realized you two knew each other," he said.

What was he talking about? Liza could not focus, for now the viscountess was addressing her. "So good to see you," Lydia said, and she, rattled enough to forget whom she was dealing with, leaned in to kiss the viscountess's cheek.

Not a warm and cuddly sort, Lady Sanburne. Reformed spinsters so rarely were. But she proved surprisingly game for Frenchness, even giving Liza's shoulder a squeeze before retreating to her husband's side. "What lovely gardens you have," she said, and darted an abashed glance toward—Michael. "Lord Michael said you had a way with roses. I'd not realized you favored horticulture."

Lord Michael! *Roses!* The brazenness! Liza gritted her teeth. "Prowling about, was he?"

"De Grey was always a bit slinky," Sanburne said.

De Grey? "This man . . ."

Michael *de* Grey. She knew that name.

Lord Michael. The de Greys. Why . . .

"Ah, yes," said Nigel to Michael. "Now it comes to me where I've seen you. How fares your brother?"

"Didn't he just sack you from your own hospital?" asked Katherine with a pleasant smile. "I believe I read something about it."

Sanburne touched her arm. "Lizzie," he said in an undertone, "are you quite all right?"

No. She was not all right. Sanburne *knew* this man. Nigel knew *of* this man. Which meant her doctor was no country rustic, but a *fraud*.

And he was watching her with a smile that was distinctly unkind. "More accurately, I would say I stepped down," he replied to Katherine. "Other matters required my . . . *particular* attentions."

Why did those words ring a bell?

She gasped. Those were *her* words—spoken to him . . . about *him*. For, God help her, she had no choice but to conclude that he was the brother of . . .

"The Duke of Marwick is not seen much of late," Nigel said. "Katherine speculated he might be ailing. But I reminded her, with a doctor for a brother, he'll have to use another excuse."

The ringing of the dinner bell saved her. Were it not for the bell, the entire room would have heard Liza whimper.

CHAPTER TWELVE

"So curious," Katherine Hawthorne said, her voice cutting clearly through the conversations of the six people who sat between her and Liza. "How on *earth* does one miscalculate the number of place settings?"

The answer was simple: one did not know that a *rat* would crash one's party. But one did not confess such, lest one wished one's relationship with said rat to receive a very uncomfortable degree of speculation.

Instead, from her place at the head of the table, Liza pretended not to hear. Her wine made a good excuse for inattention. She reached for it—her third glass; she'd managed to drink two, very quickly, as the table settings were rearranged. Yet somehow she wasn't tipsy. Or perhaps the wine's effect was indistinguishable from the shock that had already set her head to spinning.

Not only a liar, but brother to the *Duke of Marwick*. No playwright could have designed a better irony. How Nello would have laughed!

Lord Weston leaned in from her right elbow, his face

full of sympathy. "Good help can be very hard to find," he said.

He had a very nice nose, did Lord Weston. Straight and firm, not at all oversized. His lips were not so full as one might wish, but they were *honest* and did not speak *lies*. "How *true*," she said.

"Is Ronson slipping? I'll be glad to steal him away." This from Sanburne, who sat at her left and, until this moment, had been entertaining himself by flirting with his wife. They made a curious couple, Lydia being a prim and reserved scholar, James being one of England's handsomest men—and, until recently, one of its most dissolute scapegraces, to boot.

"There is nothing wrong with Ronson," Liza said. He was probably standing behind her right now. She didn't dare look. Her butler was capable of the most *tremendous* scowls.

"Dementia, is it?" James asked with interest.

Liza looked very quickly over her shoulder—but Ronson had abandoned his place by the sideboard, probably to check on matters in the kitchen. Thank God! "Only bad tempered," she said as she turned back. "But his *hearing* is excellent, mind you."

"All the better," said James cheerfully. "We can sic him on my father, and hope for a homicide."

"James," said Lydia in a chiding tone.

He sighed. "You're right, Lyd. It would be too cruel to Ronson."

Liza finished her wine and was gratified by a footman's quick approach with more. Her staff was excellent. And very prideful. "If you don't wish your soup poisoned, James, I would confine your witticisms to the guests."

Lydia abruptly laid down her spoon.

Goodness. That was a clumsy misstep. She cast a quick look at Weston, who was frowning into his own soup. "Only a joke," Liza said, and tried to laugh reassuringly, for nobody liked a bitter hostess. Instead her laughter squeaked like a rusty hinge. Or perhaps like something *unhinged*.

No wonder poison was on her mind! Against her will, her gaze swung across the table, to the man who sat diagonally across from Lydia.

Michael de Grey was doing a splendid job of ignoring her. Currently his attention focused on his dinner partner, Baroness Forbes, who had been delighted to meet "the famous doctor." Apparently she knew *all* about his hospital. Probably she also knew about his *other* talents. That would explain her quivering interest in him.

For Michael de Grey was nothing more than a *rake*! Her *decent,* upstanding country swain was in fact *notorious* for his womanizing exploits—or at least one of them, for Lady Heverley herself still fed the rumors, fanning herself and sighing every time his name was mentioned in public. She was desperate, probably, to remind the world that a man had once wanted her. She must be fifteen years older than de Grey.

But what of it? Michael de Grey was not known for his *select tastes.* No—he was known simply as widows' catnip!

A flush stung Liza's cheeks—a violent blush fed by her mortification. Why, now *she* had become one of his desperate widows! One among a great number of women generally characterized as grasping and hungry, avid for the smallest crumb of attention a man like de Grey might cast their way—

"Mrs. Chudderley," called Katherine Hawthorne in a gay, bright voice. "How grim you look! I suppose I should look grim as well, were my staff so forgetful! How on *earth* did they miscount the table settings?"

A dozen pairs of eyes swung in her direction—but not, she noticed, those belonging to the widows' catnip. *He* remained focused on the baroness. Somebody should point out to him that she was not a widow. The *baron* remained very much alive, presiding genially over the foot of the table.

The rat's hair was too long for a duke's brother. Where had he gotten that jacket? It molded to his body in a manner that suggested bespoke tailoring from Savile Row. Had he hidden his finer clothing away in that little house he'd rented? Oh, what a laugh he must have had when she recommended Mr. Broward's haberdashery!

"I'm quite well," she said. And she would be once she'd kicked the cad out of her house. It would have to be a quiet expulsion, done while the others were distracted. That did not mean it would be *peaceful*. "I confess, it was my fault that we were lacking one cover—will you forgive me, darling, if I admit that it had quite slipped my mind that you were coming?"

Katherine did not miss a beat. "Oh, not in the least," she said with a laugh. "Why, *I* almost forgot I was coming. These little events do tend to slip my mind!"

On a deep breath, Liza reminded herself that she had invited Katherine for a reason. Excellent training for Jane, and a guaranteed diversion should boredom set in. Nevertheless, at this moment, she wished the woman to the devil, for she needed no distractions beyond the liar two seats away. "I'm sure your social calendar is packed to the gills, darling. But take care; I find regular rest very beneficial to one's looks. You really should try to make more time for it."

"Point to Lizzie," Sanburne said, and picked up his wineglass. But where a year ago he might have drained it and joined Liza on the fourth round, marriage had altered his habits: when he returned the wine to the table, its level was barely diminished.

Liza, looking from his glass to hers, grew conscious of a strange unhappiness on that count. It was so much easier to drink deeply when one had a companion in it.

Michael was not drinking at all.

Her eyes fixed on his untouched glass. How malicious were his intentions here? The possibilities were dark, though she could not bring herself to believe the worst of them. Even if he knew that Nello had cuckolded his brother, it would make no sense to punish *her* for it. When Nello had taken up with the duchess, Liza had also been betrayed.

Perhaps he didn't even know about the affair. Perhaps this was some cosmically unhappy coincidence. In which case . . . she felt nothing but *wrath.* Of course he required no wine to be comfortable at her table. His brazenness served him better! He practically *lounged,* and if he was aware of Katherine's ongoing effort to brush her breasts against his arm, he showed no sign of it.

God in heaven. She had warned him that her grand friends might discomfort him—when his brother outranked everyone in this room!

She wanted to take his comfort and *smother* him with it.

The force of her glare finally registered on him. For a second, across the span of the candlelit table, his eyes met hers. In the candlelight, he looked like a medieval icon, his strong cheekbones underlaid by dramatic shadows. The light even softened the line of his nose. He looked positively, *typically* handsome. No wonder Katherine kept trying to win his attention from the baroness!

"Perhaps we need more light in here," Liza said. "It's very dim." That nose would benefit from the glare.

"Good God, must we see what we're eating?" asked James. "How barbaric—" Wincing, he came to an abrupt stop.

"It's a very fine spread," Lydia said. "I should love to see it more clearly."

"*Ouch,*" said James. "That leg you kicked belongs to your loving husband. Have a care with it."

"Such *lovely* centerpieces," Lydia said emphatically.

"Really, Lyd, you could have played football."

"Oh, let the lights be," said Weston. He offered Liza a warm smile. "You're the consummate hostess, Mrs. Chudderley, and I can think of no finer atmosphere. Indeed—I'm informed that you have a great roster of wonders in store for us this week!"

Liza called up an answering smile. To the devil with de Grey! She would deal with him later; in the meantime, let him flirt with whomever he liked. Her quarry was *here.* And tomorrow, with the less conventional seating she'd arranged, she would evade the tiresome rules of precedence and give Hollister a chance to be her dinner escort. A fair contest between her eligible bachelors. "Someone has been telling secrets," she said. "I wished to keep the entertainments a surprise!"

Weston's teeth were lovely, even and strikingly white. After Nello, she had not expected ever again to be fond of a blond man, but one's mind could change. "Mrs. Hull only gave hints," he said, "and in strictest confidence, I promise you."

Jane? What was *she* doing, sharing confidences with *Weston*? Liza shot a look down the table. Jane had tried to intercept her on their procession into the dining room—

too unskilled to know that she must conceal her shock at de Grey's unmasking. But now she seemed to have recovered. Indeed, by Liza's estimation, she was inclining a bit too *eagerly* toward Hollister. Why weren't Tilney and Nigel making themselves useful?

Liza held on to her smile. "Dear Mrs. Hull. I'm so pleased that she consented to join us. I fear she still mourns for her late husband—it was a great romance, you know. She says no man will ever match him."

From Sanburne came a soft, knowing laugh. She would have to speak with *him* later.

"I'm sorry to hear that," Weston said somberly. "I did not realize she was so recently widowed."

"Yes, she just cast off her weeds."

Weston nodded slowly. "We must endeavor to cheer her, then."

"Indeed," said Liza. "Only, lest we reawaken her grief, we must go about it very carefully, I think."

"Ah," said a voice two seats away. *His* voice. "Is Mrs. Chudderley sharing her rules with you, Weston?"

Her heart skipped a beat. Such low, purring words. Surely everyone must hear the taunt in them—and see it in the smile he gave her.

She had not imagined her country doctor capable of malicious pleasures. But . . . this was not her country doctor, was it? This was a stranger, well versed in the barbed ways of high society.

She swallowed. How curious that for the briefest moment, she felt a violent pang of loss.

"Rules?" asked Weston.

She shot Michael a warning look. He leaned back, a faint smile playing on his lips. Damn that smile. She did not care how well his suit became him, how sharply the snow-white neckcloth set off the square angles of his jaw, or how cleverly he could make her pay for having believed his ruse. She would not let him ruin this for her. "No," she said flatly. "You misheard us, sir. We are speaking of the entertainments I've scheduled." And if he persisted with talk of the rules, she would—she would *hurl* her soup at him.

"Oh, my apologies," he said smoothly. "Entertainments, of course. Though they seem a touch superfluous, with you as our hostess." The widening of his smile deepened the creases that bracketed his mouth. The effect should *not* look becoming. Wrinkles were signs of premature aging. He was too *young* to have them. Only thirty! He was a *puppy.*

Weston, blissfully ignorant, took Michael's remarks as an invitation to break etiquette; he leaned around the baroness to reply. "I confess, de Grey, I'm surprised to see you here. Hadn't imagined anything could drag you from London. But I suppose if anyone could work such miracles, it would be Mrs. Chudderley."

"Oh, yes," Michael murmured. "Our very own Miss Nightingale."

Her hand closed over her knife, a spasmodic clench. How *dare* he bait her with the memory of that? Galling to recall how flattered she'd been—how very much she'd wanted him to approve of her.

Her judgment was rotten. Ever drawn to the deceivers.

"Yes," she said, "I promised Lord Michael a *very* amusing departure from his normal routine. Namely, a host of experts who specialize in the broadcasting of curious truths. I expect he was drawn by the danger in it— for as we all know, some truths may be very *unwelcome.*"

With a soft laugh, Michael lifted his wineglass, an ambiguous gesture, not quite deliberate enough to be considered a toast. The candlelight spilled through his wine and gilded his throat with a crimson glow, which seemed a fine foreshadowing. If she gutted him with her fish knife, he'd be redder yet.

Why, his fraud surpassed even Nello's. Nello, at least, had lied only about his intentions and his fidelity. His true name, she'd known from the start!

"How intriguing," said Weston. "A riddle. Dare I guess it?"

She would never trust her own instincts again.

"Oh, it's very easy," piped up Lydia. "She's hired a lot of—"

"Don't say it," said Sanburne. "Not while she's holding that knife."

Liza snatched her hand back beneath the tablecloth. This dinner could not conclude rapidly enough.

"Oh—very well," said Lydia, sounding puzzled. "But do you know, Mrs. Chudderley, I meant to tell you— after I recommended that book on mysticism, I encountered a shaman outside Alberta who claimed to be able to divine truth from a bundle of bones. And he quite contradicted Beloit's claims about tribal magic."

"Did he?" She had no idea who Beloit was. The book's author, maybe? Michael had turned back to Lady Forbes, as though he were not perfectly aware of her rage—as though it did not concern him in the *least*. She stared at his back and loathed him.

"Indeed," Lydia was saying. "Had I persuaded him to return to England with me, I believe he might have set off a new fad. As a society, we incline quite ardently toward all manner of mystical nonsense, don't we? I wonder if it indicates something significant about our broader need for a bit of mystery to flavor our faith."

And here Lydia went, turning a proper dinner into

a lecture on her anthropological curiosities. Bless her! Liza was grateful for the distraction. She sat back and breathed deeply in an effort to temper her pulse.

"An interesting question," said Weston gamely. "I suppose there's something deeply mysterious about the Christian concept of miracles, for instance. But wouldn't you say that mystery is a common characteristic of all religions? For who can know the face of God?"

"Ah, too true! Perhaps I misspoke, then!" Lydia leaned forward, animated now, as her husband smiled on her dotingly. *Doltishly,* more like. Liza was not in the mood to admire lovesick puppies. "Rather than religion, perhaps we should consider this obsession with mysticism as a symptom of some societal lack—or a need; a need to believe in the existence of mysteries that science cannot explain. Why, yes! Yes, indeed! It was Hobart, I believe, who argued that one could characterize individual societies by their central preoccupations. His example, of course, was the Albanians and Hakmarrja, but for our purposes—"

James touched her elbow. "Don't forget to translate for us, darling."

"Oh!" Lydia blushed. "Hakmarrja is the Albanian philosophy of revenge."

Liza nodded. She was calmer now. She could handle this mess. "I like that philosophy," she said. "Revenge, you say? Tell us more, please."

Michael swallowed a laugh at the transparent taunt. He'd be glad to give her a chance at revenge—later, in private, preferably near a bed. A wall or couch would serve as well.

God save him, but he was a shallow rotter for enjoying this. The moment she had disinvited him from this party, his course had been decided. No gently worded confession from him. He would change strategies. Force his brother's hand, and confront Elizabeth Chudderley on equal footing.

It was damned bracing to have a clear mission again. She was angry, so he would soothe her. Apologize, and explain himself. They would make a game of figuring out common acquaintances. She would realize she no longer needed to condescend to him, to apologize for her airs. And then, the matter settled, he would have her again.

For once could not be enough. Not after *that* interlude. Her newfound concern for propriety might still be an obstacle, but it was a thin pretext that he would finish off in the course of five minutes alone with her. He would remind her again of how thoroughly she'd enjoyed the advantages of widowhood in that spartan little cottage.

"How do you know Mrs. Chudderley, Lord Michael?"

With difficulty, he dragged his gaze from their hostess back to the baroness—a pleasant woman, round and sweet as a muffin. "We met only recently," he said. "A pleasant piece of serendipity. And you?" Though he did not know the Hawthornes, five minutes in their presence had explained their inclusion on the guest list— they defined "fast company." But Lady Forbes seemed a puzzling choice.

The baroness smiled. "Oh, I've known her practically since her infancy—or since her debut into society, which I imagine is quite the same thing."

"Oh? What was she like as a debutante?" He could not imagine Elizabeth stripped of her knowing air. The attempt, after a moment, grew strangely unsettling. Her composure was her armor. He had stripped her of it briefly in that gamekeeper's cottage, but he did not like to think of her thus disarmed in public. Without that invisible shield, a beautiful woman would make easy prey for any number of wolves.

"Oh, she was gorgeous as the moon, of course—" The baroness paused as a footman switched out their soup bowls for the fish course. "No surprise in that, nor in the great stir she caused. But were you to go back in time, I vow you may not have recognized her. She was shyer then—softer, too. Such a waste! That rotter never deserved her." She made a tsking noise before spearing her fish.

"Rotter?" Had she suffered some unhappy love affair before marrying?

"Her first husband," said Lady Forbes. She paused to chew. "Nobody credited me when I called him a nasty piece. Bland as a banker, Mr. Chudderley—that was the worst anybody else could say of him. But what others mistook for sobriety, I saw very clearly as a lack of charity, and an *inflexible* temperament."

Elizabeth had never mentioned her husband. All her complaints had centered on a more recent disappointment. The realization left Michael feeling rather . . . out of sorts, in fact. Abruptly, he realized the depth of his ignorance about her.

Vexing thing, to take an interest in a woman with a history.

He frowned. No, that wasn't right. He *preferred* women with histories. Innocents were the problematic ones: they expected things he would never give.

Why, he supposed he'd never objected to lovers' complicated histories before because he'd never had any interest in knowing those histories.

Christ. He himself was more of a rotter than he'd realized. And this interest he felt in Elizabeth . . .

It was different, somehow.

Else why was he here? He had come because he wanted her to see him as an equal. An . . . eligible man.

The realization astounded him. *Eligible?* The notion was laughable. He had no money—his brother had seen to that. And Alastair would never consider Elizabeth a suitable match.

That thought triggered a hot anger. The hell if he cared whether or not Alastair approved of her.

Glancing up, he found the baroness watching him—and realized only then that he'd let the conversation hang.

He mustered his thoughts. "Bad luck in love, then." He heard the leading note in his voice, and it unnerved him further. Why was he asking these questions? Wiser to leave the mystery intact, wasn't it? Mystery was the spice of any affair. Surely he could not want . . . more.

"Oh, she's had the worst luck, no doubt of it." Lady Forbes lifted her wineglass, exhaling so forcefully that her breath set the Bordeaux to rippling. "The poor thing is putting on a very bright face, of course, but this most recent news must have left her furious."

She must be referring to the unnamed cad's betrothal. *Furious* seemed to Michael to be a very curious choice of words. "Or heartbroken," he said.

The baroness laughed as though he'd just told a very good joke. "Heartbroken! Elizabeth Chudderley! I should like to see the man who could manage *that*! A very thick axe he'd require for *that* armor."

He disguised his astonishment in a sip of wine. Did her friends know so little of her? For he had looked into her face on Midsummer's Eve, and he had not seen a woman incapable of heartbreak. Far from it.

"At any rate," Lady Forbes added idly, "it would take a far better man than Mr. Nelson."

Nelson. His brain locked onto the name like a sharpshooter on his target. He felt a sudden, itching need to retire to Elizabeth's library and comb through a volume of DeBrett's. *Nelson.* The name rang no bells. "I can't say I've met the man. But if he had Mrs. Chudderley on the line and chose to cast elsewhere, he's a fool."

"What a romantical statement," came Nigel Hawthorne's voice from across the table. He sat beside Jane Hull, who was alternating between avoiding Michael's eyes and staring at him avidly. "And how surprising that such romantics should come from *you,* my lord. May we assume the countryside has awakened your chivalry?"

Michael had never met either of the Hawthornes, but they certainly seemed to keep track of *him.* "What can I say? Fresh air works wonders on me." He recognized Hawthorne's type from his school days: pinch-faced and malicious, but only when in a crowd. In private, he would whimper and tuck his tail between his legs. Harmless, then, and rather pathetic to boot. "I do hope you enjoy a similar effect," he said. "You might find the novelty refreshing."

Hawthorne laughed and lifted his wineglass, giving it a contemplative swirl. "I do wonder . . . how long have you been enjoying the fresh air? The rest of us ran into each other at St. Pancras, but I don't recall seeing you at the station."

"You mustn't twit him," said his sister sweetly, from Michael's right. Katherine Hawthorne had been quite content all evening to confine her conversation to Tilney, who sat diagonally opposite her, on the other side of Jane; but even as she'd spoken with him, she'd been attempting to teach Michael's right arm the precise shape of her breasts. "Perhaps he wasn't in first class," she went on, turning her bark-brown eyes toward Michael. "Some can't afford it, you know."

Tilney leaned forward, eager to join in. "Do you know—I didn't see your luggage brought in, either."

Mrs. Hull's eyes were widening rather comically. She darted a nervous glance around their immediate company, as though only now realizing she sat in the carnivorous corner of the table. "I'm flattered," Michael said, and then smiled at her in reassurance when her panicked gaze touched on him. "I had no idea my whereabouts were of such interest to those who had not met me before this evening. But I suppose friendships spring up in the unlikeliest of places. Even if the friendships themselves are unlikely."

As Tilney's eyes narrowed, Michael realized he was enjoying himself. It was not so hard to slip into his old skin, after all. There were mannerisms and attitudes a country doctor was not allowed to employ, that the son and brother of a duke might exercise at will—arrogance being one of them.

Katherine laughed, a low and sultry sound. "Cornwall *is* rather unlikely, isn't it? I don't know how we let Liza talk us into such shenanigans."

"Ah," said Tilney, "this is nothing. Do you remember last winter in Monte Carlo? My God. I lost half my year's income in one night."

And so the conversation turned again, to matters that had nothing to do with Michael. But he listened closely over the remainder of the dinner, gathering from the lively discussion a good picture of what Elizabeth had meant when she had told him she was different among her London friends.

She was the very definition of fast.

Normally, he had no interest in such routines. But when it came to her . . .

As the dessert course concluded, he deliberately turned his attention toward the head of the table. She was waiting and ready to meet his regard. Her jaw firmed. Her shoulders squared. A laugh started to rise in his throat—she looked like a soldier preparing for battle—but when she stood, his mirth died.

The candlelight licked over her skin like an ardent suitor. Her beauty at this moment could have stopped any man's breath. But it was her presence that arrested him. She silenced all the conversations without a single word. Her composure was queenly, though the smile she showed the table was false. No one else would have guessed it, but he knew it in his bones.

"I believe we will skip the usual formalities," she said. "To the drawing room, if no one objects."

As everyone rose and began to file out, he deliberately slowed his pace. As soon as the last of the guests had passed him, he was not surprised to feel a hand close on his elbow.

He turned. "Yes, Mrs. Chudderley?"

"You," she said in a sharp whisper, "are coming with *me*."

CHAPTER THIRTEEN

Michael let her lead him out of the dining room. But when he opened his mouth to speak, Elizabeth cut him off. "Not another word," she said in a low voice. "Not until we are somewhere where I may *scream*."

He made an interested noise in his throat. "That sounds promising."

She dropped his arm as though it burned. Onward she stalked, her plum-colored skirts frothing around her ankles, her train hissing over the polished wood floor.

He followed her into the little salon off the entry hall. When she turned to face him, his uplifted hands—palms out, in the gesture of surrender—won not the slightest hint of a smile. He said, "I owe you an explanation—"

And then ducked the vase that flew past his head and shattered against the door.

"And an apology to boot," he said as he straightened.

Bright spots of color burned in her cheeks. "I want nothing from you. Nothing but the sight of your back as you leave! Which you will do, *at once*. You—"

Abruptly she stopped, pressing her lips together very

tightly. But she could not control their trembling, and that small sign of distress caused a startled shock to ripple through him.

He stepped toward her out of instinct. She took an answering step away, her brief look of surprise transmuting to a contempt so transparent that he froze.

Perhaps he had . . . miscalculated her reaction. But he'd supposed she would be *relieved* by the truth. If she had liked him as a doctor, surely she would find him even more pleasing as the son and brother of a duke. What woman would not?

This one, apparently. The look on her face left no doubt of it. "Listen," he said slowly. "My purpose was not to fool you. I told nobody the truth. I was trying to avoid my brother's notice here."

She took a quick, audible breath. "Your brother," she said. "The Duke of Marwick."

He tried a rueful smile. It did not hold, for she was looking at him as though he were a stranger, and he did not like it. "That's the one."

She walked around a silk-upholstered armchair, stopping behind it as though she required a shield against him. "Make your explanation, then. But keep it short. I have guests waiting."

"It's . . . rather too complicated for brevity," he said. "But I can give you the bare outlines, and later—"

Her brows flew up. "Later? There will be no *later*."

He exhaled. "Elizabeth, I—"

"I rescind your right to address me so informally." She gave him a slight, chilling smile. "And I tell you now, if you ever speak of—*us*—abroad, I swear you will regret it. I am no Lady Heverley, *Lord Michael*. I will not sigh when I speak your name."

Lady Heverley, *again*. His small, disbelieving laugh made her scowl. "You think this is funny?" she asked.

"No. Not in the least." Not any longer. "I was wrong to misrepresent myself. But I confess, I did not realize . . . that is, you seem strangely . . . furious that I'm better born than you thought."

She gave him a stony stare. "*Higher* born," she said. "But far from *better*."

He stared at her, trying to puzzle it out. "Then it's simply that I lied. Is that it?" His own words belatedly made him wince. Put so plainly, yes, he could see cause for her anger.

"Don't flatter yourself," she said coldly. "I am well accustomed to frauds."

Ah. That smarted. "Slotting me in with the other rotters. I suppose I deserve it."

She shrugged. "One rotter is much the same as the next. Did you imagine you were somehow different?"

"I never meant to lie to you." How bloody insufficient, even to his own ears. "That is . . . I should have told you sooner." He had tried to do so in the gamekeeper's cottage, but . . . he did not think she would care now to hear of his excuse. *It turned out I was more interested in shagging you than taking the time to explain.* No, that line would not serve. He was an ass. "Elizabeth. I'm sorrier than I can say."

The silence, for a long moment, was broken only by the ticking of a distant clock. She looked down at her hand, rubbing her gloved thumb over her fingertips, and then shrugged again. "I find I do not particularly care for your apologies."

"Then I must hope my explanation suffices." He took a deep breath. "My sister-in-law, as you'll know, passed ten months ago." How best to tell this tale, without spilling secrets that were not his to share? "The duchess's death . . ." No more lies, now. "Her death, and certain truths that emerged thereafter, sent my brother into a decline."

"Truths." She put her hands on the back of the chair, gripping it so tightly the fabric wrinkled. "What kind of truths?"

He grimaced. "They aren't mine to speak. I promise you, if I could . . ."

She stared at him a moment, and then her chest rose and fell on a great breath. "Yes, of course. I suppose they don't concern me." She made an odd pause, then shook her head. "Go on, then."

"My brother's decline was gradual. At the beginning, he simply seemed less inclined to go into company. Mistrustful of his friends." Michael hesitated. He did not like to divulge this. But . . . he trusted her. Ironic, that it should take betraying her trust to realize he had faith in her never to betray his. "In February, he ceased to leave the house entirely. This is no ordinary hesitance, mind you. He isn't ill, he simply refuses to step outside. Not even in the garden. It's almost as if . . . the world has begun to frighten him."

"I see." She watched him narrowly; he had the sense from her of quivering alertness, of powerful impulses leashed by hard effort. "And so, in response, you have undertaken a masquerade in the wilderness. Yes, it all makes *perfect* sense to me now."

He acknowledged her mockery with a grim smile. "He gave me little choice. He will not sire an heir, he says, so I must do it for him, with a woman of his choosing: otherwise, he will use all his powers to close the hospital."

A line formed between her dark, winged brows. "The hospital in London. The one that he sponsors."

"Yes. The one I *founded*."

"How . . . Machiavellian," she murmured.

"You don't know my brother. Machiavelli would be a mere apprentice to him." He paused. "At any rate, you see why I cannot concede to his terms."

She averted her face. He watched the plume bob in her coiffure as she smoothed one elbow glove. The stroke of her hand hypnotized him: from the fingers to the elbow, twice, then thrice.

"No," she finally said, very quietly. "I suppose I don't."

He exhaled, an explosive burst of disbelief. "Is my life to be sacrificed for his own pleasure? He is—" He took a deep breath. "You don't know my brother. I *want* to help him. By God, I tried my best to do it! I lie awake at night worrying over it."

Her head bowed. The naked desperation in his voice had embarrassed her, he supposed. Probably it should embarrass him, too. But for some reason it felt vitally important that she believe him on this count. "I would *not* abandon him," he said.

"All right," she said slowly. She did not look up.

"But you must see, the solution he proposes will help no one. Far from it! He wants the line to continue? Then he will have to leave his house and find a wife of his own. *That* is the medicine I have prescribed. *That* is my cure for him."

"Ah. So your motives have been purely noble, then." She lifted her head, and the look on her face made him feel as though some shutter banged hard in his chest.

Lady Forbes imagined this woman immune to hurt?

He had proof to the contrary before his eyes right now, and it cast *him* as the villain. "I have betrayed your trust," he said, very low. God damn his clumsiness, his stupidity. "That was not noble. And it was never my intention, I promise you."

Her one-shouldered shrug was no doubt meant to telegraph her indifference. "Rest easy on that front. We made no promises. You were only an afternoon's distraction, after all."

The breath went from him, ragged like a laugh, though he felt no humor. Now *he* was the one wounded. How peculiar was that? "I'd hoped we might distract each other a bit longer than that." A good deal longer. He was only now seeing what potential they had. "What passed between us in that cottage . . . was unlike any passing pleasure I've felt. Elizabeth, it did not feel like an afternoon's distraction to me. Indeed, the more I've thought on it—"

"Stop." When she raised her gaze, her eyes looked suspiciously bright, and the sight struck him like a heavy weight to his chest. She blinked as though to bring him into focus, and then looked beyond him toward the door. "The guests," she said. "I must . . ." And then she straightened, visibly gathering her composure. "I've heard your explanation. And now, sir, you will hear mine. In a minute, you will go into the drawing room and make pleasant conversation with my guests. Within the half hour, a letter will arrive that informs you of some trouble in London—you may come up with a story for it, if you like. Perhaps your hospital, perhaps your brother. Either way, you will make your excuses and announce your departure."

Her voice had hardened during her speech. But her

hands told a different tale. They were flexing on the chair, knotting and unknotting, and he wanted to take them in his grasp, pull them to his face, and fall to his knees before her and beg her to forgive him. To let him try again.

The image was so vivid, the impulse so foreign, that it made him stupid. Tongue-tied and amazed.

Which was well and good, for she had not yet finished. "As your concerned *hostess,*" she said, "I will arrange for my coach to carry you away—to your amusing little cottage, where the driver will wait while you pack your bags. John Coachman will then take you onward to the station. If you miss the last train, there will be another at nine o'clock tomorrow."

He exhaled. A very neat dismissal, that. Rather as if she owned the entire district.

Which he supposed she did.

Releasing the chair, she swept up her skirts and strode for the door.

"Wait," he said. As she passed, he caught her by the elbow. Without hesitation, she spun on her heel and slapped him.

The flat of her hand cracked spectacularly. But he did not release her, though his cheek stung viciously. She stared up at him, her eyes wide, her expression strangely blank.

He did not like that look on her face. "I deserved that," he told her.

"You did." She shook her head as though to clear it. "I will *not* apologize."

"Don't." He could feel her trembling where he gripped her, and it gutted him. What had he done here? He reached out to cup her cheek, and she averted her face. But she did not knock his hand away. That was something.

She swallowed audibly. "I must go write that letter."

"In a minute."

"Let go of me," she whispered.

He knew he should. But his hand would not obey him. What was happening here? What was happening within him?

He hadn't known until this moment. But suddenly it was plain, and he was a fool. *He* was the fool, not she.

"Elizabeth," he murmured. Elizabeth, who laughed like a barmaid and parried his jokes with a philosopher's wit, who forwent sleep for distant cousins whom other women of her station would never have acknowledged. Who drank ale with villagers and guided rude country doctors to the shores of a lake, simply to share the beauty of this place she loved.

Elizabeth, whose vulnerability her friends believed long dead. But she had wept in his arms in the gamekeeper's cottage. She had wept, and then smiled at him, and kissed him as he'd never been kissed before.

She had offered him friendship, and in return, he had disappointed her.

How had he not foreseen this moment? How had he not glimpsed, until now, how little she could afford to be disappointed again?

How had he not divined the great cost to him for having done so?

"Elizabeth." Her name felt delicate on his lips, precious. "Let me make this up to you."

She would not look at him. "I am sick of you," she said. "I want you to *go*."

"No." He stroked her cheek. "I'm not going anywhere."

Now she glanced around at him, and though he did

not fully understand her expression—for it seemed balanced between surprise and pain—he knew better than to waste the opportunity. He would remind her of why she might wish him to stay. Before she could look away again, he leaned down to kiss her.

For a brief, sweet moment of relief, he felt her yield. Her hand rose to cover his where it cupped her cheek, and he tasted her tongue, and the heat leapt between them as consumingly as ever. The small sound she made might have been a sob, but it might also have been surrender. He stepped into her, gently guided her back a pace, and then another, until her shoulder blades touched the wall.

He had hope as he kissed her. All his experience, all his skills, could be put into this single kiss of apology, a kiss to persuade her, a kiss to atone. "Let me," he whispered into her mouth, and her grip on his hand tightened, tightened to the point of pain—which was fitting; he did not mind it; he would encourage her to hurt him if that was what she required to forgive him. He leaned into her, his free hand finding her waist, gripping her there, pulling her solidly against him, letting her feel what she had enjoyed before, and what he would put into her service once again. "I will make it up to you," he murmured into her ear, feverishly, as he covered her throat in a hot, open-mouthed kiss.

"You can't," she whispered.

"First let me try."

"I must marry."

For a moment the words made no sense. Her collarbone, the grain of her skin—

"Money," she said. "I must marry. Have you any money?"

He froze. "You . . ." *Marry?* "What?"

She gave a strange little laugh and slipped out from his hold. "I said I must *marry*," she said. "The look on your face—have no fear, sir. My need is too great for a *second son* to supply."

"Your need?" He sounded as witless as an automaton. "What need?" She was the last woman he'd imagine in desperate straits. "What do you mean?"

She blew out a breath. "I am pockets to let. Why else should a widow remarry?" Her smile was not pleasant. "Surely not *love*? We are too old to be so naïve, are we not? Or *I* am, at least. Older than you, and wiser, too."

"You're . . ." He could not put it together. She gave no sign of suffering financially.

An unpleasant prickle moved through him, a tightening in his chest that spelled comprehension. "*Weston*," he said.

She shrugged. "Or Hollister. Either will serve."

A knocking came at the door. That black smile did not leave her face. "How shocked you look," she said. "I do hope you were not planning to ask me to be your keeper? I'm afraid I can't afford it. Ask next year, when I am once again some man's angel in the house."

Before he could reply to *that* fine insult, she pulled open the door. "Jane!" she said. "Excellent! Lord Michael was just leaving."

And taking her friend's arm, she hurried out of view—never once looking back.

He did not follow her instructions, for he never returned to the drawing room. Liza passed a black hour with one eye on the door before Baron Forbes's fatigue brought an end to the assembly. Travel-worn, the company agreed that there was no shame in concluding this evening, and only this evening, at a shockingly reasonable hour.

Liza walked with her guests to their rooms, bidding them one by one good night, ignoring Weston's idle remark—and Katherine's more pointed one—about Michael's disappearance. Once everyone was safely installed, she hurried back to the entry hall.

Moonlight was falling through the skylight onto the checkerboard tiles. A shadow detached itself from the wall: the night porter. He had let his lordship out the front doors over an hour ago, he said.

She opened the doors before she realized what she was doing. Not a breeze stirred. The night was still and warm and empty.

Her heart gave an odd, hollow knock.

Another lie to lodge against his account: *I'm not going*. But he had gone, after all.

Which was what she had wanted.

Coming to her senses, she pulled the doors shut. The porter was giving her a sideways look; in the servants' quarters tonight, gossip would fly.

She picked up her skirts and started for the stairs. *Good riddance, then*. Lying ass! His explanation had not made him look any better. How lovely it must be to live as a man, and take to one's heels whenever the threat of marriage was raised. If *she* could earn a living—

But no. She sighed as she laid her hand on the balustrade, handsomely carved walnut, waxed to a high polish. This house was its own burden, absurdly expensive to maintain. But it had been built for her mother, to Mama's own specifications, and Liza could no more sell it than she could part with her own soul.

No living she could have earned, even as a man, would have supported her obligations. Nor would the earnings of a second son, as well he knew. He had not even tried to argue with her on *that* count.

She swallowed. Such ludicrous thoughts! Of course he had not argued. The *widows' catnip* was, by definition, a bachelor.

"Liza!" This breathless call came from above. Jane was creeping down the stairs, casting thrilled glances over her shoulder—the very picture of a four-year-old awake past her bedtime, nervous that the elders might catch her out.

Liza felt a great weariness swim through her. It was all still a game for Jane. She had so much time remaining in which to play without consequences.

"You should be in bed," she said.

"Not before we speak!" Drawing her shawl more tightly around her, Jane bounced on her feet. "You put me off earlier, but now you must tell: *why* was he in hiding? Did you know who he was all along?"

Liza did not pause when she reached Jane. The girl turned and hurried after her.

"There's nothing so mysterious in it." Her voice sounded sluggish and flat, but she could not muster a better performance. Her head ached. Her mind could barely grapple with whatever odd emotion was pulsing through her like a bruise.

He had kissed her, and it had felt . . . not like a kiss, but something more. A promise. She grew drunk on him within the space of a breath.

That made her doubly a fool. But when he touched her, her brain ceased to function. All she wanted was *more*. Frightening effect. With Nello, she'd finally learned about desire—but her desire had always been tempered by anxiety. Even as she'd touched him, she had calculated his response, gauging whether he was pleased, and how she might please him better.

With Michael de Grey, she thought of nothing at all. Greed consumed her. *More,* was all she thought.

Enough, she thought now. And: *Never again.*

"But of course there's a mystery!" Jane sounded breathless and slightly cross. "A duke's son, masquerading as a plain doctor—"

"He had his reasons." If he truly intended to oppose his brother, perhaps he'd been right to flee. She had never spoken at length with Marwick, but his reputation did not recommend him—not as a friend, and certainly not as a man to cuckold. Her shock at Nello's betrayal had been edged by her amazement at his stupidity. Margaret de Grey, of all people! Marwick was famously possessive.

Machiavelli would be a mere apprentice to him.

She shivered. Nello had been full of remorse when she'd discovered the affair. He had pleaded and begged for another chance, and been so terribly sweet in the weeks afterward—in order to win her forgiveness, Liza had assumed. Only now did it occur to her that perhaps it hadn't been her forgiveness he was desperate to secure, but her silence.

"What reasons did he give you?" Jane asked.

Cresting the stairs, she turned to pin Jane with a steely look. "None that concern us. And I hope you realize that you mustn't speak of this to anyone. It will only make *you* look the fool for having believed him."

"Oh." Jane frowned. "Of course. But . . . will he join us for the remainder of the party?" She brightened.

"And perhaps call down his brother? His grace is widowed, I believe."

Her calculations were as transparent as glass. "No," said Liza. "Lord Michael has gone back to London. And as for his brother . . ." She shook her head. "They call the Duke of Marwick 'the Kingmaker.' Did you know that?"

"Oh!" Jane looked entranced. "But why?"

"Because he has put men into power," Liza said. "Men like Hollister, in fact. But when they grow disagreeable, he also destroys them."

"But surely he would not do so with a *woman*!"

"Better," Liza said, "that we don't find out."

Michael woke with a start. No light from beneath the curtains. For a moment he was disoriented. His flat? His office in the hospital?

No. *Bosbrea*. He had sent Elizabeth's coachman away from his doorstep. Had needed time to think before making a decision regarding his departure.

Thirst gripped him. He sat up, rubbing his face, and swung his feet off the bed. The chill of the floorboards reminded him of something—

He'd been dreaming.

He sucked in a breath, for it came back over him so vividly—the feel of the dream, the dark suffocating hopelessness of it. Himself a boy, hiding in the wardrobe as his parents fought. Alastair curled beside him, pressing a finger to his lips to keep him quiet.

Not so much a dream as a memory, then. That summer before he'd first gone away to school. The last summer his parents had still lived under one roof. A house party under way, their parents the hosts. His father had invited his mistress du jour—flaunted her beneath their mother's nose. And when Maman had raged, he'd slapped her. Alastair had seized Michael to keep him from bursting out of the wardrobe. "You'll make it worse," he'd whispered.

Through the wardrobe doors, left an inch ajar, they had watched as Maman gave nearly as good as she'd got. She'd scored their father with her nails, raised a trail of blood down his cheek. *Good,* Michael had thought. *Good.*

I'll let the world know you have the pox, she'd screamed. *We'll see how your lovers like you then!*

Their father had charged toward her. Alastair had pulled Michael's head into his chest, as though blindness would protect him from the sounds.

He exhaled now. Stood and walked to the basin. The cool water was soothing to his throat. On the desk a few feet away rested the letter that had been awaiting him on his arrival home—a note from Alastair, sent by Halsted. His brother was closing the hospital unless Michael reappeared in London by the end of the week.

Was it an empty threat? He wasn't sure. But while the letter had enraged him earlier, he gazed on it now and felt nothing but . . . grief.

As children, they had survived a hell together. Alastair had helped him to survive it. And now his brother had discovered a fresh hell, and was striking out from that place of darkness.

He returned the tin cup to the table, the metal so cold against his fingertips. Yes, he felt grief. But not hatred. Hatred was born of relationships like his parents'. They had hurt each other so terribly. Alastair's threats could never approach that level of betrayal.

That was good. Michael never wanted to be betrayed like that.

Marriage had always seemed to him like an invitation for such betrayals. Behold, for instance, what had happened to Alastair. But . . . he supposed marriage was not required to betray someone.

"Fuck." He sat back down on the bed, the ugly word still ringing in his ears.

His father had tried to walk away from their mother. She had fought back against his abandonment—for the custody of her children, which she had lost; for money to live on, which she had been denied; and above all, for her dignity, though in the end, the publicity attached to her legal efforts had destroyed that, too. She had not been able to move in public without being cursed and accosted. *Loose*: Michael had not known the word could be a slur until he'd heard it applied to his mother by his classmates. *Whore. Slut.*

She'd been none of those things. But such were the ways of the world, which cared little for facts—or creativity—when it came to condemning a woman.

One rotter is much the same as the next, Elizabeth had said to him. *Did you imagine you were somehow different?*

He was *not* his father's son. Not in the ways that counted. He'd done wrong by her? Then he was not going to walk away before he made it right.

He lay back down, staring at the ceiling. She needed money. How was that? He could not imagine that her parents would have wed her to Chudderley were the man unable to support her in style.

Well, whatever the cause, she needed money. He would not quarrel with that; he would never scorn a woman's mercenary concerns. He had seen what the want of funds might do, even to a lady of high birth. His mother had possessed friends in the highest places, but they had not, in the end, protected her. Poverty was not *fashionable*.

He'd been too young to help his mother. Had she not died while he was at university—well, medicine would not have been his choice. Instead he would have made it his business to make money, the better to see her comfortable. He would not have depended on Alastair for that. Alastair had been too inclined to take the middle road, to strike compromises, to claim their father had his own reasons that mitigated his sins.

No, he would never have trusted Alastair with their mother's surety. But instead she had sickened, and Michael had loathed and mistrusted the bumbling doctors' treatments, and so he'd decided to learn how he could help her recover.

He'd learned too late. She was gone by the time he'd entered his practice. But if he had not been able to help her, he could help now. He had no money to give Elizabeth, but he had knowledge of men who did. Weston, in particular.

The pain in his knuckles startled him. His hands had curled into fists. He forced them to flatten on the sheets. His own feelings were immaterial in this. He *had no money*. And Alastair would never approve of her. God, no. His brother was too much a pompous prig to give her a single chance.

So. He would do this. And then he would go back to London. For suddenly his exile seemed foolish. He had proved a point, but now he was no longer interested in protecting his own pride.

Weston. Weston it would be. A decent fellow. But Michael would wager he had never once thought of Elizabeth as a marriage prospect. Weston had such tedious tastes in women. Conventional femininity appealed to him. Knitting, and watercolors, and skill at the piano, and needlepoint . . .

A smile twitched his lips. He recalled her confession at their first meeting. No artist with a needle, she. Her flowers emerged as blobs.

But that talk wouldn't suit Weston. He would admire her wit only when it did not cut too sharply. Would be drawn to blushes rather than saucy flirtations. If she had a talent for the harp or piano, all the better.

She would need to know these things. So, tomorrow he would tell her. And he would begin, too, to work on Weston—encouraging the man's awareness, and ultimately aiding his courtship, of the woman whom Michael . . .

He rolled over to smother his groan in the pillow.

The woman whom he *owed*. And that was all it could be. That, he told himself, was *all*.

CHAPTER FOURTEEN

Liza was dressing when Mather burst in with the news: she had spotted Lord Michael strolling with Lord Weston on the east lawn. "Wasn't he supposed to have left?"

"Yes." Perhaps the exhaustion of another sleepless night had stupefied her, but Liza could muster only the smallest flicker of outrage. She knew he hadn't gone on to the station; the coachman's message had been awaiting her with her morning tea.

Perhaps . . . in some part of her . . . she was *relieved.* He had kept his promise not to go.

That did not mean she would let him stay, though. "I'll deal with him when I've dressed," she said, and dispatched Mather to go keep an eye on him.

Not half an hour later, Mather returned. "He has joined the breakfast table, madam. Mrs. Hull was . . . *loudly* delighted by his change of plans."

Liza now sat at the dressing table, where Hankins was pinning up her hair. "Something simple," she murmured—archery and croquet did not support high style. "I suppose everyone thinks he's actually a proper guest, then."

"Yes, madam." Mather shifted her weight. "Shall I have the footmen toss him out?"

"No, of course not. I've told you, we mustn't cause a scene." Hankins stepped back, and Liza nodded her approval: a simple bun, high on her head, with a fringe of Josephine curls over her brow. "The pearl earrings," she said, and Hankins went to fetch them.

"He's eating all the food!" Mather was twisting her wrists. What she thought of Michael's sudden elevation in rank, Liza could only guess, but judging by the girl's ferocious scowl, she disliked being fooled as much as Liza did. "There were at least six eggs on his plate, by my count!"

Despite herself, Liza laughed. "Matters aren't quite so desperate as *that*, you know. Why, I believe we can even spare eight eggs, should his appetite require it."

"I thought you didn't wish him here!"

In the mirror, she watched her smile slip away. "You're right." Her humor was misplaced. *What is he about, here?*

A knock came at the door. Mather went to answer it, cutting off Hankins by two long strides.

Michael stood in the doorway.

Liza spun around on her stool. She was impressed, despite herself, by this newest evidence of his temerity. Finding his way to her bedchambers required the kind of audacity she'd thought native only to Americans.

"You can't come in here!" Mather hissed. "She's still dressing!"

"No," said Liza, "do let him in." She turned back toward her reflection, eyeing herself. She would not lose her temper today. Indeed, the memory of her distress last night was embarrassing. She'd reflected on it all through the night. That he had almost driven her to tears! She barely recognized herself around him.

That would not do. Her guests had come to Cornwall to be entertained by Elizabeth Chudderley, fashionable beauty, consummate hostess. Michael de Grey had sprung a surprise on her, but he would not manage to discompose her again.

She smiled at herself, very deliberately: the same smile she wore in all the photographs. *Your face is like a beautiful mask,* an admirer had once told her. *I can see nothing of your thoughts.*

It was quite the compliment. Only now did she realize that.

Michael came into view in the glass. "Good morning," he said.

"Another fine suit," she observed. Pinstripe, this one. "I suppose you must have an entire wardrobe hidden away. Did you think the countryside could not bear such well-cut jackets? I assure you, even mere doctors may dress well."

A rueful smile tipped his mouth. "Compliments to my wardrobe, when I came prepared to duck a vase. My luck is turning."

She sighed. "All my vases are carefully chosen. I regretted the loss the moment I threw it."

He caught the insult. "Not worth it, was I?"

She shrugged. Yes, her smile was holding.

"Perhaps your mind will change when you hear my proposal," he said.

Mather gave a violent start—interpreting the comment, no doubt, as an overture to seduction. Liza returned her scandalized look with a benign smile. "Mather, darling, I'll ask you and Hankins to leave us be for a few minutes." For her maid had just returned with the jewelry case, which Liza took before nodding toward the door.

"But—" The girl looked between them. "Madam, you're in your *dressing room*!"

"Then make certain not to tell everyone where we are," Liza said. "You shouldn't like to foment a scandal—or a marriage." She winked at Michael. "God knows that would serve neither of our purposes. Lord Michael requires a saintly virgin, and I . . . well, you know what I require."

Mather's mouth formed a perfect O. Hankins, who had seen worse—she had, after all, known Nello—took Mather's arm and guided her out.

Once the door had closed, Liza turned back toward her dressing table, busying herself with a jar of powder—dipping her brush, then carefully smoothing it over her skin. She had spoken truly to Katherine Hawthorne; these sleepless nights were very bad for the skin. "Your proposal, sir?" If he *was* bent on seduction, she had a laugh prepared for him.

"I propose to help you land Weston."

A puff of powder flew up, dispersing in a brief haze. "I beg your pardon?"

"I know him." Movement in the mirror: he took his hat out from beneath his arm, then turned it around in his hands. "From school. You're going about it wrong. He likes the demure ones. Blushes instead of quips."

"I see." She laid down the powder brush and reached for the rouge.

"No cosmetics, either."

Her hand stilled over the pot as her temper began to kindle. She welcomed its return; without it, she'd felt very much like a burned-out candle, cold and dark. "I believe I know how to snare a man's interest, but *thank* you for your advice."

He took a step toward her. "I mean what I say. You offered me friendship once. I mean to be a friend to you now. You need money. I have none. But I have knowledge that can help you secure it. And, more than that, I can influence Weston. Or Hollister, if you prefer. A well-placed comment here; a suggestion there."

She stared at her hand atop the rouge pot. A new freckle, damn it. Right atop her middle knuckle. "You mean to . . . help me win a husband."

"I do."

She glanced up at her own expression. A very pretty face, though too round to belong to a great beauty. With Michael's cheekbones, age might not have terrified her so. But she still looked young, though perhaps that was a trick of the emotion on her face. Surely only the young were still vulnerable to such a great and illogical sense of *hurt*.

She blinked very rapidly, then reached for the earring case. So. Her lover—her former, one-time lover—wished to help her secure the attentions of another man. "How amusing," she made herself say. The pearls were slippery, troublesome little devils. One of them simply did not want to go in.

Suddenly he was behind her. "Let me," he said, and the air carried the warmth and scent of him, that faint musk that her body had grown to know. He bent down and she froze, disbelieving, strangely unable to protest. *Get away.*

His breath coasted across her cheek. His fingers gently brushed over her hair and a shiver rippled through her. His touch on her earlobe was warm and light. Large hands, so skilled at delicate operations. The earring slid through her piercing. His mouth—it must have been an accident—brushed the rim of her ear as he withdrew.

Her hands hovered uselessly over the dressing table. She let them fall to her lap as she exhaled.

The silence felt charged with something unspeakable and fragile. Yet it seemed to accumulate weight by the second, until her throat was full and she needed to swallow. When she braced herself sufficiently to look at his face in the glass, his eyes were shut. But he opened them immediately, as though he felt her regard.

"They become you," he said. He visibly swallowed. "The earrings."

She managed a faint smile. He looked ridiculously out of place in her dressing room. In another mood, she might have appreciated how the light through the lace curtains limned his tall, broad-shouldered body.

He was clutching his hat so tightly that the brim was bending.

The realization touched off a strange welling in her breast—regret mixed with . . . other things, undeserved and unwelcome. Sympathy.

And longing.

"You want to help me find a husband," she said.

Was that a flash of pain she saw in his face? No. She must be imagining it. His jaw squared. "Yes," he said.

The syllable was adamant. He had no doubts. "Then don't look at me like that," she said.

He laughed softly and turned to the window. A muscle flexed in his jaw. Then he faced her again. "I could say the same to you."

"But that would be unwise," she said. "For as I told you, you were only an afternoon's distraction."

"Indeed." He took a deep breath, then his eyes crinkled at the corners as he smiled. Devastating smile. It caught at her heart like a hook. "A very pleasant distraction, but a fleeting one."

A pang ran through her, which she ignored. They were striking a bargain here, in coded language. "Nearly forgotten by now," she said, to test him.

"Circumstances being what they are," he agreed.

Very well, they would be civilized about this. She would not throw him out; he would not make a scene. She closed the earring case, running her fingers along the velvet nap. "Circumstances can be so annoying. Always popping up. But I suppose they can be managed civilly. Between friends."

They looked at each other another moment in the mirror. Then, on a deep breath, she rose and turned toward him. He was a full head taller, but from this distance, standing did give her some advantage. She felt firmer on her feet, and firmer yet when she did not have to look at her own reflection and see what was revealed there. "Your brother will find out you're here," she said. "The Hawthornes posted a dozen letters this morning."

He sighed. "I'd foreseen that. But it's time I came out of hiding. I received a letter he'd written . . . it seems my brother has decided to increase the stakes in this ridiculous game. Or perhaps I'm wrong to call it a game, for he . . ." He shook his head, and she felt a weird shock to see him look so openly troubled.

My brother raised me. Suddenly she remembered him telling her so, that long-ago day when they had visited the Browards', before Mary's baby had come. Some ancient scandal had surrounded his father, the late Duke of Marwick . . . a very public, very unhappy divorce. It came to her now, sending another shock through her. *My brother raised me.* Why, he'd told her more that day than she had known to listen for.

She gritted her teeth. Civility was one thing. Compassion was going *much* too far. "I know very little of your brother," she said. "But he does not strike me as forgiving."

"Be that as it may," he said, "I cannot afford to hide any longer." He hesitated. "In fact . . . in that regard, perhaps you might help me."

"Oh?" She couldn't think of how.

"Mrs. Hull seems a respectable sort," he began, and everything in her tightened as though in preparation for a blow. "Do I have that right? No rumors circulating about her that I've yet to hear?"

No. No, no . . . "No," she said with great difficulty. "I suppose she hasn't spent enough time with me yet."

His slight smile was his only acknowledgment of that barb—which, belatedly, horrified her. She would not betray herself that way. Never would she make herself the target of her own unkind witticisms. "Then she's precisely what I require," he said. "Some pretty pretext to keep my brother appeased. I will make a point of paying particular attention to her. Perhaps even drop a few unguarded compliments to her in the Hawthornes' presence. Word should travel quickly."

"No need for that." She felt removed from herself, suddenly, speaking by some script designed to keep conversation flowing when she'd much rather be alone, alone in some dark, shuttered room. *Jane Hull.* "I can write letters, too. I have a very full roster of gossiping friends. Shall I say you've stated your intentions, or shall I paint your interest to be of the fledgling variety?"

"Somewhere in between," he said after a moment. He nodded. "Yes—say that I've spoken highly of her, and made discreet inquiries about her prospects. Does that sound right?"

"Yes, very believable." This conversation needed to end. *Now.* Yet her mouth kept moving. "You think your brother would approve of a widow, then?"

He paused before replying, as though widowhood— the mere fact of ill luck—might indeed cast a black mark on a lady. "I should think her previous marriage would not disqualify her," he said. "At the least, he'll not be able to object straightaway. And that's the main thing—to keep him occupied."

"Right." She felt light-headed. Where was her anger? She should be angry. "Well, then . . . I should go down to breakfast, I think."

"Of course. Now that the bargain has been struck." He came toward her, holding out his hand, and for a second she was too much a coward to take it.

But she forced a smile onto her lips and shook his hand, his callused palm pressing against hers all too briefly before he retrieved it.

Yes. She could do this. She *would* do this. There was no choice in it.

He smiled back at her. "And so we will be friends again," he said. "Comrades with a common cause."

"To our joint victory, then," she said, and gestured him out the door.

*   *   *

Since mysticism was best experienced after dark, Liza had instructed the spiritualists to remain concealed throughout the day. To keep her guests amused, she had scheduled a variety of entertainments: lawn tennis, bowling, and shooting at clay birds; a picnic luncheon by May Lake . . . nothing too original, but the company made all the difference.

As it transpired, the company was game for anything so long as champagne was provided. Nigel and Katherine (who, experience told Liza, would drink until she slurred her words; nap until sober; and then reappear for another drink) began the fun by challenging Jane and Tilney to a game of tennis. Already Katherine's steps were slightly unsteady, which made the game quite entertaining to watch—to say nothing of her terrible, or perhaps very *accurate,* aim. Three times in the first five minutes, Jane was forced to duck to avoid a black eye.

Down the field, far enough not to disturb the tennis match, Lady Forbes and Lord Hollister practiced their gunmanship, aiming their shotguns at the clay pheasants shot up from behind a small fence erected for the occasion. The regular punctuation of explosions added to the festive flavor, as did the growing evidence that between the two shooters, Lady Forbes possessed the superior aim.

The archery butts drew no interest. The remainder of the guests—apart from the Sanburnes, who were once again suspiciously *absent*—loitered beneath striped awnings beside the tennis court, sipping drinks and nibbling on dishes of fresh strawberries and clotted cream. Conversation flowed agreeably. Everybody who had seen

The Mikado deemed it perfectly splendid. The recent appointment of Cecil as prime minister occasioned a heated debate over Irish Home Rule that Liza put to an end by calling for a toast to good company. The weather was marvelous. Nobody thought it would rain tomorrow.

Slowly she worked her way toward Weston, who had broken off during the Home Rule debate to converse privately with Michael. Her stomach felt strangely fluttery as she made her approach. The two men were of a height, but next to Weston's brawn, Michael's lean strength put her in mind of a greyhound.

Many women preferred bulk. She supposed it might be like oysters: one must learn to acquire the taste.

He glanced at her briefly as she joined them. The faint curve of his lips seemed somehow conspiratorial. And then, to prove it, he *winked*.

She was betting a great deal on the sincerity of his offer, because he could as easily sabotage as aid her.

She knocked aside the fluttering ribbons that trimmed her hat to show Weston her kindest smile. "Important talk?" If they were still on the Irish question, she was going to intervene.

"No other kind," said Weston.

"I suppose that depends on one's perspective," said Michael. "We were discussing horseflesh. Weston has recently been in the market." As the breeze ruffled his glossy brown hair, he tilted his head slightly, probably to shift the stray wisps from his eyes.

That mannerism struck her suddenly as painfully familiar. A lover would appreciate it for the excuse it provided to brush his hair away with her hand. She knew how his hair would feel, soft and smooth, warmed by the sun . . .

She curled her itching fingers into her palm. "But I love horses," she said brightly. "Have you found one to purchase?"

"There's a very promising stud I've my eye on," said Weston. "Dam Pandora, sire Apollonius."

"Ah!" She could speak to this. "The same Apollonius who won the Queen Anne Stakes four years ago?"

Weston's visible surprise gratified her. "Why, yes, the very same. Do you follow racing, then?"

"Yes, I—" But a look at Michael made her hesitate. He was shaking his head slightly. "That is, of course I read the papers." Until recently, she'd made a great sport of wagering, too. "That's bound to be a very profitable foal."

Michael, who had retreated a subtle pace from Weston's view, now winced.

"No doubt," said Weston. "Of course, I consider racing more an art than an industry."

She bit her cheek. *Bat your lashes,* Michael had instructed her on the way down the stairs. *Imagine yourself fresh from your mother's leading strings, wide-eyed and eager and naïve.*

She'd snorted at his advice. Everyone knew Weston was somewhat tightly buttoned, but she could imagine no model more unlikely to snag a man's interest.

Nevertheless . . . it was true that profit did not make a genteel motive. Very sweetly, she said, "Oh, I quite agree, Lord Weston. In fact, my admiration for horse-flesh is deplorably shallow. It's as simple as . . . some of them are very *pretty*."

As easy as that, Weston was smiling again. "Ah, yes. Ladies and their ponies."

Ponies? "Ladies and their ponies," she agreed. What on earth? She had not sat on a pony since her sixth birthday.

"I have a niece who demanded a snow-white mare, the better to pretend it was a unicorn." Weston's smile was softening, growing fond. "Insists on collecting every equine dolly she comes across. A great stable she has, all of them no taller than two feet high!"

She joined in with his laugh, though she did not, in truth, find it a particularly flattering comparison.

On the other hand, he was thinking of children in connection to her! And that could be nothing but encouraging. "Yes," she said, "how perfectly adorable ponies are!"

Weston cast a look over the parkland. "Prime country for hunting, here. I suppose you chase the foxes now and then?"

She stole a questioning glance at Michael, whose impassive expression now afforded her no clues. Surely Weston did not consider it unfeminine to hunt? That would make him the oddest Englishman she ever knew.

Oh, this was rubbish. She was not going to second-guess *everything* she said. Michael was not so credible a witness as *that*. "I have been known to hunt," she said. "I confess, more for the chase than the kill."

Weston chuckled and shot a wry look toward Michael. Abruptly she became aware of the double meaning in her statement. Such a remark might also come from the mouth of a committed bachelor . . . or a merry widow.

But Weston, thankfully, did not remark on the unintended humor. "Have you scheduled a hunt for us, then?"

She had not. She truly did not like the slaughter of foxes.

Inspiration struck. "No, I haven't, for foxes are too,

too adorable to kill," she said. "Nearly as adorable as horses! And—they put me in mind of dogs," she added quickly, for Weston was blinking as though amazed. Drat it—foxes *were* darling. And if he did not like dogs, he was a Frenchman in disguise. "Puppies!" she said. "I do so love *puppies*!"

Weston shrugged. "A pity, of course, that they do tend to grow up. Shed hair all over the place. But foxes, you know, are vermin."

"Weston always has three or four behemoths in his drawing room," said Michael. "Monstrous ugly dogs. I don't think he ever combs them."

She nodded politely, willing her smile—and her out-fit, a cream lawn suit with cunning pink trimming—to veritably *scream* her girlish charm. "I adore all kinds of animals," she said. "Anything . . . fluffy."

Good God. She felt her smile waver toward a grimace.

Weston was studying her, his expression one of be-nign amusement. "Is that so? Can it be that our famous Mrs. Chudderley, toast of all the town, was also once a girl who dreamed of unicorns?"

Was that a veiled joke about her virginity? She blinked innocently. "What girl does not long for a uni-corn, sir? Why, perhaps I still want one!"

His brief laugh smacked of surprise. "Goodness! That's a—well, I must say, Mrs. Chudderley, I never imagined that you might be . . ."

She waited for him to finish that sentence—which, in all fairness, might as easily turn into an insult as a compliment. But he trailed off, turning toward Michael as though in search of aid. Michael stepped forward im-mediately.

"Mrs. Chudderley is many things," Michael said as

his eyes met hers, "all of which surpass a mere mortal's ability to imagine."

Look away, she told herself. *Now.* But she was as helpless as a snake before its charmer. His eyes were the most extraordinary, heart-piercing blue. And he was making no move to look away, either.

"Very prettily put," said Weston. His transparent relief at being rescued did not, precisely, cheer her. But it did free her from the spell. She looked out over the lawn, and when she peeked back, Michael was frowning in the direction of the tennis match.

As for Weston, he seemed disinclined to speak again, and the silence began to strike Liza as awkward. She cast about for another topic, increasingly frustrated when nothing came to mind. This was so unlike her! She wished Michael would walk away; she could not focus with him standing there.

The lull was shattered by a cry from the direction of the tennis game. Liza turned in time to see Jane regaining her feet with Baron Forbes's aid. Somewhat mysteriously, her tennis racket lay about ten feet away. "Watch where you're aiming that!" she yelled.

Katherine, on the other side of the net, gave a toss of her head. "The point is to *hit it back*."

"I do believe someone's going to die on that court," Michael remarked. "One solid strike to the temple . . ."

"Had no idea tennis could be so gladiatorial," Weston replied. "Are you prepared to play doctor?"

"I don't *play* at it, Weston."

Was that . . . a note of aggression? "I imagined you would be the first on the tennis court," she said quickly to Weston. "Do the rumors mislead me? I hear you're a great sportsman!"

"Such kind rumors," said Weston, "that I believe it would be rude to deny them. No, you're quite right, madam; spectatorship has never been my strength." Good heavens, was that a subtle flex of his arms he'd just performed? *That* was encouraging. "I've already challenged de Grey to a match."

"Which you will lose," Michael said cheerfully.

"That would be a first," said Weston, just as cheerfully.

The two men locked eyes, grinning fiercely. Oh, dear. Masculine rivalry. Well, she knew how to take advantage of that.

With a gentle, fleeting touch to Weston's elbow, she said, "I have every faith in you, sir."

"As you should," he said, a touch too seriously. "This one may look strapping, but I promise you, at university, he was a perfect stranger to the playing fields."

"Imagine that," said Michael. "I rather thought we were there to learn."

"And what can't you learn on the playing fields?" Weston demanded. "Honor, courage, proper bottom, a sporting spirit—"

"Oh, indeed," said Michael. "All of which would be very helpful when I'm playing doctor. *What ho, a fever? Well, chin up, man; can't let down the team!*"

"Always had his nose in a book," Weston said to her, then tsked and shook his head.

She managed a distracted smile at this bait, but her mind was wandering. Michael as a bookish boy: the image rather caught her off guard. What had he been like in his youth? Gangly and gawky, she would wager. But already dedicated; already unlike any of the other men of his class that she had known. It made sense that he would have been studious: one did not become a doctor by following the usual path by which the nobility traveled through their university days—namely, drinking, wenching, and sporting.

"Ah, that's us," said Weston—for Jane had stalked off the court, and Katherine and Tilney were jeering. "Shall we, de Grey?"

She mustered herself to the task. After another brief touch to Weston's elbow, she ducked her head as though her own temerity had abashed her. "Good luck, Lord Weston."

"Oh, I won't need it," he said briskly—a rather off-putting kind of reply.

Michael gave her another wink, to which she replied with the haughty lift of one brow.

As they walked off, she turned to watch them. For a self-proclaimed athlete, Weston moved with a strange stiffness, almost as if he had a steel rod in place of his spine. Very little swivel to his hips, either. A very . . . masculine walk, she supposed. Whereas Michael . . .

Michael *strode*. His movements were decisive. His stride firm and long-legged.

His hips moved fluidly.

He would make an excellent dancer. She already knew what else those hips could accomplish.

She swallowed and turned on her heel. High time to go find Hollister.

CHAPTER FIFTEEN

During a lazy luncheon by the lake, Liza sussed out Hollister's potential. They sat beneath an umbrella large enough to screen them both from the sun—a blessing, for he was paler than she, in that manner only dark-haired Irishmen could achieve, his mother, he explained without embarrassment, having hailed from Cork. She decided she admired a self-made man. His eyes were a pleasant, mossy hazel, and nobody would find fault with his features, which were finely, even exquisitely molded. If anything, he was *too* handsome, for a lady did not like to be outranked in that regard.

She forgave him for it, though, because she liked his manner better than Weston's. He had sculpted lips made for sneering, and his humor matched his capacity: his wit was sharp and his repartee tremendously delicious. On their stroll together back to the house, he commented on Jane Hull, walking ahead of them, her head close to Michael's: "Climbing like ivy," he said, "and no blade to hand. Do you mean to fetch one?"

She cut him a surprised look, but after a quick calculation, did not pretend to misunderstand him. "I have no designs on Lord Michael," she said.

He lifted his brow briefly. "I do admire bluntness in a woman."

She'd imagined he would. He was something of a climber himself—a financier who had all but purchased his title. That he should judge Jane for similar ambitions struck her as curious and perhaps concerning. "And what of feminine ambition? Do you approve of that as well?"

"Certainly," he said. "Though I will admit I reserve my admiration for the more subtle displays."

His faint smile left no doubt that he recognized her flirtations as the overture to her own ambitions.

Feeling so transparent might normally irritate her. But his frankness left her peculiarly unruffled. When he took her arm to help her over a very unthreatening tree root, she turned her hand in his grasp just so, the better to drag her fingers suggestively over his palm when he released her again.

His smile faded, the look he gave her turning somewhat hotter. But it called forth only the mildest physical reply in her—nothing to compare to the pull she'd so recently known.

She forced away the beginning of a frown. Ahead, Michael was making no similar attempt to touch Jane. A very stupid part of her was gratified by that. The rest of her was irked. If he wanted her aid in circulating rumors of his interest, he needed, at the least, to *act* interested.

Back at the house, she went to her rooms to bathe and rest. After a few lazy hours set aside for unscheduled amusements, the guests once again assembled in the larger drawing room, this time to be entertained by the clairvoyant, Signora Garibaldi.

The signora, dark and sloe-eyed and quite trim for a woman of about fifty, might have passed easily for an Italian had her craft not required her to speak. When she did, her vowels slid madly across a geography that had never existed in the real world: a curious combination of France, Trieste, and the slums of London.

For all its unlikely provenance, her low, growling voice caused the assembly to quiet immediately. "I have been summoned here tonight by Madam Chudderley," she said, pulling her black lace shawl—a peculiarly Spanish touch—tighter around a gown of plain black wool, cut high at the throat and loose over her waist and hips, reminiscent in its own way of the habit of medieval nuns. "But I do not come to serve her. I serve no one and nothing but Truth."

Oh, that was very good. Liza stepped back a little from the cluster of guests, discreetly watching as two footmen circulated the perimeter of the room, turning down the gas lamps and lighting great branches of candles in their stead.

"Must we endure this without a drink?" came Sanburne's voice in her ear.

She felt disinclined to humor him. Not turning, she said, "Oh, you're still here? I wondered if you and Lydia had gone back to London."

"Went for a walk around ten in the morning," he said cheerfully. "It turned out to be longer than expected."

"Oh, I'm *certain*. Will I hear scandalized reports from some farmer whose crops you crushed?"

"No, but Lydia is absolutely fascinated with these cairns. She'd never been to Cornwall. Can you imagine?"

She glanced over at his sigh. He had a dreamy, distracted look on his face. She followed his attention and discovered his wife creeping through the doorway, still smoothing her evening gloves over her elbows.

Liza cleared her throat. "James, it simply grows embarrassing now."

"In what regard?" He sounded genuinely puzzled.

"The way you fawn on her. You're in friendly company, of course—"

"Yes, the Hawthornes would make our lord and savior *weep* with approval."

"You'll be mocked to kingdom come, all right, if you carry on in town this way."

"Oh, come now, Lizzie. Are you saying a man can't be madly in love with his wife?"

Another voice replied for her: "It runs contrary to popular wisdom," said Michael as he stepped up.

"And how goes that wisdom?" asked James.

Michael shrugged. "Why, that marriage is the quickest cure for love."

"Ah, yes," said James. "I believe I've heard you say that before. One would hope you'd developed some new witticisms since your school days. If you'll excuse me . . ." And with a bow to the both of them, he crossed the room to join his wife, who was listening to the signora's low speech. Indeed, everybody looked rapt save Jane, who was leaning around the baron to steal a peek at Michael.

Liza squared her shoulders. "You're doing terribly," she said. "I didn't see you touch her once today."

"Must I touch her?" He looked surprised. "I spoke to nobody else at the picnic."

"You were lecturing her on medical hygiene!"

He pulled a face. "She asked me whether it wasn't true that soap was injurious to the skin. Really, Elizabeth, I don't know where you found her—"

"She's sharper than she seems. Perhaps if you'd treat her as though you take her seriously, instead of preaching at her as though she were a child who didn't know to wash her hands—"

His hand closed on her arm, exerting a subtle pressure that forced her to turn toward him. In this dim, temperamental light, his face was mostly lost in shadow; she saw only half of his rueful smile. "And now you're instructing me on how to flirt? Perhaps I should return the favor. Does Hollister really wish to know the mineral composition of your properties?"

She tried to tug free, but his grip only tightened. "He's a businessman," she said. "He expressed an interest in the state of the mining industry in these parts."

"Oh, and I'm sure he has no employees to answer such questions." His gaze dipped to her mouth. "In fact—I'm wrong. Probably wouldn't have mattered if you'd nattered on in gibberish. He simply wanted to watch your lips move as you spoke."

For some reason the implicit compliment irritated her. She jerked free. "Actually, I think he was *quite* intrigued by what I had to say. He complimented me on being so learned. Imagine that: a man more enamored with my brain than with my face!"

He frowned. "And you think I'm not?"

She huffed out a breath. "Recall yourself, Michael. Your interests are not my concern."

A titillated murmur rose behind them. For one horrible second she feared that everyone had overheard her—that their reaction was for this silly spat.

But, no, Signora Garibaldi had issued some apparently impressive pronouncement. The space around her had widened considerably, as though everybody had taken a step back.

Liza exhaled. Suddenly she felt very foolish. What was she doing over here, quarreling with him? Quarreling like . . . lovers?

"Take heart," Michael said. "I had it from Weston that Hollister longs to settle down with a woman who will help him win a welcome in the more fashionable corners of society. I imagine you might qualify . . . even if he hasn't looked this way once."

"How kind of you to keep track for me," she said through her teeth. "But don't trouble yourself. If you'll watch, now, you'll see that I require no aid in my own flirtations."

As she walked away, she caught his murmur: "Oh, I'm always watching."

His words sent a shiver of pleasure up her spine. She tried to battle it down as she stepped into hearing range—and then promptly forgot it as she absorbed what the signora was actually saying.

"A great war," she said, her eyes closed, her brow knit fiercely. "Blood in the fields, blood and iron and smoke, unnatural smoke, smoke that kills with the first breath—"

Good God! This was not at all the thing! "Signora," Liza said stridently, but then Weston cut her off.

"Germans, I'd wager? It must be the bloody Germans!"

"*Ja,*" affirmed the signora, "*ohne jeden Zweifel*"—evidencing in the process that her accent did *not* stretch so far east as Germany. *Without a doubt,* she'd said, but she'd mangled it almost beyond recognition.

"And now for something a bit more *cheerful*, please," said Liza.

"Oh, but it's terribly interesting," called Lydia. "She was speaking of giant iron horses, which, as you may know, is also the phrase by which many Indian tribes in North America refer to trains."

"I wonder if this army shall be transported chiefly by train, then," said Baroness Forbes.

"Why not in a magical puff of poisonous smoke?" drawled Tilney. "Emitted, no doubt, by very large dragons."

Titters went up from the Hawthornes, and as simply as that, the eerie mood was dispelled. Signora Garibaldi opened her eyes and drew a great breath. "The vision fades now. But if you'll give me a moment . . ." Encountering Liza's glare, she visibly started. "Ah—that is, I am seeing a new vision. A vision of . . ."

"Love?" suggested Jane shyly. Weston beamed at her, and she ducked her head, blushing.

Drat it. How did she so perfectly manage that routine? Liza unobtrusively edged closer to Hollister, who was idly examining his nails.

"Oh, yes, love," said the signora gustily. "I see . . . so much of it. Fated, destined. Give me your hand, child!" She reached toward Jane.

"We have hired a palmist," Liza said pointedly. Jane's fortune was *not* the one at stake here.

"But of course," the signora said smoothly as she withdrew. "Then let me see . . . oh! A vision of *you*, Madam Chudderley!"

Oh, that was too transparent. She did not like how Katherine was smirking. "Why not Miss Hawthorne?" she asked, gesturing toward the woman. "Has the vision any bearing on her?"

As the clairvoyant obediently turned, Hollister leaned down to murmur in her ear. "Have *you* some mystical powers, madam? For you seem curiously able to direct these visions."

She gave a light laugh. "And if I did, would I tell you, sir? A woman must guard her mysteries."

"Perhaps true," he said, "if her mysteries are few in number. But I feel certain that a man could study you at his leisure and never find himself short on the most . . . pleasant brands of speculation."

She felt a very agreeable quickening of her pulse. Was Michael watching? Against her better judgment, she took a quick glance over her shoulder.

He was staring at her as though no one else was in the room.

Breathless now, she turned back to Hollister. He had followed her look, which was a very bad piece of luck. "I do wonder why some people refuse to join in the fun," she said brightly. "As the hostess, I can do only so much. Merriment, I think, is an inborn talent."

Hollister recovered his smile. "One that you possess in full measure, I think. Your invitation made me the envy of all my friends."

From the corner of her eye, she saw Weston turning to focus fully on Jane. Very well, let her have him. "And your acceptance won me the envy of all of mine," she replied.

Hollister's eyes narrowed slightly. He gave her a slow, deliberate smile.

And so it begins. On a thrill of triumph, she set her hand lightly atop his arm. "Would you walk with me around the room, sir? Perhaps we might learn whether our mutual envies were justified."

"It would be my pleasure." He tucked her fingers more firmly into the crook of his elbow before leading her along the wall.

He was witty. Open in his interest. Surprisingly erudite for a financier. And as she parried his repartee, her attention grew curiously divided. Half of her laughed and flirted and focused on her posture, shoulders down, spine straight, the better to show her figure to its best advantage. The other half fixated on the man who stood on the opposite side of the room, watching so closely that she could *feel* his attention, like the stroke of a finger along her cheek.

It . . . affected her. Of course every woman carried with her the constant knowledge that she was being watched, her actions evaluated and judged. But Liza had never set out to woo one man under another man's auspices. To have Michael's eyes on her as she flirted . . . it felt, to her growing unease, deeply erotic.

It should not be so. She should not find herself angling her face so he could see her smiles as clearly as Hollister could. Should not find her glance wandering to him every time Hollister bent to murmur in her ear.

But every time she looked over, his eyes remained fixed on her. And it was not her imagination that his face grew stonier and stonier.

Perhaps he had *more* than half her attention, for when he abruptly stepped away from the wall and launched himself into the group still riveted to the clairvoyant, her words hitched. The barest pause. She recovered herself almost instantly. ". . . But I prefer Monte Carlo," she said. Where was he going? *To Jane.* Of course! Well, it was high time he took her advice. "The stakes are higher, and if one enjoys gambling, there's really no other place to do it."

"You're preaching sin to the Devil," said Hollister. "I am a gambler not only by trade but also by nature, Mrs. Chudderley. Having made a fortune wagering on the market, I intend to make several more, for the sheer pleasure of knowing that I can."

His frankness grew more startling by the moment. "Very bold," she said. "You must know such talk will not endear you in these circles."

"Ah, but I have no great interest in these circles," said Hollister. "I am speaking only to you now, am I not?"

That comment finally riveted her entire interest. She eyed him, suddenly uncertain. He spoke almost as if he knew her predicament—and was listing his qualities as though to persuade her that *he* was the solution.

Why should that unsettle her? Shouldn't that properly be a very welcome relief?

"I certainly don't carry tales," she said finally. "If that is what you mean. Your words are safe with me, sir."

He laughed. "Oh, you may tell whomever you like, Mrs. Chudderley. I do not apologize for myself to anyone."

She blinked very rapidly. That was *her* philosophy.

"But I will confess to you," he went on, "that I should be most disheartened if you felt I *should* apologize for it. For I thought I'd found in you a kindred spirit." His smile lingered as he looked her over, his appreciation so frankly sexual that she felt her pulse skip once despite herself. "A woman unafraid to flout convention, and to embrace—how did you put it? Ah, yes: an inborn talent for merriment."

She should be encouraged. For he was handsome, and confident, and he *did* seem a kindred spirit—and the very kind of man she would have been, had nature given her the opportunity. How much better to gamble on the market than on marriage!

Yet her unease only grew. She slipped free of his arm. "That sounds like the prelude to a proposition—and not, perhaps, the proper kind."

"Then you mistake me," he said. "There are easier places to seek a brief affair than a country house in Cornwall."

She stared at him. Her heart was beating very quickly, disbelief being the goad. Hollister was all but dancing around the main question—and so quickly!

Too quickly. He knew nothing of her.

"From the moment I first saw those photographs of you," he said in a murmur, "I knew I'd found a woman who knew her own worth."

"Ridiculous!" This bellow came from Baron Forbes, causing them both to turn. All the people gathered around the clairvoyant were shaking their heads.

She manufactured a laugh. "What can she be saying now?" she asked. "More talk of a strange war?" She was infinitely grateful for the distraction. *Those dratted photographs.* He had fallen in love with her face.

But why should she feel so stung by disappointment? Her face was her greatest hope, was it not? She had always depended on it.

"It will be war, or love, or an unexpected fortune," drawled Hollister. "Perhaps a long-lost family member. These performers have their set routines."

"I believe what Mrs. Hull wishes to know is whether she will find her *soul mate,*" said Weston loudly.

Jane covered her eyes with one gloved hand, precious as a kitten. "Oh, goodness," she said. "Do not tease me so!"

Michael was finally feeling competitive, Liza saw, for

he stepped forward to gently pry Jane's hand from her face. "Don't be shy," he said, in tones so rich with affection that a brief, startled silence fell over the room. "You've every right to be curious."

Katherine and Nigel Hawthorne exchanged a speaking look.

"Well," said Liza. That remark had served its purpose, and suddenly she had no more stomach for flirtation. Not without several glasses of wine first. "Shall I ring for refreshment?"

At ten the next morning, Liza swept into the entry hall, lowering her voice in case it carried up the stairs. "Any notable mail?"

Ronson lifted a brow to telegraph his disapproval, but he had the pile ready for her, promptly handing it over.

She thumbed through it quickly, one eye out for her guests. She was keeping track of who was writing letters to whom. Tilney *and* Katherine Hawthorne had written to Nello—but not Nigel or anybody else. It was good to know who were her friends, and who were mere spies.

One particular letter gave her pause. It was addressed to His Grace, the Duke of Marwick, in a hand she had never seen before. The penmanship was bold, confident, but not at all elegant.

Ronson cleared his throat. "From Lord Michael, ma'am."

Yes. She would have guessed that he would write like this. His script somehow conjured the way he walked. She could see it in her mind's eye, that confident, aggressive pace.

How starkly it contrasted with his manner when

he spoke of Marwick. This letter might contain a bold challenge, but she would wager what remained of her assets that instead it expressed his earnest concern.

They had not spoken again last night after the clairvoyant's talk had turned to soul mates. He had been too busy showing his particular considerations for Jane, and she . . . She had taken respite in her obligations as hostess. Sparing smiles here and there for Hollister, for she meant to keep him on the hook, she had drifted from person to person, producing her best witticisms, her most daring jokes.

The evening had been a great success. Jane had looked very gratified by Michael's attentions.

Liza had been sure to drink enough to fall directly to sleep on her return to her rooms.

But he had stayed up. He had stayed up to write a letter to his brother, who certainly did *not* deserve letters from him.

The impulse was on her to go find him. To ask him what he had written. He had looked so troubled when speaking of Marwick . . . and he had nobody to talk to about it, for he was keeping the secret of his brother's odd behavior from everybody.

Everybody except her.

She bit her lip. She did not want to feel tender toward him. But one could not help but admire a love that survived bullying and threats. Such loyalty spoke so *well* of him.

Bah! What was she *doing*? She thrust the letters back at Ronson. "If you see Mather, tell her I've gone to consult the palmist," she said briskly. She meant to ensure there would be no more talk of wars, and smoke, and *Germans*.

*   *   *

Michael made a late start to the morning. He'd been up for hours composing a testing letter to his brother—a few bland, careful lines to hint at an interest in a demure young widow. Easier said than done to compose bait that did not also seem like a challenge or a taunt.

As he walked through the gallery, bound for a late breakfast, he caught sight of Elizabeth hurrying down the hall ahead of him. Instantly he withdrew behind a statue, guided by some fleeting instinct. The look she threw over her shoulder before rounding the corner rewarded his suspicion: it struck him as distinctly furtive.

He wrestled with an impulse to follw. That letter had not been the only thing to keep him stewing into the wee hours. It was clear to him now that he had a bad case of . . . jealousy. Was she stealing off to find Hollister?

The thought made him impatient with himself. If she was pursuing her prospect, it was none of his business. He was hungry. He should be at the dining table, making calf eyes at Jane.

Ah, but curiosity was the devil. He stepped silently out from his hiding place and stole after her. As he turned the corner, he caught sight of her climbing the stairs above. "Oh!" she said, and drew to a stop to address someone out of view. "Miss Trelawney! There you are!"

He stepped beneath the staircase to listen.

"I was looking for you," she went on. "Did you not receive my note?"

The reply was too soft to make out, but after a moment, the stairs creaked: Elizabeth and her companion were coming back down.

He withdrew farther into the cramped space, and in the process, nearly knocked a Roman bust off its pedestal. Damned strange place to hide it. The senator, noseless but still resplendent in his wreath of laurels, glared reproachfully.

"—compose my thoughts," came a serene female voice, not Elizabeth's. "A clear head helps me receive the messages from beyond."

One of the spiritualists, then.

The creaking ceased. From the sound of it, they were standing directly over his head. "About that," said Elizabeth. The uncharacteristic hesitance in her voice caused his ears to perk. "I was wondering if perhaps . . ."

"Perhaps?" came the polite reply. This one sounded quite young.

"Perhaps you might direct the visions a bit."

He swallowed a laugh. The little rogue! Her intervention last night had been too public; now she employed more surreptitious measures.

The spiritualist did not catch on as quickly as he had. "Oh, no," she said earnestly, "I can't control what I see in a person's palm. I would strongly urge you to mistrust any who claim to be able to summon specific knowledge—"

"Yes, yes, I understand that the—spirits or what have you—rove where they may," said Elizabeth. "However, for the sake of my guests, I do wonder if you might not focus your insights *specifically* on matters of the heart."

A pause. "The palm does have much to tell us about love," came the cautious reply.

Well spoken, Miss Trelawney.

"Mm," said Elizabeth. "Splendid. Mind you, though, there's a certain lady in our group, recently widowed, who would not be able to bear such discussion if it concerns her specifically. I believe it would, in fact, *offend* her should you predict a successful romance in her future. Mrs. Hull is her name. Young, very blond. Barely out of mourning, you know."

He frowned. Was she working against him now? Or did she mean to divert Weston's attention from Jane? Yesterday she'd seemed quite intent on Hollister.

"I see," said Miss Trelawney. "I should not like to offend, of course."

"Indeed not! But as for the rest of us—well, I would say that I, for instance, am *perfectly* willing to receive any happy news provided by your visions. Indeed, nothing could cheer me more greatly than to hear that my soul mate was in attendance at this very party!"

"Soul mate?"

"That's the term I've heard used, yes."

Weston had used it. Michael supposed that answered his question. He felt oddly cheered. He did not like Hollister in the least. Monopolizing jackass. Bent far too close to her when whispering.

"Soul mate." Said slowly, in accompaniment to a scribbling noise. Miss Trelawney, Michael realized with delight, was taking notes. "Any particular hair color?"

"Oh, goodness, I can hardly guess," Elizabeth said. "This is your talent, after all. Whether his hair is black or blond . . . there's simply no saying."

"The vision is hazy," Miss Trelawney said in tones of compassion.

"*Very* hazy, I assure you!"

"Well." More creaking as they resumed their descent. "Rest assured, madam, I have a great deal of practice in refining on such matters. You will not be disappointed."

All cozy warmth now between the two women. "Oh, I know I won't," Elizabeth exclaimed.

A long moment of silence followed, in which Michael began to wonder if they had slipped out through some exit he'd not yet noticed. But as he took a step toward fresher air, the conversation resumed, freezing him in place.

"There is *one* other thing," said Elizabeth, her voice much more distant now.

"Oh? Pray tell me, Mrs. Chudderley! I am here to entertain your every concern."

"A certain gentleman. Dark hair. Roman nose. Lord Michael is his name."

He grinned. *Roman?* That was . . . flattering. And had the dust at his feet parted to reveal a venomous asp, he would not have stirred an inch now.

"I do wonder," Elizabeth went on, "if he is not . . . in terrible need of some sign from the beyond."

"We all stand in need of guidance," Miss Trelawney said solemnly. After a beat, she added, "In which direction, do you suppose, does Lord Michael require encouragement?"

He waited, prepared to swallow his laugh as she threw out a suggestion sure to lacerate him.

"His brother. If you could subtly assure him his brother will be well, that would be . . . lovely, I think."

His humor died.

Miss Trelawney murmured some reassurance, and then the women's footsteps retreated. Silence closed over him again, deepening. Yet he could not move. He stood

there, feeling as brittle as glass, one hand still resting on
the Roman senator's head.

He had not expected that.

He did not deserve it.

He closed his eyes.

An afternoon's distraction. Nothing more.

What liars they were.

CHAPTER SIXTEEN

He'd found it easy last night—in the manner that a tooth extraction might feel easy—to witness Elizabeth's flirtations with Hollister. In a crowded room while some charlatan rattled off nonsense, it was . . . easy not to take such matters seriously. But now that he'd overheard her conference with the palmist, her every remark to the *eligible bachelors* grated on his nerves. He stewed silently over the noon meal, letting the repartee flow over and past him like so much flotsam and jetsam; feeling, at times, as though he'd lost the skill of smiling, so stiffly did his lips respond to the natural cues.

He begged off the boating expedition, and retired to his allotted chamber to read. Or to try to read. Instead he found himself sitting at the window, sulking like a young girl denied her supper, watching the trees for a glimpse of the party's return. And then, when that, too, became unendurable, he went to the writing desk and pulled out a sheaf of paper.

He'd written to Alastair yesterday, a cordial note that made no mention of their quarrel. But that was not his intention now.

I write to you, he began, *of a woman I have met. Your first impulse will be to disdain her. But if you are as wise as I once imagined you, and if even a shred of brotherly feeling remains to you, I beg you to read patiently. For I would make my choice.*

Four hours after dispatching this note to the staff, he caught the sounds of laughter and conversation floating up through the window. Looking out, he saw the boaters returning, Elizabeth arm in arm with both Weston *and* Hollister. She was talking animatedly, and had a wildflower stuck in her straw hat.

A man's pride was a damnable thing. It bucked like an unbroken colt at this sight. It bade him ring the bell and call for his letter to be returned. To be burned. *You choose her? She does not choose you.*

Instead he pulled on his jacket and stepped out of his room. It was time, he thought, to go hunting a widow.

He found her, after a half hour's search, alone on the terrace that overlooked the house garden. She was sipping a glass of wine and staring out at the sunset.

"Success?" he asked as he stepped out the doors.

Her laughter was edged. "Failure," she said as she turned toward him. "Miserable failure."

"It didn't look so from the window."

She took a swig from her wineglass. "Watching, were you? Hollister was attentive, but Weston—well, he's not so easy a target as you said. I tried my very best routine, innocently coquettish, bashful glances and all. Do you know what he asked me?"

"I can't imagine," he said as he walked toward her.

"Had I injured myself while boating? For I looked as though I had a terrible crick in my neck!"

He tried not to smile. "Perhaps he wanted to rub it."

"No, he's not so forward."

"True," he said after a moment. "Not sure there's a forward bone in his body, actually."

Their eyes met. She lifted her brows. "Oh, God above," he muttered. He slapped his palm against his forehead. "Terrible double entendre."

"I'll pretend I didn't catch it, shall I? So long as I'm aping modesty."

"Many thanks." But when he lifted his head again, he made no effort to hide his grin. Had he ever met another woman with whom he could jest with such pleasure? It wasn't only their silences that were comfortable. "Come now," he said, "he *really* asked if your neck was sore?" What a blockhead!

"Surely if I wanted to lie I'd have made up a more entertaining story than that," she said. "Or a more flattering one! Do I *look* as though I'm in pain?" She scrunched up her face and crossed her eyes.

He spluttered out a laugh. So simply she destroyed his dark mood. "Oh, very charming. Surprised nobody ever tried to photograph *that* look for sale in the high street."

She dropped the mugging and sighed as she turned back toward the parkland. "Those blasted photographs."

Her disgusted tone surprised him. He was feeling easier now, amenable to a gradual and casual introduction to the matter on his mind. Propping his elbows on the railing, he leaned forward, craning his head to get a look into her face. "Never say you don't enjoy your fame?"

"Enjoy it!" She shook her head and laughed under her breath. "They were one of the stupider exploits of my youth. Freshly widowed, dying to kick up my heels. My husband was not, shall we say, a free spirit."

He recalled Lady Forbes's words. "Bit of a killjoy, was he?"

"Killjoys are too animated," she said. "He was a stick-in-the-mud. Terribly staid. He liked the fact that I was pretty—until we wed. And then he disliked the fact that men tended to look at me. He was convinced I was doing something to encourage them. Which I wasn't," she added more softly. "But his accusations grew wearing. And once he was dead, I thought—why, let them look. Let them look as long as they like. For I *am* pretty, and I'll no longer apologize for it." She shrugged. "Mr. Readey—a photographer, quite fashionable a few years back—asked me to pose at just the right time."

"But you regret it now?"

She retrieved her wineglass from the ledge beneath the rail. "Well," she said into her burgundy, and then took a deep swallow. "I can't say I fancy the notion that every Tom, Dick, and Harry might fall asleep staring at my face. *If* you know what I mean."

He smiled despite himself, for he knew exactly what she meant. But it still came as a surprise to encounter a woman willing to allude to matters that women were not meant to know about.

His smile dropped as the implications struck him. If she knew how men pleasured themselves . . . then perhaps she had figured out how women might do it.

She gave him a look from under her lashes. "I wonder where your mind is wandering."

Her purr had much the same effect as her hand might have, between his legs. He shifted uncomfortably. "I don't think you want to know."

She eyed him a moment longer, the smile playing over her lips an added goad to his already fevered imagination. He swallowed a groan and trained his eyes on the green field rolling away toward the trees. If Alastair did not see reason, she would be another man's wife. For he had nothing to offer her. And these thoughts . . .

Oh, the hell with it. These thoughts would remain with him until he was old and gray and too infirm to do anything about them, even with her photograph as an aid. And he was—he drew a great breath—resigned to it. His letter today proved as much.

"My, what a sigh," she said lightly as he loosed his lungful. "Now I'm burning with curiosity." She took another long drink of her wine, and he wondered, not for the first time, if her drinking was a tell, as clear and predictable as a bad poker player's grimace.

Or perhaps it was medicine—a sort of anesthetic, for she looked away from his regard and said quietly, "To safer topics, perhaps."

"Indeed." He cleared his throat and straightened, gripping the rail now with his hands to give them something to do other than wander toward her. In the dying light, she looked gilded with gold, a sylvan creature, small and neatly curved and blemishless. But the beauty of her face—though it would, perhaps, always astonish him—no longer interested him nearly as much as the brain working behind it.

It was the brain he needed to figure out.

"So you've given up on Weston, then?" he said.

She shrugged. "No results."

"And Hollister?"

Her grimace was fleeting. "I should prefer Weston, I think. Hollister's regard is too . . . *marked.*"

That was a pretty piece of illogic, for eagerness would only serve her greater purpose. But he would not be the one to point out the error in her thinking. Indeed, he found the statement profoundly encouraging.

"Weston, then," he said. Privately, he now agreed with her: having observed Weston very closely these last few days, he'd noticed the man's attention growing particularly sharp whenever Jane Hull was about. "Don't give up on him yet. Perhaps you're simply going about it wrong."

"I told you—"

"Let me see what you're doing."

She flashed him a startled look. "The . . . coquettish look, you mean?"

"Precisely."

Her white teeth flashed, a grin that made her look properly girlish, indeed. "Really?"

He waved encouragement. "Give yourself a good start."

"Very well." She set down her wineglass and spun on her heel. Sashaying a few steps away, she cast over one shoulder a brief, coy look, her chin angled downward.

If Weston had not responded to that, he was dead inside.

"Terrible," he said. "You're smiling too much."

She spun back, her hands fisting on her hips. "I'm not smiling in the least!"

"Yes, you are. With only one side of your mouth, granted, but that's half a smile too much. Almost worse than a full smile, really, for it suggests you have some secret. The key, of course, is to look as though you haven't a brain in your head."

Now she crossed her arms. "*That's* the key to Weston?"

"Afraid so." He tried to sound sympathetic. "He likes simplicity." And the man mistakenly thought he'd found it in Jane Hull. Best of luck to him.

She shook her head in evident disbelief. "And you really want me to marry such a man?"

No, he thought. *No, I do not.*

But he would not play his hand now. Not until he knew Alastair's response. So he merely looked at her, and watched as she realized her mistake, and what his silence signified.

She broke from his gaze and quickly stepped to retrieve her glass. One swallow and it was drained. When she looked around, he knew she was searching for the bell to ring for more.

And he did not want to be part of this—to be the man who, even by accident, drove her to drink more deeply. Happily, he knew now how to distract her.

"You should study Jane," he said. "She manages a vapid, flirtatious look very well."

For a moment she went quite still. And then she turned toward him, forgetting about her bell and her empty glass, too. "Jane? You're using each other's Christian names now, are you?"

"Not publicly," he said. Which was true enough. Not privately, either, but he saw no need to mention that.

"My." She stared at him. "Has the sham become something more, then?"

The question sounded so bright. Suspiciously so. He waited a moment, and sure enough, out came her wide smile: her clever and most dependable mask. "But what happy news!"

"Don't be foolish," he said. "I and Jane Hull—that would be a match made in hell."

"Or perhaps not." She twirled the glass by the stem before setting it aside. "Perhaps you'd suit each other *perfectly*. Your brother would approve of her, which means you'd have the money you need to keep your hospital afloat. And she would marry into one of the foremost families in England. Why, an ideal match all around."

He didn't know how to reply. All the honest answers would not make this conversation more comfortable. "Of course, you forget that a loveless marriage is never a happy bargain."

Her laugh sounded brittle. "You're preaching to the wrong congregation, sir. You forget my aim."

"I don't forget your ideal," he said softly. "I have heard you speak of your parents." And it frightened him, he realized suddenly. For her ideal was the only thing that might persuade her to surrender the chance of a brilliant match—a match to a moneyed aristocrat. And that ideal was a very high standard for a man to meet, particularly if he knew nothing of happy unions.

She was staring at him. He offered her a slight smile. She stepped away from it, then spun on her heel, bound for the bell that stood abandoned on the terrace ledge. He moved too quickly, though; when she started to ring it, he caught her hand.

She went very still. Her wrist was so small. *She* was so small, to contain such a ferociously vibrant force of life.

"Listen," he said very softly, his entire brain focused on this speech, this damned important speech, a desperate bid to win them both more time. Even if Alastair balked, he might figure out some financial solution, but it would require *time*. "I've been thinking on this. Your need can't be so great that it won't survive another season. Come

March, London will be rife with bachelors of means. You needn't resign yourself—"

"Yes, I must," she said through her teeth. "Do you think I've undertaken this course for the fun of it? I know exactly what I need to do."

"But to enter a loveless marriage, simply for the sake—"

She yanked her hand free. "Do *not* presume to lecture me—*you*, of all people! Michael de Grey, he who says marriage is the quickest cure for love!"

He exhaled. "I did not say that to you, Elizabeth."

"But I heard you. You said it with conviction. And not for the first time, apparently! It's your lifelong philosophy, Sanburne said!"

"Never . . ." *Never in reference to you.* "Never with the right woman," he said slowly. Christ. They were torturing each other, weren't they? This whole bloody situation was intolerable.

"So what does that mean?" she asked. "Is that why you refuse to follow your brother's bidding? Are you holding out for the *right kind of woman*?"

He stared at her, biting back words—and pushing down *thoughts*—which he could not voice. She lifted her head, her chin tilting proudly, the angle nearly defiant. After a long moment, it was he who looked away, biting his tongue so hard it was a wonder he did not taste blood.

"Well," she said. "I wish you much luck, my lord. You may find your wait does not disappoint you. As you say, the season is always rife with moneyed prospects— even for the *men* among us."

He turned on her so suddenly she flinched. "God damn it, Elizabeth. Do you want me to say things that can't be unsaid? For I will, you know. I will say them to you, and to anyone else who cares to listen, my brother included."

Her silence—so stubborn, so *cowardly*; she would drive him to the brink but then step away from it herself—snapped his patience. He seized her by the elbow and hauled her toward him. Planting one hand in her hair—pins scattering, clinking against the bricks—he savaged her mouth. No warning. No polite notice. With his tongue he penetrated her.

And, by God, this, *this* was where he'd needed to be. Where he needed to be again, and again, and again: inside her, his tongue and his cock, every hour of the day, as her small, hot hands closed on his waist, then on his shoulders, grasping, squeezing, as though she were as hungered, as desperate as he. She gasped into his mouth as he bent her over his arm, but he did not care; he was past caring. Let her be, for once, pliable; *he* would set the course here. There were windows above, glass doors to their right; he did not care. He licked and sucked at her; he took her lip between his teeth and growled when she tried to step to one side. "Be still," he said, and sucked her earlobe into his mouth, and breathed against her as she shivered. She liked that. He had discovered it. This was *his* to know, *his* to employ.

"Did Hollister kiss you like this?" he said into her ear. "Did he?"

"He hasn't—touched me," she said. Her palms framed his face, pulled his mouth back to hers. Her lips were not clever now, but crushing, brutal; he would have winced had he not wanted more of it, more of her brutality; he wanted her over him, on top of him, her hands fisted in his hair, pulling to the point of pain.

And there were windows above, and glass doors to their right.

"Here," he said hoarsely, and tried to move her into

the lee of the building, out of sight of the windows. But the first step broke the spell; and then, just as suddenly as she'd responded to him, she was pulling free, shaking her head, gasping a denial. And though there was savagery in him—which pulsed like a red angry haze, urging him to ignore her, to take her bodily into the darkness, to persuade her, as he knew he could, to like it—he released her. Because, God damn it, he was *not* his father, not a bastard, he would—he would *not* contravene her will—

She backed away, stumbling over the bell and causing a discordant jingle. The sound brought her up short. She looked down to her feet and uttered a curse, a low word that would have shocked Weston beyond all possibility of redemption. And then she snatched up the bell and clutched it to her chest. Turning, she fled to the double doors, letting herself inside without another word.

Once on the other side of the glass, though, she paused to look back. He did not know what his face revealed to her, but whatever she saw, it made her press the flat of her palm to the pane, a gesture that lanced through him more sharply than a knife before she turned and walked away.

That gesture looked so much like a good-bye.

She ran from the terrace. Ran like a coward, her steps only slowing as she neared the drawing room, for fear that somebody might witness her flight.

The murmur of voices within caught her attention— and as she passed, she glimpsed Tilney crowding Mather into a corner. The sight brought her up short. Spinning on her heel, she marched back.

"Very striking eyes," Tilney was saying as Mather blinked myopically.

Good lord. All thoughts of her own distress evaporated. Had she come upon a boy poking a puppy with a stick, she could not have been more irritated. "Tilney!" she said sharply, causing him to jump and straighten. "Off with you," she snapped, before he could muster some witticism to cover his fluster. "Go find Katherine or Mrs. Hull if you wish to flirt. My *secretary* has more important matters to manage, and I expect you will remember that in the future."

With a lifted brow, Tilney looked between the two of them. "Understood," he said stiffly, and then sketched a bow before exiting.

As Liza closed the door behind him, Mather spoke. "I had that well in hand, ma'am."

"Oh, I'm certain you did." The girl's color was high, and the sight pricked Liza's temper more sorely. She could not abide men who abused their station to prey on the staff. "Such a wide experience of men you have! No doubt your path to the typing school was *littered* with broken hearts."

This sarcasm won from Mather a slight smile. "You might be shocked. Typists attract a very rash lot, you know."

The girl's color had begun to recede, and Liza could see no other sign that might indicate Tilney had misbehaved with her. Still, she wished to make certain that Mather did not labor under misapprehensions about what her employer would and would not tolerate from guests. "Should anyone ever bother you, darling—and I do mean *anyone,* even if he owns a small country—you know how to scream. And also, I hope, how to kick a man in a way that makes him regret himself?"

For a brief moment, Mather looked struck. Then her smile widened, and she laughed. "Madam, how remarkable that you should ask! That is the *very first lesson* given at typing school!"

"Very good, then. We understand each other."

"Yes," Mather murmured. "We do. You are very kind, ma'am."

"Nonsense. And where are your spectacles?"

"I dropped them," said Mather. "Mr. Tilney offered to help me find them, but . . ."

Toad. Liza glanced over the room, surveying with lifted brows the detritus of a very gluttonous high tea. A plate of half-eaten scones lay abandoned in an armchair—directly next to Mather's spectacles. Removing the plate and handing over the glasses, she took a seat. She would use this opportunity to recover her composure.

Do not think of him.

Mather replaced the frames on her face and blinked experimentally. Watching her, Liza felt exhausted. "Tilney is a rotter," she said. Men were such endless trouble. *All* of them—even the worthy ones. "I expect he saw your spectacles and decided to ignore them."

Mather shrugged. "If you mean to warn me, there's no need, ma'am. I could never take Mr. Tilney seriously. He sneers so regularly that I suspect he shaves his mustache only to spare his nose the whisker burn." She paused. "As you suggested, Mrs. Hull will do nicely for him."

Liza laughed in shocked delight. "Mather, I request you never to change. It would be *so* disappointing if you discovered a beneficent streak."

Mather lowered herself onto the chaise longue opposite. "Then I shall strive at all times to remain a perfect curmudgeon."

"Such a lovely quality in a secretary!" The rumble of Liza's stomach reminded her that she had eaten very sparingly today. Food would make an excellent distraction, for her mind wished now to wander back to the terrace, the *last* place it should go. If she thought on how he had kissed her, the things he had said . . .

Her attention alit on a nearby pastry, nearly intact save a bite or two. "Whose plate was that?"

"Lady Sanburne's, I believe."

"Oh, that's fine, then." Liza picked it up—adding, at Mather's shocked look, "Well, I certainly wouldn't have wanted to eat *Katherine's* leavings. Rabies is fatal, I believe."

Mather put a hand to her mouth, smothering a giggle. "Madam, you've a wicked bite yourself."

"I suppose that's why we get on so well, you and I." Liza took a moment to chew as she glanced around for other likely plates. Sugar was excellent medicine for the sore heart. Why, a slice of poppy seed cake sat untouched by the window! What fool had discarded it? Cook's cake was a work of genius. "Do you know whose cake—"

But as she glanced back, she forgot her next remark. For once, Mather had set aside her dignity and iron-spined posture. Slumping a little amid the ruffles and flounces of her sapphire satin skirts, she looked like a figure in a romantic painting. The deep blue of her dress brightened her eyes and caused her pale skin to glow. Her vivid hair, the scarlet of oak leaves in autumn, had been curled into ringlets that softened the square shape of her jaw, and her face looked poreless and opalescent, a pearl wreathed in fire.

"Why, you're utterly beautiful." Liza heard the surprise in her own voice, but decided not to append an apology: it would require vanity to take offense, and Mather lacked that entirely.

Sure enough, Mather glanced up with a startled smile. "You're teasing me."

"Not in the least." How had it taken so long to realize the girl's beauty? Mather had been in her employ for almost two years now.

Mather's smile slipped into a more wistful curve. "It's the gown, then." She looked into her lap, giving the silk an admiring stroke.

An awful thought occurred to Liza. "Have you never used a milliner before?" For now she thought on it, all Mather's dresses were ready-made affairs, save the few Liza had ordered for this party. "How awful of me! I should have arranged to purchase a wardrobe for you in London."

"No, ma'am." Mather spoke calmly. "That is not the usual call for an employer with her secretary."

"Do I not pay you enough, then? For you know that there are very reasonable milliners—"

"You pay me handsomely. But I fear I'm a penny pincher."

"Oh." Nonplussed, Liza paused. "Well, that's virtuous," she said. An example she'd do well to follow. "But what are you saving for?" Mather had no family; she was orphan, by her own admission.

Mather shrugged. "A rainy day, I suppose?" Before Liza could inquire into that answer, she added, "I must thank you again. The gown does become me very well. I confess, I find it rather . . . amazing, the illusions such clothing might work."

Liza smiled. "But it's not the gown that makes you

beautiful, silly goose. Or perhaps it is, but only because the gown is an invitation to really *look* at you. And your spectacles do quite the opposite, you know. They allow *you* to see, but they blind the rest of us entirely."

Mather bit her lip. "Perhaps that is their point," she said after a moment.

"Is it?" Casting caution to the wind, Liza crossed the room for the poppy seed cake. The first bite rewarded her courage: moist, flavorful, utterly perfect. "Was typing school so dangerous, then?"

Mather's eyes bounced from her hands in her lap to the window, then back to Liza. She rarely talked of her past. This look in her face now was the reason Liza had never pressed her on it. The headmistress of the typing school had recommended her handsomely, and that had been enough for Liza.

"You needn't answer," Liza said gently—although her curiosity was suddenly aflame, eager to seize on this puzzle, which offered a very welcome diversion indeed. Seeing Mather dressed as though to the manor born— and so very *comfortable* in the role—made her wonder a great many things. Mather spoke in refined accents, but if she had been forced to look for employment, then surely her family had not been sufficiently moneyed to provide a governess for her. "Did the typing school also supply your French?" And her piano skills, and her fine knowledge of geography?

A line appeared between the girl's russet brows. "No. The typing school was concerned with more useful things."

"How boring that sounds."

"Not at all. It's lovely to learn to be useful. To *feel* useful. French . . ." Mather pulled a face. "French is not useful."

"Spoken like one who has never braved Paris!" Liza took another bite of cake. Because it was Mather, she did something very savage, and talked with her mouth full: "Besides, darling, you are the *definition* of useful. I suspect you were born so. I am more curious about the French. If not at school, where did you learn it?"

"From my mother," Mather said slowly.

"And did she play the piano, too?"

"Anyway, it's quite the opposite, ma'am—I was born utterly useless. And very noisy, I'm assured."

A neat evasion. "A bawling baby," Liza said. "Yes, I can imagine that: you *would* be colicky. Sometimes I think you still are."

Mather laughed. Here was another riddle: the unlikely whiteness of her teeth. Indeed, now that Liza was looking for them, little clues appeared everywhere, contradicting one's prior assumptions. Mather's graceful deportment; her height, which suggested hearty meals in her childhood; her self-possession: these things did not suggest a child raised in poverty.

"Your mother was a Frenchwoman?" Liza guessed.

Mather shifted a little, her satin skirts crunching. "No, ma'am. She was quite English. Nobody of note," she said, which struck Liza as odd—for who would imagine a typist's mother to be otherwise?

"And your father?" Liza asked.

"It was only my mother and I."

"Widowed, was she?"

Mather's mouth thinned briefly. "Abandoned, ma'am." Her clipped words suggested she'd now grown weary of interrogation.

"I see." Liza felt a new suspicion forming.

"You mustn't think the worst," Mather added, making Liza wonder what had come into her own face. "We always had enough to get by."

Not living on charity, then. Liza's intuition strengthened. "I imagine she was very beautiful, your mother."

Mather smiled widely now. "Yes, she was. A great beauty, I believe."

A rich man's mistress. It would account for Mather's caginess, and also explain how an abandoned woman might nevertheless possess an income that would support her child's education.

"Then your looks are from your mother," Liza said. "For in that dress or out of it, you're a beauty as well. For all that you disguise it." She reached for a half-drunk cup of tea.

"I hope I am not a beauty," Mather said somberly. "For I see how that fortune treats you, madam."

The cup halfway to her mouth, Liza froze. "I beg your pardon?"

Mather sighed. "You are not enjoying this party, ma'am."

Liza set down the cup. "Have you overheard something from the guests?" The last thing she needed was tales circulating about her downcast spirits. Good God, Nello would assume *he* was the cause. How irksome!

"Nobody else has noticed, I think. But it's quite clear to me." Frowning, Mather leaned forward. "Madam, I know you feel some urgency to marry, and were aiming at first for a very grand match. But I wonder . . ." She hesitated. "I do not wish to offend."

Liza waved this away. "You have always been frank with me," she said. Then, with a smile: "At least in regard to my own circumstances. So, out with it, darling."

"I wonder if perhaps a title is not what you require."

Mather adjusted her spectacles, her blue eyes round and earnest. "You said once that Lord Michael required a . . . *saintly virgin,* were your words. But that does not strike me as the case."

"Ah." Liza felt the breath and good cheer slip out of her. How instantly and completely her hard-won composure shattered.

Do you want me to say things that can't be unsaid? For I will, you know.

"I should not have spoken," Mather said instantly. "Forgive me, I—"

"No. No, don't worry." Liza reached again for the teacup, turning it in her palms as she sorted through her thoughts. Good *God,* she was in trouble. "Mather, you've been over the accounts with me. You know how sore my need is. And a second son . . ." She swallowed. "He cannot supply it."

In the silence, she kept her eyes on the tea, the bits of leaves at the bottom of the cup. Some thought fortunes could be read in the patterns of the leaves. What a depressing notion—that one's fortune might literally be located in the dregs.

"I am no romantic," Mather said finally, her voice hushed. "You mustn't think that."

Liza's low laugh ruffled the surface of the tea. "Goodness, Mather. I assure you, I'd never imagined it."

"But that's precisely why I feel emboldened to say this. Marriage is the *greatest* risk a woman ever takes. I know you have some experience of it, but there are so many shades of unhappiness in a union. And the darkest shades—why, even poverty is not nearly so dangerous."

Liza looked up. Mather had bent her head to study

her hands where they lay locked together in her lap. The set of her shoulders was stiff.

"Have you some personal cause to know that?" Liza asked softly.

Mather looked up, her face unreadable. "I have two eyes, ma'am. And I have seen a great deal with them."

Liza hesitated, puzzled by the mystery her secretary had become. "You know I am always here to help you, Mather."

The girl's expression softened. "I do, ma'am. But I speak now of you. I would not like to see you unhappy."

Liza tried to smile. "Well. I agree with you that the opposite of unhappiness is not money. Money cannot buy happiness. But love isn't a very reliable currency, either, you know. And I don't think only of myself when I think of marriage. I think of Bosbrea. Of the hundreds of tenants who work the land, who rely on me for their support and livelihood." She could sell the land—but the men with the money to buy it no longer looked to farming for their incomes. Men like Hollister looked beneath the ground to minerals for their fortunes, or to timber, or acres for factories . . . "My future is not only my own, darling."

Such good sense she spoke. Would that she could *listen* to herself!

Mather was studying her. "Is it love, then?"

Her throat closed. "Oh, Mather," she said with difficulty. "Don't be ridiculous."

Oh, Liza, she added silently. *Please,* please *don't be ridiculous.*

CHAPTER SEVENTEEN

Mr. Smith, the spirit writer, had insisted on particular scenery: dark, dimly lit, with high ceilings to allow for "circulation of the vapors" . . . whatever that meant. In conference with Mather, Liza had chosen to host his event in the portrait gallery, which she had filled with standing candelabra to aid the mood. He took a seat now beneath a portrait of her father and laid out his utensils—a pot of ink; a feathered quill; a stack of vellum—atop a small writing desk, which he'd brought with him all the way from York.

Mysterious glyphs had been carved down the desk's polished wood legs. Liza might not have noticed them had she not been trying so intently to avoid Michael's eyes. He stood two feet away, and he was making no effort to disguise his interest in her. She felt his steady look like a hot hand on her skin. He wanted her to look back at him. She couldn't. The scene on the terrace seemed to have left her sensitized almost beyond her ability to bear. If she looked at him, she would go to him; if she went to him, she would take him by the arm and drag him out of this scene.

He'd lit a fire she did not know how to put out.

It's not love. It's not.

Desperate to distract herself, she leaned toward Lydia, who had walked in with her. "Those symbols on the desk." *Yes, very good, Liza. What of them?* "Aren't they remarkable? Do you recognize them?" Lydia was something of an expert in such things.

"Not in the least," Lydia replied. "They're vaguely reminiscent of hieroglyphs, but I suspect some artist had a very good time inventing them."

"A fraud?" said James. "Denounce him, Lyd."

This exchange made both the Sanburnes laugh loudly. For her part, Liza gathered it was a reference to how they'd first met—James had been taunting his father in public with some artifact that Lydia had decried as fake.

A vivid vision opened in her mind . She and Michael might trade such jokes—a sly allusion to the trustworthiness of mere country doctors. He would laugh, and so would she. And nobody else in this room would understand.

A shudder went through her, powerful and bittersweet. How had she ever imagined herself in love with Nello? The jokes between them had been malicious, and always at somebody else's expense. He had excited her, of course—and angered and annoyed her; every moment with him had been tumultuous, and in the interludes between their meetings, she had fretted, parsing every moment of their past interactions. But that was not love. Love, she saw now, did not feel at all the same.

Love was more than passion. It was built on *intimacy,* a history woven of private moments, knowing looks, and silent smiles. She had *known* that as a girl. How had she grown so confused? She had seen such love between her mother and father—and now, for the first time, she had seen the prospect of it for herself. She saw in a single moment how it might go between her and Michael, if she . . . abandoned everything else of worth.

Her parents' legacy.

Her own surety.

Her tenants' futures, and the hopes of smart young boys like the Browards.

This was too cruel. Her very thoughts seemed to be gouging out her own heart. She could not stand to listen to James and Lydia murmur to each other a moment longer. She walked around them to join Tilney's conversation with the Hawthornes. Their barbed tones suited her better.

"Ah, Mrs. Chudderley," said Nigel in greeting. "I was just speculating on the unlikely idea that spirits might incline toward the *written* form of expression."

"Nigel lacks imagination," said Katherine. She was dressed head to toe in gunmetal gray satin that reflected the candlelight in strange ripples. "After all, letters are the natural medium for all manner of delicious and shocking tidings. If you know what I mean." She lifted one thin, dark brow.

The words were clearly pointed, and invited a leading reply. "How intriguing," Liza said. "That sounds like the view of a woman with *tremendously* interesting correspondents."

"So it does," said Tilney with a sly laugh. "If only Katherine were tasked to read *her* letters tonight! *That* would be true entertainment."

Katherine tilted up her chin, striking a supremely satisfied pose. "I would never betray my correspondents' trust. I will say, though, that I received the most *fasci-*

nating letter in today's post." She lifted a brow at Liza. "I don't suppose you also heard from Mr. Nelson?"

How predictable. "Darling. Had you not gathered that my interest in Mr. Nelson has diminished considerably? Why, I've not thought of him in weeks."

"I see." Katherine exchanged a charged look with Tilney. "What a pity. I suppose we mustn't mention his name, then."

What on earth had happened to Nello? Oh, she did not care. The memory of him felt like a fading itch, mildly annoying but not worth her notice.

Mr. Smith clapped his hands, calling the group's attention to his little desk, where a single candle burned next to a slim stack of vellum. "If you please," he said. "I will require full silence for my labors here."

Conversation collapsed into whispers—and then died entirely, as Mr. Smith lifted his candle to his face to display his strenuous frown. For the unsteady light painted a strange and fearsome mask on his bulldog face, which was hatched by deep lines, and sagged at the jowls and brow. His eyes were beady and dark and glimmered strangely.

A very good effect. Liza cast a smile over her friends— holding it brightly as her survey passed over Michael, letting it linger as she met Hollister's regard.

Any stranger would judge him handsomer than Michael.

But how wrong that stranger would be! For a single glance could not uncover the skill in Michael's hands, whether to caress or save a life—and the wry humor lurking behind his easy smiles, or the way, when he looked at a woman, she felt seen in all ways, exposed to him, yet so utterly *safe* . . .

"I will now take up my quill," said Smith, "and I will wait for divine instruction. Should the silence be broken, so, too, shall my trance, and then we must begin anew. Thus, for your own patience and satisfaction, my lords and ladies, I will beg your brief indulgence."

She was not paying attention to Michael. Yet somehow she was sharply aware when he retreated a stealthy pace from the circle; when his attention focused on the painting to the right of the spirit writer. Her heartbeat quickened. He was looking at *her* as a young girl, her face still round with puppy fat, innocence personified in that ridiculous white gown that her mother had insisted she wear, tied at the waist with a blue silken sash. A girl whose expression was shy and hopeful, nothing like the professional beauty whom Mr. Readey had captured with his photographs.

Did Michael recognize that girl? Did he wonder what she had been like? For Liza wanted him to wonder. She *wanted* to be known by him.

What a curious thing. A woman's charms were premised in mystery. But to him, she wished to be transparent as glass.

"Here," said Mr. Smith suddenly. "Here . . . *here*."

His quill began to move.

Very old-fashioned, to write with a quill. But Liza understood his motive, for the scratching sound made a dramatic accompaniment to his frenzied grimace as he wrote, and wrote, and wrote. Now and then he would gasp and snatch his quill from the page, as though what he spied there was too, too awful for words; and then, his mouth twisting open as though in a silent scream, he would jab his quill violently into the ink pot and begin anew.

Despite herself, she was overwhelmed with the urge

to laugh. She bit down hard on her cheek, for it was very poor form to spoil her own entertainment.

At long last—five minutes, or thirty; forbidden to find it hilarious, Liza instead found it very boring—Mr. Smith gasped and threw down his quill, causing the ladies closest to him to shriek and stumble backward, lest the ink splash their hems. Then, evidently oblivious of the scowls aimed at him, Smith stood and waved the paper in the air, perhaps to dry the ink, perhaps to lend to his overall effect as a deranged lunatic with very bad penmanship.

"Hark!" he cried. "Messages from the beyond!" He lifted the page to conceal his face and began to read—his voice dropping to such an indistinct mutter that the group was forced closer to hear him.

"The sylph with the sunlit hair will emerge from the shadow triumphant," he said very rapidly. "From grief she rises, the Phoenix born anew."

"Mrs. Hull," said Weston excitedly. "That must be you, Mrs. Hull!"

"Oh, I don't know." Jane had mastered bashfulness; Liza predicted a wedding before Christmas. "I shouldn't like to think—"

"But it's a fine message," Weston assured her. "You will triumph!"

He was, Liza thought with distaste, a bit *too* enthusiastic for all this charlatanry.

Mr. Smith switched to a growl now. "When the mirror shatters, twin images will be split. A new vision will rise between them, to their peril! Beware the shattering!"

Now everybody turned to look at the Hawthornes, who came as close to twin images as anybody in the group. Katherine rolled her eyes. "Oh, bollocks," said Nigel.

"The warring crowns will topple," Mr. Smith cried. "Struck down by an asp that emerges from underground! Only one shall live to retrieve the princely crown, but to him all the spoils shall redound!"

"That makes no sense whatsoever," Tilney complained. "Unless we've a secret pair of princes among us? No, I didn't think so."

"Lord Forbes is distantly related to a Hapsburg prince," Lady Forbes said brightly. "But I assure you, he quarrels only with his hunting dogs."

The baron harrumphed. "I could handle myself in a fight."

"Of course you could, dear," the baroness said comfortably.

Mr. Smith cleared his throat. "*Shall* I continue?"

Liza idly wondered if in a past life he'd been somebody's butler. His stony air of authority put her very much in mind of Ronson.

"By all means," Hollister said. "Our breath is bated, good sir."

And what a *pity* Hollister had rushed his fences. She'd always admired a dry wit. She might have brought herself around to him if only he'd displayed more subtlety.

She bit her lip. What a *liar* she was! Why did she bother pretending? She needn't fall in love to marry. And she needn't marry for her heart to break. She was breaking it herself, with every look she stole toward Michael.

"The dark-haired enchantress will silence the voice by naming its true origin," said Mr. Smith. "A new life, herself the ally."

She felt an unpleasant start of recognition.

"Is that you?" Katherine asked her.

"Only the spirits know," she said lightly, but could not prevent herself from discreetly rubbing the chill from her nape. Gibberish from an accomplished performer. Silly to let it give her even a moment's unease. She did not *truly* hear her mother's voice. It was a figment of her imagination, no more.

Smith grew pompous. "The king's brother will see his history repeated," he intoned. "Wanton for mother, and so wanton for wife, and he becomes the fool, the jester whom all the court ridicule."

She caught her breath. Nobody needed to ask to whom *this* message pertained. There was only one man in the room whose brother had ever been described in kingly terms.

Michael's reaction was lost in the dimness. But not by the smallest movement of his body did he seem to react. The silence felt edged with glass—and her own dawning anger.

She stepped forward. "Go on," she said sharply. "What is your next prediction?"

Mr. Smith huffed. "They are not predictions, madam, but messages from the vaporous realms."

Insufferable pomp. "Your next message, then."

He looked back to his sheet. "False royalty for an unsound mind: the king himself will wither in the prison of his own making—"

"Enough of kings," she said, but some movement on the periphery of her vision drew her notice, and she saw once again the Hawthornes exchanging a significant smirk. A *self-congratulatory* smirk, in fact.

So perhaps she knew, after all, what tidings Nello's letter had brought them. Michael's brother's strangeness had grown public. And it seemed she was not the only one who had thought to bribe a spiritualist.

"Another message," she said in a warning voice. "Something more—"

She stopped as Michael stepped into the dim circle of light. "In fact, I find it quite interesting," he said to her. "By all means, Mr. Smith—continue."

His tone was pleasant, his expression utterly neutral. But as he spoke to Smith, his eyes switched from Liza to the Hawthornes, and the smile he gave them put Liza in mind of a wolf spotting his dinner.

The siblings' smirks faded. Even the spiritualist looked suddenly uncertain of his material. Glancing between Michael and the page, he fumbled a little. "Ah— the, ah—" He turned the page over. "The Midas who paid in good coin for his rank will learn the—"

"Oh, I do believe that's enough," Hollister drawled. The wits whispered that he had purchased his barony. He did not look amused. "Who wants a drink?"

"Sounds lovely," said Lady Forbes.

"A fine idea," Liza said quickly. "To the terrace, then." She waved broadly down the hall, then wasted no time in leaping forward to snatch the page from Smith's hands. "I will speak with you later," she said in an undertone. Her employees, temporary or no, did not take bribes from anybody but *her*.

With the company reassembled on the terrace for a hastily arranged round of champagne and charades, it dawned on Liza that she had lost a guest. Michael was nowhere to be seen. Making some excuse to Jane and Weston, who stood nearest her, she walked back into the house. A maid, scurrying past with fresh pitchers of water for the bedrooms, said that yes, she *had* seen Lord Michael—entering the library a few minutes ago.

It was there that Liza found him. He had turned up all the lamps and was browsing a shelf full of Shakespeare, and the smile he threw her as she entered looked disconcertingly cheerful. "You've a fine library. I hope you don't mind?"

She waved this off. "I'm so sorry," she said. "I take full responsibility for Mr. Smith's rubbish. I should have made certain beforehand that he would not get up to tricks."

He did not immediately reply, but the thoughtful, measuring look he gave her communicated some message that bypassed her brain entirely. Her next breath came shorter, and she reached back to lay one hand on the doorknob. Perhaps coming here, alone, to find him had not been wise.

He noted her movement with a slight smile, then looked back to the bookshelf. With the tips of his fingers, he traced the length of a volume's spine. The gesture seemed oddly graceful . . . sensuous, somehow. His hands were magical. Their capacity never failed to fascinate her.

"Did you apologize to Hollister as well?" he murmured.

Her fingers moved nervously over the brass knob. "Should I? What Mr. Smith said of him was true."

He shrugged. "And so were his remarks to me."

She did not like that. "What rubbish! You know somebody fed him those lines to—"

"Goad me?" He turned away from the bookshelf, prowling to a long sofa where he dropped into a seat.

"I'm not goaded," he said. "If you come out of concern . . . I assure you, I didn't steal off to sulk. It's only that I lack interest in charades." He laughed. "Which is rather ironic, when you think on it. For what is this between us, if not one great charade?"

Go. Go now. They had already danced around this matter once today, and it had left her bruised and full of horrible, impotent yearnings.

But the strange edge in his voice arrested her. She found herself gripped by a suspicion that overrode her concern for herself. Letting go of the door, she took a step toward him. "You can't think it's true," she said. "That you will end up as your father did. That your . . . wife will follow your mother's path."

"My mother did no wrong," he said flatly.

But that did not answer her question. "Forgive me," she said. "I don't know much of your family's history."

"I find that hard to believe."

She winced. Of course she knew the bare outlines: a scandalous divorce, a trial filled with shocking tales of infidelity and violent quarrels. But she'd been a girl when the newsp⟨...⟩ had advertised the de Greys' troubles, and ⟨...⟩ rarely found new circulation. "I can't c⟨...⟩ ⟨...⟩ he truth," she said. "I, of all people, know ho⟨...⟩ ⟨...⟩rs might twist facts to their liking."

"⟨...⟩f the rumors were true," he said with a on⟨...⟩ ⟨...⟩ shrug. "At least in regard to my father. He w⟨...⟩ ⟨...⟩very inch the abusive, violent philanderer. And if my mother made . . . ill choices, then one cannot blame her for it. With my father as her husband, what choice did she have? He brought out the worst in every person he encountered."

"I'm sorry," she said softly. She hovered awkwardly a

moment, then folded her arms over her chest. She could not imagine what it would be like to know such things about one's parents. "That's awful."

"Yes, I suppose it is." He smiled, an unpleasant smile that showed teeth. "But that is what I know of love, Elizabeth. And they say we learn by example. So tell me, how can you be certain that the soothsayer was wrong? History repeats itself, does it not?"

His mood of self-pity struck her as foreign and disturbing. She took another step toward him. "History repeats because we do not *learn* from it," she said. "Of all people, then, you're the *best* prepared to avoid such an unhappy match."

He put an arm up along the back of the couch, leaning back to consider her. "And you?" he asked quietly. "Where does that leave you? Did you learn nothing from your Mr. Nelson?"

She went cold. Her affair had not been a secret to him; she supposed she should not be shocked that he'd learned it was Nello with whom she had dallied. But it mortified her all the same. "Don't imagine I loved him," she said. "I knew better than that!"

He lifted a brow but made no reply.

"I *didn't*," she said. "I fooled myself for a time, but . . ."

The urgency with which she spoke this denial confused her. But she had not imagined that when he looked at her, he did so with knowledge of Nello. It made her feel oddly panicked. She . . . why, she wanted him always to see her as he'd come to know her in the days before this party. In those days with him, she'd been a woman who'd had nothing to do with cads like Nello. She'd been the woman she would *always* like to be.

The thought unbalanced her. She sank onto the chair opposite him. "Surely you can see you're nothing like your father," she whispered. He brought out the *best* in her. He did miraculous things. "You only do good in the world. Look at how you saved Mrs. Broward! And what you've done with your hospital! How can you say you're anything like him?"

He leaned forward now, his elbows on his thighs. "Because I look at you," he said softly. "And I do not care for your needs. I do not care for your choice. I look at you and I think only of wanting you. And I am very tempted, Elizabeth, to take you, and to hell with your concerns."

She took a startled breath. Those dark, hot words struck a primitive thrill through her. She would not deny it. "Then I, too, am like your father," she managed. "For I feel the same."

His eyes narrowed, and he gathered himself as though to rise—but she sprang up from her seat and took a step back.

"But it is *wrong*, Michael." The words rushed from her; she barely knew what she meant to say; she listened to herself as though from a distance as she quickly continued. "It is so terribly wrong. For it is not just you and your hospital—people depend on me as well. So *many* people, and I cannot disappoint them. I know my duty! And still, despite it, I want . . ." His eyes were devouring her. She felt as though she could not breathe. Did not want to. She would drown in his eyes and relish the death. "I think only of wanting you." That was truth.

"Then come here," he said quietly. "And take me."

For a single, suspended moment she hesitated. His

eyes were all that bound her. And then, as if in a dream, she watched herself step forward. Her better sense slipped away like the tethers of gravity. She floated the two paces across the carpet. His hands closed on her hips, and she lowered herself into his lap.

He leaned forward and pressed his mouth to her throat. Her palms on his back felt the hard pull of his indrawn breath, and all along her chest she felt the burning warmth of his fierce exhalation.

"Listen to me," he said into her skin. "I have been a liar to you, but I won't lie about this. I know what love is, after all. And for all the people who would suffer for it, for the shame I would bear and the guilt that would keep me awake at night, I still think I would dismantle the hospital and sell it stone by stone if that would give me what I needed to have you for my own."

She closed her eyes to stop the prick of tears. "But I wouldn't let you," she said miserably.

"No." Softly he kissed her collarbone. "And I love you all the more for it, Elizabeth."

Shock prickled over her skin—wonder and fear chasing after it. "Stop," she whispered. He was saying things that could not be unsaid. Things she would have to live with, to remember forever.

"Why not say it? We both know—"

She covered his mouth with hers. From her position atop him it required an awkward angle of her neck, but what matter? Let her bend, let her break; she needed to have this kiss from him. She cupped his cheek in her palm and showed him with her lips what she felt: *I love you,* she thought, and *I love this,* and, *I cannot have this again,* but it felt so right, so glorious in this moment. When his lips parted and he suckled her tongue into his mouth, she moaned with a pleasure that felt almost vicious.

He twisted beneath her, sinking down lengthwise on the sofa and carrying her down atop him. Their kiss grew more feverish; they would devour each other, or melt into each other. One or the other, *now.* His hands swept down her back, palming her buttocks through her skirts, but it was not enough. She threw her calf over his legs, wanting to surround him; to feel him against every part of her. He was warm, strong, so solid beneath her, his bones as dependable as stone, cradling and supporting her. She felt the points of his hipbones pressing through her petticoats, digging into the soft flesh of her thighs. *Not hard enough.* She bit at his lower lip, and then froze, shocked by herself—by how suddenly and violently her need had mounted.

His laugh was soft and strange. "Again," he whispered, and ran his hand up her nape, his fingers sliding through her hair and closing so hard that she felt a twinge of pain—at first startling, and then, all at once, terribly right.

For they were going to hurt each other beyond repair. That was their fate. It might have been written in the scriptures, so certain she was of it. She would never again have him—never lick his lower lip, very gently now, to trace its firm shape, so pliable and so perfect. She pulled back a little to smooth it with her thumb, to admire the sight of it, to see her own hand against it, and to know, at least for this moment, that this was her right.

Never again after tonight would she feel the edge of his teeth as he took her thumb into his mouth. He sucked it slowly, his eyes on hers, pale and beautiful as the light through stained glass. His tongue curled around her and a sound caught in her throat, animal with need. She pulled her hand free and bent her head to his throat to smell him, to inhale that scent, wholesome and hot, as though his body were her medicine, the cure she'd been hungering for her entire life. She would never again know the taste of his neck, his skin smooth-grained and hot beneath her open mouth.

So much to memorize. So little time. She shoved off his coat, almost resentful that she must let him help her, cursing his waistcoat as she ripped it open, loathing the recalcitrance of the buttons on his shirt. She ripped them apart, and there, *ah,* was more of him, his skin taut and pale over the rippled musculature of his belly. She put her mouth to his navel and felt him shudder. Other women would do the same; they would share this same memory that she was making, and she detested them for it. She wanted to claw out their eyes, and *his,* for letting them have this precious sight, another that would not be hers again.

She moved lower yet, following the thin trail of hair that led into his waistband. His hands found her hair again, stopping her descent as he breathed, "My God—"

She caught his wrists and set them to either side of his body. He had said his piece already; she would have hers before they were done.

The buttons on his trousers knew their place; they yielded without a fight. His erection sprang free, long and thick and straight, the veins prominent in the light. She ran her tongue up his length, and tasted the pearl of liquid at the tip.

A curse came from him, low and fervent. "Elizabeth—"

"Yes." Her voice was fierce. He would always remember her. She closed her mouth over him and he gasped. With her tongue she laved him, and felt a hot bolt of triumph when his hips bucked beneath her. *Remember this.*

"Elizabeth . . ."

She looked up his body. He wore a look of stunned amazement as he stared back at her, his breathing ragged. And then he blinked, sense slowly returning to his features.

"Be still," she said, and then lowered her mouth again. It was a kiss unlike any she had ever given, beyond intimate, fraught with the curious pleasure of knowing how vulnerable he was. With her teeth, she might have punished him. Instead she sucked, gently and then harder, and he writhed under her, uttering a broken moan before he caught her hands. His fingers braided through hers. "Wait," he said hoarsely. "I can't—"

She ignored him, moving her head rhythmically now, wanting to destroy him, to make him incoherent. He was close to surrendering himself; she could hear it in the small noises he made. But then his grip tightened further yet, and he pulled her up his body in one brute move.

She tried to break free—and then forgot herself, for her hands found his wrists, thick and solid, and then his forearms, so tightly knit, and then the points of his elbows, and the bunching of muscle in his upper arm, all these precious places that she had to chart, to commit to memory. His biceps flexed; his hands closed on her hips; but she could not focus on that, for now she had discovered his shoulders, which she squeezed without mercy. His body had been designed with such elegant, tightly muscled economy; there was no give to him.

And he'd said he loved her, and she would never unhear those words.

The thought spurred her to turn her nails into his shoulders, digging savagely as her mouth found his again. Her anger confused her, but it blended into her hunger as he kissed her back, feverishly, his palm sliding up her nape, gripping her to hold her in place. She rolled her hips against him and he hissed into her mouth, then began to sit up.

She tried to back away on her knees to make room for him, but her dress was too ornate, and her frustration escaped her in a snarling syllable. "Be still," he whispered, and slipped an arm beneath her, around the back of her knees, before lifting her bodily off the sofa. For a moment the room rocked wildly, and then he was sitting again, and now she was squarely atop him. His erection pressed against the juncture of her thighs, and her entire body went still for a moment, everything in her focusing on that spot.

He paused, too, and for a strange, fraught second, they stared at one another. In that moment, fear bloomed through her, cold and delicate as strands of ice.

Never again.

He cupped her face in his palms. Very gently, he kissed her lips.

And the strands of ice snapped, and what came out of her mouth was, "You will never forget?"

He exhaled against her mouth. "I would wear you like a suit," he said hoarsely. "I would never let you go."

She reached for her skirts at the same time he did. Their hands collided, and she almost laughed, only the look on his face—hard, concentrated—dried up the laughter in her throat, and made her bones dissolve.

Together they gathered up the slippery silk, handful by handful, and then he reached between them and fitted the head of his cock against her and she sank down onto him, seating herself until it seemed she could take no more—and then his hips flexed beneath her, and she gasped as his full length penetrated her so deeply that for a moment she feared she could not bear it.

In the next breath, he lifted her by the hips and fear turned to panicked need, to feel him so deep within her again. Slowly, her skirts rustling around him, she moved. With his lips against her cheek, and then her temple, he whispered to her: "Yes, like that," and, "Ah, the feel of you . . ." Soft, hot words, explicit words, that she had never heard anybody speak. "You like that," he said into her mouth as he swallowed her gasp; he flexed again, the angle just so, and her body shuddered like a plucked string. "Moan for me," he said, "aloud," and she did; she had no choice in it. His words wound through her and took command of her as his body did. Against her ear, his voice low and rough, he said, "I mean to make you scream."

And he would. His hands were hot and ungentle and they seemed to move according to her own thoughts, finding every inch of flesh that craved him. "Harder," she whispered, and his laugh was broken and soundless. Into the hair at her temple he breathed, "I love you."

No. She stopped his mouth again with hers. *Not that.* She begged it of him with her tongue deep inside him. *No promises. Only this.*

But when his grip directed her to grind against him, her concern evaporated, for his promise to make her scream began to come true, the whimper in her throat building toward something louder. Hot darts of pleasure began to coalesce. He ripped free of her mouth and his tongue found her ear and swirled a hot message there before he whispered, "Come for me, Liza."

And she did, with a cry that she could not have smothered had her life depended on it.

Never, she thought, and the thought opened inside her like an oncoming night, dark and full of loss. *Never again.*

CHAPTER EIGHTEEN

A soft knock came at her bedroom door. Liza rolled away, hoisting the blanket higher around her shoulders. The light slipping beneath the curtains had reached the fringe of the carpet. Probably it was past noon. At one time in her life, she'd been quite skilled at sleeping the day away. But now it took an effort.

Too many things of late took an undue effort. Flirtations. Laughter. Denying herself, ignoring her own longings. Hadn't she acquired that skill during her marriage? Hadn't she perfected it when enduring Nello's poor treatment? Why should she forget the way of it now?

You cannot have him!

The door creaked open. Irritation brought her up to a sitting position. "What—"

"Viscount Sanburne," said her maid miserably, stepping aside to reveal James.

Hands in pockets, he rolled up on the balls of his feet and gave her a lopsided grin. "So here's where you've been hiding all day."

Liza threw off the blanket. "Go away! I have a head-ache!"

Instead he came strolling toward her—then paused quite suddenly. Eyebrow cocking, he made a sardonic survey of the room. "Oh, this is charming," he said. "No wonder you've been neglecting us."

As she followed his look, the warmth of a blush only spiked her temper higher. A discarded tea tray, two books lying facedown on the carpet where she'd flung them, an empty wine bottle, and a cold compress still dripping water on the side table. Had a theater director required a set that screamed of self-pity, this might have been the model for it.

She took a breath to speak some devastatingly sharp set-down—but her wit failed her. Her brain felt as soggy as the compress, a useless mush. Last night, she had ripped herself off Michael's body and walked away without a backward glance. And he had known better than to try to stop her, because he knew what her stupid brain must accept:

You can't have him.

She had made terrible decisions before. But this was different. Walking away from him had felt like stepping on knives, like dragging her heart over glass. She had become enamored of the wrong men before; she had erred in so many ways. But never before had she deliberately and knowingly betrayed *herself.*

And walking away from him had felt like such a betrayal.

Which was *nonsense.* She had no choice!

She fell back onto the mattress, causing a flurry of startled feathers to dance over her. "Go away," she muttered. "I'm terrible company."

The mattress tilted as James sat down on the edge. Incorrigible ass.

"Does Lydia know you're barging into another woman's bedroom?"

"Oh, it was her idea," he said casually. "I know better. One doesn't beard the lioness in her den."

She laid her wrist over her eyes. "So insufferable, am I?" She rather agreed. What idiotic impulse had caused her to seduce a man whom she'd known from the start she couldn't keep? No matter whether he was a mere country doctor, a duke's brother, or a pauper prince—he was *not for her*. How had she ever imagined this would turn out well?

James made a *tsk*. "Come now, Lizzie." His hand closed over hers, gently tugging it free. When he saw the tears, his smile faded and he frowned in truth. "What's wrong?"

The concern in his gray eyes made her feel worse. "Nothing." She couldn't love Michael. Love would not survive poverty. Or more precisely, *they* wouldn't. A duke's brother and a professional beauty—yes, much luck they would have scraping by on pennies as her estates crumbled and her tenants turned against her!

But even poverty seemed lovely when she envisioned it with him.

She swallowed a groan. What a *ridiculous* notion. Her brain was clearly scrambled. All the more proof: this was infatuation, maddening, intoxicating, *fleeting*. It would pass.

"Oh, yes," said James, "you *look* perfectly well. Really, Lizzie, recall to whom you're speaking."

She sighed. James did, indeed, know her better than most. He'd become a kind of brother during the summers of their childhood, for his parents had often summered at Sitby, an hour's drive to the north, and had invited her parents for long stays by the ocean there.

But he had been gone so long . . . and she barely recognized him now. Once he'd been beautiful and dissolute and a touch cruel. Now, in his face, she saw the kind of compassion he would once never have allowed himself to show. Lydia had taught him happiness. And truly happy people . . . they were willing to try to understand anything. But as a result of their own comfortable lives, they so rarely *could* understand.

Her stars were crossed. She had ill luck in love. Some primitive bolt of panic made her fear it might be contagious. She wished James only joy, truly.

So she said only, "Everyone must be wondering where I am."

James leaned back on one palm, eyeing her. "Oh, you've kept them pretty busy, I'd say. That secretary of yours marched into breakfast this morning with a list of activities two miles long. But, yes, I do believe the Hawthornes, at least, are wondering rather pointedly how long a headache can endure."

She rolled her eyes. "I should slap their puffed-up heads and let them learn the answer firsthand."

"A very good idea," he said. "But I don't think you really have a headache. I'll ask once more, and then I'll simply start spreading rumors about possible answers: what's going on?"

She turned her face away toward the window. "You were gone so long," she said. Only as she spoke the words did she realize how much she'd resented his absence. She'd *needed* him.

He sighed. "Well, *Canada*," he said, as though that were an answer. "Bloody hard to get to, and even harder to get out of. The ports freeze, the roads freeze, the snow mounts higher than your head. I was afraid, for a bit, that I'd have to *dig* us back to England—the long way, mind you, for we'd have emerged in China, and set sail from there."

She smiled despite herself. "But you enjoyed it." She could hear that in his voice.

"I certainly wouldn't have done," said James. "Only seeing it through Lyd's eyes was something . . . quite new. Quite different."

She swallowed. He was not going to be able to cheer her, not when his every promising witticism kept sliding back, so predictably, into love-struck praise for his wife.

How small hearted you've become.

She bit her lip. *Oh, Mama.* Mama had been over the moon at James's wedding. *Finally, a woman who deserves him. I knew one would come along. And so, too, with you, my love. Only wait, and he will come.*

"Look here," James said. "I should have come home. By the time I got your telegram, we were two days out of Montreal. I should have turned around—"

"No." She made herself turn back—discreetly wiping her nose before facing him. "I mean—that's kind of you, James. But she was gone by then. And afterward . . ."

Afterward she'd been in no mood for solicitous consideration. She'd wanted only wildness, the sweet oblivion of forgetting. Nello had supplied that very satisfactorily, for a time. "I wasn't alone," she said with difficulty.

James was watching her, his expression sympathetic. "Bastard was bound to let you down. You're better off without him."

How well he knew her, to have followed her thoughts. "So you'd told me. I should have listened."

He tilted his head slightly, his tawny hair slipping over his eye. "But that's not why you've been weeping, is it?"

"No." She hesitated, gripped by the urge to confide in him. But if she laid out the whole sad tale of her restricted circumstances, he'd try to solve the problem for her. Pay off her debts at the expense of his own welfare, perhaps. He could not afford that. Not yet. His relationship with his father was strained, his living drawn mainly from the profits of his factories in the north. Until he came into the title, he could not play the hero.

And regardless of what he might offer to do, Liza could not imagine his wife would appreciate such a marked demonstration of their friendship. Liza had not always been at her best in front of Lydia, who had been cut from a very bourgeois cloth. Such strict notions of propriety she had!

"It's silly," she said finally—her voice steady, no hint in it of the ache she felt. "I'm only . . . very anxious, I suppose. First you married. Then Phin." For Lord Ashmore, too, had been part of their summer confederacy as children, most often as James's guest at Sitby. At the thought of his new wife, Liza pulled a face. "Married to an American, of all people! And what a peculiar girl. She's beautiful, I won't deny it, but the last time we met, she tried to persuade me to go rolling down a hill for fun. I was wearing a Worth gown at the time, mind you—and worse yet, so was *she*!"

James gave her a sideways smile. "Phin's rather peculiar himself. Perhaps we're the ones who seem odd to them."

"I suppose." And Phin could probably afford any number of Worth gowns. She sighed. "At any rate, it does seem like everyone in the old childhood gang is finding their way. And I'm very happy for all of you, only perhaps I . . . perhaps I'm coming to realize that it's not in my fate to be loved as you are."

James laughed, a soft sound of disbelief. "As far as I can tell, you've at least two bachelors downstairs hanging on your every word. Not saying that either is the one for you, but certainly you've no cause to despair of finding love, if that's what you want."

She rolled her eyes at him. "Weston and Hollister? Would you really match me with either of them?"

Now his brows climbed. "Who mentioned Weston? I was thinking of de Grey."

For the space of a moment she could not catch her breath. If only Michael were eligible for her purposes! If only life provided such fairy tale solutions . . .

"Lord Michael is a second son." Her voice emerged roughly. She cleared her throat and tried again. "Surely you would aim higher for me! Am I not worth a prince or a king at the least?"

James studied her. "Without doubt," he said after a moment. "Of course, I'm not blind to the way you look at him. There's a tale there, I expect."

Her throat closed. *Do you want me to say things that can't be unsaid?* Michael had demanded on the terrace. *For I will, you know. I will say them to anyone who cares to listen.*

In this instant, she knew precisely what he'd meant. The urge to speak of him, to *boast* that he'd laid his hands on her and it had been *glorious,* was almost physical in its ferocity.

But the Duke of Marwick wanted for his brother a wife that nobody would criticize. That would never be Liza. Michael would lose his hospital for certain.

"Your face is speaking volumes," James remarked.

She shook her head. "A volume of rubbish."

"I confess, it did surprise me when I first considered it. You and Saint Michael? Always holier-than-thou, that one. And now a bloody hospital. I'm surprised he hasn't earned a knighthood yet."

The description startled her. "You misunderstand him. He's not self-righteous in the least."

"No?" James shrugged. "Well, I was never close to him at school. But he always seemed damned fierce in his convictions. Though knowing what I do of his brother . . ." He smiled, not pleasantly. "Marwick seems a fine tyrant, a man after my father's own mold. So I'll reverse my opinion, then, and say I like de Grey simply for having had the guts to defy the bastard—for I'm certain Marwick envisioned a more glorious path for his brother than mere medicine."

She frowned, irked by the notion. "But the hospital is a very fine achievement! The . . . lowest death rates in the country, I believe. If Marwick doesn't see glory in that, then he's a fool!"

James looked at her but did not speak. In the silence, her own words rang in her ears, and she heard them as he must have—so earnest and defensive—and closed her eyes again. Who was the fool here? Not Marwick, it seemed.

"Lady Elizabeth de Grey," James said. "Has a fine ring to it."

She bit her lip. "James, don't."

"People do like him. You'll have no trouble introducing him to our crowd. Of course, he's a bit somber for my taste—"

"Somber!" She gawked at him. "Says the man who married a lady lecturer!"

He grinned. "But Lydia is the last thing from somber. You'll come to see it when you know her better. Her brain, Lizzie . . . it's a thing of beauty; I cannot *begin* to track how it works. That I don't bore her is a constant amazement to me."

What rubbish. "You could never be boring. And if she isn't somber, then Lord Michael *certainly* isn't."

"Ah, but he *works,* you know. Makes the rest of us chaps look a bit lazy." He hesitated. "And then there's the mess with his parents. Not surprising if he always had a . . . hard edge to him."

She toyed with the lace detailing on the blanket beneath her. "Some court battle, I recall?"

"Yes, a very ugly divorce. The old duke accused his wife of any number of sins, some of them too indecent for print. And the duke himself emerged as no prize." He sighed. "Granted, my own recall is somewhat vague—mostly collected from stupid jokes at school. De Grey was a target from the moment he enrolled—endured a good deal of taunting, as you may imagine. But he gave as good as he got." With a faint smile, he added, "Quite a savage little beast, very good with his fists. Not that I disapprove." His voice turned darker. "No honor in surrendering to bullies. Reply in kind, I say."

Now it was Liza's turn to divine where his thoughts had led him. Much of James's hatred for his father was owed to that man's abandonment of James's sister, Stella, when her husband had turned abusive.

Stella had killed her husband. She now remained in an asylum in Kent.

"She doesn't answer my letters," Liza said softly. She and Stella had been very close, once. But all her overtures were rebuffed with silence. "You said she was . . . better. But she doesn't reply. I wonder why that is."

He shrugged. "Can't say. I'd spring her free tomorrow if only she wished it. But she seems to be waiting for something. Our father's death? I wouldn't blame her." His mouth flattened. "But she doesn't belong there, Lizzie. She's as sane as you or I." He laughed without humor. "Saner, in fact. I *saw* her—right before the wedding. Did I tell you that?"

"You did," Liza murmured.

He shook his head. "I can't tell you how well she looked. Only she *insisted* she must stay—locked up there, like an animal—" He exhaled, a violent sound. "Lydia says I must leave her be; that I mustn't try to persuade her. That I must wait until she's ready."

Liza put her hand over his. The pain in his face broke her heart a little. "Lydia is right," she said softly. "Give Stella the choice. She'll come back to us in her own time."

His hand turned underneath hers, his fingers squeezing hers briefly before he withdrew them. "So, the devil take it," he said. "I've nothing but admiration for de Grey. Fight back when struck. Rage against injustice. Hell— burn the place down. Far better than making nice."

She drew back, slightly alarmed now. If he had decided that Michael somehow resembled his sister, then nothing would stop him from championing Michael's case to her. "James, I have no designs on Michael." For his sake as well as her own, she *mustn't*.

He nodded once. "You're a jaded little pessimist, and I adore you for it. But take it from one who has learned: love may make you into an optimist yet."

Her smile felt brittle. "That is not optimism but idealism speaking through you, James. Why, even if one were to find love . . ."

He waited a moment, then said gently, "One such as you, perhaps?"

Her heart felt as heavy as a stone. "Even if one finds it, that does not mean one can keep it."

"Oh?" He smiled as he rose, a smile that was far from reassuring. "Then prove it," he said. "Come down and flirt with Weston for me."

In Liza's absence, the dynamics of the party had grown complicated. Katherine Hawthorne had developed an inexplicable interest in Weston. Jane was sulking. And as soon as Liza entered the observatory for high tea, Hollister pulled her aside to request a private conference.

Looking into his calm, handsome face, she felt, all of a sudden, very *annoyed*. To propose marriage after such a short acquaintance seemed insulting. Could he not at least *pretend* to care about what she was like as a person? Or, at the least, to seem a small bit nervous around her! Clearly he assumed that with his money, his looks, and his new title, she was his for the taking.

She turned down his invitation by pleading a hostess's obligations, and then did her best to avoid him by making sure that she was constantly in conversation with someone else. Anyone else, save Michael. Michael, she avoided.

And in this effort, he seemed determined to aid her.

As they drifted into the drawing room at half past seven, she mistakenly approached a group before spotting him in it—realizing her mistake only when he turned away and moved onward to join Jane and the Forbeses. And illogically, his tacit cooperation wounded her. Like an arrow through her heart, the sight of his retreating back left her crushed and breathless.

This had to stop. It *must*.

Through an interminable dinner, she mustered quips to trade with the Hawthornes and Tilney, managed persuasive laughter at the guests' recounting of the clairvoyant's predictions, and issued mysterious demurrals when pressed for details of the night's particular entertainment. She did not intend to drink so very much, for there was no point to it; she felt light-headed already, her wits benumbed. But keeping up with the toasts was only polite, and the food on her plate could not interest her. When she rose from the table, the ground seemed to tilt beneath her. She had to catch the edge of the table to steady herself.

"Goodness!" She managed a laugh, high and bright, and said something about the carpet—tripping on the carpet; how ridiculous! But it was no good. She saw that in Lydia's quickly averted gaze. Lydia had a gift for looking away in the most *judgmental* manner possible.

The next second, Hollister was at her elbow, solicitously offering his arm. Had she not dispensed with the formalities the very first night, he would not have had the chance to escort her; the women would have retreated into the drawing room while the men enjoyed their cigars. But as soon as she'd risen, everyone had come to their feet as well, and now they were filing out of the room, chattering excitedly about the next spiritual demonstration. And her head was spinning and she could not pull away from Hollister's grip without risking her balance again. Not yet. Her heart felt as though it were trying to knock straight out of her chest. Too little food; too much wine.

"Perhaps a brief rest before you join the guests," Hollister was saying, and now he was urging her away from the direction of the others, and when she tried to tug free, the dizziness assaulted her again, freezing her in place. For the first time in her life, she felt truly panicked. For the first time, she truly wished she had not drunk at all. Her body was not responding properly to her commands. A wave of panic, irrational and overstated, swept through her. She was in her own home. She was perfectly safe.

"I'm fine," she said, but the room spun again, and Hollister laughed and said, "Before the fifth glass, you were."

The laughter in his voice held no unkindness, but her panic seemed to swell larger yet, for what woman would welcome the news that a man had been tracking her liquor consumption with an eye to privacy? She planted her feet. "I don't—"

"I only mean to see you to your rooms," he said. "I shan't take advantage."

"No, you won't." This level statement came from Michael, his voice washing over her like a cooling relief. He stepped up and slid his arm around her waist, in the process knocking away Hollister's grip.

He turned her a little, and blurrily she grew aware that the Hawthornes had paused in the doorway to watch—James now stepping up to urge them onward.

My God. She wanted the earth to open. She wanted

to sink into the ground. It was one thing to drink to excess deliberately, and quite another to discover oneself overset by accident. She had a sudden, vivid memory of the Stromonds' ball last year—her most vicious fight with Nello; far too much champagne, like oil on the flames of her rage—and James rescuing her from the water closet, where she'd woken sometime later, flat on the floor.

How had that not frightened her? How had she laughed about it the next day? Now, suddenly, she wanted to weep over the memory. What had happened to her this year?

Who have you become? Mama whispered. *You never dreamed of this for yourself.*

She made herself straighten. "I'm fine," she said. She would not collapse *tonight.* "Lord Michael will escort me."

Hollister looked between them. "Are you certain?" At her nod, he retreated a pace. "Very well. Until later, Mrs. Chudderley."

When he walked away, she would have followed, but Michael held her in place. "In a minute," he said.

He stood beside and slightly behind her. She did not want to look at him. This was not who she was when she was with him. When she was with him, she did not enjoy this spinning feeling; she did not need it. "I'm fine," she said. And truly, the dizziness was passing.

"Good. But take a few deep breaths. And some water. Here—" His arm still around her, he leaned over to snag a half-drunk glass from the table. "Mine," he said as he handed it to her, as though she would not have known that; he was the oddity at the table, the guest who asked for water along with his wine. His hand closed over hers to keep her grip steady as he directed the glass to her lips.

Like a father with his child. It should have mortified her. But the tears that pricked her eyes felt born of a different emotion. *Will you—would you always look out for me so?*

Would you never lose your patience?

She sipped hesitantly, fearing for a second that her stomach would reject the libation. But as soon as she'd swallowed, she realized it was exactly what she'd needed. Only then a drop went down wrong, causing her to cough.

His arms closed fully around her, pulling her back into his chest, crushing her bustle between them. "Finish it," he said into her ear. "Lean on me."

For a moment, though, she could not bring herself to obey. The feeling of his arms around her was more than a revelation. It was relief in its purest, physical form. *Lean on me.*

This, her mother whispered. *This, here.*

Her throat was so tight that she was not sure she could swallow. Had the Hawthornes popped back in to see this damning tableau, she would not have cared.

"*Finish* it," he said, his curt voice jolting her back to the moment.

She did, quickly. And then twisted in his embrace to return the glass to the table—becoming aware as she did of the footmen clustered in the doorway, obviously uncertain of whether this scene would bear their intrusion.

She nodded to signal her permission, then used her study of the table to compose herself. Dessert plates and crumbs. Ivy twined cunningly around the silver candelabra.

She could not bear to look into his face and see contempt.

"Better?" he asked.

Reluctantly, she stepped free of his embrace. His face was grave in the candlelight. She could not tell what emotion might underlie his sobriety.

She did not apologize for herself to anybody. Did she?

Perhaps you should apologize to yourself.

"At least I didn't end up in the water closet," she said. "Ask Lord Sanburne about that, if you like."

His expression did not change. "Do you think it would make a difference, Elizabeth?"

She wasn't sure what he meant by that. Or perhaps she *thought* she knew, and was afraid to discover that she was wrong.

Or that she was right. He was not for her.

"I wonder if you should go," she said. Her voice was not steady. "If it would be . . . easier. For both of us."

"If I'm the cause of your drinking," he said quietly, "then I'll leave tonight."

She sucked in a breath. "No." It felt terribly urgent to make this clear to him. "That started long before you. And it . . ." It was not always so bad. "I never drink when I'm alone. I would not . . ." *Drink with you.*

"Then perhaps you should rethink the company you keep," he said.

Now came the gentle clink and rattle of china being collected. She found herself afraid of what she might say if they continued to stand here. His blue eyes were so steady on hers. So pale, ringed with gold around the irises. The most beautiful eyes in the world. "We should join the other guests," she said. *We cannot be alone. Not any longer.* "Tonight is . . . the medium. Table rapping." Her laugh was weak. "An old favorite."

He tilted his head slightly. "You look steadier," he said. "But perhaps you should bid us an early good night."

She brushed her hand across her mouth—and then froze as she realized what she'd done, the girlish rudeness of it.

He gave her a slight smile. "I think you missed a spot." He leaned forward and very gently ran his thumb along her chin, flicking away the last drop of water.

A sound escaped her, more formless than an *Oh.* His smile faded. She stepped backward, breathless. The way he was gazing at her! "I really didn't drink so much," she said quickly. "Only I hadn't eaten anything until dinner."

"And you barely touched your plate," he murmured.

He'd been watching. She'd felt his eyes on her. She had to leave. Now. "I'll be fine. I only—"

The door flew open. Mather burst into the dining room, breathless and harried in one of her new gowns. "Madam," she said. "A coach just arrived from the station, and it seems—Mr. Nelson is here!"

"Who?" she asked stupidly. And then: *"What?"*

"I'll handle this," said Michael, scowling—and *that,* at least, she had the wits to reply to immediately.

"No, you won't." The look on his face left no doubt that his treatment would *not* be diplomatic.

"You're in no condition to deal with uninvited guests," he said coolly, and then strode out of the dining room—leaving her no choice but to race after him, Mather at her heels. She never, ever wished him to meet Nello. The very thought drove her mad with panic.

Nello was not . . . not a man she ever wished to have to explain. Or to have Michael associate with her.

She caught him by the arm just as he turned into the main corridor. "Stop! *Stop*," she said. "This doesn't concern you!" What Nello's visit concerned, she could not begin to imagine—but he had no part to play in it.

He swung around with a curse. "Doesn't it, then? Don't I have the right—"

There was violence in his face. The sight shocked her. Pure instinct drove her to recoil from him, snatching back her hand—and her reaction, in turn, seemed to shock *him*.

He blinked and then scrubbed a hand over his face. On a long breath, he let his hand fall.

"Of course, you're right," he said coolly. "It does not concern me in the least. Forgive my presumption, Mrs. Chudderley. I will join the other guests, then."

The bow he gave her was painfully formal. She swallowed hard and waited until he was out of sight before turning to Mather.

"Nello?" she asked.

"Yes, ma'am!"

"What does he want? Did he say?"

Mather shook her head. "Ronson did not know what to do. He let himself into the little drawing room. You'll have him thrown out, of course. I'll handle it myself—you needn't even see him."

"No. No, that would be unwise." As their relationship had deteriorated, Liza had come to realize—too slowly, and very reluctantly—that Nello was cut from the same cloth as the Hawthornes. He made a game of other people's miseries. To turn him away now, when he obviously had some reason for visiting, would be like turning away from an oncoming vehicle whose horses were shying and bucking. Better to figure out his aim.

She squared her shoulders. "Do I look well?" Amazing how her dizziness evaporated at the hint of danger.

Mather frowned. "Very well," she said solemnly. "But I don't like—that is, shall I listen at the door, in case you . . . need assistance?"

"That won't be necessary," Liza said. She had already broken one vase in that room, but there remained several heavy objects that would make excellent weapons.

CHAPTER NINETEEN

When she entered, Nello was standing at the mantel, examining some piece of bric-a-brac. He turned immediately, his lips crooked into a sideways smile—a favored weapon in his patented arsenal of charms. But that smile, which had once made her heart turn over, now gave her a strange, prickling sensation, akin to the icy breath down one's spine that often followed a brush with mortal danger.

He looked far from menacing. With a startled sense of coming awake, she saw that she had misremembered him. He looked smaller, somehow diminished, and his blond hair, which had always been thin and fine, seemed to have receded an inch since they'd last spoken. His coat, cut in the latest style, seemed a poor choice, the broad lapels emphasizing the narrowness of his build.

Had he always been so small?

Calm fell over her. Her pulse slowed, and she drew an easy breath. "What are you doing here?"

"Right to the point," he said. "Shan't we share a drink first? I've traveled a long way."

"You'll be traveling longer yet. I've no intention to house you tonight."

"Oh, come now!" With a laugh, he fell into a nearby chair. When he stripped off his gloves and folded them, his hands looked as pale and slim as a girl's. "Will you really be so cold? We're old friends, you and I."

It gave her a shudder to remember how those hands had once touched her. "Not cold," she said. "Bored, already. And you've barely spoken five words."

"Intriguing," he said. "You seem to be doing splendidly without me. You know I can't resist a lady's indifference."

How had she ever found his malice-tipped humor so diverting? And really, was there anything so demoralizing as meeting a former lover? Never did a woman have more cause to doubt her judgment than when confronted with the pathetic evidence of what she had once somehow found appealing.

"Won't you return the compliment?" he asked, winking.

That wink annoyed her. She had seen him dispense it across a dozen ballrooms, but she had never liked the boyish affectation.

That memory encouraged her. Yes, from the start she had seen all the warning signs that had eventually made him intolerable. "Surely you didn't come all the way to Cornwall for compliments."

"Perhaps I missed you," he said.

She smiled. "How amusing! Has Miss Lister broken off the engagement, then? The Hawthornes *had* been wondering why a date hadn't been set for the wedding."

He laughed and gave an idle flip of his gloves. "Good heavens, no! That child thinks I hung the stars for her.

No, she has no idea I'm here. Her father, on the other hand . . ." He sighed. "More difficult. I really do wish you would sit down, Lizzie."

That was James's name for her. That Nello used it now, when he never had done before, announced very plainly how *determined* he was to be chummy. The realization was mildly alarming.

She took a seat. "There," she said. "Now explain yourself."

"Well, if you must know—I've a proposition for you. A delicate one. Didn't want to put it into writing." He laughed again. His laugh was one of his chief charms, low and lovely. His teeth, on the other hand, were yellow. She had always known that, too.

"I can't imagine any proposition that would concern the both of us," she said.

"Can't you?" Now he began to bounce his foot. He'd always lacked the talent to sit quite still. His eyes wandered the room, latching onto the liquor cabinet, which he nodded toward. "Just one drink, then," he said.

"Pour it yourself." She folded her hands. "I'll wait."

His mouth flattened. "Had to let go of staff? I knew you were pinching pennies, but I never dreamed it would go south so quickly."

"My staff is busy entertaining my guests."

"Yes, Katherine said you had a houseful of perfect lunks. Very well." He rose and loped to the cabinet, rummaging about until he found a decanter of whisky. Uncapping it, he took a whiff and grimaced. "Economies here, too?"

"Uncreative," she remarked. "I've already told you of my difficulties. If you mean to insult me, you'll have to find a novel approach."

"Insult you?" He splashed himself a generous few fingers and then returned to his seat. "No, I've no interest in that. And of course I haven't breathed a word to anyone . . . yet."

She lifted her palm to disguise her mimed yawn. "And now threats. But surely those could have been communicated by post. It only requires a bit of subtlety."

"Too true," he said, and took a healthy swallow. "But I mean it when I say I've no wish to harm you, Liz. You're lovely. And I look back very fondly on our time together."

Her skin crawled. It would be far easier, she realized, to hear that he loathed her. "Don't think of me at all," she said. "And I will return the favor."

"No, I have a different bargain in mind altogether," he went on.

She could not begin to imagine what devil was dancing in his brain-box. "Then propose it, so I may return to my party."

"Very well," he said. "To the chase, then. What got me thinking of you was Hollister. Ennobled three years ago, yes?"

A very bizarre tangent. "I don't keep track of such things. You may ask my social secretary. Shall I summon her?"

He waved away this suggestion. "Well, no matter. It was three years ago. I hear the Duke of Marwick had a great deal to do with it."

She tried not to tense. The last time Marwick had entered their conversation, she had been awash in tears over Nello's betrayal with Marwick's wife. It was horrifying now to remember how very hurt she'd been. This man had not deserved a single sleepless hour. "What of it?"

He crossed his legs and leaned back in the chair, making himself comfortable. "To be clear—I speak now on the understanding that you and I, we will keep each other's secrets, as a favor to each other . . ."

"Yes," she said impatiently. "You needn't spell it out; I don't wish to hear my private business advertised abroad."

"Very good," he said. "Then to be blunt: my future bride's father was less than enthusiastic about our match. Some nonsense to do with thinking his daughter deserves a title."

Liza laughed, blackly amused. "Imagine that! And I suppose you had nothing to do with his expectations." Nello had been spinning the same story for years: a title was coming to him any day now. He was related to the Queen through a second cousin, and made an attempt, occasionally, to appear at court, though his welcome had waned after the Queen had witnessed him drunk at the theater last spring. Yet he persisted in believing that his blood connection to her, and the few brief years he'd served in the Horse Guards, somehow merited ennoblement.

"I may have hinted," he said with a shrug. Always shameless, Nello. No parson or priest in the world could have put him to the blush. "That is, if Hollister can win a barony—a nobody whose parents were raised in the penal colonies! Well, then I can't see why I shouldn't be so lucky. They're practically on sale these days. Disgraceful, really."

She sighed. A very old polemic. "If they're for sale, then Hollister certainly had the wherewithal to purchase his own. But I suppose, once you've wed your heiress, so, too, will you."

"There's the rub," he said with a grimace. "Her father wants some more solid assurance of my advancement *before* we wed."

"But that's absurd." Despite the editorials in the conservative papers, it was not, after all, so common for titles to be created. Yes, a handful of baronets every year, and a new baron or two, perhaps—but titles were not given to men who'd achieved nothing of import.

"Isn't it?" Nello sighed. "It would be ever so much easier with his daughter's fortune bankrolling my chances. But he's insistent, and I've made discreet inquiries. In fact, I've had assurances from several quarters that my name *might* yet be placed on a particular list, to be submitted to Her Majesty for consideration early next year—but it will require funds, you understand, to guarantee it. And, more important, a word or two from the right people."

"Naturally," said Liza. "I've no idea what on earth this has to do with me, of course."

"Nothing, really," said Nello. "Only I've certain information that you'd not like divulged, which ensures your discretion—and you've a certain proximity to someone who can help me. Or rather, to his brother."

She had an inkling now of where this roundabout nonsense might be headed, and it made her very uneasy. "Go on."

"Since you're doing so very well without me, I hope it won't distress you if I tell you that Margaret de Grey was quite chatty in bed," Nello went on. "Even more so out of it. Very indiscreet in her letters—and one in particular. To be blunt: I've not only a list of the other men with whom she shared her favors, but also some very amusing anecdotes about these men and their use of secrets shared with her by her husband. Now, we all know the Kingmaker is *most* sensitive of his reputation. It seems to me that he might appreciate it very much if these letters were never to see the light of day. But I'm not stupid enough to approach Marwick directly."

"Oh, indeed," said Liza. "I seem to recall you groveling in fear at the prospect of him finding out about your liaison."

"Fear seems a bit strong," Nello said sourly. "But a healthy respect, yes, of course. So I'll entrust the negotiations to you."

She scoffed. This was more preposterous than anything she could have imagined. "To *me*? I've barely spoken with the man!"

"Yes, but it would take a miracle for him not to have heard of you—and of our affair. Besides, I imagine he'll be quite intrigued when a great beauty comes sniffing at his door. He's widowed, you know. For your part, you'll play the heartbroken lover. A widower might appreciate that. In exchange for handing over the letters, you'll insist that Marwick put in a good word for me when it comes to advising the Queen regarding new titles. Why, I expect he'll find it very touching proof of your continued devotion to me. Who knows? Perhaps you'll even end up a duchess for it." He smiled. "Do you see? I truly am hoping the best for you, Liz."

Liza came to her feet, her laughter now entirely genuine. "Charles Nelson! Truly, I believe you've taken a hard knock to your head. I wouldn't lift a finger to spare you from a runaway carriage, and you know it."

"Oh, come now, darling, you might at least shriek a little, surely?"

She rolled her eyes. To think that she'd once found his flippancy amusing!

Nello came to his feet as well. "But more to the point, you could always demand a payment of your own," he said. "I won't be selfish—I'll have no need of money once this title business is settled and Miss Lister and I walk down the aisle. Ask for whatever you like from Marwick. Save this pile, and your little parish. See? I bring you a gift!"

"Goodness," Liza said. "How kind of you. Do I strike you as a blackmailer?"

"No, but I have faith that you could learn." He smiled slowly. "You were always very . . . inventive."

Had he been closer, she would have slapped him for that smug leer. "You will leave now," she said. "Or I'll have you thrown out."

He *tsked.* "Think, Liz. If not for your own sake, perhaps you'd care to spare Marwick the embarrassment of those letters going public. It would hardly reflect well on his brother."

She froze.

"Yes," he said. "You were never very good at discretion, were you? The Hawthornes' letters have been terribly suggestive."

A bluff based on empty suspicions. She'd done nothing compromising in front of the Hawthornes. "I have no idea what you mean."

"Oh?" Nello bolted the rest of his drink and set his glass on the coffee table. "Very well. I suppose they were wrong, then. It makes no difference to you if Lord Michael de Grey is once again made a laughingstock by his family. Very well."

No, that prospect did not agree with her in the least.

That *Nello* should be the one to effect it made her heart pound with pure, elemental rage. She took a deep breath and thought very carefully. "For all I know, you're lying," she said. "What woman would be so stupid as to commit all this to writing?"

"An opium eater," said Nello with a smirk. "Oh, don't look at me so—as I've said, it was a mistake to sleep with her. But one I'm quite grateful to have made, now that it offers such a neat solution."

"Charming," she said. "So you propose I waltz into Marwick's house and inform him of all of this? I'm sure he'll be very amenable to championing you after *that*. Provided he even believes me!"

"Well, you'll have proof in the form of the letters," said Nello. "As for Marwick . . . surely he'll recognize his own wife's handwriting?"

She stared at him. "You have no shame."

He offered her a bland smile. "Once you rather liked that."

With a noise of disgust, she waved this comment away. "If this is true, you should go to Lord Michael, not me."

"As I said, I wish to maintain my anonymity. And about that . . ." He paused. "Should you breathe a word of this to de Grey—should it come out that I'm behind this—well, the letters will be published. And your own sad circumstances will become public knowledge on the instant."

Beside the scandal of the letters, her private circumstances would barely register. But she wouldn't point that out to him. He'd only look for another way to compel her. She did not think he'd find one, but . . . Michael would pay the cost for it.

Perhaps she could do precisely as Nello bade her: take the letters to Marwick and let *him* ferret out their source.

If word reached Michael of her involvement, he would never forgive her for it.

Michael. Michael knew Nello was here. "Lord Michael will put two and two together," she said. "He knows you've come down to Bosbrea. He's not an idiot. He'll divine that you're behind this scheme."

"So you must convince him otherwise," said Nello. "Or the copies of the letters will be distributed."

She bit her lip. There was some solution, but she required time to find it. "I must think on it," she said. "Figure out how to make my approach to Marwick."

"Don't think too hard," he said cheerfully. "Don't want to injure your pretty little head."

Bastard. "Were you always such a rotter?" she asked. "Or have you taken a hard knock to your skull recently?"

"Again—you used to like it," said Nello with a laugh. He started for the door. "I'll let myself out, shall I? Write to me with your decision, if you can still afford the postage."

The door shut behind him, closing her into a suffocating silence.

Elizabeth never returned after her conference with the bastard. That none of the other guests remarked on her absence turned Michael's mood all the blacker. These were her *friends*. Did they not wonder where she had gone? No, it seemed they were content to sit about drinking themselves to death, and trading ridiculous conversation.

Late in the evening, the conversation turned to the question of beliefs: did anyone credit these mystics? And Viscountess Sanburne, a lovely but serious young woman who had spent most of the night smiling silently at her husband's repartee, leaned forward to argue that magic was real. The jeers that answered her statement— even Baron Forbes chuckled—did not discourage her. Jaw squaring, she explained that she did not believe in *sorcery* and the like, but felt that faith was in itself a mysterious and perhaps magical power, insofar as one could not argue with its transformative properties.

"For instance," she said, "a certain tribe in the northwest of America favors a ceremony which they undertake for three days and nights without sleep." To the beating of drums, she explained, the men of the tribe inhaled intoxicating smoke, and spoke at first of the visions that came to them. On the third night, however, they did not speak at all, for by then they had entered a speechless trance in which neither sound nor sight had any grip on them. "It's only after they wake again," she concluded, "that they are considered men—for they have reached a place beyond reason, a very sacred place, in which they have come to learn a deeper truth about themselves, beyond all logic. And in many cases, they do seem transformed—some discover new skills, and others are remarked to have altered their very personalities."

The Hawthornes had made light of the speech, as was their wont. But long after the gathering had broken up, the viscountess's words continued to echo through Michael's mind, until their sense seemed perfectly plain to him. Perhaps all great truths emerged from compulsions. For as he prowled down this darkened hallway now, nothing—no piece of logic, no reasoning—could have compelled him to turn back. He was driven in this course, though it would change him irrevocably.

He could not let her go.

Even if the price was his honor, and everything else he'd thought he knew of himself—his dedication to the hospital and the people he served there; his purpose to heal; his cynicism that love ever made a wise gamble—he could not let her go.

He was almost to her door when a shadowy figure stepped out ahead of him. "Up to no good," it said.

He recognized the voice, and came to a stop. "Sanburne. Why are you up?"

The viscount stepped forward into the dim circle of light shed by a nearby sconce. He wore a dressing gown, and his eyes were heavy-lidded. "I'm up because I have a wife who dislikes me yanking the bellpull at half past two. Those pastries we had at high tea," he said wryly. "She's a terrible craving for them. And peculiar ideas about servants, whom she thinks require their sleep."

Michael smiled despite himself. "You're off to prowl the kitchens?"

"Indeed." Sanburne eyed him. "And where are *you* off to?"

Michael did not reply to that. Elizabeth's bedchamber was three doors away. He'd known that for days now, and the knowledge had kept him burning well into the nights.

After a moment, Sanburne sighed. "If you hurt her, I will see that you regret it." His tone was pleasant and steady. "I will make it my main business, in fact."

Michael did not pretend to misunderstand. "I have no such intention. And I'm glad that she has friends to look after her."

Sanburne rolled his shoulders, an impatient gesture. "She has more than one."

"Then I'm all the gladder for it."

A brief pause followed, during which Sanburne studied him with frank curiosity. "Here's the thing," he said. "You're a decent sort, which is more than I could say for myself before I met Lyd. And I suppose Lizzie might also have a taste for pastries one day. Would you know where to look for them?"

This conversation was rapidly approaching the surreal. "I suppose I'd try the larder first," Michael said.

Sanburne nodded. "And if she only wanted the strawberry kind?"

For God's sake. "I suppose I'd take all of them, and let her pick out the ones she wanted."

Sanburne laughed. "I like that." Stepping forward, he delivered a solid clap to Michael's shoulder. "Remember this ambition. *All* the pastries. She wouldn't settle for less, you know. Nor should she. And now . . . I believe I'll pretend I didn't see you here." With a tip of an invisible hat, he walked onward.

Michael stood in the darkness, listening to the viscount's footsteps fade. He felt oddly disoriented—as though he truly had been entranced, and only now had he come awake.

All the pastries. He smiled a little. While Sanburne was slightly deranged, he was also right: Elizabeth deserved everything.

But Sanburne did not know the circumstances. No matter what Michael did or did not do, she would be hurt in the end. Love could not save her estates.

Turn back. Walk away.

That was the honorable course.

His temper lit. He had already walked away once tonight, when he rightfully should have followed her and laid Charles Nelson out with one swift snap of his fist. And afterward—afterward he would have turned to her and said, "*That* was my right. And it will remain so."

Why had she not come back after meeting the bastard? Michael could force himself to respect her need for funds—but if she meant to take up with that ass again . . . then she had abandoned her plans. In which case, she might as well dally with *him*.

He covered the remaining distance in less than a minute. The door to her sitting room opened without a squeak. Across the moonlit expanse of carpet, he saw the next door standing ajar. And through it . . .

On silent feet he advanced.

Her eyes opened suddenly. In the dark of her bedroom, Liza knew she was not alone.

Fear never touched her. Later she would find it curious that she had known from the first moment that it was he who stood at the foot of her bed. Clairvoyance, her spiritualists might have told her. But her knowledge was more mundane, born of a faint current of air that brought to her the suggestion of his warmth, the precise chemistry of his skin.

Animal spirit to animal spirit, she sensed him nearby.

She sat up. A shadow detached itself and approached.

"I am going tomorrow," Michael said.

She knuckled her eyes, which felt gritty for lack of sleep. Only ten minutes ago, it seemed, she'd still been tossing and turning, looking for a way to foil Nello, to protect this man.

Going, he said. Yes, that was best. For both of them.

"If you mean to go back to him," he growled, "I cannot stay to watch."

It would be wiser not to correct him. But she could not bear for him to think her such a fool.

"I'm not going back to him," she said.

She heard him exhale. And then the mattress dipped as he settled down at her side.

"I could never go back to him now," she whispered.

The warmth of his fingers on her face drove her eyes shut. In a long moment's silence they sat together, as through the open window came the sound of a warm summer breeze ruffling the leaves.

He had never been in her bedroom before. How surprising and wrong that seemed. He belonged here with her as she slept.

Urgency quickened her pulse. She had seen the pain in his face when he worried for his brother; she had heard it in his voice when he spoke of his parents' legacy. What kind of love would hers be, if she did not protect him from fresh agonies?

She made herself say it. "I am glad you are going. It's best."

"Yes," he murmured. The mattress creaked as he leaned down. His lips were barely a whisper over hers. The kiss, so gentle, broke something inside her.

She wrapped her hand around his nape and kissed him back, earnestly. *I must protect you.* The thought, a moment ago so panicked, now felt sweet and strengthening. She could do this for him, so gladly, with no regrets.

But not before he loved her one more time.

"Come," she whispered, and took him beneath the arms to urge him to lie down beside her.

*   *   *

He let her guide him down—wishing, for the briefest moment, that he had thought to open the curtains, so he might see her in this thin, slippery shift she wore. But then her mouth found his again and all other thoughts faded but this: how soft she was beneath him, how scented, some subtle floral note blending with the more natural perfume of her skin; the cool weight of her hair through his combing fingers, and then the delicate slope of her nape and the sweet, bony spur beneath it. Her arms closed lightly around his back, but he felt the strength in her when she arched against him. He suckled her tongue, and ran his hand down to her waist, curving over her hip.

He would touch her forever. He felt no rush, no physical urgency. All he wanted was to stroke her like this, in the dark of her room, wondrous with her acceptance of his right to be here.

She moved over to make more room for him. He settled by her side, exchanging with her long, lazy kisses. No rush, none. He traced her hairline as he kissed her, delicate feathering touches along her temple, the curve of her ear, the tender spot at the top of her jaw. She sighed, and he felt her eyelashes flutter against his cheek. It caused a shiver down his skin. He felt by memory for the mole beside her eye, pressing his lips to it. *I know you.*

Her lips found his ear, causing him to shudder again. His groin tightened, and he knew a fleeting disappointment that his body would not, after all, prove better than his appetites. He slid down a little to suck her neck, to trace the slope of her breast down to the nipple that stiffened so invitingly beneath the thin cloth. Very lightly he took it between his teeth, wetting the fabric with his tongue, sucking strongly until she whimpered.

But that was not enough. So much required his attention. He lifted the silken shift off her, raising it by slow inches, moving down to kiss what he bared: her ankles, small and bony, and the gentle swell of her calves; the tender place behind her knees, and the soft give of her thighs, which trembled under his mouth.

Time, he thought, was a privilege, and in a just world this would be their bed, and this night not worth counting, it being the first of innumerable shared nights to come. But now he knew why men married, for then time was theirs, a privilege and a claim; *your time is all mine,* he would tell her. And he saw, too, that lovemaking was a very particular kind of sex, one he had never enjoyed before, but the way of which was so clear to him, seeming to emerge from some ancient place of knowledge within him. This was a world away from mere congress, his desire unrecognizable—no less fervent than when he'd taken her in the gamekeeper's cottage, but profoundly redirected. The goad that spurred him onward, the pleasure he craved, had nothing to do with his own pleasure, save that her pleasure became his.

He licked up to the sweetness between her legs, gripping her hips when she would have twisted away. She tasted of the ocean, and she sighed like the sea. With his tongue he found the little bud that made her gasp. Again and again he licked into her, making her buck, making her sob. And when she cried out, going limp beneath him—when she whispered to him to stop; she could not bear any more—then that was only the beginning, still. This was still the beginning.

He moved back up her body, his mouth leading the way, his hand cupping her firmly between her legs, using the heel of his palm to torment her sensitized flesh while he suckled hard again at her nipple. Her whispers broke apart into incoherent fragments, sobbing entreaties that made no sense; he palmed her harder yet and then growled into her mouth when she tried to squirm free.

"I want you inside me," she said raggedly into his ear.

Not yet. This was still the beginning. He was intent—

A groan escaped him as her hot little hand closed over his cock. She was freeing him, three clever tugs, seating him firmly against her quim. His cock slid down through her folds, wet, wetter than the ocean.

"Please," she whispered.

He took her mouth as he thrust into her. No longer innocent, no longer pure; his appetites were roaring, and he resented them for making him so helpless—until she wrapped her legs around him and arched, and the beauty of it broke over him like a wondrous revelation.

Nothing of resentment in this. Only gratitude.

"God, you are beautiful," he said.

Her laugh hitched. "You can't even see me."

As if that mattered. "You are a wonder," he said. "Were I blind, I would see that."

But he did not like that she could still manage to put together words. He rolled his hips and her breath caught. Leaning down, he tongued her lobe and thrust harder. Her thighs tightened around his hips and that was the signal he'd required. Again and again he stroked into her, deeper, faster, as her rapid little breaths turned into keens, rising the scale, breaking—

She contracted around him and the top of his skull

seemed to lift away. One, two, three more thrusts, and then—ah, God, he did not want to do it, he did not—

Her hands gripped his buttocks, her nails cutting into him in demand. And with a gusty groan, he spilled himself in her.

A mistake. He knew it the moment he rolled off her. But it did not need to be so. "Marry me," he said.

Her ragged breathing fell silent. And then he heard her draw a great, shuddering breath.

"I can't," she said. "You know I can't."

"Forget why you can't," he said. "Only tell me that you want to. That you will."

Her hand found his throat. Groped very lightly to his face. The soft press of her lips destroyed him.

"I *can't,*" she said very gently. "Nor can you, my love."

My love. "Don't use those words," he said roughly. "Not if you don't mean—"

"And you will go in the morning, and my heart will break," she said. "But I do love you. That won't change, even with my heart in pieces."

He held himself very still, curious to see what would be first to break—her heart, or him.

And then, suddenly, all these words, all this turmoil, irritated him beyond measure. He sat up. His brother had not replied to his letter. It was time for a confrontation. "If I came to you with money," he said. If Alastair could be persuaded—or threatened, for by God, he had it in him. "Then, would you—"

She sat up, too, and kissed him again, lingeringly, her cooling skin moist against his own, moist with their combined sweat. On her lips he tasted a message he would not, he *refused* to hear.

He pulled back from her. "Answer me!"

"I want the best for you," she whispered. "That is what love means."

"The best for you is me."

No reply to that. He gritted his teeth. "And if a child comes from this?"

"I will tell you," she said. "We will deal with it then. But I think it unlikely. My cycle only just ceased."

She had all the answers, and none that he wished to hear. He stood, grabbing at his clothes. "Promise me you'll make no decisions until we see each other next."

"Yes," she said. "I promise."

Michael left the next morning, an hour after dawn, as the sun climbed the sky through banks of scarlet clouds. But Liza was not at Havilland Hall to see him off. She had kept a brave face for him until he'd left her bed-chamber, and then she had let herself weep until her throat ached. For a time, terrible thoughts had trans-fixed her—ways to make Marwick bow to their will; ways to *make* him approve her—and then sanity had settled over her again.

Finally, at the first hint of light, she had abandoned her bed for the woods. The lake gleamed under the dawning light, but she lingered there only a quarter hour before continuing onward.

Until the last few minutes, she did not admit to her-self where her footsteps were taking her. The graveyard looked a peaceful sight, the headstones casting long shadows across the grass. Her mind was curiously quiet as she opened the gate, the latch squeaking.

A bundle of fresh roses lay atop her mother's grave, the scarlet leaves gleaming with dew. She reached down to pick them up, drops of water soaking through her sleeves, the flowers' rich, dark scent making her dizzy. She blinked hard. Lack of sleep, and perhaps a few lingering tears, blurred the words chiseled into her mother's headstone.

Set me as a seal upon thine heart, as a seal upon thine arm: for love is strong as death.

"Mama," she said softly. The lifting breeze gently touched her cheek; it carried the scents of summer, a hint of the day's oncoming warmth, the trace of smoke from some hearth where the morning meal was being warmed.

She went to her knees in the grass. Carefully she laid the roses back in their place. *From me, Mama. They were always from me.*

She'd been so afraid to face this place. Shame had kept her away. But her mother was not here. And even if her mother had lingered in this place . . . she would never have judged Liza so harshly.

That voice in her head . . . it had always been her own.

"I miss you," she whispered.

A flutter of movement from the corner of her eye: a small brown finch had alit on her father's grave. The bird tilted his head, eyeing her.

How had Mama borne the separation from him? She had mourned, but she had never lost herself in her grief. Her kindness, her compassion, her gentleness—they had never diminished. She'd always had love to spare.

Michael was right. Every child required an example. And Liza would learn from her mother's.

She rose to her feet. Strange, that even as her beloved left her on a London-bound train, as she stood in a graveyard surrounded by fading names and forgotten souls, she might, at last, feel her loneliness lift. Alone, but not lonely.

With her mother's death, she had imagined that she would never again find someone to love her unconditionally. But she had forgotten that there would always be someone who did so: she, herself.

You are a wonder, Michael had told her.

She was determined to be nothing less. But if she failed, sometimes, to live up to his view of her . . . then she would love herself anyway. Never again would she allow herself to do otherwise.

"Sweet dreams, Mama."

Turning on her heel, she started back for the house.

Two hours later, she sat at her dressing table, half listening to Mather's recital of the morning's business. Tomorrow the remaining guests departed, and their travel arrangements involved a good many particulars, all of which Mather seemed to have well in hand.

"And the Forbeses are taking the earlier train," Mather said, "but that should not pose a problem, for Lord Hollister arrived with his own equipment, and is glad to take Lord Weston and Mr. Tilney to the station in his vehicle."

"That's fine." Liza looked over her powders and rouges and kohl. Her hope was to assemble a face that did not look puffy and red from last night's weeping. "You and I will go in the pony cart, then. No need to rush Jane; she can join us at her leisure."

Mather frowned. "But . . . where are we going, ma'am?"

"To the station. I want to be on the first train as

well." She tapped the lid on the powder jar, then decided against it. No amount of cosmetics was going to make her look beautiful today. The idea, strangely, did not bother her in the least.

"I—I hadn't realized," stammered Mather. Poor girl; she never liked sudden changes of plan. "But the town house is closed, ma'am. I'll need to wire the staff there at once—"

"Oh, they can open the shutters after we arrive," Liza said. She had two pieces of business that could not wait on such niceties—an appointment with Nello, followed immediately thereafter by a visit with the Duke of Marwick.

"Another thing," she went on as she turned on her stool. "You must prepare to soothe the staff. My financial plight will soon become public. I expect the staff will be very uneasy about it. You must assure them that I have no intention to let anyone go." *Yet.* "Not without proper notice," she added. She could hold on for another six months, give her employees a generous measure of time in which to find new positions.

It was a mark of her surprise that Mather fell into a seat without asking for permission. Such a stickler, she was. Liza would miss her terribly.

"I don't understand," the girl said. "Why would— that is, how would anyone know of it?" Her russet brows dipped suddenly. "*Mr. Nelson.* You mean to . . ." Her lips folded abruptly, trapping the thought unspoken.

Liza shrugged. "It was bound to come out eventually." And certainly would, once Nello realized she had thrown him to the dogs—or rather, to the Kingmaker. For she had no intention of protecting him. The more fool he, for imagining she might place her pride, and her prospective financial gains, over the chance to see him squirm.

Mather studied her a moment. "Very well," she said slowly. Then, as Liza started to rise: "There is one more thing, madam." She held out a letter.

Taking it, Liza caught her breath. It was not addressed to her.

She looked sharply up at Mather. "Why bring me this? You should have posted it onward to Lord Michael."

Mather's lashes lowered, veiling her expression. On a girl best known for her bluntness, this abashed look screamed as loudly as a confession. "I thought you might like to read it."

Liza realized she was gaping. "Why, you cunning little thing! Have you been taking lessons from the Hawthornes? I would not read another man's letters." No matter how burning the temptation was, now that Mather had suggested it. "Why on earth—"

But she stopped as Mather's brows rose to a speaking arch. *Come now,* that look said. *I'm no fool.*

Liza sighed. "Was it so obvious, then?"

Mather shrugged. "Sometimes I eavesdrop, madam. It's a vice."

"Heavens, Mather. Do I even *know* you?"

The girl reddened. "I worried last night that Mr. Nelson would not behave. I wanted to be ready to help should he . . ." She scowled. "And one can hardly say he behaved, at that! Such a nefarious scheme."

So she knew about the matter of Marwick? "Gracious, what *else* have you overheard?"

"From the Hawthornes' talk, enough to gather that you were right: Lord Michael is not a suitable solution to your financial difficulties." Mather's jaw was assuming its most mutinous cast. "However, it took no eavesdropping to see how you might wish it otherwise."

A brief silence opened, which Liza did not know how to fill. Her secretary would have made a very good spy! "You understand most of it, then. I still won't read that letter."

Mather's hands twisted together in her lap. "Then I have another suggestion. You won't like it, though." In a great rush, she said, "You may use those letters to blackmail the duke into accepting you. To—to force him to pay off your debts, as Mr. Nelson suggested, but also to give his blessing to your wedding with his brother."

Liza sighed. She might have been shocked . . . had the idea not crossed her mind in the hour before sunrise. "But I couldn't," she said—gently, for judging by the increasing pallor on Mather's face, her secretary was also seeing the ill in it. "Lord Michael loves his brother. When the truth came out, how would it serve me any good for him to know that I had held those letters over his brother's head?"

Besides, she had a very different threat in mind for the duke. Not being in the habit of blackmail, she could only assume that threats were best issued in the singular.

"No, of course that wouldn't suit," Mather said. "But if somebody *else* were to employ the letters for your sake—"

"Goodness, no. I wouldn't drag anyone else into this mess." Her eyes fell to the letter in her hand. It seemed to grow hotter the longer she held it. "And I can't read this," she said, thrusting it back at the girl.

"But . . ."

Mather looked highly agitated now. As Liza studied the girl, a terrible suspicion overcame her. "Mather, how did you know that Lord Michael required his brother's approval to wed?"

If possible, Mather went even paler now. Her freckles looked livid.

Liza groaned. "Do *not* tell me you read it." Her eyes fell to the seal, which appeared unbroken. Mather was gripping it so tightly that her knuckles were white.

"I . . . won't," said Mather, her tone muted.

Liza covered her eyes briefly. God help her. "You are *not* to tamper with correspondence! Never, ever again!"

"I won't, ma'am! I *promise* you!"

"Then . . ." Her hand fell, and she drew a great breath. "You seem to think I would find its contents interesting. Tell me—why is that?"

Mather swallowed audibly. "I expect . . . if you were to read this letter . . . you would gather how deeply Lord Michael cares for you . . . and how much an *ass* is the Duke of Marwick!"

Liza managed a smile. "Well," she said. That put paid to the last of her hopes—a hope she had not realized until this moment that she'd been nursing in the most private corner of her heart. "No need to read what I already knew."

"He has closed the hospital! Shut it up and turned out the patients!"

She sucked in a breath. That, she had not known. And it made her mission in London all the more urgent. "Mather, be *sure* to book those tickets for us—the earliest train, please. I mean to be in London by tomorrow midnight." She paused. "And—post the letter onward for me, will you?"

"You are a better person than I," Mather said hoarsely—startling from Liza another laugh.

So. It seemed she *would* keep laughing, then, no matter what. That was good to know. Perhaps she did not have her mother's kindness—but her gift for merriment would never fade, even in sad circumstances such as these.

"Mather," she said, "that is a *very* flattering verdict for me, and a very *grim* one for you—*despite* your talent for espionage. Now, take that letter away—and make sure the seal appears unbroken."

"Yes, ma'am. At once."

CHAPTER TWENTY

For the second day in a row, Michael sat down across from his brother. Today he would not scream. Today he meant to match his brother for coldness.

"Thank you for seeing me," he said calmly. If they were going to end up in court—if history was determined to repeat itself—then he would, at least, edit it somewhat. The newspapers would have no cause to report screaming fights and vitriol. The aggrieved party would provide no nasty quotes.

"I confess, I was surprised to hear you announced," Alastair said. Once again, he sat behind his desk. Jones said he spent most of his days here in the study, and still refused to budge from the house. His decline had grown more marked, particularly in his alarming gauntness; had he been a patient seeking help, the sight of him would have alarmed Michael into ringing for hot broth and a hearty repast.

But though Alastair's flesh was sallow and withering, his will remained hard as diamond. *It is for your own good,* he'd said yesterday. *A widow, a notorious whore, no,*

*I will not approve of such. You waste my time and insult my
intelligence with this proposition.*

The memory made it easy to hand over the sheaf of
papers. He felt nothing as he watched his brother look
over them.

"I don't understand," Alastair said flatly.

"This is a legal action drawn up by Smythe and Jack-
son." The solicitors had accepted him as a client yesterday, agreeing to draw their fees from his winnings. "If
you will not surrender the allowance vouchsafed to me in
our father's will, then I will take my request to the courts.
In addition, I am suing for your removal from the hospital's board of directors. You overstepped your bounds in
ordering its closure. I have asked Weston to replace you.
Hollister may come aboard as well." Michael had spoken
to both men before leaving Havilland Hall.

"Interesting," Alastair murmured. He cast aside the
papers, his hand fluttering down to rest anemically atop
them. His signet ring hung loosely on his finger, sliding
all the way to his knuckle. "Yet I doubt they have any
interest in funding your efforts."

"As to that," Michael said, "Weston has offered a sizable amount, and both men support my proposal to
expand our services to patients of the middling class.
Fees from the new clientele will support our charitable
operations." He had gone over the budget last night.
Provided the bourgeoisie would consent to be treated
at a charity hospital, it might work. He was not overly
hopeful, of course. But it was a chance, and that was
more than he'd had three days ago.

Alastair's smile was slight, and faded so quickly that it
left the impression of exhaustion. "I would not count on
Hollister remaining involved. I have been a great friend

to him, as you may know." He pushed the papers toward Michael. "And I do not appreciate men without loyalty. Indeed, I tend to make sure they repent the lack of it."

Michael gritted his teeth. "Funny thing, that. Until recently, I had imagined that *brotherhood* might entail loyalty. But I see your understanding of the term is a far match from mine." He shoved the papers back toward his brother before coming to his feet. "And now, I'll bid you good day."

"Wait." Alastair stared up at him. "You . . ."

Michael waited impatiently, trying to ignore how his brother's eyes seemed to be sinking back into his skull. Alastair looked more and more like a death's-head. *"What?"*

"You really mean to do this," Alastair said. "To take *me* to court."

Michael called up his grimmest smile. "A fine irony, is it not? And here you wished to keep your name free of scandal."

A muscle flexed in Alastair's jaw. He started to stand, and—*Christ,* but he had to use his hands to do it; palms down on the desk, he shoved himself up with visible difficulty.

His jacket hung limply from his shoulders. There simply wasn't the flesh to fill it anymore.

And despite his best effort to remain cold—for Alastair deserved nothing from him; *nothing*—Michael felt his indifference crack. "Good God," he said. "Good *God,* Al. You are killing yourself. You—"

But what was there to say that he had not said already?

There was one thing. "I love you," he said with difficulty. "That has not changed. My God—you and I were in hell together as children. And you were *everything* to me. My only ally. My dearest friend. My protector and support. If I emerged whole, it was only because of you. How can I ever forget that? You will *always* be my brother."

A scowl was dawning on Alastair's brow. "And how nobly you show it," he said. "This *brotherly affection*."

"You leave me no choice." Michael shook his head. "Alastair, you have become the man you once sought to protect me from. You are our father reborn—but I am not our mother. God knows, *you* raised me better than that. So, yes—I will show you no mercy. I will take you to court and fight for what is mine, and I will win. And I vow to you, that day will mark the end of our connection. Though it grieves me, I will leave you to our father's fate—for by your own hand, you will have earned it."

Alastair stared at him for a long, unblinking moment. And then he laughed, a laugh that sounded like the rasp of dry leaves. "Very dramatic," he said. "But I fear you misunderstand my disbelief. I only wonder at your foolishness. You'll win, will you? No. I will crush you. So easily. So easy to suborn Weston and Hollister! And I have solicitors on retainer who specialize in ending these cases quickly . . . and always, *always* to my opponents' detriment."

Michael sighed. "Right. You forget now to whom you're speaking. I've had years to witness your operations. But if it cheers you to dwell on what power remains to you—for all of London whispers now that you've run mad—then by all means, dwell on it. And exercise it against me as you must."

Alastair narrowed his eyes. "It is not *me* whom society will mock. *You* are the one who once again will make us the object of ridicule. And for what—some *woman*? What do you imagine people will say? De Grey makes a spectacle of himself, bankrupts himself for a hussy who sells her photographs for money; who collapses at balls from too much drink; who, by all reports, has taken lovers who—"

"*Enough!*" Michael stepped backward lest he lunge *forward*; lest he smash his fist into his brother's face. "I would hit you," he said through his teeth, "only I think it would kill you, in this pathetic condition you're in. But listen to me carefully now: that *woman* is the woman whom *I love*. And unlike my love for you now, what I feel for her is *earned*." A black laugh escaped him. "And you would judge her based on the tales your *spies* collected? *You,* who saw how eager the world was to believe the worst of our mother? My God, I would ask you where you'd misplaced your sense of shame—but I expect you left it where you left your sanity! I wash my hands of you, Alastair. But I vow, if you raise *one finger* to trouble her, I will change my mind. I will come back here and strike you down like the wrath of God."

The words had been washed out of him by a red wave of rage. He stepped back again, for the rage had not abated; it wanted to tug him forward, to make him do something he'd truly regret.

But he controlled himself, and saw at last his brother *react* as a human might. Alastair blinked very rapidly and all but fell back into his seat. He looked, finally and at last, shaken.

Michael did not let himself hope, though. He was through with praying that such signs portended a revelation. "I am done with you," he repeated softly—as much to himself as to Alastair. *Done.*

And then he turned on his heel and walked out.

In the hall he passed Jones, who threw him a scandalized look. Perhaps the old scoundrel had been listening at the keyhole. Michael quickened his step, desperate to be out of this house, to drag in a breath of air not poisoned by his brother.

At the top of the stairs, though, he stopped dead. For below, in the entry hall, stood a figure that made his heart turn over once.

By sheer instinct he retreated to the alcove that screened the entrance to the west wing from view. His heart, which had sat in his chest like clay throughout his interview with Alastair, now suddenly came back to life, pounding wildly.

What in God's name was *Elizabeth* doing here?

Jones passed by him again, oblivious to his covert position. Quickly the butler went down the stairs. He exchanged some murmured conversation with Elizabeth that Michael could not make out. Then, together, the two of them mounted the staircase.

Alastair was *receiving* her?

His muscles contracted, his pulse beating harder yet, his entire body tensing as though in preparation for battle. It took his last shred of will not to reach out as she crested the stairs, to stop her from entering that study. His brother was not a man to be trifled with. If Alastair lifted a hand to her—Christ, if he so much as *raised his voice*—

He waited, barely breathing, as Jones returned again, alone, to descend the stairs.

Not wasting another moment, Michael stole out from his hiding place and raced silently down the hall.

The door to the study stood closed. But there was indeed a keyhole for spying. He knelt and put his ear to it, dimly aware of the indignity of the position, not giving a damn about it. At the first sign of goddamned trouble he would burst into that room and—

"Forgive my presumption," said Elizabeth. "I know we have not been introduced. But I have a matter of great urgency to discuss with you, and it could not wait for the usual niceties."

Michael knew that his brother's appearance must shock her—and that Alastair would be eyeing her with steely distaste. But she sounded utterly composed, if a touch cool.

"I'm sorry to hear that," Alastair replied, "for as you may imagine, it is my fondest desire that we remain perfect strangers."

"Then the polite thing would be to thank you for the kindness of receiving me," she said. "But I won't thank you. I see no reason to be mannerly with a man whose recent actions toward his brother rightfully deserve only my contempt."

Michael exhaled. It was a curious thing to hear her defend him. A curious and . . . misplaced pleasure, in such circumstances.

What was she *doing* here?

"That is frank," said Alastair.

"Yes," she said, "I am known to be frank. And I will be franker yet. You see—"

"Did you encounter my brother on your way up?"

This idle question was answered by the briefest pause. "No," she said. "Is he . . . here, then?"

Michael dug his nails into his palm. *That* notion clearly rattled her as his brother's words had not. By God, but he wanted to see her—

He schooled himself with a long breath. *Patience.* He had to know why she was here.

"I suppose he has left already," said Alastair. "Well, make it quick, then. I do not have time for women such as you."

Her laughter was low and dark. "Then your standards have risen considerably of late—and certainly since these letters were written."

A longer silence now. Michael peeked through the keyhole. Her back was to him, but she had handed Alastair a bundle of papers. He was leafing through them with a good deal more energy than the legal documents had merited.

"Where did you get these?" he said then, and his voice might have been cut from glass.

"From one Mr. Nelson," she said. "He tasked me to bring these to you, and to beg, in return, your sponsorship of his bid for a barony at the least. And I was to ask a bequest of my own, perhaps eighty or ninety thousand pounds, the better to pay off my debts—which he will be glad to advertise, when he learns that I divulged his part in this scheme. But instead I have a different proposition for you entirely."

Michael shook his head slightly. Nelson had *blackmailed* her? Threatened to reveal her impoverishment?

He was going to kill that bastard.

"Nelson," Alastair said.

"Charles Nelson. Your wife's lover. One of them, at least. As you see."

"Barclay," his brother muttered. "And Patton!"

"Yes," she said, "and Huston as well. The late duchess was quite busy, wasn't she? One wonders what *you* were doing all this time. Ah, yes—I remember now: you were playing politics, and promoting your favorites. But it seems your wife disagreed with your politics, for her affections favored the opposition—and they seem to have profited greatly by it. Why . . . your grace, I daresay that your *wife* was something of a kingmaker as well!"

Michael sucked in a soundless breath. Now it was clear to him. The letters she'd handed over were connected to Margaret.

Somehow Nelson had gotten hold of Margaret's private correspondence.

Christ. Nelson had been one of her lovers.

In his disbelief, he nearly laughed, a wild laugh that would have exposed him in an instant. Instead he bit down hard on his knuckles and strained to hear their next words, even as his mind raced. *Why had she not told him?* Why had she not come to him?

"These are the originals?" Alastair asked.

"A sampling of them," she said. "I will hand the rest to you later. Yes, I know—there are more! Imagine that. Very prolific, was your wife. But before you receive her collected works, first you must do me a particular favor."

Michael's breath stopped. Why, with this leverage over his brother, she might demand . . . anything from him.

Abruptly he stood. He did not want to hear this. No wonder she had not told him of Nelson's threat—for she meant to blackmail Alastair, just as Nelson had done to her. He could not breathe, for a great volcanic rent seemed to be opening in his chest. It was a disappointment, a *betrayal,* beyond all endurance—

No. She would not do this. Not to his brother.

The next second, he *knew* she would not do it. She would never disappoint him. Never betray him in such a way—or in any way so fundamental.

The certainty of this belief unwound through him so

rapidly and powerfully that it nearly crushed the breath from his lungs.

Why, he had no doubt of her. *None.* And this certainty, which he had once believed, *known,* he would never feel for any woman—why, it did not seem so miraculous, after all. It felt . . . natural. Trusting her was the most natural and simple thing in the world. He had no choice in it; his faith in her was like his breath, steady and involuntary.

For so long he had been afraid to repeat his parents' tragedy. But *this* was love: not something separate from trust, but *woven* of it. *This* was what his parents had lacked.

His parents' story would never be his.

Feeling dazed and strangely weightless, he knelt again, just in time to hear her say, "You will reopen your brother's hospital. That is my favor. And you will resume—whatever it was you did for his work before. I want your promise in writing, drawn up by my solicitors, that you will fulfill your bargain to *him* for as long as he requires it."

Michael closed his eyes. *Elizabeth, you idiot.* She hadn't needed to do this. He'd had it well in hand. Damn it, she *should* have demanded money for herself. She—

He stood and threw open the door.

Alastair looked up from the letters. Elizabeth, turning on her heel, went pale.

"Eavesdropping?" Alastair said. "How charming."

"Give her the money," Michael said. "Eighty, ninety thousand pounds. Do it, or the letters go public."

"No." She stepped toward him. "No, that isn't the right way. Michael—"

"I don't need his support," he said. "God damn it, I *don't need it.* But you need the money."

Her face changed. She stopped in her tracks, her hand at her throat. "And you think I would take it? From *him*? You thought better of me yesterday!"

He'd offended her. His idiocy appalled him. "No," he said, striding forward and catching her hands. "No, you misunderstand me. All I want is that you—" He tightened his grip when she tried to break free. "Listen to me, Elizabeth! You cannot marry another man. I won't *allow* you to do it. You will take the goddamned money!"

A scraping sound came to their left. Alastair had cast the letters into the fire, and was stabbing them with a poker.

"There are more," Michael said to him. "And by God, I'll print them myself, I'll distribute them in the streets—"

Elizabeth's hands turned in his, her nails against his wrists calling him back to the moment. "You will not," she said sharply. "You've no business in this. He is your *brother*, Michael." Releasing him, she faced Alastair. "But my own threat holds good. I will have that promise from you, sir, ensuring that the Lady Marwick Hospital reopens—and remains open—from next week onward. Or you *will* regret it."

She turned back to Michael, lifting her hand to touch his cheek very lightly. But when he would have caught it in her own, she shook her head and stepped away.

"I must go," she said softly, and walked toward the door.

"No." The hell with *that*. He moved without thinking, catching her by the arm and hauling her around. "You will not walk away from me. Did you not hear? I have found a solution for the hospital. And—"

"And no solution for me," she said gently. "Michael,

if it were only my future at stake—I would so gladly put it in your care. But . . ."

"I *love* you," he said. "I will find a way. I will find a solution. You cannot walk away."

She stared at him, her lips parting. They trembled visibly, and the sight hurt him. He reached up, very gently, to still them with his thumb.

"Trust me," he whispered. "As I trust you. We will find a way."

A strange whimper broke from her. "But . . . I . . . if it were up to me alone . . . but so many people are depending on me . . ."

"And we will find a way." He nearly had her now. Victory was leaping in his blood. "Only say you trust me, and I vow to you, I will never disappoint you."

She blinked up at him, and a single tear slipped from her magnificent eyes. Green as jade. He could not bear to see her cry. Slowly he leaned down and captured that tear with his lips.

"I am going to forbid you to weep," he said. "I'll make the parson put it into our vows."

Her shuddering breath singed his ear. "Oh," she said. "All right, then . . . if you . . . promise."

"I promise you everything," he said, very low.

With a broken noise, she grabbed him by the hair and pulled his mouth to hers.

It was a hot, deep kiss, and it tasted of—*relief*, by God, she was his, he had her. He wrapped his arms around her and hauled him to her. "You're not leaving me," he said.

"No," she said. "I—can't, I think."

"Oh, for Christ's sake!"

Elizabeth flinched in his arms. He'd forgotten his brother, too. He ignored Liza's attempt to step away, but he loosened his embrace just enough to let her turn toward his brother as he did.

Disgust lent more animation to Alastair's features than Michael had seen in months. "This is a pathetic display," Alastair snapped.

"I hope his charm does not run in the family," Elizabeth said flatly.

Michael was startled by his own snort of laughter. "Come," he said, and urged Elizabeth toward the door.

"I will have those letters!" came the panicked call behind them.

"Ignore him," Michael advised. "No time like the present to begin to develop the habit."

"You can have your money!"

At that, Michael stopped dead. When Elizabeth frowned up at him, he arched a brow.

She shook her head. "I don't want it. Not like this."

"Your money, and funding for the hospital to boot." Alastair sounded truly desperate now. "Enough money to see you both comfortable."

"Dirty funds," said Elizabeth, but now she was worrying her lip between her teeth.

"Cleaner than marrying for it," Michael pointed out. "And you were willing to do that—or briefly consider it," he added quickly, for she'd begun to scowl.

"God curse you! I'll pay off your debts as well! And that is my *final* offer!"

Elizabeth spun back toward his brother. "Accepted!" she said brightly.

And Michael laughed in astonishment. By God, he'd thought she'd had a tell—but she didn't. She'd been bluffing these last few moments, waiting for the stakes to be raised.

"Very well, then," Alastair said. "I will have my solicitors draw up a binding contract. And *you* will deliver the letters. But I have one more condition."

"No," said Michael instantly.

Elizabeth touched his arm. "Wait. Let's hear it first."

Alastair, bracing himself by one hand against the mantel, took a visible breath. "And . . . as to the matter of your wedding . . ."

"Goodness, how fast he runs," Elizabeth murmured.

"Only logical," said Michael. "For I do intend to marry you."

"Won't you ask first?"

"In a minute, yes. I'd rather we have some privacy."

"It must be a public wedding," Alastair growled. "And I must be included, lest there be talk about my absence."

Elizabeth looked to Michael. "That must be your decision," she said softly.

Michael bit his cheek. It seemed possible to him that Alastair's condition was, in fact, a veiled gesture at an apology. But perhaps that was only wishful thinking. He no longer knew his brother well enough to say.

"Our wedding will not be held in this house," he said. "So the choice is yours: you will be welcome to come, but only you can say if you'll be able."

Alastair's eyes narrowed. "I'll be able," he said. "Dear God—do you think I would miss your wedding?"

And Michael felt something in him relax that, unbeknownst to him, had been constricting his lungs for months.

It was a poor start at recovery on Alastair's part . . . but it was a start all the same.

CHAPTER TWENTY-ONE

There was no question but that Michael would come home with her tonight. The novelty of a happy ending was too new, and felt too fragile, to risk with a single moment's separation. As soon as they entered her carriage, her hands were on him, and his mouth was on her, and she somehow got onto his lap, and they were kissing feverishly. But the drive was too short—frustratingly short; they exited the vehicle breathless and disheveled. And then, once in the house, up the stairs, en route to her bedroom, Liza encountered a very unpleasant surprise:

The box in which she'd stored the late duchess's letters—the box she'd shut away in her wardrobe—stood on her dressing table.

In a panic, she opened the lid. "No," she said. "The letters are still there."

No, wait—there weren't *enough* of them.

Pulling them out, she counted quickly.

"*Half* of them are gone," she cried. "There should be twelve!"

"How can that be?" Michael took them, counting again. "Seven. Are you certain there were twelve?"

"Positively certain! But who would have taken them?" She turned a tight circle, as though the cozy confines of her boudoir might contain a thief. But nobody save Hankins and herself ever ventured here.

A cold finger touched her spine.

"Mather," she whispered. Mather had entered just as she'd been shutting the wardrobe.

No. It couldn't be.

"What about Mather?" Michael demanded.

She shook her head and raced into the hallway, where her haste caused two startled maids to stop in their tracks. No, they had not seen Miss Mather this afternoon. Nor, it transpired, had the housekeeper—nor Ronson, who had only just arrived from Bosbrea.

But one of the footmen had spotted her leaving the house an hour ago, with a valise under one arm and a portfolio beneath the other.

"She can't have done this," Liza said to him as they climbed back up the stairs. "*Why* would she have done this? And what will your brother do when I can't give him all the letters?"

"There are enough there to satisfy him," Michael said. "You didn't tell him how many you had left." They went back into her boudoir, where he rifled through the remaining sheets. "Enough details to satisfy him," he said. "He'll never know that some are missing, and perhaps she—"

He went still.

"What is it?" she asked anxiously.

His face grave, he reached over to her dressing table

and plucked up a single sheet of paper that she had not noticed in her panic.

Mather's script unfurled in tidy, angular rows.

Madam,

You are indeed a better woman than I. But perhaps my sins might prove of use to you. I have taken certain of the duke's letters for safekeeping—a careful selection, to ensure his honorable treatment of you. Should his grace continue to stand in your way, you may tell him that I will ensure his deepest regret.

You will wonder why I have done this. For separate reasons I cannot divulge, I am forced to conclude my tenure with you. But you have been very good to me, and whether or not you agree, I do owe a debt to you. This is how I repay it. I am sorry to do so in such an underhanded manner, but I beg you, if you are able, to consider this not a betrayal, but my parting gift.

Sincerely,
Olivia Mather

P.S. It may interest you to know that I caught Mrs. ~~Hussy~~ Hull closeted with Weston in her boudoir on the morning of our departure, speaking of marriage and . . . other things. I predict that the bride will need to loosen her corset considerably before the wedding.

"Where on earth has she gone?" Liza whispered.

Michael was reading over her shoulder. "Does she have any family?"

She shook her head. "Her mother is dead. She never spoke of anybody else."

"A former employer?"

"I found her at a typist's school," she said. "I've not the first idea where to look for her!"

His hands closed on her shoulders, a comforting grip. "It seems she doesn't mean you any harm," he said.

"What? No, of course she doesn't! This is *Mather*! But why has she run off?" She reread the note very quickly. "I do not like the sound of this. It almost sounds as though she was *forced* to go. But by what? She showed no sign of any plan to leave me—"

"Shh." Michael began to massage her, his fingers digging deeply. Despite herself, she felt her muscles unwind. "Wherever she's gone, it shouldn't be too hard to track down a redhead the height of a man. The police will make quick work of it."

She bit her lip. "You don't understand. I'm not . . . *angry* with her so much as concerned. That is—yes, this was quite wrong of her . . . and I'd *never* have expected— that is, she gave absolutely *no* sign—" But that wasn't quite true, was it? Now that she thought on it, Mather *had* hinted at her plan during that last conversation they'd had at Bosbrea. She'd asked, *What if somebody else were to employ the letters for your sake?*

"No police," Liza said decisively. Something was awry with Mather. These mysterious circumstances that compelled her to flee—they suggested she required help. "We'll find her ourselves."

"Very well," he said. "We'll find her."

"If we can," she fretted.

He turned her to face him, dipping his head to look into her eyes. "We'll find her," he said. "That is a promise."

She took a great breath, and then felt a smile come

over her. "Why is it," she said, "that you can make me believe anything?"

"Because I would give you anything." His manner had suddenly grown serious.

She started to lean into him—and the letter, forgotten in her hand, crumpled between them. Michael blinked down at it. "Is that writing on the other side of the page?" he asked.

She turned over the note—and frowned in befuddlement. "It's a copy of the rules! The ones we concocted for suitors." A little laugh slipped from her. "She kept this? But—how absurd; she *edited* it!"

He was studying it upside down. "What did she strike out, there?"

"That business about words matching actions."

"Ah, yes. She never liked it, if I recall."

"Objected most strenuously," Liza said. "In retrospect, that should have given me pause."

He laughed softly. "She was most worried, I believe, about the potential harm to gentlemen's dogs . . . My God." He gave her an astonished look.

Her heart quickened, panic touching her. "What is it now?" she asked. Too many more revelations, and she feared she'd become apoplectic.

"Only that I've realized I never poured your tea for you."

She blinked. "Oh. That's all right. Wait—where are you going?"

For he had turned on his heel to cross the room. Over his shoulder he said, "To ring for tea. Must mend my ways quickly, lest you change your mind and decide I'm not eligible."

Silly man! She lunged after him, catching his wrist to

tug it away from the rope. "No need for tea right now." Dropping her voice, she murmured, "You can . . . prove yourself in a different way."

He followed her nod toward the bedroom and a new light kindled in his eye. Grabbing her by the waist, he pulled her toward him. "My pleasure," he said, and leaned down to kiss her.

She looped her arms around his neck and returned the kiss eagerly. With her skin against his, their lips pressed together, the worries slipped away from her like raindrops off a pane. For a long moment she luxuriated in the feel of him, his broad hands firm on her spine. Hers, hers to *keep*—to have here, and in Bosbrea, and anywhere else she liked; but above all, to have *now,* for desire was quick to rise, leaping through her and brightening all her senses. The sweetness of the moment expanded; she felt the afternoon light from the window behind her like a warm caress on her nape, and smelled the roses in the vase atop the coffee table, and heard the distant rattle and hum of the city, the busy crowds passing on the road without, oblivious to the perfection unfolding here.

The whole world was theirs now.

And then he ruined it by lifting away his mouth. When she tried to pull him back, he shook his head.

"Something more I need to say."

"*Now?* Can't we—"

"Next time someone attempts to blackmail you, you come to *me*. You do not attempt to handle it alone."

She sighed. "Oh, very well. You may add that to our vows as well, if you like."

But his mouth had flattened, and his gaze had unfocused. "And that's something *else* I must do: hunt Nelson down and make him pay for threats to you."

"I don't think you'll need to," she said. "You didn't see your brother's face when he heard my tale. In fact, I believe he will seem to you like a man reborn in the next few days, for I've never seen anyone so instantly transformed by the mere act of learning his enemies' names."

He focused on her. "Do you really think so?"

Ah, but he loved his brother. It made her heart clutch to behold the hope in his face, so fragile, so precious. And he was trying so hard to check it, to conceal it from her.

She touched his cheek. "I want your brother to be well," she said gently. "For your sake." She could not like Alastair, but for Michael's sake, she would hope the best for him. "And I believe he will be well, with time."

Slowly he smiled down at her. "If he does recover, it's by your doing, then."

The notion pleased her. "So you aren't the only healer here."

Lifting her hand, he kissed her palm. "Indeed not. One day I'll tell you all the ways you've healed me. For now, let me say only that I've chosen to marry a *very* clever woman."

"And I'll add that you're a very lucky man to have gotten me," she laughed. Then, sobering, she brought his hand to her own mouth, kissing his palm in turn. "And what a fortune beyond compare it is, to have you."

For a moment they stared at each other raptly. And then, at the same time, they both pulled a face.

"Terribly sentimental," she said.

"Pure mush," he agreed.

"At this rate, we'll be as bad as Lydia and James. Or perhaps worse—for Lydia does not incline to public displays, you know."

His brow cocked. "And you do? How intriguing." The slow survey he gave her was distinctly lecherous, and made her pulse trip.

But two could play that game. "So many things you don't know about me yet," she said. "However, I know a place where you may begin to learn. It's conveniently near, and quite comfortable."

He tracked her thoughts exactly. "Then with all due haste," he said, and bent, scooping her up in his arms so suddenly that she shrieked and grabbed onto him. "To the bedroom, my love."

She sighed. "And afterward, to the chaise."

"And eventually," he said, shoving the door open with his shoulder, "the lake?"

"Everywhere," she said, and kissed him.

Rules for Reckless Ladies,
to Distinguish Eligible Gentlemen from
Cads, Blackguards, and All Other Breeds of Ruffian

1. The eligible bachelor must be handsome, but must never believe that he is handsomer than you.

2. The eligible bachelor is charming without being insincere. His blandishments are never guided by ulterior motives or self-interest.

3. ~~That said, he also knows how to put his tongue to purposes more varied and rewarding than speech.~~

4. He has no debts, is generous ~~but not too generous!~~ with his friends, and does not begrudge a lady her fripperies, even if said fripperies have too many *ribbons* for his liking. ~~Beware he does not prove overly fond of your ribbons, either!~~

5. The eligible bachelor makes himself useful in unexpected ways: ~~Pouring a lady's tea, for example. For example, by providing an ingenious solution for headaches. For example, by never inspiring a headache to begin with!~~ For example, a cloak for every puddle.

6. He is dapper without being a dandy; his suit fits him properly ~~and he looks all the better once his suit is removed.~~

7. The eligible gentleman is a crack hand at apologies. He confesses his mistakes and begs very earnestly for forgiveness, for which he is willing to wait at least a day or two, ~~during which, if he is wise, he acquires a very nice piece of jewelry for you!~~

8. The eligible bachelor gazes at his lady with admiration, but recognizes that her other talents ~~somehow nearly inconceivably manage to~~ outstrip her remarkable loveliness.

9. The eligible bachelor's words must be matched *at all times* to actions. He makes no empty promises, as there is little worse than an empty promise (save, perhaps, an empty head or an empty pocket!).
Addendum! The eligible gentleman will treat his dogs very well, but no better than his staff, whom he will treat very well, indeed.

10. Above all, the eligible bachelor is fearless and faithful in his love, but never idly sentimental. ~~The eligible gentleman is capable of making love, that softest of sentiments, have a *hard* dimension indeed.~~